DIRE STRAITS

MARSHALL FRANK

Dire Straits

Printed In the United States of America
54 24 66 74 12 98 15 01 14

by
EVERLY BOOKS
P U B L I S H I N G CO.
Everly Books Publishing Co., 1918 BOUL.SAINT-REGIS
DORVAL, QC, H9P 1H6
CANADA

www. EverlyBooks.com

LIBRARY OF CONGRESS CATALOGING-IN-PUBLICATION DATA
ISBN: 978-0-9949809-9-1

PUBLISHER'S NOTE

Editor-In-Chief: Chris S. Douglas
Cover design by Everly Books Publishing Group

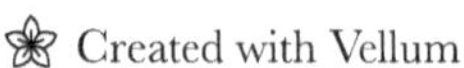
Created with Vellum

CHAPTER 1

M*IAMI, FLORIDA - SATURDAY, 10:30 P.M.*

HIS BROAD NOSTRILS sated with the aroma of sea air, Orestes Fernandez had just moored his twenty-four foot Mako at the far end of Dinner Key Marina when he heard footsteps approaching along the oak wharf. Odd, he thought, for anyone to be heading out to sea this time of night. But Orestes was one to mind his own business until he looked up at the three men standing quietly in the shadows over the bow.

"Can I help you men?" he asked in Spanish, wiping sweat from his brow.

The tall one in the flowered shirt looked furtively left, right, then spoke. "Si. We want to go fishing."

"I'm sorry," answered the seaman with a nervous smile. "There are no more boats leaving until tomorrow..."

In an instant, Orestes was peering into the muzzles of three semiautomatic pistols. Two of the men in black tee shirts jumped into the vessel as the tall one interrupted. "Perhaps I was unclear. We are going fishing now."

"Please. Please don't hurt me. Take the boat. Take whatever you want, just don't..."

"Drive the boat," ordered the leader. "Do as we say and you will not be hurt."

Trembling, wracked with fear, Orestes started the twin Mercury engines while the gaunt, skinny one pressed the muzzle at the back of his head. "Please..."

"Shut up," he barked, whacking him over the ear, twice.

"Drive slowly out to the bay so you do not attract attention," ordered the leader.

As he aimed his beloved craft toward the center of Biscayne Bay, Orestes lowered the throttle gently, shaking, whimpering, wondering what lay ahead, wincing at the cold, hard steel against his temple. "Where are we...?"

"Shut up."

Several minutes passed when the one referred to as Javier barked another order. "Stop here."

"Here?"

Idling in neutral, the Mako rocked calmly to the motion of the darkened waters. There were no other boats in sight, no other movement in the bay as Javier scanned the city horizon. He ordered Orestes to the stern with his hands atop his head, facing them.

"What, what are you going to...?"

As the short stocky Spaniard looked on from the side, Javier and the skinny one called Chico lifted their weapons, smiling.

Orestes sobbed now, his face contorted in fear. "No, please, I beg you..."

"I told you, we were going fishing."

A volley of muzzle flashes pierced the darkness. They were his final images. The Mako headed south while Orestes' corpse rested peacefully at the bottom of the bay with an anchor attached to his ankle.

Twenty minutes passed as the three Latinos idled quietly through a labyrinth of residential waterways five miles to the south of downtown. The droning hum of engines and the slap of the bow cutting gently into the placid waters were the only sounds to pierce the August night as they slowly passed one mansion after another, careful not to create a wake. Occasionally they could see figures of people moving about through pane windows in the distance.

"Which one is Sylvester Stallone's?" asked Chico, nervously.

"Shhh. Stay down." Javier checked his watch. It was after eleven.

"Are you sure you know which is the right house?"

"Quiet. Trust me."

"Javier, look at the size of that house. Carrumba. What a score that would be, eh?"

"Chico, I told you to be quiet." Javier, the tall one, stood at the helm peering house to house, searching for a coral pink mansion at the end of a small peninsula and a statue of a small, black jockey standing on the dock. Only a quarter moon existed, but the spray of sparkling stars provided enough illumination to see houses, but not the statue. "Felix, turn on the spot," said Javier in a whisper. "Not on the houses, just the docks."

They made a slow left turn around a corner where the three-story house appeared, sitting alone at the end of the finger of land. Felix pivoted the spotlight to the left as they passed by. The davit was empty. Suddenly, the beam glared upon the statue of a miniature black man wearing a jockey uniform, extending a golden ring in one hand.

"Ah, this is it. A little further," whispered Javier as they turned off the spot. "There is supposed to be another house nearby under construction."

They deadened the motor and docked the boat at the rear of a half-built structure near a cull de sac two lots from their target. Quietly, all three deboarded, tied their lines and glanced over at the distant glow from the city to the north. Felix slapped at a mosquito. "Let's go," he ordered. "Chico, bring the tape and the ropes."

Perspiring from dense humidity, they stealthily penetrated the darkness and stopped in the lush foliage at the east corner of the mansion, then recoiled at the sound of a door slamming. Peering through hibiscus, Javier and Chico watched the silhouette of a young woman stepping briskly toward a sports car, enter, rev the motor and drive away. Moments later, Javier felt the vibrating of his cell phone. Illuminated numbers. Three zeroes. The signal.

"Who is the woman?" Chico asked in a hushed voice.

"Who knows? Es Bueno. One less to worry about."

A dark Chrysler convertible was parked in the circular driveway. Two other cars were parked a hundred yards away beside a dark field of cabbage palms and tropical weeds. They remained unnoticed.

From a bay window in the gated lanai, Javier peered through a crack in the drapery and saw a large woman lying on a sofa beside another woman with jet black Borneo-wild hair. They appeared to be sleeping. The faint humming sound of a distant television was barely audible over the pestering, squeaky bark of a small dog.

"Felix, you are the pizza man. You knock, say you are delivering a pizza. Say it in English; do not forget." Quiet, obedient, Felix was built low and strong like a fireplug, with connecting eyebrows and a face with more craters than the surface of the moon. "Hurry. Conyo, that fucking dog is barking."

They pulled semiautomatics from their waist bands, racked the slides and raised them at shoulder height. Javier and Chico assumed positions on each side of the door while Felix beat his fist on the frame, disregarding an illuminated door bell. The little dog erupted into a frenzy.

"Knock again, Felix," said Javier, impatiently.

Before his fist struck the frame, the voice of a young English-speaking male asked through the door, "Yes? Who is it?"

"Pizza. Domino pizza," answered Felix hoping he would not have to converse in English.

As the dead bolt unlatched, the door slowly opened. Javier moved Felix aside, raised the boot of his right foot and slammed it forward with the force of a battering ram.

THREE MILES TO THE NORTH, a drab gray Ford Taurus driven by a black man pulled out from the glitzy Mayfair Hotel. By his side, a slick, well-dressed Cuban jotted notes on a pad. An old lead which could have solved a 2010 murder hadn't panned out. The witness, a barmaid, died of an overdose a year before.

"Hey, the Grove's jammed tonight, Zeke. Why don't you take a side street and head over to Bayshore Drive?" Detective Sergeant Mike Estevez checked his Seiko and saw there was less than an hour left on duty. "If nothing's going on, we'll stop at Monty's for a nightcap to celebrate. I'll buy."

"Celebrate what?"

Mike smiled. "A murder-free Saturday night in the city of Miami. Would you believe it? Tonight, my friend, we are going home." He took a photograph from his badge case and showed it to his partner.

"That your old lady?" asked Zeke, glancing over. Mike nodded. "Good lookin'. You're a lucky guy."

Mike checked the glossy print himself. "Christ, I need a picture to remind me what she looks like," he said, wistfully.

It was one of those humid summer nights in the city of sunshine when clothing sticks to the body seconds after walking out of an air-conditioned room. But the temperature didn't deter the throngs of fun seekers, theater goers, rickshaws, side-alley masseuses, itinerant musicians, imbibers and eccentrics crowding the bistros, shops and streets of lively Coconut Grove. Zeke drove silently as Mike peered out the window, contemplating his life, his illustrious career, what the future might hold, reflecting on the pressures, the effect it had on his family and pondering a change for the first time ever. Perhaps it was time to move on, he thought. He had made his mark. Life existed beyond homicide. Then, he had a notion. He lifted the cellular phone from the glove compartment and punched seven numbers. Zeke listened with one ear to the police radio and the other to Mike.

"Corrina. How are you, honey?"...Is your Mom there? ... Oh, yes. I forgot. Scandinavian. Right. ... Well, do me a favor, okay. Leave her a little note, uh...no, better yet, don't we still have some of those Hershey Kisses in the jar? ...Good. Listen, honey. I want you to take two of them and just lay them on top of her pillow ... She'll understand ... I don't know, baby doll. Real soon, I hope ... I know it's been a long time. Maybe EPCOT Center, next month ... Sure ... Don't forget the Hershey Kisses. Love you. Bye."

He looked to Zeke. "My daughter. She's thirteen. Great kid."

They stopped at a traffic light when, suddenly, the sounds of screeching brakes in the distance. A small car caromed off the sidewalk and came to rest between a bus bench and a row of small trees. "Jesus, what now?" Mike growled. "Head over there." They attached the small, blue rotating beacon atop the unmarked car and sped through the intersection.

A young woman rested her chin on the open window from inside a metallic blue Mustang Cobra, grinning at the detectives. Strands of carrot-red hair slovenly covered a freckled face. "My God, you're gorgeous," she mumbled to Mike in a slurred but distinctive southern accent. Her lids were half closed while her eyes seemed to focus somewhere at his collar. "Hey, I'm sorry. Is there any damage?"

Mike flipped his shield which drew a breathy "Oh, shit" from the drunken lady. When he asked her to step out of the car, she stumbled and grabbed his arm. "I'm really sorry, you know. Really."

"Any damage, Zeke?"

Zeke stepped around the car. "Nope. Maybe a little scratch on her bumper. Want me to call for a unit? You know," Zeke winked to his partner. "Oh-nine, thirty-nine, reference a sixteen?" They were code numbers for a drunk driving arrest.

Mike checked his Rolex again. It was eleven twenty and his plans for an early homecoming were not to be foiled by a mere traffic matter. An arrest meant waiting for a uniformed unit, calling a tow truck and an hour of paperwork. But she was too drunk to drive.

"Are you going to arrest me, officer?" she asked.

"No ma'am, but I want your keys. Your car will be parked here tomorrow when you come for it." He turned to Zeke. "Call her a taxi."

"So, you don't wanna see my license?" she asked provocatively, looking him over. "You married?" She wore a candy-striped sun dress with spaghetti straps and a sagging neckline revealing a modest cleavage and, obviously, no bra.

Mike parked her Cobra next to Monty Trainer's On The Bay, an upbeat seafood restaurant and watering hole abutting the Biscayne Bay in Coconut Grove. "Make sure she has another set of keys at home because I'm locking these in the car," he shouted to Zeke.

A warm breeze whipped the woman's skirt as she stepped from the curb to the taxi. Then, she turned to face Mike across the lot and waved her fingers. "Too bad," she said to Zeke with a sloppy grin. "He's quite a guy."

"Yes ma'am, he is. And you're quite a lucky lady."

Minutes later, Mike twisted Zeke's arm and sauntered into Monty's open air waterfront bar, hoping to pass the final duty hour without a call. The lively atmosphere consisted mostly of young people sitting at picnic-style tables bobbing heads and shoulders to the sounds of the Reggae band, while a parade of power boats and sloops drifted into the marina. The pungent aroma of sea water and dead fish drifted through the lounge.

Zeke was Mike's rookie, working his first week in homicide. The term did not set well with the giant black officer. Not only was he five years older and a head taller, he had already been a uniformed cop for eighteen years. But this was the golden opportunity of a long career, finally to work in homicide with the best cops in the department. He knew how lucky he was to pull the esteemed Mike Estevez as his trainer.

Mike felt out of sorts sipping on a Johnny Walker Black in one of Miami's most popular bars while Zeke hoisted a glass of chocolate milk. Another waft of salty air blew strands of hair onto his forehead while his mind churned with thoughts of Robyn and Corrina, murder trials, lesson plans and the department bureaucracy. He barely listened while his partner chatted about his dream of owning a farm in North Florida. Zeke said he wanted pigs and horses, to go fishing on the Suwanee with his grandchildren and maybe even get married again one day to a good Christian lady. Just maybe. It had been nine years since Agnes died.

At eleven fifty-two, Mike straightened the gold rings on one finger of each hand and called for the tab. At that moment his cell phone jangled. Caller I.D. showed it was central dispatch.

"You're not going to answer that, are you Mike? I mean, like only seven more minutes – it can wait for the graveyard crew. Right?"

Mike chewed on a piece of ice. "Well, Zeke, you never know. You just never know."

"Man, they were right about you."

CHAPTER 2

TWO DANCING STUDS, one white, one black, had stripped down to silk jock straps, prancing and gyrating barefoot across the plush green pile carpet, their bare toes sinking into the fibers with each step. As the music thumped on, pulsating, beating, breathing, four of five fervid women sat on the edges of chairs and sofas clapping, shaking their heads and screeching like peahens each time one of the studs humped before their noses. Stale cigarette smoke pervaded the mansion.

Her inhibitions unharnessed by seven glasses of Dom Perignon, the conservative Janie Tucker spontaneously whipped off her pumps, leaped to her feet and danced face to face with the white stud. The ladies hooted, raved and clapped. Hot rhythms of the Pointer Sisters' song "Jump" blared from quad speakers at four corners of the palatial room. Janie's silver-streaked hair swooped over her face while the fullness of her well-defined implants wobbled inside her tee shirt like a pair of water balloons. The shirt displayed the words, "Don't Worry Be Happy".

"Do it Janie. Do it. Go, Janie. Yeah. Yeah. "Whoooeeeh!"

"Hey, Lillie, any more champagne?"

"Yeeeaah. Go, go go!"

A professor of English literature and the wife of an out-of-town antique distributor, Janie was letting it all hang out, hootin' and hollerin' at the shaggy blond haired stud with the chiseled features. He danced with fluid, sensuous movements but a forced rictus smile gave a detached appearance to his persona. Janie, on the other hand, played to the audience more than the dancer himself.

When the music stopped, Janie turned to Lillie Diefenbach, their hostess. "More, more. We want more. Come on. Let's keep it going."

"We need some new music," Sylvia Cicerone shouted in her indisputable Bronx accent, coughing and hacking between fits of laughter. Wedged between her nicotine-stained fingers, a burning cigarette dropped gray ashes to the carpet. Jet black hair stood out from her head like she'd been zapped with a thousand volts of electricity. Sylvia was the drunkest of all and loving every minute of it. "Oh sweetheart, give him some of our music, you know, from the fifties and sixties. Got any Elvis?"

"One better, dahling," yelled garish Lillie from the kitchen. "How about them Righteous Brothers?" Widowed by two elderly millionaires, Lillie's money allowed her to revel in her freedoms of expression and eccentric lifestyle. If it felt good, it was done. "You only live once," she'd always say.

Like a three decade throwback, her hair was teased and lacquered in a yellow bouffant and she wore a huge, variegated muumuu festooned with layers of beads and pearls. With oversized lashes and enough face paint for a circus clown, Lillie looked more like an old drag queen than a respectable resident of the most affluent neighborhood in Miami. Pepito, her blue-gray toy poodle with painted toenails and bows on his ears, followed her every move with petite exuberance, chasing after her bare feet as she thumped from the kitchen with a bottle of Dom in one hand and a CD of the Righteous Brothers in the other.

"Yeah! Take 'em off. Take 'em off," shouted Sylvia and Lillie, their furtive party at its height.

Carolyn Webb rose to dance with the white dancer, bumping and grinding to the music, her crystal champagne glass elevated as though offering a toast. A Sissy Spacek look-alike, the earthy redhead was the youngest of the women, spirited and lurid as the rest of her party mates. A one-piece candy-striped dress hung from her shoulders by spaghetti straps, flowing and swaying to the movements of her body. Tonight, it was a festival of raw sex, alcohol, drugs and wanton abandonment.

Whump whump. "Ooooh yeah!"

Seated away on a single chair, mesmerized by the erogenous rhythm of the black dancer, Mirage posed a stark contrast to the crass exhibitionism of the others. The mood, the music and the alcohol had taken their effect as she watched and fantasized the contrast in color, his blackness, her whiteness, his natural power, his primal passion. Alluring and softly beautiful, she wore clear wide-rimmed glasses, very little make-up and her dark brunette hair in a full length pageboy with bangs to her eyelids. Outwardly, she seemed distant. Inwardly, she was cooking.

Extremely handsome, the young black man was sinewy and muscular, and his movements to the music seemed as natural as a dolphin swimming in the sea. He reminded her of a young Denzel Washington. A strange intoxicating warmth consumed her as his eyes locked upon hers. More so than his white counterpart, he was absorbed in music, thrusting his bulge and flexing his muscles to the beat. Nearly hypnotized by erotic fantasies, Mirage remained oblivious to the antics of the other guests.

Whump whump. "Yeah! Yeah! Whoooeeey!"

Nestled within an array of tropical landscapes near the shore of sparkling Biscayne Bay, Lillie's coral three-story stucco mansion sat off by itself like a deserted island at the end of a cul de sac in the lavish and gated residential development known as Cocoplum. Upscale and very private, it was a neighborhood where armed uniformed guards took names and numbers, and no one was permitted through without clearance. Residents often commuted via small yachts and cabin cruisers through man-made waterways fed from the bay, leaving automobile traffic to the less bountiful. Home to celebrities of various genre, the water-based community sat in close proximity to the Brickell Avenue banking district, making it equally alluring to money-laundering cartels.

Lillie's sunken living room comprised an immense chamber of mirrors, white leather, multicolor cascading track lights, French impressionist art, chalk white sculptures and glass tables set upon a field of emerald green carpet. On one end, sliding glass doors curtained by white silk drapery bordered in gold braid led to a dimly lit pool patio. On the opposite end in full view, a glossy white

Steinway grand piano sat in a mirrored anteroom upon an Italian marble floor.

Besides all the free flowing booze and the pate de fois, the caviar and the carvings from carnard a l'orange, an arrangement of ten, neatly rolled joints centered on a silver tray among the hors d'oeurves. Lines of freshly imported cocaine were available in the kitchen if anyone was so inclined, the best dope money could buy.

A hair dresser and Lillie's best friend, Sylvia arranged the party in honor of Lillie's sixtieth birthday. Like Lillie, she, too, was a long time widow who never remarried.

Janie Tucker also lived in Cocoplum, two cul de sacs away. Her husband was away on a business expedition to Hong Kong.

The pretty mystery guest, a customer from the beauty shop, was known only to Sylvia. She had accepted the party invitation with the stipulation that she be introduced only as "Mirage".

The music was raging with The Righteous Brothers singing Little Latin Lupe Lu when Janie and Sylvia emitted joyful shrieks. Both studs had unsnapped their tiny jocks leaving bare appendages swinging and swaying to the women's delight. As she began to feel numbness set in, Mirage's head spun in a double-take, gasping, blinking. She couldn't believe her eyes.

Arms raised, Lillie wedged herself between the dancing boys while Pepito danced in circles on hind legs emulating his mistress.

"Yes, yes...Lillie, ahhh, go for it. Whoooeeey!" The music roared on. Lillie rotated with the dancers stuck to her, while Janie Tucker gyrated into a shimmering frenzy, their passions inflamed by the booming rhythm.

Whump, whump. "Ooooooh yeah."

Sylvia, coughing and hacking, called to Mirage, "Come on, honey. Get with it."

Another two glasses of champagne brought Mirage to the threshold of complete inebriation. Succumbing to the lure, she slowly rose from her chair, stepped barefoot toward the group and slunk into the licentious milieu of dancing women and naked boys. Wearing blue jeans and a blouse tied at the midriff, her eyes fixed upon his as she began friction dancing with the dark-skinned stripper, a single body in movement with no touching of the hands. Her hair swung like a pendulum to the music as they pressed against each other. A bead of perspiration trailed down her cleavage; the black dancer captured it with his finger and brought it to his lips.

"Yeah, yeah, Mirage. All right!" Whump, whump.

Sylvia danced the Watusi in circles while Janie continued shaking her shoulders and breasts, hands combing her body high and low, grasping, moaning. Unabashed, twirling around the room, Carolyn Webb dropped the straps of her dress.

Finally, the music, dancing and booze had taken its toll. The mood subsided. The music softened. Exhausted, Lillie sprawled out on the sofa, raising one of her immense, ugly feet onto the cushion, an empty champagne glass hanging from her hand. "I'm maxed, girls. Whew. Go ahead. Keep on. Don't mind me."

Carolyn Webb slow danced with the unclad blond boy to the sounds of The Platters. *Only youuuu, can make me feel this way. Oh oh, only youuu...*

Feeling like her head was levitating from her body, Mirage followed Carolyn's lead and danced with the black naked stud, slowly, sensuously, eye to eye, lips a breath away, drunk, sweating, languid. His smooth ebony skin glistened from perspiration as she ran her hand across his back and then lower, and lower. His firm buttock muscles tightened with each movement. She paid no attention to Janie who had collapsed on a chaise on the pool patio, nor to Sylvia and Lillie kissing each other on the sofa. The lights were dimmed. She was burning inside, inflamed by his masculine scent and the bare brown torso pressed against hers. *Oh oh, ho ye es, I'm the great pretender ... pretending that I'm all...*

Disheveled, cross-eyed, Sylvia looked up, puffed her cigarette and announced to the two dancing couples, "It's bonus time, girls. Have a nice time."

Lillie snorted, "Yeah, kids, it's all paid for." Embracing, the two women released hearty laughs and locked lips.

MIRAGE STAGGERED up a short flight of stairs into the master bedroom while the black fellow balanced her by one arm, carrying his satchel in the other. She nearly tripped to the floor. "I feel so woozy," she mumbled, smiling silly, head lolling. "You're really some beautiful guy, you know. So, uh, wowie, those muscles." Snickering childlike, she brought her fingers to her mouth sensing the numbness. The room began spinning as she yearned for unconsciousness, wishing for the awful feeling to go away.

"You're not too bad lookin' yourself," he answered, holding her shoulders now, his two hands leading the staggering woman to the back of the room.

She was still wearing jeans and a blouse as he embraced and fondled her next to the waterbed. Her arms hung listless, submissive, seemingly unaware, her eyes half closed, her lips mumbling. Her blouse slipped open at the stomach as he pressed his dark skin against hers. Stupefied, she held his erection for a moment, then passed her hands over her face saying, again, "I feel sooo woozy."

"It's okay. It's okay. I'll take care of you."

"Who are you? What's your name?" she asked slovenly as he fumbled with her jeans. Her knees buckled and she felt the room spinning faster now.

"It's Ken."

"Mine's..."

"Yeah I know, Mirage. Is that your real name?"

"I don't know. I don't know who, what..." She felt her body recline, then his. "I feel sooooo, sooo..." Then…deep repose, silence, precious darkness.

NOT LONG after Mirage and Ken disappeared into the master bedroom, Carolyn emerged fully dressed from the guest room and sauntered past Lillie and Sylvia dozing on the sofa. Languid and blasé, the blond dancer, called Chad, followed a few steps behind. On unstable legs, Carolyn raised her shoulder purse and checked for her car keys. She stopped for a moment and studied the flaccid features of the two women as Pepito lifted his tiny, decorated head with an inquiring expression. In a South Carolina drawl, she muttered, "My luck, wouldn't you know it. Mr. Stud here is gay as a caballero. Well, I gotta call to see if my boy friend's available tonight." Carolyn used the kitchen phone but hung up seconds later without uttering a word. She fluttered a short wave saying, "Ciao, Sylvia; happy birthday, Lil. 'Twas fun."

Carolyn walked out the door, entered her Mustang Cobra and quietly drove into the warm Miami darkness toward an empty bed in Key Biscayne. Happy to be five hundred dollars richer, Chad scrounged a peach soda from the fridge and turned on a rerun of Maverick in the family room while he waited for his partner in debauchery. Suddenly, there was a pounding on the front door. Pepito went into a barking frenzy.

Party time was over.

"NO, NO DON'T," she pleaded.

"Come on, baby. You know you want me."

He had her completely undressed now. "No, no, I can't. I can't. The room, it's spinning. I feel...I feel awful. What are you doing?"

Kneeling on the bed between her, he raised her legs but she recoiled suddenly, her glasses falling from her face to the floor. The reaction startled him, but he was still aroused, feeling emotions of anger, frustration and desire all at the same time. She was milky, soft, so utterly tempting.

He didn't want to take her by force, but neither could he just walk away at such an irresistible moment. He lay down beside her, reaching, cupping her breast, kissing the back of her neck. For a moment, as it seemed she was willing again, he arose between her once more and mounted.

As he started to enter, she gasped, widened her eyes as though in shock and pushed him off. "No, no. What are you doing?" She started slapping, uncontrollably. He backed away, defensive, holding his arms before his face.

"Hey, take it easy. I thought you wanted to make love?"

It was a sobering moment peering at his suspended hardness, throbbing, his eyes showing complete disbelief. She knew that she had somehow allowed the situation, perhaps even led him into thinking she would be his. Grabbing sheets to cover herself, Mirage sat up, disoriented and ran her fingers across her face trying desperately to recover, to gain control again. "Look, um, listen, whatever your name is..."

"It's Ken."

"Okay, Ken. Listen, I'm sorry if...um..."

"I get it. I understand. Don't worry..."

Still naked, part angry, part embarrassed and aching with anxiety, Ken alit from the bed and reached into his satchel for clothing. "I'm not going to do anything if you don't want. I thought you..."

"Okay, it's my fault. I was wrong. I just want to get dressed and go, okay?"

After donning their clothes, little was said until they started to walk out the bedroom door. Ken noticed two small bandages wrapped around each of her big toes. "What's wrong with them?" he asked, pointing.

"Oh, that. Oh, yeah. Hey, my shoes. They're still out there somewhere."

Suddenly, sharp smashing sounds exploded from the living room. Mirage and Ken leaped back from the door as a ruckus of shouting voices blared throughout the house, sounds of angry men, demanding, threatening, almost hysterical. Mirage jerked Ken by the arm. "Shhhh." She laid her index finger across her lips and cocked one ear back to the door.

"What the hell...?" he said.

"Jesus Christ, Ken." She took several deep breaths, holding her face, her heart pounding. "Shit. This is bad. This is real bad. Oh no, God no! It's a robbery." Panic surged through her body as she ran from the door and searched the room for a place to escape, to hide. "Oh my God...oh no, please. This can't be happening."

CHAPTER 3

LITTLE PEPITO erupted into one of his irritating barking fits as Lillie and Sylvia were semi-aroused by the beating on the door. With Ken and Mirage in the upstairs bedroom, Chad remained the only person conscious enough to answer.

"Yes? Who is it?" Chad asked peering with one eye through the wide angled peep hole at the pockmarked face.

"Pizza. Domino Pizza," replied the man with an accent.

He unlatched the bolt, turned the knob then felt the force of a bomb blast against his head. Chad caromed off the wall and slid to the floor, dazed.

"Grab him," Javier ordered in Spanish. Brandishing guns, Chico and Javier rushed into the living room leaving Felix holding the dancer in a choke hold.

By the time Sylvia and Lillie were alert, they were staring into the barrels of two nine-millimeter Glock semi-automatic pistols.

"Oh my God! Oh my God!" Sylvia screamed, hacking.

"Who ees the sonny boy, Lillie?" asked the tall Spaniard named Javier, standing over them waving a pistol. She wondered how he knew her name.

Lillie gawked at the open end of the muzzle. "Just some kid, a friend," she stammered. "Hey, who the fuck are you? What's this all about?"

Petrified, the women trembled, speechless as their saucer-sized eyeballs shifted from one intruder to the other.

"Scream again and you are two very, very dead *mujeres, comprendes?"*

Nodding in panic, they watched as Felix dragged Chad across the floor by his collar then hog-tied him with a nylon cord, arching his back so his feet nearly touched his head. A strip of three-inch surgical tape was wrapped across the boy's mouth. Javier ordered Chico to check the windows, making sure the vertical blinds and drapes were drawn. Janie Tucker remained out on the patio chaise undetected.

"The mooney, beetch. We want the mooney," barked Javier in slow, deliberate English pressing the muzzle of the gun against Lillie's enormous head.

Frenzied, Chico paced the floor, teeth gritting, eyes in perpetual motion, hyperventilating, waving his pistol back and forth from the women to Chad. Felix never uttered a sound.

"Take it all, fellas. Take my watch, my rings, my purse is on the table." Lillie was pleading as Sylvia went into shock, her bulging eyes locked onto the muzzle of the Glock.

"I mean *the* mooney, Lillie. *The* mooney. No sheeting with me now; no fookin' around. I want *the* mooney. You know what mooney I talk about."

Lillie winced as the Glock pressed harder. Javier backhanded Lillie across the face with the weapon as Sylvia screeched a series of uncontrollable screams until she was whacked also, only harder. Both women bleeding, they gasped for breath. The leader ordered them tied like Chad who squirmed in the center of the plush green carpet.

They taped Sylvia's mouth and deposited her on the floor between the sofa and a glass coffee table. Lillie remained on the sofa with her hands bound behind her back and her feet tightly wrapped at the ankles, but no gag. They wanted her to talk.

Aroused by the strident sounds of Sylvia's screams, Janie Tucker boldly opened the glass sliding door, only to find her left arm suddenly twisted behind her back and an olive-skinned hand wrapped around her mouth. Felix had seen her movement from a wall mirror. She squealed, grunted and writhed but in a matter of seconds, she was trussed, gagged and dumped on the floor beside Sylvia and Chad.

"Anyone else in thees house, Lillie?"

Her mind racing, Lillie spat out, "No one, godammit; no one else is here. Come on, fellas. There's no need for all of this."

"Then you will geeve us the mooney? That ees two million fookin' dollars and we know you have it."

"What in the hell makes you think I have that kind of money? Jesus Christ, I'm just a widow with some investments. Look, you give me a little time, untie me and tomorrow I'll liquidate and give you part of what you want. Just don't hurt anyone." Pain shot through her shoulders as she twisted and squirmed on the couch.

"Lillie, maybe you no have the big picture," said Javier facing Lillie and straddling the back of a white enamel dining chair. His voice echoed through the house. "Like what weel it take? Keeling all of you?" He sniffed and snorted and with great pleasure, he raised his weapon and casually aimed at a Georgio Armani figurine next to the fireplace. One shot rang out. The hog-tied party goers wiggled frantically, grunting in horror. Chico raised his eyebrows in a fiendish grin, giggled and fired a senseless, random shot into the ceiling. Then he giggled again. Felix stood taciturn at the entrance to the patio, a good sentry waiting for orders.

Lying frozen, his mouth sour, Chad prayed to survive the ordeal. Janie Tucker, sweating profusely, writhed and moaned hysterically. Sylvia coughed and hacked uncontrollably, sounding like she was drowning in her own phlegm.

Frustrated by Lillie's stubbornness, Javier nodded to his companions who heaved the glass coffee table across the room, caviar, duck and all. A free-swinging dining chair played havoc with the wall unit, stereo, bar, liquor cabinet and a collection of ceramic art pieces. They smashed everything in sight. Tough Lillie was just as irate as she was frightened. Within seconds, a cyclone of violence had turned the once lavish setting into a virtual shambles. Pepito fled into a guest room under the bed.

From the kitchen, Chico yelped "*Amigo, oye tu, mira.* Look at this sheet in here. We can have a party."

"Leave that sheet, you ass. We have beezness here. No fooking around."

Still straddling his seat, arms crossed on the chair back and dangling his gray weapon from one finger on his left hand, Javier turned to look into Lillie's darting eyes.

"The two million, Lillie. The cash. Two million for the Freeport payoff. The mooney you're holding for Marco. You know Marco, your fooking weasel lawyer. Before I tear this house to pieces and keel all of you, you weel tell me where it ees. Okay? Now, where ees the safe?"

"I ain't got no two million dollars," she said, barely able to breathe. "Not in cash anyway. Jesus Christ, I got arthritis and this is killing me."

Javier turned his eyes to crazy Chico and gave a succinct order in Spanish. *"Oye, imbecil, aqui no. Mira ve y hazlo en el piano."*

Chico giggled, took three steps, raised Chad by his sun-bleached hair then dragged him to the sofa where he presented his petrified face to Lillie, the semi-automatic pressed at his temple. She glanced pathetically at the boy, looked up at Javier with contempt then turned her head away. Chico dragged Chad like a sack of feed to the anteroom which housed the glossy white Steinway grand, top raised. It was surrounded by a half dozen panels of mirrors and a crystal chandelier hanging from the vaulted ceiling.

With pleading eyes, Chad writhed and twisted. A resounding dissonant chord echoed throughout the house when Chico heaved the boy onto the harp of the piano, the top collapsing. Titillated by the boy's panic, he thrust the muzzle to Chad's temple, giggled and unceremoniously fired one shot. Chico laughed and leaped away as a geyser of blood pulsated from the boy's head. There was an involuntary twitch, then another, then stillness.

Ears ringing from the gunshots, Sylvia and Janie grunted and quivered in sheer fright. Hyperventilating, Lillie turned away from the spectacle in the anteroom. Chico paced like an animal, returning three times to the piano to gawk at his accomplishment, death in action.

"You fucking animal," screamed Lillie, horrified, glaring at the smug Latino.

"The mooney, Lillie," he repeated slowly. There was no answer. He faced Chico and Felix ordering them in Spanish to search the entire house. *"Busca por todos lados. Vira esto boca abajo. Me estoy ponieno impaciente!"*

Her mind racing, desperate, Lillie tried to think of a plan. They were certainly not going to leave Janie and Sylvia alive, she figured, so they were a write-off. No bargaining chips there. She assumed Mirage and Ken were still in the master bedroom, innocently caught up in this web of terror. She could show good faith and turn them over to the killers. They would think she was being honest. No, that would not be reason enough to let her live. She had to think of something, anything to save her ass.

If she surrendered the money, there would be no explaining to Marco or the cartel. Resolution would be swift. She would simply become a police statistic, a situation made clear long ago. As a reputable American, she was entitled to one percent of all proceeds for holding and protecting cash derived from drug trafficking. There were risks and this was one of them. Her only hope of survival would be to leave the country before she was caught, and she didn't even have a passport. Her tit was in the proverbial wringer. Die now or die later.

"Look," she squealed, straining, "If I give you the money… Look, I'll take you to it but you gotta let my friends go. Don't kill them. Please don't."

"You want to leeve, Lillie? You geeve us the mooney. Fook your friends." The comment was not music to the ears of Sylvia and Janie who locked onto each others' eyes with horror.

"Okay, okay, but it's not in the house. You don't think I'd keep two million in cash in my house, do you? Don't kill us and I'll take you to it. And, godammit, loosen these ropes. My arthritis."

"You see, Lillie, I know it ees all here and you are lying to me."

There was a pause. "You no answer? Okay, lady."

Her words were labored. "Come on, fellas. You know, we could do a lot of business."

Chico bellowed from the upstairs hall. "*Javier, Estas puertas estan cerradas. Creo que hay alguien mas aqui adentro!*"

The one called Javier turned to Lillie and translated. "Who ees in the bedroom, beetch? The doors are locked."

"No one, godammit! I always keep my bedroom locked."

When little Pepito heard Felix and Chico kicking in the French doors to the master bedroom, he scampered back to find his Mama on the sofa. The diminutive animal scooted to and fro, confused and nervous, not knowing what to make of the tall man holding the gray object in his hand. Javier looked at Lillie, then the puppy, then Lillie again.

"Oh no, Goddamn you. Don't, don't please..." She turned her head away as another shot rang out.

ON THE BRINK OF HYSTERIA, Mirage scampered through the dimly lit room searching for a phone, but the clutter of piled sheets and utter disarray of clothes made it impossible. "Gotta call 9-1-1," she said. "Gotta call 9-1-1."

Ken grabbed her arm and whispered, "Look, we gotta hide, baby. There's no time. By the time they'd get here..."

"You're right, but where?"

Trembling amid piles of wrinkled garments and boxes, they entered the walk-in closet and slid the mirrored door closed.

She exclaimed, "Oh God, no. Oh please. This can't be happening." As Ken turned to the overhead light, Mirage grabbed his hand. "No lights, no no."

They could hear harsh voices from the living room shouting at Lillie, demanding money. For a moment it sounded like Sylvia shrieking and then she stopped abruptly. Ken and Mirage huddled in the darkness behind a malodorous wardrobe that smelled like it had never been washed. Suddenly, a gunshot, *BANG*!

"Oh my God, no." She shrieked. Then another. *BANG!*

"We gotta get outa here," Ken said, peering up and around, trying to adjust his eyes to the darkness. "Look there," he whispered, pointing to the ceiling. "It's the attic."

They heard the clamor of breaking glass and furniture crashing. One of the men laughed constantly. It was time to move. Get somewhere. Anywhere.

The plywood cover to the hatch seemed about two feet square, wide enough for their bodies he figured. "We're going up," said Ken. "Link your hands together and then lift me."

"I can't lift you."

"Yes, you can. Come on. There's no other way."

Another shot rang out and they could hear Lillie's ominous screams, "Oh, Jesus, you fucking animal." Someone had been shot. They had to escape or they were doomed.

"Hurry, let's go," whispered Ken.

He then placed his right foot in Mirage's hands serving as a stirrup. She raised herself from a squatting position giving Ken enough lift to push open the scuttle lid, grab on to the edge of the hole and then hoist himself with the pull-up of his life. He peered into the darkness and saw there was room for crawl space, enough for hiding. As he lay prone, looking downward, he reached for Mirage. "Grab my hands!"

With a surge of power, Ken raised Mirage up and through in one sweep as though lifting a child. He placed the hatch cover over the square opening. That moment, from below, they heard menacing sounds of bedroom doors being smashed. "My God," breathed Mirage, "we madc it."

Another shot rang out. Lillie screamed again.

"Come on," whispered Mirage. "Move away. Just in case." Like a pair of wartime GIs in darkness, they crept blindly on elbows and bellies across rafters and sponge-like fiberglass away from the bedroom area until they reached another hatch cover from which a sliver of light appeared. From below, they could hear voices.

"Where are we?" asked Ken in a whisper.

"I've never been in this house before," she answered. "Let's see."

With a hard fingernail, Ken carefully raised one end of the scuttle lid, allowing a small crack to see through. They were above the staircase, at least ten feet from the floor. At a distance, Mirage saw the reflection in the mirrors of the anteroom where the lifeless bound body of the blond dancer lay within the white Steinway, a coffin dripping now with crimson fluid. Ken looked away while Mirage opened the lid a bit further, aghast at the carnage below.

Across the room on the green carpet, hair covering her face, a pathetic, quaking Janie Tucker lay next to Sylvia. The gregarious hairdresser, tied and gagged with her eyes squeezed shut, writhed about like a fish fresh out of water. Atop the sofa, fat Lillie lay flat on her back, her bulbous face a bright pink, hands beneath her, ankles tied, moaning and rolling her head right to left, back and forth. A wiry, dark-haired Spanish man with intense, deep set eyes held a gray gun as he straddled the back of a kitchen chair at Lillie's feet. His pale green eel skin boots were partly covered by cuffed trousers. He looked to be about thirty-five.

Ken shivered and looked away. Mirage took control of the hatch cover. Steeled to the scene fifty feet away, she studied the tall Latin with a frisson of fascination. Safe now, a furtive spectator in the dark cavity above, she continued to watch.

Javier glared at Lillie as he called to his goons in Spanish to return to the living room. "*Vamos...vengan para aca. Tenemos mas cosas que hacer.*"

They had found nothing in the master bedroom. Out of patience, Javier looked to Chico and nodded toward Janie. "The beetch with the gray hair. Over there. She can play *Malaguena* for us." He spoke in English so that everyone could understand. Then he broke into a nefarious grin and gave an order, *"Matenla!"*

Janie writhed, her eyes darting in fear, head shaking in desperation as Chico giggled and grabbed the rope that bound her feet together. He dragged her across the floor to the execution chamber where Chad's body lay encased in the blood-drenched piano. Lillie turned her head away from the direction of the anteroom and shut her eyes. Chico grasped a handful of Janie's silver gray hair, forced the woman to face herself in the mirror and with the Glock pressed at her right temple, fired a single shot that echoed throughout the house. Janie flopped like a fish as blood spurted from her head, then she slumped to the marble floor. Chico smiled and ran back into the carpeted living room, blubbering excitedly in Spanish that he wanted to kill the next one.

Above, Mirage silently gazed in horror while Ken curled up in a fetal position holding his ears, whispering, praying.

"The mooney, Lillie. What ees it going to take?" shouted Javier.

Her head turned facing the back of the sofa, the yellow-haired virago sobbed hysterically. "Please, I beg of you. I'll tell you where the money is. I'll even tell you where there is another five million. But you gotta let me live."

"Okay, Lillie. Just you only. You leeve because you are the trail to the mooney." Javier nodded to Chico once more.

Wrapped tighter than a bale of hay, Sylvia Cicerone had been weeping and spewing mucous from her nose until all movement ceased about the time Janie was shot. She was limp and heavy as Chico attempted to drag her to the execution chamber. Then he saw that her eyes gazed into nothingness. He kicked her but no response. "Hay, mierda," said Chico, ruefully. "The beetch ees already dead. She take away all the foon."

"Bring her over with the rest of them," ordered Javier. Felix and Chico carried the ponderous corpse and dropped her like a sack of potatoes on the marble floor next to Janie's body. Then for good measure, Chico fired a shot into the back of her head. This time, there was no blood.

OTHER THAN MOVIES, pictures and funeral parlors, Mirage had never seen a dead body. She had never been a part of violence. It was all surreal, as though a dream, had it not been for the piercing gunshot blasts and the sounds of Lillie sobbing which brought it all to stark realism. This was really happening. A chill crept over her as she watched the expressions of the three executioners obviously delighted by the act of killing.

She whispered to Ken, "Poor Sylvia. She was already dead."
Ken lay silent in his fetal position, unresponsive.

"THE MOONEY, LILLIE," demanded Javier.

Lillie began to dry heave. Her only hope was to forfeit the money. "How do I know you'll not kill me anyway?" she asked, barely audible through gritted teeth.

"Hand over the mooney and we leave you here to answer questions," he said, snorting. "You no can tell the cops the truth, right, Lillie? You know, you no can tell the cops you are a go-between lady in the drug beezness. You want to tell them that? You go 'head. I think you weel come up weeth a good imagination when they get here. We get the mooney and you get to leeve. Now, you no can turn down an offer like that? Eh?"

"Then Marco will have me killed."

"I guess we all got problems, lady."

"There is a wall in my bedroom closet that's not a wall. It's false. Behind the shoe rack," Lillie said resignedly. She recited the combination.

Javier translated quickly to his henchmen who then rushed back up the stairs.

"Please don't kill me," Lillie begged in a strained and almost inaudible voice. The side of her face had turned blue from the pistol whipping. "I'll work for you guys. I know lots of people and we could make a lot more money."

Within a short time, Chico and Felix returned carrying three athletic satchels filled with two million, one hundred thousand dollars in five, ten and twenty dollar bills. Javier used a handkerchief to wipe his gun and laid it on the mantel, then ordered Chico and Felix to do the same. In Spanish, he explained they could not risk being stopped with murder weapons in their possession. As the three Cubans stealthily departed out the door, bags in hand, Lillie breathed a sigh of relief. She wriggled her corpulent body off the sofa, falling heavily to the floor, then rolled onto her side. She was trying to free her hands when she heard the door open once more. Her heart pounded as she watched the eel skin boots stride slowly toward the mantel.

"Just want to say thanks, Lil," he said with a smile, straddling her.

"You son of a bitch." At first she closed her eyes then looked up at Javier with utter contempt while he slowly raised the pistol. She never heard the shot.

"ARE THEY GONE?" Ken asked.

"Yeah. Let's just wait a minute," she answered in a whisper. A pall of eerie silence now cloaked this elegant mansion where, in a matter of an hour, music and laughter had been transformed into a night of terror and death. Ken shivered even more. She smacked him on the leg saying, "Come on. Let's get out of here. I got to get my shoes."

"What about the cops?"

"Right, Ken, the cops. You go ahead and call the cops while I get my shoes."

They crawled back to the opening over the bedroom closet, lowered themselves and saw that the wall was peeled back, baring an empty vault. As Mirage tiptoed through the macabre scene, four of her party mates lay in pools of blood, bound and slaughtered like animals. She could not bring herself to look in the direction of the anteroom with its nauseating blood odor. She wondered about Carolyn and figured she may have been raped and killed in another room. She was not about to check it out.

Ken headed for the kitchen phone, dropping the receiver several times from nervous trembling. Meanwhile, Mirage found her high heel shoes under the curtains by the glass sliding doors. Then, as Ken spoke to the 9-1-1 operator, he heard a door slam. Mirage was true to her name.

CHAPTER 4

AS MIKE AND ZEKE ARRIVED, flashing lights from patrol cars painted the three-story mansion in an array of moving colors; a cacophony of squawking police radios echoed in the night air. The Forensic Crime Scene van pulled in behind them, driven by a pudgy woman with stringy, shoulder-length hair. Yellow barrier tape already surrounded the house and the Chrysler parked in the driveway, but not the entire property.

Another unmarked Taurus was next to the Chrysler. Mike's eye caught the figure of a corpulent grey-haired man in a limp brown sports jacket stepping out to the lanai. It was burglary Sergeant Gus Grimanski.

"Hey Mike, good to see ya. You're gonna love this one. There's four stiffs in there, giving a piano concert."

"Please, Gus, stay out of the crime scene and for Christ's sake put out that cigarette. Why are all these cars parked on the driveway? Why isn't this tape set up further down the street? Whose SUV is that down the road? Who's the lead officer? I want to know everyone who has been inside this house."

Mike was a take-charge cop and everyone knew it. He buttoned his jacket, straightened his rings and checked his watch.

It was twenty past midnight. Zeke Ferguson stood by, the dutiful student.

"Just me, Mike. Don't sweat it, kid," said Grimanski, fifteen years senior to the Cuban sleuth. "I only went in a few steps to check for other victims. Didn't touch a thing. Honest."

"Gus, get more tape and seal off the entire street past that SUV down there. I also want your shoe impressions for eliminations."

Mike asked about the Mustang. "It's the witnesses, I think," answered Gus. "Some black kid scared shitless. He can hardly talk."

"Witness? Where is he now? What's his relation to the victims?"

"He's in my car," replied Gus, gesturing. "I talked to him a few minutes but he's shakin' like a leaf. Some kinda male stripper hired for a party tonight. Wrong place, wrong time, that's all. He's lucky to be alive." Gus smiled, leaned closer and lowered his voice. "Probably a fuckin' faggot. His white buddy is lying in there with three dead broads. It's pretty gruesome, Mike. You ain't seen many like this." Gus gave the detective a brief account about the young man's escape to the attic while three crazed Spanish males demanded two million dollars from a woman named Lillie.

"What's his past?"

"Clean as a whistle."

"Name?"

Gus referred to his little note pad. "Jonathan Kennedy Lancaster. He's twenty-two."

Multiple victims in a posh neighborhood set this case aside from other routine murders. Media coverage and scrutiny from city hall would be intense. Decisions made here were critical. The living witness was Mike's first priority. The scene investigation could wait a few more minutes. He took a cursory look inside and ordered Gus to stand sentry at the door while technicians took photographs outside. As he entered Grimanski's car, he felt a tap on the shoulder. Spinning around, he was face to face with Gloria Menendez, the department's public information spokeswoman. He paused a moment to absorb her dark eyes then said, authoritatively, "I'm glad you're here."

"The army is on the way, Mike. Channels four and six are

already here..." Mike looked down the dark road and saw news vans setting up their antennas. "...and there'll be dozens more. This is Cocoplum you know, not Liberty City. What can I tell them?"

"Christ, Gloria. You got to be kidding. Look, four people are dead. Okay? All appear to be shot. For now, that is it."

"Suspects?"

"None."

"Witnesses?"

He thought briefly about his response. "Nope. None at this time." He took her gently by the arm and walked aside. "Gloria, dear Gloria. Give me a little time okay? At this point, I don't know any more than you. Keep the vultures away and I'll be in touch. Fair enough?"

"I'll try."

Mike stuck his head into the window of Grimanski's car and made eye contact with the youthful black who was leaning over, his forehead planted in the palms of his hands. "Hey there. I'm Sergeant Mike Estevez. I'll be in charge here."

"Yeah, I heard about you." Ken muttered, shivering. He was still wearing gym shorts, tee shirt and Nikes.

"You okay?"

"Oh yeah. Real good. Surviving mass murder. Well, you know, that's an every day thing, man."

Estevez ignored the wisecrack and sat inside. From the window he saw the end of the road jammed with cars and vans, people moving about. The air was humid as Mike took a folded handkerchief to his forehead. "Look, I know what you went through. I heard. I saw the scene inside. It was horrible, I know." He paused to study the young man for a few moments. "It's important that we find these animals before they kill other people. You know what I mean? Can I call you John?"

"I use my middle name. It's Ken."

"Okay, Ken. One important question. Can you make an I.D.? Can you identify their faces?"

Ken glanced out and looked at the elegant death house aglow under the bright police lamps. He paused, then replied, "Listen man, I saw one of them through the attic cover. It wasn't a good look. Uh, I honestly don't think..." he was still shivering.

"Scared, Ken?"

"Shit, wouldn't you be?"

"Damned right. But we have ways of protecting people in your position. You'll have nothing to worry about. Nothing." It was an assurance the shrewd detective had to make, but it went against his grain, particularly when he liked the person he was lying to. "What were you doing in the bedroom, Ken?"

"I'll tell you what, Sergeant...like, you know, you should be out looking for that woman. She saw them real good. All of them."

Mike alerted. "Woman? What woman?"

"She and I, well...we kinda got it on after the dance party and then all hell broke loose. We were lucky to be in that bedroom. Shit...it saved our lives. She was a fox, man. A real class lady."

"Her name?" Mike asked softly, comforting.

"She called herself Mirage. That's all I know. Mirage. Never met her before."

Ken Lancaster tried answering Mike's questions but the shivers and the trauma made his story sound disjointed. He repeated his account of three hysterical Spanish men demanding two million dollars from the woman called Lillie and that he overheard one being called Felix. But it was Mirage, he claimed, who had watched the entire massacre through the hatch cover. Without a doubt, she could identify all three.

"She was amazing," he said. "When it was all over, she disappeared out the door while I was on the phone with the nine-eleven operator. Gone. Just like that."

"Try to relax, okay? I need a description, Ken. Did she have any identifying marks. She tell you anything about herself? Anything?"

"I'm gonna throw up." Ken opened the rear door to the unmarked police car and heaved onto the driveway. Helping him, Mike glanced down the road again. The crowds had grown larger. He had to shuttle Ken from the area before the media learned of a living witness.

The dancer composed himself when Mike insisted for her

description once more. "Uh...well there was a long scar on her stomach, six inches maybe. She had dark hair and she was soft, man, real pretty. She was, uh, about thirty, I think. Wore jeans and a shirt tied up at her stomach. It had a lot of colors, flowers I think. And glasses, big designer looking glasses and..." Ken raised his head suddenly. "Wait...you know, there's another woman."

"What?"

"Hey, man... I just remembered. I don't know if she's in there anywhere or if she left the party before all the shit happened. I think they called her Carol. Red hair, bright red, about thirty. She had freckles, man. Lots of freckles." Ken was huddled now, oscillating to and fro.

Mike pressed him. "Are you serious? Can you describe her?"

"Yeah, she wore a one piece dress with red and white stripes and skinny little straps always falling off her shoulder."

The detective pondered. "Wait a minute. What kind of car did she drive?"

Ken glanced up from his hands. "Shit, how am I supposed to know that?"

Freckles. Red Hair. Spaghetti straps.

Mike's image flashed on the drunken woman he had sent home in the taxi an hour earlier and never even bothered to get her name. "Hey, Zeke, come here a minute." The giant detective poked his head through the window. "Ken, this is my partner Zeke. Tell him about the woman with the freckles and what she was wearing."

Ken repeated the story again. When he finished, Zeke looked at Mike. "Hey, that's the lady who..."

"You got it, my man. Aren't we lucky? And her Cobra is still at Monty Trainer's. I want a uniformed unit over there right now. Get an I.D. from the tag and have someone sit on the car until we can find another detective. Jesus, we need some people here."

"Right on."

Ken was safe now and they were probably closing in on another witness. But the mystery woman called Mirage was his highest priority. Perhaps she was part of the conspiracy. Doubtful, but not impossible. How did she get out? Why did she vanish? Who was this woman, the key to the whole case? She saw it all and could identify the killers. He had to find her.

He made a calculated but risky decision. Mike ordered a be-on-the-lookout (B.O.L.O.) broadcast via dispatcher to all police units with a description of the woman known as Mirage, wanted for questioning. Without knowing the connection, everyone monitoring the scanners would now be aware they were searching for her. She was crucial. They had to get to her before anyone else. When the dispatcher asked the nature of the situation, Mike replied, "Negative at this time. No other information. Just put it out."

"ALL UNITS B.O.L.O. A WHITE FEMALE, APPROXIMATELY THIRTY,

DARK SHOULDER LENGTH HAIR, WIDE RIMMED GLASSES, FIVE FOOT

FIVE, ONE HUNDRED TWENTY POUNDS, WEARING BLUE JEANS AND A

MULTI-COLORED BLOUSE. USES THE NAME, MIRAGE. WANTED FOR

QUESTIONING REFERENCE A THIRTY-ONE. NO OTHER INFORMATION."

"LISTEN KEN, Zeke here is going to stay with you to make sure you're safe and to get a statement from you. It's routine cop shit. You going to be okay?"

"Yeah, I'm okay," he answered morosely, shivering again.

Mike exited the car and took his partner aside. "Call the department shrink, Zeke. This guy went through hell and I don't want him falling off the edge, if you know what I mean. He's vital, Zeke. We gotta keep him alive and talking. Bring him downtown and stay glued to him like a Siamese twin." Mike raised a closed fist. "Okay?"

When Mike turned around, the pretty media lady was there once more, pad in hand, eyes wide. "Anything yet?"

"No Gloria, I'll tell you. I promise."

"Who's the black guy?"

Mike stormed away with exasperation written over his face. "Later, Gloria."

Bright television lamps glared from a distance behind the yellow tapes. The police B.O.L.O. had been monitored and reporters were buzzing, anxious for any tidbits of information but Mike ignored them.

CHAPTER 5

BEFORE RE-ENTERING THE HOUSE, Mike organized a textbook scene search, huddling with forensic personnel and ordering that no other persons be permitted inside unless it was the Medical Examiner. Even then, he would escort the pathologist step by step. "Remember," he said, "we are walking where the subject's walked. Every step you take could be a prime location for evidence. Shoe prints, fingerprints, blood drippings, threads, fibers, trace evidence of any sort. Watch every step you take."

He ordered Gus Grimanski to conduct a neighborhood canvass and to bring one of the bulky uniformed officers along. "Hit all the houses between here and the gate, Gus. Find out who was home between ten and twelve, what they heard, what they were watching on TV, who they were screwing, what cars went by, who walked their dogs. Then talk to the guard at the gate. See if he took names and tag numbers."

"You got it."

The pressure was mounting. Mike needed technicians and detectives, experienced homicide detectives, not the assembly line gumshoes from Auto Theft and Burglary who always seemed to arrive first on the scene. His request via radio was met with a swift reply. The voice of Lieutenant Raul Gonzalez bellowed over the air reminding him of the chief's policy regarding overtime call-outs without authorization from a supervisor. Gonzalez announced he was on the way, as was the mayor, the chief, the assistant chief, the chief of detectives, the head of the Crime Laboratory, the supervisors of Property Bureau, Communications Bureau, S.W.A.T., Mounted Patrol and every other curious quidnunc with a gold badge and access to a police radio.

"Conyo!"

The clock was ticking. Mike had yet to start probing the crime scene. His only assistant was gone, tied to a key witness and he desperately needed manpower. Meanwhile, he had four bodies and a mansion draped in blood, an army of news media, the department brass swarming in and two women out there, somewhere, one of whom was the key to the entire case.

With customary arrogance, Lieutenant Gonzalez swaggered up to the driveway wearing a ratty, faded green Polo shirt with a B.L.O. logo on the breast pocket standing for "Brotherhood of Latin Officers". His shirttail draped over his belt in a futile attempt at concealing a beer gut. Just behind him, the youthful Chief of Police, George Amos Howard, III, thin lanky and black, unabashedly stooped under the crime scene tape along with two assistants and headed for the front door.

"Can I help you, sir?" Mike asked, raising his arm. He then gave the chief a brief, obsequious account of the facts and convinced him that he had already made an important contribution by simply appearing before the public.

"Where is Captain Davidson?" asked the Chief.

"Not here, boss. Don't know."

"Well, he's the Homicide Bureau Captain. Has he been notified?"

"Undoubtedly sir." Inwardly, Mike was relieved that he hadn't shown up. Old Barnie Davidson was best known for three little figurines arranged on his desk; See no evil, Hear no evil, Speak no evil.

"We would like to see the inside, if that's all right, Mike," the chief asked.

What could he say? With caution and deliberation, he showed them no further than a few steps through the front door where they each stood spellbound at the macabre death scene. Later, with the city manager and Gloria Menendez by his side, the chief addressed the media throng.

Mike pulled Raul Gonzalez aside to the corner of the house. "Look, I need help, Lieutenant, big time. This isn't exactly a nickel-dime rip-off. I want a Spanish detective and I want Randy McAdams working with me. I need them now, on scene."

The portly lieutenant smoothed his thick mustache with the curve of his index finger and held a cigar with the other. "You know the orders, Mike. No call-outs on overtime. You have Zeke Ferguson with you now and you can use the on-duty burglary man for leg work until Sunday's crew shows up tomorrow."

Mike responded angrily, "With all due respect, sir, perhaps you haven't taken into consideration that this is a fucking massacre in the wealthiest community in this city. You're not going to give me the resources I ask for?" Mike paced off and back, then turned around. "Zeke's great, but he's fresh out of uniform and I have to lead him by the nose. And, Gus Grimanski? You gotta be kidding." Gonzalez puffed his cigar, listening as beads of sweat poured down Mike's sideburns. "Then again, what the fuck do you know about homicide."

"Watch how you talk to me, Mike."

"Fine, I'll be happy to report your decision to the public information people so they can assure *The Miami Herald* and all the local channels that the City of Miami Police Department is holding the fucking line on the budget while the millionaires of Cocoplum can await their next slaughter. It can easily make the difference between finding these killers or not. Are you ready to take that responsibility?"

"That's department business and you can't..."

"That's public record, sir! Look, I got more important things to do than stand here and argue with you. I'll tell you what, Raul. This case is yours. You can transfer my ass."

"That will get you time," answered the smug lieutenant as Mike stormed off. Gonzalez thought a brief moment about his threat and called after him petulantly, "Okay, okay. Who was it that you wanted, Mike?"

As the crime scene technicians prepared to follow Mike into the house, Gonzalez insisted on tagging along.

"Three stipulations, Lieutenant, that I ask for. First, no one else tramples on this scene without my okay. You can help me with that. No captains, no chiefs, not anybody except the M.E. Agreed?"

"Agreed."

"Second, please don't offer to help. Look, listen, but try to stay out of the way. Please, sir."

Gonzalez looked indignant at his cool subordinate. "Maybe you have forgotten who's the lieutenant and who's the sergeant here, amigo."

"Fine. But if it's my case, then I run things. It's your call, boss."

Gonzalez curled his finger around his thick mustache, nodding.

"Third, sir, you can put out that cigar. In your own car, please."

With a legal pad in hand, Mike passed through the front door asking the police photographer to take a series of shots as they entered in order to show the crime scene in its most pristine condition. Every move they made, anything touched, collected, moved, even their notes could eventually be subject to cross examination.

A shoe print centered on the face of the front door was photographed using oblique light. Drops of dried blood on the tile floor were also photographed and collected. The pungent odor of human blood permeated the entire house. A chubby technician named Gail took the pictures while her partner carried the equipment box and collected samples of blood, fibers and cigarette ashes.

Except for the faint sound of a television in the background, silence prevailed. Absorbing the grisly ambience, they halted in unison and gazed at the three corpses in the brightly lit anteroom and then the large blonde woman lying on the floor beside the sofa.

Raul Gonzalez held a handkerchief over his face, *"Jesus Christo, carrumba Miguel..."*

Mike and the technicians had witnessed hundreds of death scenes but this was like none other. It seemed a herd of raging bulls had wrecked havoc throughout the palatial residence. Hardly a piece of furniture, pane of glass or a single fixture was left intact. The camera strobe flashed again and again as Mike recorded copious notes and diagrams with the comportment of a surgeon in an operating room. After all, that was supposed to be his calling.

As they reached the kitchen, Mike spotted several lines of white powder in a row upon a mirrored tray next to the sink. Plastic cocktail straws lay to the side undisturbed. The wall telephone was dusted first for latent prints to set up a communications link with the outside. Then he pressed the redial button only to find it was the 9-1-1 number last dialed by Ken Lancaster.

When Gus Grimanski returned from his neighborhood canvass, Mike called for a critique outside in the pool patio. By this time, Al Sanchez and Randy McAdams had joined the team. Gus had checked on the Mustang Cobra parked at Monty Trainer's. "It's registered to a Carolyn Webb, DOB 4/18/79, 315 Seagrape Lane, Key Biscayne," he announced with a small notebook in hand.

Mike spoke up. "That fits with Ken's description. He said she was about thirty and her name was Carol. Al, get over to that address ASAP. When we saw her, about eleven-twenty, eleven thirty, she was drunk and happy, too happy to have been there when all hell broke loose. But find her. She's got to know something. Her connection to the victims. What went on before the murders? Who else was here? And find out who the hell Mirage is."

"Any help from the canvass, Gus?"

"Neighbors heard nothing, saw nothing," he replied. "This house is kinda isolated you know."

"What about the guard at the gate?"

"The evening guard went off duty at eleven. I got his name and number. The log book has a note about a party scheduled at the home of a Lillian Diefenbach. Anyone giving her name was sent on through. No tags." Grimanski shrugged his shoulders.

McAdams was in charge of coordinating functions outside the crime scene so that Mike could concentrate on the evidentiary matters inside. He would assemble all data from reports, canvasses and the grey Cutlass still parked down the street registered to Sylvia Cicerone. He would also arrange contacts with all the victims' next of kin.

Before wrapping up, Mike had to make a point. "Listen, guys. This could be Organized Crime connected. We have two, possibly three witnesses that are still alive. We have to keep them that way. The media is to know nothing about eye witnesses, is that clear? Be careful what you say and who you say it to, even within the department. It's a need to know basis only. Don't even tell Gloria Menendez. She's a sweetheart, but she doesn't have a need to know."

They all nodded in agreement.

Mike had told McAdams about the critical witness, Ken Lancaster. "Help Zeke if he needs it, Randy. Tell him to get details. Lots of details. Especially about Mirage. We must find her."

At that moment, the Assistant Medical Examiner stumbled in the door. "Good to see you, Dr. Gavilo," Mike said enthusiastically. Having organized many seminars together, the doctor and Mike Estevez enjoyed a long established fellowship of mutual admiration. He was a small, nervous man of Puerto Rican and Filipino descent with bulging eyes magnified even larger through thick lenses. A Nikon camera, a scalpel and a small tape recorder were the simple tools of his trade.

Gavilo examined Lillie first. "She's fresh, no rigor. This happened in the last two or three hours just like your witness said," muttered the pathologist. Facing the ceiling from the green carpet, Lillie's hands were bound behind her back and her ankles tied so tight with nylon rope that her fat, crusty feet had turned purple. Blood trickled from a single entry hole in the middle of her forehead just above the bridge of the nose. Under her head, the carpet was soaked in blood. Her expression seemed almost alive, her eyes partly open and her brow low as if to be asking, *"Who in the fuck are you?"*

The pathologist explored further and discovered the crotch area of Lillie's muumuu was also blood stained. "Check this out," he whispered. Dr. Gavilo reached under the garment with surgical gloves. "Stuck the poor little critter right in her snatch." Gonzalez, Mike and the technicians looked on as he held out the pathetic, limp carcass of a grey toy poodle crusted in blood. On its collar, a gold tag was etched, *Pepito.*

The team carefully walked into the anteroom that housed the white Steinway and three corpses all bound like hogs on a spit. It was the eeriest scene of Mike's career. He had to take a step back to regroup his emotions. They all visualized the terror that the victims must have endured before being taken to slaughter.

He looked closely at the young man in the piano, then the two women side by side on the marble floor; their grotesque images reflected a dozen times from mirrored panels surrounding the once beautiful instrument. Doctor Gavilo took particular note of the woman with the wild, black hair. "I think this one was already dead before she was shot," he surmised, probing. "There's hardly any bleeding."

Lieutenant Gonzalez shouted from the area of the fireplace. "Hey, Mike, look at this. Ever see this before? Two nine millimeter Glocks just like the city issues. Right on top of the mantel, over here." He raised one of the guns with his ball point pen inserted into the muzzle.

Mike quickly stepped across the sunken room, took Gonzalez by the arm and into the hallway out of earshot. "Very good, Lieutenant. You've learned much by watching Columbo. Or was it Naked Gun? I asked you not to offer any help. Jesus Christ, Raul! You never stick anything down the fucking bore of a suspect weapon! Sir!"

"Sorry."

Mike breathed deep and calmed himself before his temper took over. "But I will admit, that's a first," he said. "I've never seen killers leave their murder weapons behind, not deliberately anyway. Wanna bet they're stolen?"

One by one, wearing surgical gloves, they inspected each victim while the forensic team went on shooting pictures, dusting for prints and collecting blood samples. The dead woman with the grey hair had defecated in her panties, which added a fetid stench in the immediate area. "She took a contact shot to the right temple," blinked Doctor Gavilo, squatting. "Same as the boy in the piano."

A red leather purse found on the kitchen table revealed the identity of Sylvia Cicerone. Her driver's license photo was unmistakable.

Chadwick Alan Hawkins had all his papers in the athletic bag found in the family room where the television was softly tuned to an old black and white film. A driver's license confirmed he owned the Chrysler in the driveway.

The fourth body with the silver-grey hair was yet to be identified. No vehicle or any personal items were associated with her. "I have a hunch she's from the neighborhood," Mike said. "Unless she came here with the Cicerone woman."

The pathologist dictated into his recorder and snapped photographs from every angle of every body, stooping, probing, sweating, jotting little notes down on a pad, imagining all the slide shows that would rapture police and pathology audiences for years to come. In the midst of his technical dissertation, the phone ran. It was Al Sanchez at Carolyn Webb's apartment.

"Hey Miguel, this lady is whacked out. I mean, we had to beat on the door with a night stick to wake her up. Now, I'm standing in her apartment with a Key Biscayne cop and she can barely keep her eyes open."

"Anyone else there, Al?"

"No one. Just a furry little cat. She says she's divorced. The ex-husband's a pilot."

"She there with you now?"

"Yeah."

"Ask her if she was at Lillie's house tonight. Don't say anything about the murders. See what she says. Then ask her about Mirage."

After several minutes, Sanchez picked the phone up again. "It's no use Miguel. I think it's drugs. I asked her about Mirage, but she just shook her head."

"Get a unit to stay on her house until later tomorrow. She's going to be looking for her car and I doubt she remembers where it's at. We'll talk to her then, when she's sober."

Desperate for any clues that would lead him to Mirage, Mike Estevez and his entourage searched every corner of every room in the house. They rifled through drawers, address books, trash cans, Lillie's purse but it was a lost cause. Finally, a sweat-soaked Raul Gonzalez complained of fatigue and abruptly left for home. "You guys finish up," he said, acting like he was in charge. "I've had it. We'll meet in the morning."

Mike was relieved.

CHAPTER 6

ON THE WAY TO HIS CAR, a frustrated Gloria Menendez approached Gonzalez pleading for a statement to appease a waiting press corps. It was the lieutenant's moment to shine. In the midst of the humid darkness, a blast of white heat from the lamps of four television cameras bathed him in the attention he had always envied.

"All I can say at this point, ladies and gentlemen, is that there are four victims of a homicide in the house and we are doing everything within our power and resources to get to the bottom of it. As you know, we have assigned Detective Sergeant Miguel Estevez to the case and provided him with additional detectives for as long as it takes. We will set no limits in solving this horrible crime." Beneath the officious facade, Gonzalez was glowing.

"Do you have any information on the woman called Mirage? We heard the B.O.L.O."

"None."

"What is her connection to this case?"

"Sorry. I can't answer that."

"Are there any suspects at all?"

"Well...no not really." His answer was tentative, too tentative. News interviews were foreign to Gonzalez.

"What do you mean by not really, Lieutenant? Are there suspects or aren't there?" A young, male reporter was persistent.

"Well, no suspects...like we don't know who committed the murders. Not yet anyway."

"Then why did you say, 'no not really?'"

"Look here, the only thing I can tell you is that there were three Latino males involved. Who they are or how they're involved, I cannot tell you at this time. Sorry. That's all I have."

Realizing he had fallen into a trap, Gonzalez strode hurriedly toward his car, reporters on his tail. "Is there a description of the three Latinos? How do you know they are Latino? Are they the killers...three Latin males?"

"No names, no descriptions. No more information, all right? That's all I can tell you." He slammed the car door and drove off, wheels spinning. Minutes later, the gloating lieutenant would stop at a pay phone to tell his wife to record the Channel Seven News.

UNAWARE OF THE INTERVIEW that had taken place outside, Mike now probed the master bedroom. He ordered the mattress and the linens combed for any trace of the mystery woman, lost jewelry, pubic hairs, body fluids, anything. Like the entire house, the room was a shambles. The dresser drawers were dumped and strewn about the room, lamps were broken, wall paintings ripped apart and shattered glass was everywhere, including the bathroom. Processing for fingerprints would be a challenge, indeed, not to mention Mike's order to dust the scuttle opening, as well as the entire attic.

Besides pubic hair, the forensic team collected several long strands of dark brown hair that may have come from a woman. They certainly were not Lillie's.

Later, the female technician searched inside the closet, beneath the attic opening. On the carpet, she spotted what looked like a small pink bandage, still crumpled in a circle like it was pulled off a finger. The center of the gauze pad showed no traces of blood or any other substance. "There are ridge patterns in the adhesive," she remarked holding it up to the light with tweezers. "Had to come off someone's finger. I'd say it's good enough for an I.D. Check who's had a cut on their finger."

Mike examined the twisted piece of evidence and surmised that it must have belonged to Lillie Diefenbach or, less likely, one of the survivors. He returned to the sofa but when he examined Lillie's fingers, there were no indications she had been wearing a bandage. He thought of only one other person who could answer the question so he headed for the kitchen phone.

"How's it going, Zeke? How's our boy? Did he give a statement yet?"

Zeke was somber. "We got problems, Mike. This boy is really screwed up. The shrink is here now, been with him for the last hour and a half."

"What happened? Tell me."

"It was the Spanish language, Mike. I walked him through Detective Bureau passing by a couple of the guys kiddin' around in Spanish, you know, macho like. The kid went nuts. Berserk. He was hearing the killers all over again. I had to restrain him until he calmed down."

"Any chances of getting his statement?"

"Mike, you may have got all you're going to get, for now anyway. Jogging his memory starts him shivering all over again. He's getting worse. Doc Ammons says he needs medical treatment, a shot, or something."

"What about family. Has he got family? Jesus, Zeke. We need this guy. He's like gold. Right now we have nothing without him."

"Yeah, I know. We're doing everything we can. He lives with a girl common law, but he doesn't want us to call her. She knows nothing about him having sex with other women and all. So we let it be his call. Doc Ammons and I are going to bring him over to Jackson Memorial. I'll call you from there."

Mike hung the phone and took a moment to ponder.

It can never be easy. Two great eyeball witnesses to the most horrific crime in this city's history and sure enough, one is losing his mind and the other is lost altogether.

It was four forty-five in the morning when the first of four bodies were loaded on to a gurney headed for the Medical Examiner's autopsy tray. Zoom lenses went into full gear and a row of camera lamps came alive, illuminating the entire street as two men, one small, one tall, wearing white short sleeve shirts and black ties, awkwardly placed the shrouded body of Lillian Diefenbach into the van.

Out of range from cameras, the sharply dressed but frazzled Gloria Menendez pulled Mike to the side, paused a moment to admire his raw pulchritude and fired her wrath with both barrels. "Hey Sergeant, come on. I'm holding these people back all night sweating my buns off, but I can only do it so long. They're eating me alive. Christ, do you realize this is already national news? Tell them something, anything. Even if it's bullshit, okay?"

Mike saw her French twist falling apart as strands of black hair draped across her shoulders. "All right. All right. After the bodies are gone. Give me ten minutes."

"Thanks. And don't forget, the chief and the mayor want you at the news conference tomorrow at five."

He looked at his watch. "You mean today, don't you?"

A few minutes later, with his double breasted jacket properly buttoned, Mike stood in the middle of an illuminated street dutifully fielding reporter's questions. He spoke openly yet told them nothing more than they already knew. They were pleased to get their footage of the handsome and popular detective articulating in police jargon about the macabre murder scene. Careful not to reveal specifics, he titillated them with harmless anecdotes and adjectives that they couldn't get from the Public Information Officer or the chief. "Grotesque." "Bizarre." "Pathetic." "Savage."

Then a young, male reporter asked, "Do you have any information yet on the three Latin males?"

Startled, Estevez swung his head toward the reporter and with emphasis on the first word, asked, "What three Latin males?"

"We were told there may be three Latin males involved."

Stunned, Mike boomeranged a question. "And who told you that, sir?"

"Lieutenant Gonzalez. Your boss."

Bewildered, off guard, he paused to formulate a careful response. "Well, that's unconfirmed speculation at this point, and I would appreciate if you would not put that out. I mean really appreciate it."

Mike was stewing. If the killers saw any report that the police were looking for three Latins, they would instantly realize a witness was left alive. It spelled disaster.

It was eight-thirty that Sunday morning when Mike wearily donned his suit jacket and huddled his crew together for a final checklist before securing the crime scene. The glowing Miami sun had risen as burning eyeballs yearned for a cool, air-conditioned bed.

CHAPTER 7

AMID CROAKING of frogs under a dark and muggy sky, they moored the Mako next to a small park facing Biscayne Bay. Whispering merrily in Spanish and reveling in newfound riches, they heaved the satchels onto the concrete sea wall and looked in every direction before making their way toward the car. Javier admonished crazy Chico a dozen times to keep his voice down.

The three bags fitted easily with room to spare in the trunk of the 2004 Lincoln sedan prized by the short husky one. Six months had passed since Felix was rescued by the Coast Guard from a small dingy in the middle of the Atlantic. It was his first car ever. He called it his baby.

Javier sat in the back seat while Felix drove and Chico babbled in Spanish from the passenger side. They stopped at the corner of a closed service station along Coral Way where Javier could make a phone call, while his accomplices remained in the car. When he returned, he told Felix to continue driving west and to watch his speed. There were many plans yet, much to do. Everything had to be carried off with precision. Now they were off to meet the boss, he said, where they would change vehicles then rendezvous at a secret, neutral point and divide the money.

"Who is this boss?" asked Chico.

"It is better you don't ask his name," Javier answered. "When our work is done tonight, you will never see him again and you will never know who he is. You understand, don't you? It is to protect you as well as him."

Both men nodded, then laughed as Felix quipped, "I guess that means the boss is not a *mujer*, eh?"

"I can tell you he is the one who set up the whole deal, who knew the cartel money was in there. That's all I can tell you." Javier lit a cigar and blew the first puff out a small opening in the window as he took notice of the passing shops, bistros and restaurants along colorful Calle Ocho.

"Where do we go?" Felix asked in Spanish.

"Drive, Felix, until I tell you to turn. It will be a while."

Chico was ecstatic, rambling in excitement. *"Carrumba,"* he exclaimed over and over again. "Did you see that gray-haired bitch, like a fish flipping around out of the water? Ha! And that kid. He never thought he would die inside a piano. The blood was like a fountain. Ha!" Javier listened, his eyes dancing as Chico recapped the joy of violence. Felix spoke not a word. "I will buy a Cadillac and enough dope for a lifetime. First thing, I need a woman. A good woman."

"You were in Castro's prison much too long, Chico," said Javier. "You must be careful or you will be in the prison of Uncle Sam. Watch how you behave and who you talk to. Keep your mouth shut and you will stay out of trouble. Like Felix here. See, he just does his work and no talk."

Chico looked to the taciturn one driving the car and asked, "And you, Felix, what are you going to do with a half a million dollars?"

Felix never took his eyes off the road. "*Mi madre en Cuba.* I am trying to arrange for my mother and my sister to come to the United States. My mother, she is very sick." Then Felix looked at his leader in the rear view mirror. "I want to thank you for choosing me, Javier. My mother would thank you, too."

"Do not tell her about me, Felix. Just say it was a friend."

At one a.m. the streets were nearly deserted as they sped west from the suburbs on a four lane road. Felix looked to his left and commented, "Ay, the Krome Detention Camp is down this road, a hell I will never forget. How much further, Javier?"

The road narrowed to two lanes. "Another couple of miles; just keep driving. We'll be turning off soon," he answered chewing a cigar.

"And you, Javier, what are you going to do with the money?" asked Felix.

"Business, *amigo*. You'll see, I will double or triple this by being smart."

Now they were more than thirty miles west of Miami penetrating through the blackened Everglades when Javier ordered Felix to turn left on a gravel road in what seemed like a dark ocean of wilderness. The Lincoln slowly jiggled its way parallel to a canal for half a mile until they came upon a sharp left in the barren road.

"Stop the car here; do not turn," he said to Felix. "This is where we are meeting the boss. He should be here in fifteen minutes."

"Who is going to hold the money?" asked Chico, warily.

"We will transfer one of the bags to the other car. Don't worry, Chico. You will be paid for your work. Trust me. Meanwhile, keep the windows up in here. Damn mosquitoes."

With the air-conditioner on, the three men waited amid the sea of grass with only the sounds of crickets, frogs and the purring engine to break the eerie silence. Javier stepped from the car saying he needed to piss, then returned two minutes later. When all conversation had ceased and Javier saw that Chico and Felix had rested their heads back, he quietly lifted the same Glock semi-automatic pistol that dispatched Lillian Diefenbach two hours earlier, pointed it under the elevated headrest and fired one shot into the back of Chico's neck. Javier turned the gun to the left and fired another shot into Felix's right eye. Felix slammed back against the window while Chico listed to his left side, gurgling and drowning in his own blood. Javier waited in the back seat for several seconds until the gurgling stopped and he knew Chico was dead. He reached across and removed the keys from the ignition, careful to avoid touching the bloody corpses.

The night was silent again when Javier stepped out of the car, walked around the corner and past a hummock of palms and foliage to make sure the dark blue 1999 Buick Regal was still parked there facing the opposite direction. He opened the trunk to the Lincoln and made two trips, transferring the satchels to the Buick. Then he re-entered the Lincoln through the rear seat and reached across to turn the wheel to the right, careful to avoid contact with the dead man's blood. He started the ignition, lowered the gear shift into drive and hopped backwards onto the gravel road, watching as Felix's "baby" sank into a murky grave.

CHAPTER 8

LONG, FINE HONEY-GOLD HAIR fluttered from the open window of her speeding red Toyota Supra as tall buildings shrouded in colored spotlights across Biscayne Bay provided a warm glow to the midnight skyline. But she paid no notice. There were no noises now other than the whoosh of air and those that haunted the inner sanctum of her brain.

Wracked by grotesque images, the sounds of death, and the stench of fresh blood which lingered deep within her nostrils, she found herself driving aimlessly across the Rickenbacker Causeway past the Seaquarium over bridges to Key Biscayne, though there was no earthly reason to be there. She wanted to scream, to break down, to lose control.

Get a grip girl. Come on. What are you going to do? You've got to get home. You gotta play it normal. Get rid of your things, quick. You can't leave any trace.

Carefully, slowly, she spun a U-turn. She nearly panicked at the sight of a City of Miami police car cruising the opposite direction. It was not uncommon being stopped for no reason, a young woman in a flashy sports car all alone, often a hazard of being beautiful. She checked her speedometer, then the rear view mirror and breathed a sigh of relief as the cop car continued on.

Images flashed, vivid, penetrating, compelled to relive each second of every horrible minute. "*Matenla!*" shouted the tall one with the eel skin boots. Each time she saw Janie held to the mirror, her eyes darting in terror and the gun pressed to her head, she gripped her mouth. *No screaming.* Then, the crazy one — laughing. *Why was he laughing? Oh God!*

She stopped briefly in front of a Brickell Avenue motel, slipped a pair of coins into a *Miami Herald* dispensing rack before aiming her Supra toward Kendall. The car was quiet. No radio. No rock and roll. She had to think. But her brain could not seem to function. She was losing her control. It was all so ugly; blood, bodies, gunshots, screams, Lillie on the floor looking up at the tall Cuban. "*You son of a bitch. BANG!*"

The digital clock showed *12:23.* Under a star-clustered sky, she pulled in behind the sprawling Dadeland Shopping Mall only two miles from her house and wrapped the brown pageboy wig and her non-prescription glasses in a tight fold of the newspaper. She looked around nervously, exited her car and deposited the wrapping in the dumpster. Humidity was stifling as perspiration poured down her body like a shower.

Her mind mired in the nightmare, she drove back onto Kendall Drive reliving the images again and again, the shouting in Spanish, the crazy one giggling, poor Janie, the gunshots, *BANG! BANG!* Ken shivering in the attic and Chad's lifeless body rolled up inside the grand piano smothered in blood. Trembling, she pulled into the driveway of a two-story townhouse in the upscale Royal Oak development, feeling relieved that his car wasn't there. Clasping her hands together in an effort to stop shaking, she turned off the lights and took a very long breath.

Like a common burglar, shoes in hand, she tiptoed into her home and stopped to open the door to her daughter's room. She was sound asleep. She took a plastic garbage bag from the pantry which she would use to discard all her clothing, including her underwear and shoes. Orange fiberglass residue from the attic insulation had clung to her jeans and she was desperate to get rid of it.

Hurry, she thought to herself. *He'll be home any minute. Calm down. Calm down.*

Ascending the stairs, she was startled by the subtle click and soft hum of the air conditioning compressor turning on. Perspiring profusely, she opened the door to the darkened bedroom and furtively stripped her clothing off and into the bag. Then she shoved it behind long dresses hanging in her closet.

In the bathroom, she looked at herself in the mirror for the first time since it happened and saw a completely different woman than before. Her beauty was absent, as were the poise and the confidence. She felt unclean, frazzled, petrified and confused.

I've got to calm down. Stop shaking.

She opened the cabinet, reached for a vial and swallowed two Valiums, then turned on the shower tap. It was in the solitude of the steaming, tile chamber that her control collapsed. As water pulsated upon her, she scrubbed until her pink skin seemed raw. Images, the vivid horror, continued to race through her mind. *BANG!* The cold-blooded, deep set eyes and that cocky gait. The green, eel skin boots. *"Matenla!"* Janie quivering in terror before the crazy one fired the shot through her brain.

"Nooo. Nooo," she wailed as the water beat upon her breasts. Sobbing uncontrollably, she slipped to the tile floor, feeling so terribly alone. She thought about her marriage, her family and her home, wishing she could take it all back, start over again and make it right. But that was impossible.

Wrought with shame and fear of being exposed, she prayed aloud, repeating over and over, “Please God, don’t let him find out. Please God.” She would have to live through this nightmare, this dilemma all by herself. "Oh no, oh please no." And she cried until the water turned cold.

By the time the Valiums kicked in and the crying jag was out of her system, she composed herself and tried to figure what to do next. She needed a plan. She backtracked, thinking of any clues she may have left. The clothing under the bed was headed for the dumpster next trip out. Then there was Ken, the black dancer. It all seemed so hazy, he on top of her, groping, noises from outside, then pushing him off. As far as he knew, her name was "Mirage". The same with the redhead, Carolyn. That's all she knew.

Hey, whatever happened to her? Hopefully, Sylvia didn't blow her identity. Thank God, I went under another name. Thank God, I wore a wig.

Had the killers realized she was there, she would have surely been killed. Ken was the only one who could tell the cops about the mysterious woman.

About her.

For a moment, she gave passive thought of coming clean, to suffer the humility and turn herself in. Get it over with. Then she thought again.

Sure, you're going to tell your husband that you went to a sex party, got drunk and had a brief fuck with some young stud you never met before. Right!

She had to talk to somebody. She thought of her best and only friend in the entire world, returned to the bedroom and picked up the phone.

"Beth, it's Robyn. Listen, I'm sorry. Yes I know it's almost two o'clock in the morning, I'm really sorry, but... something's happened, I've got to talk to you."

Beth Ann Lieberman could hear the desperation in her voice.

"I've got to meet you. Beth, please! It's urgent. I can't tell you on the phone. I'm in big trouble. I mean now!"..."I know it's almost two in the morning."..."No, no, I can't come there. I'll meet you at the Brown Sugar Pub on South Dixie. Look for me in a rear booth. Hurry, please."

She scrambled for her purse and a slip of paper. Then she scribbled a short note for her husband; *Got an early client. Will call.*

Wearing no make up, she donned a pair of gray baggy pants and one of her husband's plaid shirts that hung nearly to her knees. With her hair stacked under a Florida Marlin's baseball cap, she was as inconspicuous as she could possibly be at that hour. No one would know her at the Brown Sugar.

The moment she grabbed the sack of clothing, she was startled by the sudden ring of the phone. She ran next to the bed to monitor the voice mail. Sure enough it was him, her husband. After the beep, she heard him talking in the background. Then, "Hi baby. It's me. Listen, uh...say, how come you're not home yet?"

Pick it up. Come on, talk to him. No, I can't, I can't.

"I'm stuck here working late. Well, what else. Same old story, I know."

He's got to think I've been home. Come on, pick it up.

"But this is important..."

Sound groggy, like you've been asleep. Hurry.

"Well, sorry I missed you, I'll try..."

Her heart pounded as she slowly raised the receiver. "Uhhh... Hello," she said, restrained.

"Hey, honey. Good, you are home. What's the matter? You sleeping?"

The images started to reappear again. Shaking, she pulled the phone away from her head a moment, swallowed and took a deep breath.

"Yeah, honey. I came home and went right to bed. I'm not feeling too good."

"Well, it's just as well then. Sorry 'bout that. I'm tied up; won't be home for a while."

"It's all right. Hey, don't you worry about it." A moment later, she realized she had hung up without saying goodbye.

Her heart raced as she lay back on the bed in the dark bedroom, composing herself, breathing deeply, staring at the ceiling. As she turned her face, she felt small, hard objects beneath her neck, irritating her. She rose to see what they were. There was his message; two Hershey Kisses lying upon the satin pillow. A shadow of the past. A message of love and desire. He would want her when he arrived home.

My God, I can't. I couldn't.

Robyn Estevez grabbed her plastic bag full of clothes and ran sobbing to her car.

ROBYN HAD PASSED BY the Brown Sugar a thousand times but went in only once. The pub was sparse with regulars, most of whom were local blue collars getting off work at midnight who never went straight home from a job. A husky woman with short brown hair served drinks and laughed heartily from behind the bar. She swaggered like a coal miner.

A Taylor Swift record bellowed from the juke box when Robyn spotted her bespectacled friend open the tinted glass door, scan the dimly lit room and step in. Robyn waved her over.

"Murders? My Lord. What murders? Are you crazy, Robyn?"

"Don't say that, Beth. Come on. Please, listen to me. I'm dead serious. You've got to help me." Trembling, Robyn started to weep again, hands to her face. It was the first time in twenty-two years that Beth had seen her friend lose her composure. She shifted seats and put her arm around her.

"Easy now. I'm with you. Tell me what happened, Sugar."

The barmaid approached and Beth ordered an orange juice. Robyn had been sipping a glass of zinfandel.

Between bouts of weeping and trembling, and omitting few details, Robyn sputtered through the ordeal, her images as vivid as the moment they occurred. Jaw agape, Beth Ann sat speechless as her best friend described a scenario that she thought only took place in horror movies. But this was not fiction.

"My God, that's the most horrible thing I've ever heard. Those poor people. Look, I've got chills. How did you ever keep your sanity? Oh, how frightening." Beth Ann took a moment to reflect, shivered involuntarily and then regrouped.

"What the hell were you doing in that bedroom in the first place?"

"Beth, oh Beth," she paused, struggling with her memory, "I don't...I was so drunk. I guess I got turned on. Both these fellas dancing balls naked and all the champagne...I never expected all that. I just...I guess I just let loose. I hardly remember. The next thing I knew, I felt him, this black guy on top of me, moving like he was in me. It was Ken, the dancer, taking advantage, thinking I wanted it.

"As soon as I realized, I shoved him away, told him to leave me alone. Actually, he was pretty decent about it and he backed off. It must have been my fault, leading him on. I don't know. It wasn't me in there. It was Mirage, my other me, my alter ego. It sure as hell woke me up."

She sipped from her glass and continued on. "It all started just after we were dressed, the shouting and screaming from outside in the living room. Things crashing. God, we were so scared. My head was pounding. We were in such a panic, so afraid. Ken spotted the attic cover when we were in the closet. I helped lift him then he pulled himself up. He yanked me up like I was a rag doll. My God, Beth, a minute later they were in there. We would have been killed with the rest of them." Robyn choked, reached for her glass, but quivered and pulled away. "We crawled in the darkness across beams and then we stumbled on another hatch. I lifted the edge just a crack and there we were, over the hall stairs with a birds-eye view of everything."

"Weren't you afraid they'd spot you? My God! How could you just watch all that?"

"I don't know. It was something, well, it's hard to explain, but it was like disgusting and horrible, things you would never want to see in your lifetime, ever. Yet, I couldn't turn my eyes away. I don't know why. I wish now I had. Poor Jane, poor Sylvia, that poor young boy." She sobbed into her handkerchief once more.

"Look, sugar, I'm here for you. What can I do?"

"Beth, I can't go home. I mean, right now, I couldn't even look at Mike, yet alone go to bed with him. He'd know. I know him. He'll see it in my eyes. He'll see the images I cannot erase." She paused and looked down at her drink. "Mike said if he ever caught me screwing around, he wouldn't kill me, beat me, shit, he wouldn't even curse me. He would just pack his suitcases and never look back."

"But you weren't screwing around, Robyn. You were taken advantage of. Surely..."

"Right. Then how do I explain being at a sex party with men hired to take off their clothes? Huh? How do I explain being in bed with that guy? Beth, that's the bottom line. I was in that bed. God knows what Ken is going to tell him. Jesus Christ, the second time in my entire life I ever shared a bed with another man besides Mike and I get caught in this, this, horror. I feel....I feel so dirty, so ashamed."

There was a long break in the conversation as Beth allowed her friend to collect herself. Robyn blew her nose again while Beth sat calmly with an arm around her shoulder. Country music played in the background.

"It was disgusting, Beth."

"I would imagine."

"Those poor, poor people."

Beth Ann looked at Robyn with amazement. Her skin was still as perfect as the day they first met, smooth and tight like a baby's bottom. This was the darling high school senior of 1991 fantasized by an entire Miami High football team until she married class stud, Miguel Estevez, the day after graduation. It was storybook. He was as brilliant as he was handsome. Together they were the dream couple, madly in love and the envy of all their friends. "It's too bad," Beth said, her arm around Robyn's shoulder.

"Too bad? What's too bad?"

"Oh. It's just a shame everything with you and Mike has fallen apart. You would never have been there tonight."

She dabbed her eyes. "Shit, Beth, he's oblivious. He hasn't the faintest. He still thinks everything is hunky dory. He's not married to me. He's married to the goddam Miami P.D. Homicide Bureau and has an illicit affair with his wife once in a while."

"Yeah, but, you know, sugar, there are a million women who would love to be in your shoes."

"Come on, Beth Ann. I don't have to tell you. How would you like it if Sam were to never come home, if you saw him once or twice a month, conscious that is, and it went on for years and years until you became strangers. You still have needs, you know." Robyn hesitated, then reflected, "Maybe you were right. Maybe I have been greedy. I wouldn't be in this mess now if I had taken your advice and let the marriage die a natural death."

"Well, I always said, you got guts."

"I can't help it if I love him. I've always loved him. I always will. I couldn't imagine sharing this planet without that man."

"I know."

Robyn's eyes gazed out into space. "I feel so dirty, Beth. So dirty. God, if he ever found out..."

Beth placed her hand over the top of Robyn's glass. "Booze is the worst thing for you now. You need to keep your wits about you," she said forcefully. "Listen to what I'm saying. I think you're in more trouble than you realize."

She raised her head, eyes darting. "You mean, you can top this?"

"Think about it. What if your husband really breaks this case? You'll have more to deal with than just Mike. What about the killers?"

Robyn raised her head and looked to the ceiling. "Oh Jesus, that's right. God, they'll hunt me down. What about Corrina?" Robyn's eyes gushed once more. "Beth, this is one time...no, Mike cannot solve this case. I can't let him. I can't ever let him know I was in that house. They'll kill me."

"Okay, Robyn. Get hold of yourself. First of all, think hard. Is there anything that could get you identified? Anything?"

"Unless I run across Ken or that girl, Carol, I think I covered my tracks well. I don't think they'd recognize me. I was in disguise. I'm Mirage. Anonymous."

"What about records? Did you check in at the gate? Did Lillie have a list?" She removed a pen from her purse and began making notes on a paper napkin.

"No. The guard passed me through as soon as I said 'Lillie Diefenbach's'. I wore a brown wig and phony wide rimmed glasses. I don't think Lillie knew who I was."

"How did you get invited?"

"Sylvia. My beautician. I don't even know her last name. She owns...well, owned a shop on Miami Beach. I went for a highlight last Saturday and while she was telling me these raunchy stories, you know, she invited me to this party where they were hiring male strippers. I wasn't going to but Sylvia said it would just be fun. No harm in it. So I thought, what the hell? It was something different than another Saturday night waiting up for a man that wasn't coming home. Sylvia was quite the woman. There was nothing she wouldn't do for kicks."

By this time, Beth had returned to her own side of the table. "Does Mike know you go there? To Sylvia's?"

"No. He doesn't have any idea what I do other than what I tell him." Robyn pondered for a moment. Then it struck her. "Oh shit. I see what you're getting at. Damn."

"Records," Beth said.

"Yes. I must be listed in her appointment book. Mike will trace that." Robyn sipped from a glass of melted ice. "Damn, Beth, how can I get to it?"

"I don't know, Sugar. We'll think of something."

The product of the rural south, Beth Ann Lieberman was reared as a preacher's daughter until the age of fourteen when her parents were divorced. Her mother moved to Miami where secretary jobs were plentiful and the pay was better than in Macon. That's when she met Robyn Saunders, far and away the prettiest girl in the school and the heart throb of every red blooded, acne-ridden kid this side of the Georgia line. But Beth wanted for nothing. She was college educated and married to a successful, real estate broker and a licensed sales agent in her own right. Her career, her million dollar bay front estate and her three Himalayan cats were the focus of her life.

Robyn was not only a friend but an employee of her company for the past five years. That was when the dutiful wife who had lurked in the shadows of the famous Miami homicide detective decided it was time to seek a life of her own. Mike would always have murders to solve, court to testify in and interviews to give. Robyn would have clients and self-esteem.

When the music fell silent, Beth Ann grabbed a handful of quarters from her purse and walked over to the juke box and punched a half dozen numbers at random. The blaring sound of Elton John allowed them to resume their furtive conversation.

"Why don't you give Charlie a call?" Beth asked. "He said he would always be there if you ever needed him. Maybe he could help in some way."

"Charlie? Come on. What could he do? Break into Sylvia's shop for me? Forget it."

"Well, you know how crazy he was about you."

"Please Beth. All that is distant history. There was never anything between us anyway. If I called him, it would only compound everything." Robyn caught Beth's expression as she looked back at her quizzically. "Oh Beth, I know you think he's such a great guy, but there is nothing there for me. Nothing. I've always wanted this marriage to work. Forget Charlie."

The barmaid approached the table once more to announce last call. Beth waved her off. Juke box music echoed through the room. "Okay, Robyn. Let's get your wits together here. I see it this way. First, you need to find some way to get your name out of that appointment book. Second, I'll find you a major client and you find yourself a safe haven out of state somewhere until this settles down. Corrina is thirteen. She's a good kid; she can handle herself just fine. I'll look in after her."

"And what about Mike?"

"I'll stay in touch with your husband. He trusts me. And I'll keep you posted. Just watch your ass."

"You're a dream, Beth. Thanks. But I can't go off, not just yet. It would be too coincidental. Anyway, by sticking around, I'll know how the investigation is going. Maybe there's a way I can throw him off. I don't know. Let me think about it." Robyn crossed her arms. "My God, my God, I'm so mixed up." "You said you couldn't get close to Mike right now."

"Oh, I think once I get over these jitters, I'll be in control enough. I think I can fake it. I have to."

Beth Ann reached across the table, touched Robyn's hand and said, "I have an idea."

"An idea? About what?"

"The appointment calendar."

"What is it?"

The music came to an abrupt halt as a bright spotlight suddenly illuminated the entire room. The barmaid announced it was closing time. Then she turned up the volume to the television which rested upon a shelf behind the bar. It was the five a.m. news:

"DETECTIVES ARE STILL ON THE SCENE OF A GRISLY QUADUPLE

MURDER IN THE UPSCALE COCOPLUM COMMUNITY IN MIAMI.

NAMES OF THE VICTIMS ARE NOT BEING RELEASED UNTIL NEXT OF

KIN ARE NOTIFIED. THERE ARE NO SUSPECTS ALTHOUGH POLICE

HAVE ISSUED A BULLETIN FOR A WOMAN APPROXIMATELY THIRTY

TO THIRTY-FIVE YEARS WHO GOES BY THE NAME OF MIRAGE.

ANYONE WITH INFORMATION CONCERNING THIS WOMAN SHOULD

CALL THE CITY OF MIAMI POLICE DEPARTMENT. NOW WITH US, WE

HAVE THE CHIEF INVESTIGATOR, DETECTIVE SERGEANT MIKE

ESTEVEZ."

"Come on, sugar. Let's get outa here."

IT WAS EIGHT-THIRTY on that Sunday morning when Mike Estevez wearily entered his Kendall townhouse hoping to catch two or three hours of sleep. He would be useless going on without rest. Corrina was gone for an early day at the beaches, normal for the weekend if there was a good sun. Robyn's note said she had an early client. It was routine. He would be crawling under those cool sheets alone. Ah, a good stiff Johnny Walker Black. *Where are you, Johnny?*

As he shed the clothing he had worn for the last twenty-four hours, he glanced over to the photo of him and Robyn taken on their ski trip at Tahoe five years ago and reflected. They had become near strangers, he thought. Such a wonderful, beautiful woman.

I'm so lucky to have her. So patient. So understanding. Someday, I will make it up to you. I promise.

Perhaps this should be his last homicide case, he thought to himself, then go on to do more teaching. Perhaps get promoted. Time to move on. He felt so tired, so weary.

As he laid his head upon the pillow, his brain brimmed with details. He cursed Raul Gonzalez for blabbing classified information to the media:

Fucking asshole! That jerk is going to get our witnesses killed. Mirage. Mirage. Who is she? Why didn't she stay?

He thought about Carolyn Webb and how lucky she was. By now, she must be awake. Perhaps she knew Mirage. He made a quick call to headquarters. Al answered.

"The Assistant State Attorney says we got to give her the Miranda warnings before taking any statement, Mike. They asked, 'what if she turns out an accomplice like maybe she set the whole thing up'."

"Who's the prosecutor?"

"Dick Jacobson."

"Good. He's the best. How's her attitude?"

"Still groggy and confused, but she'll make it. Mike, she works for some law firm in Miami and she's worried about her job and all this shit getting out."

"So, give her the warnings. Big deal. Tell her it's just a routine part of your job. You'd give your own mother the warnings. Right? Now that she's sobered up, did she tell you anything about Mirage?"

"*Nada, amigo*. She paid little attention to Mirage. Says she was sort of standoffish. Doesn't know her from Adam. Or, 'McAdams', if you get my drift."

"Hilarious, Al. Just get some preliminaries okay? But hold her there. I've got to get a couple hours sleep and I'll be in a little later to take her statement. Keep it together for me, my friend."

It was a matter of seconds after setting the clock that Miguel Estevez drifted off into slumber, dreaming about the greatest man in the history of planet earth, Doctor Jorge Alfonso Perez-Estevez, physician, cardiologist, surgeon, father, husband, patriot. His subconscious flashed to the day he and his parents arrived at Miami International Airport fleeing from a communist dictator. He remembered the waiting and more waiting, the endless lingering at the airport and the dense crowds of weeping Cubans, frantic over being ripped from their families. He was only three then. He dreamed of his father's wisdom, his advice, *"You are now an American, my son. Your children will be American. Be proud of your Cuban heritage, but you must live and act as an American."*

Visions of that terrible day flitted in and out of the deep channels of his brain, seeing his father in 1996 lying in an adorned casket, the senseless victim of street muggers in search of drug money. His was an heroic, generous and dignified life snuffed for eternity at the whim of two kids with a gun. He heard his Mama wailing. Then his father's words passed in and out of his dreams like they came from heaven, *"You will be a great doctor, Miguel. A great surgeon."* And Miguel spoke aloud in his sleep, "Yes, Father, but not before I avenge."

Then he dreamed of the soft, warm flesh of a beautiful woman with her legs around his body, her long narrow fingers combing through his hair and the most beautiful eyes in creation peering at his through moist lashes telling him, "I love you, Mike."

"I love you too, Robyn."

CHAPTER 9

MARCO SCANDIFFIO WAS AN OBESE, balding, venal lawyer who lived high on the twenty-fourth story of a luxury Brickell Avenue condominium overlooking sparkling Biscayne Bay. His wealth came not so much from attorney's fees, but from wheeling and dealing with the Columbia drug cartel who entrusted him with laundering and investing money in places where IRS and the cops could never trace. It was a craft he had mastered well. His weakness was an insatiable quest for more and more money. There was never enough.

He often boasted of owning half the judges in Miami-Dade County with enough clout to get any drug case either dropped or transferred to a court that would. Though he fancied himself a lady's man, he had been buying services from the opposite sex nearly all his adult life. A bloated face framed his large, bulbous nose, and he pulled his side hair tightly back into a pony tail. In the comfort of his plush abode, Marco wore Bermuda shorts that hung below his giant gut covered by an oversized tee shirt which identified its origin in bold letters, *Nieman Marcus*.

He remained seated in his patio chair as the tall Latino ambled through the apartment in his green eel skin boots before stepping onto the wrap-around terrace. Javier stood for a moment to admire the dark, panoramic view of glittering bay and the glow from Key Biscayne in the distance. An arrangement of multi-colored lights from gleaming cruise boats sparkled at the docks of Dodge Island a mile to the north. Marco handed his nubile blonde harlot two hundred dollars in cash and waved her off.

"Close the door and sit." Marco's voice sounded like he had just swallowed a pound of seaweed. "You got the money?"

"*Si, senor.* Everythin' went bery smooth. A leetle messy, but smooth. The mooney is downstairs in the trunk of my car ready for you to geeve the word."

Marco blotted his forehead with a dish rag. "And Lillie? You didn't make her suffer, did you? She was a decent broad. Did she hold out or what?"

"Man, she was a tough lady. She hold out until everyone but her was dead. But I make sure she no suffer. One boolet between the eyes. No pain." Javier snorted and lit a cigarette. Marco studied the Latin for a moment, awestruck by the sheer callousness. "What ees the matter with you, Marco? Everythin' all right?"

Slowly, distinctly, with his gravel voice subdued, Marco said, "Javier, I want to make one point so you understand. Okay? Now, this is not to say that I don't trust you, but I got to protect my ass, too. Right?"

"All right."

"So it is important that I tell you one thing before we go any further." He took a drag from a cigarette as Javier listened. "If anything should happen to me, you should know that I have a tape recording stashed in a safe deposit box about the entire rip-off with instructions to my confidant to send it to Carmine Escandar in Medellin. It names you and all the others, except me, of course. Now, if all goes well and I remain a healthy lawyer practicing in Dade County, I will have the tape destroyed one year from now. *Comprende?*"

"Marco, I would never..."

"Now, you understand what Carmine's reaction would be to all this?"

"Marco..."

"*Comprende?*" His tone became more forceful.

"*Si, amigo.* But you have nothin' to worry about."

"What did you do with the two aliens?"

They went for a little swim. In the Everglades. The crazy one almost went out of control." Javier snorted. Marco chuckled.

The two men shared snifters of Courvoisier as Javier amused the fat lawyer with a brief report of the grisly murders, garnering another chuckle from Marco when he heard that the blond boy had been dispatched inside a piano. He was assured no witnesses were left alive and no traces left behind. For sacrificing a few expendable lives, they each were another million dollars richer.

They adjourned into the opulent apartment where modern furnishings of black, red and white sat upon Italian marble floors partly covered with sections of tiger skin throw rugs. The mirrored wall opposite the sliding door offered a spectacular view of the eastern panorama. Hallways leading to the spare bedroom were lined with a blanket of framed photos of a younger, thinner Marco Scandiffio hugging and shaking hands with an assortment of notable personalities. They sank into huge recliner chairs to watch the local news on the sixty-one inch Mitsubishi. It was five a.m.

"Well, Javier, let's see how famous you are. After that, we will divide the money."

"...ONE OF THE MOST BRUTAL CRIMES IN THE HISTORY OF MIAMI,

HERE WITH US NOW IS DETECTIVE MIKE ESTEVEZ, THE LEAD

INVESTIGATOR IN THIS CASE. DETECTIVE ESTEVEZ, CAN YOU TELL

US..."

"AH HA, there's that son of a bitch," Marco whispered under his breath. "I swear he lied on the stand. That's the only way he could have beaten me on the Samoyez case." Marco sniffed the bouquet from his cognac. "Fuckin' bastard. He's a sharp cop. I don't like it, him on this case. He's too fuckin' straight."

As always, Mike Estevez was immaculate on camera, flawlessly speaking in articulate, resonant tones, ever cautious to limit the dissemination of classified information. Hard hitting questions were being asked about a mystery woman named Mirage but Mike refused to identify the reason they were searching for her. He passed it off as one of a myriad of leads.

Marco's eyebrows bridged at the center. "Mirage. Mirage. Who in the fuck is that?"

The reporter continued questionsing:

"DO YOU HAVE ANY INFORMATION YET ON THE THREE LATIN
MALES, SERGEANT ESTEVEZ?"

Clearly caught off guard, Mike shifted his head and asked why he was asking such a question. The reporter was tenacious.

"WE WERE TOLD THAT THREE LATIN MALES WERE INVOLVED"

Marco Scandiffio digested what he had just heard. Peering at the television, he listened carefully as Mike asked who it was that gave out that information.

"LIEUTENANT GONZALEZ, YOUR BOSS."

Mike appeared frustrated.

. . .

"WELL, THAT'S UNCONFIRMED SPECULATION AT THIS POINT. I WOULD APPRECIATE IF YOU WOULD NOT..."

A RAGE BOILED within the fat man as he pondered the reporter's question and the cop's reply. *Three Latin males? How in the fuck would they know that?*

Oblivious, Javier was more interested in the cognac, reveling in his now famous achievements. Javier raised the snifter to his lips as Marco sneered, stood suddenly and slapped it out of his hand, smashing it against the mirrored wall. Javier raised his hands in disbelief.

"Did you hear that, you fucking asshole?" growled Marco.

Javier leaped to his feet. "Hey, man, watch who you call an asshole, eh? What ees the matter anyway?"

Livid and crazed, Marco's face glowed a bright cherry. "How in the fuck could they know there were three Latin males? Huh? Who did you leave alive in there?"

"No one, godammit. They are all bery dead. Bery dead. Chico even shoot the dead one for good measure."

Marco stood, paced and burst into a vituperative tirade, flailing arms and causing Javier to shift nervously. He still hadn't figured it out.

"Someone had to tell them that there were three of you assholes. Get that? Not two, not four, but three. How else would they know? Now, do you get it, you stupid fuck?"

"Okay Marco, but dun call me asshole, and dun call me stupid." Confused, Javier searched his brain, then remembered. "Wait. Lillie's bedroom door was locked. That was strange. She say she always keep it locked. But no one was in there."

"Someone was there all right. You heard that fucking cop on TV. You better fuckin' find out who that was and take him out. You hear me? Or her, whatever." Marco shook his head in disgust and waddled over to the bar to pour another brandy. Dazed, Javier sat gazing at the television while Marco ranted on. "Jesus Christ, I don't believe this. If they get to you, they'll trace me. This is bad. Very bad."

Marco angrily played the news conference back to see what he may have missed the first time. He held the snifter to his nostrils muttering, "Mirage. Who is that fucking Mirage? Why are they looking for her?"

"I dun know, boss. But I find out. I promise you. I find out."

They remained up long after the orange sun appeared over the horizon, counting and dividing two million, one hundred thousand dollars while neither left each other's sight.

CHAPTER 10

BY ELEVEN THAT SUNDAY MORNING, Miami Police headquarters was in a state of chaos. The chief had authorized overtime for a full squad of detectives to follow a tsunami of phone leads pouring in from well-intentioned citizens. Special tape recorded lines were dedicated to all incoming calls on this one case. Arrangements were being hurried to accommodate a hungry press corps with FAX machines, phones, computers and twenty-four hour police representatives to serve as liaison with the chief.

The cramped Homicide Bureau office was dense with men in polyester suits and women in pants outfits with telephones stuck to their ears trying to hear over the din of voices, ringing phones and the non-stop clicking of computer keyboards. The parents of Chad Morrison sat weeping in a room away from the business area, waiting for Detective Randy McAdams to give some rational explanation for the insanity of his death. In another waiting room, the thirty-two year old daughter of Sylvia Cicerone was being consoled by her husband while waiting to give her statement in which she would tell all about her mother's friends and enemies. Janie Tucker's husband and two sons were somewhere on the other side of the world on a business venture. No one was there for Lillian Diefenbach. She had not a single living relative.

Chief Howard and his entourage of top staff made periodic appearances in the building to assure the media they were "on top of the situation". The mayor, with the youthful black chief standing at his side, appeared briefly for a live interview to CNN. In the lobby constantly ablaze with the glare of camera lamps, reporters scurried in and out the doors. Off camera, they asked to speak to the principals in charge of the investigation, particularly Sergeant Mike Estevez, his lieutenant, Raul Gonzalez and the captain of the Homicide Bureau who, as it turned out, had to be uprooted from a golf tournament by an enraged chief.

With much yet to be done, Mike would only sleep a couple of hours before returning to headquarters. As soon as Mike Estevez entered the building, it seemed everyone demanded his attention, the media, other detectives, the brass, the chief. He dodged everyone he could and gave the chief a fast-paced hallway briefing with Lieutenant Gonzalez scurrying along like a baby elephant keeping up with the herd. The press corps was informed that a conference would be held at five o'clock.

In a tiny interview room on another floor away from the hubbub, an attractive but weary freckle-faced redhead finally composed herself after being informed by Al Sanchez that her party mates had all been slaughtered. When Mike Estevez entered abruptly, Carolyn Webb was taken aback. "Haven't we met before?" she asked.

"I'm the one who parked your car last night, Mrs. Webb."

"Oh. Yeah."

"I see you've been crying. I'm very sorry about your friends."

"Oh, it's terrible. I still can't believe it. Listen, Sergeant, do you know how much longer I have to stay here, I..."

"Just enough time to take your statement, Mrs. Webb."

Carolyn Webb signed her perfunctory Miranda warnings and candidly answered questions posed by Mike Estevez. An older, matronly woman named Penny with blue-grey hair and prune lips sat expressionless to the side, busily recording Carolyn's statement on a steno machine. It was an extremely small office, barely large enough to fit four people and a desk and chairs. The walls were bare.

"Your name, age and address please?"

She spoke in a distinct South Carolina accent. "Carolyn Sue Webb. I live at 315 Seagrape Lane, Key Biscayne. But you already know that anyway."

"Age?"

She cast a coy look at the dashing detective. "Is that important? Well, okay, I'm thirty-three."

"Are you married?"

"I'm divorced."

"How long are you divorced, ma'am?"

"Over a year."

"Your ex-husband's name? And what does he do?"

"David Webb. He's a pilot."

"And where are you employed?"

"I work for a law firm as a secretary and receptionist."

"Mrs. Webb, I want to ask you several questions about a party which you attended on the night of...."

Carolyn unabashedly described all the lurid activities that took place at the home of Lillian Diefenbach, the booze, the drugs, the dancing and the sex. She held nothing back. When she narrated the sordid details about the naked boys and her foiled attempt at arousing the white dancer, the bony fingers of the blue-grey haired woman pounded the keys harder and harder, never wavering from a blank stare.

"He had a problem getting it up."

"That's all right, ma'am. Can you tell us how you came to be invited to this party?"

"I got a call from Lillie saying Sylvia was putting on a special celebration for her birthday and they were going to have male strippers and all. Hell, I couldn't pass that up."

"When did Lillie call you?"

"Late Friday night. Why?"

"Why would Lillie think about calling you?"

"Well, I guess she knows I like having a good time, you know."

Mike felt the urge to press, to put her on the defensive. "No, I don't know. What do you mean?"

Carolyn Webb hesitated a moment, looked at the steno then peered directly into the eyes of the Cuban detective, answering with a sheepish grin. "I like screwing around. I make no bones about it. That answer your question?"

Bony fingers continued to pound while Mike checked his notes. Al Sanchez looked away.

"How did you come to know Mrs. Diefenbach?"

"Through my ex-husband, David. She was an old friend of his parents. Known him for years. When Eastern Air Lines went belly up, Lillie was there to help David get work. She was one of

these people who just knew everyone and could do anything. She had lots of connections. She even helped me get a job in her lawyer's firm."

"And what is her lawyer's name?"

"Marco Scandiffio."

Mike knew him well. "Mrs. Webb, do you know of any reason Mrs. Diefenbach would be in possession of a large amount of cash?"

"My heavens, no. Well, she was a very rich woman. You know that, don't you?"

"Are you familiar with any of her dealings with criminals?"

"Why would I know stuff like that?"

"What kind of work did Lillie find for your ex-husband?"

"Piloting. Freelance. Private jobs here and there. You know."

Al Sanchez interrupted. "Mrs. Webb, if you don't mind my asking, but was your husband aware of your, um, extra curriculum...?"

"You mean my screwing around? Yes. That's why we were only married a year. It was my fault. But I wouldn't change a thing. I'm just not the kind to be married. Not these days, anyway. I think we're still friends. That answer your question?" She looked alternately at each detective. "I'm trying to be as honest as I can."

"Yes ma'am."

"You know, fellas, I'm pretty shook up and I've been here for four hours. Like, can we finish this another time?"

"One more thing, please," asked Mike. "About the woman named Mirage. You say you didn't know her. Can you give me a good description?"

"Honestly, I didn't pay much attention to her. She acted like she wanted it that way, sort of off to the side, you know? But she got into it pretty good. I mean, she latched on to that good lookin' black kid toward the end and turned on the steam, if you know what I mean."

"What did she look like? Please, ma'am."

"About my height. Pretty. Very pretty. Glasses, big glasses. Dark brown hair in a page boy. Tight jeans. Great ass. Hardly said a word. That's about it."

"Do you know her connection to Lillie? How did she get invited?"

"Seems something was said about being one of Sylvia's customers. Sylvia had lots of girls in her following over at the shop. Janie Tucker, I know, was one."

A young secretary suddenly opened the door and motioned for Mike, saying there was an important call. He told Al to finish the statement, stepped outside then took the phone to his ear. "What's up, Zeke."

"This kid, he flipped again, Mike. I mean he's losing it real bad."

"What happened?"

"I was dozing off next to his hospital bed when he hears a couple of doctors talking behind the curtain in Spanish. That did it. He went bonkers, man, trying to run out of the hospital until an orderly tackled him. Shit. You know Jackson Memorial as well as I do. There's more Spanish here than Puerto Rico."

"Where is he now?"

"I got him in a bathroom, still shaking. He does not want to go home."

Mike paused, thinking. "Zeke, if you don't mind, take him to your place. He'll be okay with you. I'll meet you there in an hour."

Before leaving, Mike returned to Carolyn Webb's statement

room to give her a final admonishment. "Mrs. Webb, you are not to talk about this matter to anyone. Do not even tell people that you were at that house. That means no one. It's for your own good. Do you understand?"

She smiled, coyly. "Yes sir, Sergeant."

Mike hurried out the back door from headquarters when he heard a voice from behind, shouting. "Hey, what's going on?" asked an agitated Raul Gonzalez chasing after his lead detective. "You're not keeping me informed, Mike." Gonzalez began huffing and puffing.

Mike was fuming. "Lieutenant, sorry, but I'm not telling you shit." He stopped on the lowest step and faced Gonzalez. "Not only that, I'm filing a complaint with Internal Affairs and the chief for interference with a major criminal investigation." He resumed his brisk gait to the parking lot.

"What the hell are you talking about, Sergeant?" The portly lieutenant was having difficulty keeping up.

"Like I said last night, Lieutenant, don't interfere, and you interfered."

"Interfered? What..."

"You know goddam well what I'm talking about, Raul. I'll bet you even taped that press interview, you egomaniac."

Lieutenant Raul Gonzalez could only watch as Mike abruptly trotted off to his car and squealed out from the parking lot. Friction between the two Spanish cops continued long standing, especially since Mike refused to join the Brotherhood of Latin Officers despite pressure from fellow Hispanics. When asked, Mike tersely replied, "I'm a man and I'm a cop, Raul. Don't pigeonhole me, okay. You don't see a Brotherhood of Anglo officers, or Irish, or Polish, or Jewish, do you? I don't need your pull, so get off my back."

MIKE PULLED THE CAR INTO Richmond Heights, a predominantly middle class, black residential development south of

Miami where the deacon of the Baptist church was awaiting his arrival. His name was Zeke Ferguson.

"Boy, sure glad to see you, Mike," said the giant cop. "He's calmed down some, but Jesus, don't even dare sound like you're Spanish."

Mike had no discernable accent. He grew up from the age of four in an English speaking environment where his father would talk as much in English as he would Spanish. It was his way of teaching Mike to assimilate.

Mike and his partner sat in a straight chairs leaning toward the young man who lay motionless on Zeke's bed. Calmed now, he was awake. The shivering had stopped. Without rising, he spoke in a soft, low tone. "Sorry about all the trouble, guys. I guess it's affected me more than I knew. You don't know. It was bad, man. I'm scared, real scared."

"What happened, son?"

"It sounded like their voices. That's all. Honest, I want to cooperate and all."

"Listen, Ken, you are a very important person to us. You've never been needed more in your life than you're needed now." Mike spoke slow and soft. "Now, I'm not going to bring you back there but I do need more information about that woman, Mirage. We have an expert on the way here and he is going to draw a picture from your description, so we can find her. Okay?"

"Yeah, that's okay."

"Now, Zeke here and I are your friends and we will help you get through this thing. Anything you need and we'll get it for you. Tell me every little thing that comes to mind when you think about Mirage. Anything she said. Anything she felt like."

"A real fox, man. I mean, uh, you want me to go into the sex and all?"

"Everything. Leave nothing out."

"First, the way she moved. All woman, man. Like she was made to turn a guy on. I can smell her now. Her perfume was somethin' else. I'll never forget her wonderful aroma. I think I kinda fell in love with her, at least for those few minutes. She had this real soft voice, like she always talked in a whisper. But she was real drunk, like half unconscious, ya know? We got started and all, ya know? Doing it. You want me to go on?"

"Sure, go on."

"And then she pulled away, like she changed her mind or somethin'. What a body!"

"She have any tattoos, any jewelry, religious symbols or a charm, a watch, rings, fingernails. Anything?"

"No. No jewelry. Just that scar on her stomach I told you about. She wore those big glasses. I think her eyes were blue. Not sure, really." There was a short pause as Mike watched him ponder. "Man, she was some cool chick."

"Why do you say that?"

"Hell, what we went through and she kept her cool all the time. I couldn't watch that shit, man, but she stayed glued, watching those killings. I thought for sure we'd get caught. Then, she just calmly gets her shoes on and walks out the door, like it was nothin'. Now here I am."

Mike leaned over to place his hand on Ken's shoulder. "We'll take care of you, Ken. We'll take good care of you."

"I won't have to testify or anything like that, will I? I mean, you know, I can't I.D. nobody, not for sure." He looked up at Mike's partner.

Zeke replied, "Everything will be all right, son. Yeah, we still need you to testify, just to tell what you know. You can understand that? We'll watch out for you."

"Me? Testify? Like, in court?"

"Look, Ken," answered Zeke, "it's no sweat. You stay here at my house for as long as you need. When I'm not here, my boy is. He's seventeen. Later on, I'll take you home when you're ready. Right now, we gotta get going."

Ken curled in a fetal position, tucked his hands under each arm and looked at each detective, one, then the other.

Before leaving Zeke's house, Mike Estevez tried calling home, only to hear Robyn's voice mail message.

CHAPTER 11

IT WAS ONE-THIRTY that Sunday afternoon before Robyn finally fell asleep against Beth's shoulder in the front seat of her BMW. They drove what seemed like the entire perimeter of Miami-Dade County, talking, searching for answers and strategies, anything that could ensure she would never be identified to the police or to the killers. Exhausted as well, Beth Ann saw it as an opportunity to drive home, grab a sandwich and get some needed rest of her own.

Unable to awaken her friend, Beth summoned her husband, who was engrossed in a baseball game, to help carry Robyn inside. "What's wrong with her? Where's Mike? What's going on?" he asked.

"Don't ask any questions, Sam. Please. Just help me get her into a bed. She's had a rough night. It's a personal thing."

Sam was a good man, a dutiful husband, and not one to go against the wife he adored for fifteen years. Besides, the Marlins started the game off with two back-to-back homers and he was anxious to get back to his den. Together, they helped Robyn into the house where they promptly made her comfortable in the guest room. Beth took off her shoes and saw that one of her big toes was covered with a small bandage. As she reclined partly aroused, Robyn muttered, "Oh God, she's dead. Oh my God, look..."

"What the hell is she talking about?" he asked.

"Who knows, Sam? Who knows? She's having a bad dream."

THE HANDSOME DETECTIVE stopped for a moment to study the eight by ten photo of the composite drawing in his folder, then buttoned his double breasted jacket, palmed his hair into place, checked his watch and opened the door.

Mike Estevez hated critiques. He needed to be in the field, chasing witnesses, hassling finks, organizing searches, collecting evidence, not "grab-assing" with cop egos and wasting precious time as the case cooled down. But, it was one of those necessary stages in coordinating a major investigation so that mounds of information could be funneled in a single repository, stored and evaluated. Detached and confined to a sterile laboratory, forensic experts needed to know how the physical evidence linked to the case, while detectives needed direction so they would not trip over one another.

Prosecutors treasured these discussions, a way of staying involved in a case which was certain to become a media frenzy before ever reaching the courtroom. Legal guidance to the police was essential. Preserving and testing evidence, witness statements and suspect confessions were all essential to a prosecutor, yet worthless if unable to pass the test of admissibility. With so many players comprising a criminal investigation, communications constituted the common thread vital to any solution.

Before uttering a word, he approached the green chalk board and erased all the old figures and numbers, brushing his hands after finishing. The detectives, the lieutenant, Captain Barnie Davidson, and the forensic experts remained hushed as Sergeant Mike Estevez took a new piece of chalk and began drawing an overview sketch of the crime scene with emphasis on the sunken living room, anteroom and kitchen. Still wearing his green Doral golf shirt, the glum homicide captain sat at the corner of the room, unhappy to be there. I.

Richard Jacobson, the slender prosecutor, listened studiously from a swivel chair.

They gathered in the Detective Bureau squad room which housed a dozen misarranged steel desks and as many swivel chairs, rows of file cabinets, waste cans, telephones, bulletin boards and clutter. An ugly cord hung from the center of the round wall clock. It was six p.m., sharp.

"Before we start, ladies and gentlemen, I feel compelled to make a point." His eyes lasered on Lieutenant Raul Gonzalez sitting on the edge of one desk, an unlit cigar between his fingers. "Confidentiality is an urgent matter in this case. I cannot emphasize that enough. Everything that is said in this room is classified. Any leaks of information not only jeopardize the investigation, they will put our witnesses in harm's way. You all know what fate lies in store for these people if the killers get to them first." He paced, slightly, shifting eyes from person to person. They were ever so attentive. "You are not only prohibited from talking to the media, unless first screened by myself, you are not to discuss this case with any other police officers, captains, commissioners, governors, senators, girl friends, boy friends, family members or your dog. Somebody might overhear you. Is that clear?"

A chorus of "uh huhs" and nodding heads.

"First, I want to start with the Crime Scene Unit. Gail Dow, your report. Just summarize, please."

The portly woman spoke in a raised voice, articulating as though testifying in court. She informed the assembly that three hundred and ten photos were taken at the scene, one hundred forty-five latent prints lifted, dozens of blood samples collected and seven spent nine-millimeter casings recovered along with two Glock semi-automatics. Only six spent bullets, four from the heads of the victims, were recovered, leaving one of the expended casings unaccounted for.

Also collected were five strands of long brown hair, a pubic hair from the bed sheets, dried fluids and a small used bandage recovered from the floor.

Two automobiles were impounded and processed, one a 2006

Mustang registered to Chadwick Morrison and the other a 2009 Chrysler registered to Sylvia Cicerone. Tire tread impressions found in the soft sand across the road from Sylvia's car were also photographed with oblique light. Men's shoe impressions were discovered in the bushes outside the mansion, one of which matched the dirty shoe print located on the face of the front door. Twenty-eight feet of nautical nylon rope cut into seven sections were removed from the victims. It was common material.

"Aerial photographs?" asked Estevez.

"Scheduled for nine in the morning, weather permitting," she replied.

"What about the house under construction two lots away. And the dock that's been built in the rear?"

"Sorry, Sergeant. That'll be on our agenda tomorrow."

"We also need to find that other projectile."

"Yes sir."

"Mary Ann Iversen? You're next." Mike nodded to a thin buck-toothed woman who supervised the Trace Evidence and Serology Sections of the Crime Lab. She sat adjacent to Gail Dow. "What do you have for trace evidence?"

She spoke with a nasal voice. "Well, first of all, we did a preliminary on some of the hairs this afternoon. You can forget DNA on the long brown hair. Not even blood type. It's synthetic, not real hair at all. It probably came from a wig."

Mike Estevez lifted the photo composite with exasperation. "Wonderful," he said. "You mean we spent all this time drawing a picture of Mirage and she probably doesn't even look like this?"

"Uh, well, yes. It's likely her hair, anyway, is totally different than that."

"Go on."

"Pubic hair? Haven't had time yet. Shoe prints? Well, one of our expert is on vacation and we couldn't reach the other. Might just be out of town for the weekend. No info on that yet. Uh, sorry."

Estevez's eyes darted across the room. "McCabe, what does serology have for us?"

The bearded scientist from the rear of the room said that every blood type known to man and dog was collected from the house, including a stool from an unflushed toilet bowl in the main bathroom. And, like Mary Ann said, there was no DNA to be gained from the synthetic hairs.

"Mark Sanders? Have you had a chance yet to look at any of the latents?"

A former FBI technician, the golden-skinned, black gentleman wore a thin mustache and bifocals resting on the tip of his nose. He reported there were hundreds of value latents but lacked the time yet to study any of them. "But there is an interesting patent," he remarked, reminding everyone that a patent print is one that is visible. "The band-aid exhibits an impressed print of value that can be identified. The ridges are such that we believe it came from the finger of a large person, probably a man."

"Very interesting," remarked Estevez. He glanced to Zeke Ferguson. "Zeke, we need to talk after the meeting. Maybe it's your boy Ken." Zeke nodded in agreement.

"Gus Grimanski, status please."

"Status of what, Mike?" Sergeant Grimanski leaned back in his chair, arms folded across his chest and a double chin bulging from his neck.

Mike was dumfounded by his retort. "Gus, please, the neighborhood canvass, the interviews, the guards at the gate, what you saw on your arrival."

"Oh...well, the kid, you know, the black kid, when the uniformed officer and I got there, he was sitting on the street holding his knees to his chest shivering like a ton of feathers in a hurricane, almost incoherent, rambling on and on pleading 'don't let them get me'. I just put him in my car until you got there, Mike. Neighbors? Didn't see or hear shit. Oh, sorry, ma'am."

"The guards, Gus?"

"They waved people through that were going to the victim's house. I think I told you that. But I also called the kid that worked the gate three to eleven."

"That's great, Gus. Now will you share with us what he said?"

"Oh, yeah, sure. He didn't take tags or nothin' but he remembered that a couple of the chicks, I mean ladies, sorry again, ma'am, that headed for Lillie's place were good lookin'. Like the brunette in the little red car and the one with freckles that drove a blue Cobra. Says she even winked at him."

Estevez was excited. "Wonderful, Gus. Good work. What kind of little red car was it?"

"Didn't ask."

He turned to McAdams. "Randy, will you make sure someone follows up?"

Randy McAdams and Al Sanchez, both under thirty, intelligent, eager and honest, were the proud protégés of Mike Estevez and everyone knew it. Wearing tailored double breasted suits, they sat in tandem at the same desk prepared to recite a myriad of information from their legal pads.

"Has anyone checked out the weapons yet?" Mike asked scanning the room.

McAdams rose from his chair, a little weary, but earnest. "Well, we haven't confirmed through serial numbers as yet but we think they came from a truck hijacking reported last month. Six hundred Glocks hit the streets. That would explain leaving them at the scene."

"Right. Well, I figured it. Randy, what's the scoop on the victims?"

McAdams stood to face his audience. "Lillian Diefenbach, white female, sixty. Her birthday was yesterday, August twentieth. Originally born in Hackensack, New Jersey, father was a president of a labor union, her mother died when she was eleven. Drinks champagne, does not do drugs, registered as a Democrat but doesn't vote, banks at Southeast and has a checking balance that could buy all our houses together. She had an abortion at age thirty. No criminal record, but she's connected. Her wealth comes from marriages to two elderly real estate investors who died over twenty-two and then fifteen years ago.

“Intelligence says there is a file on her where she was identified as a power broker for organized crime by an informant who turned state's witness. Like, she don't do the crimes, but she does big favors because she knows so many people. Her lawyer is Marco Scandiffio. You know him, Mike. We'll research her more and identify her associates."

"Get me a list of Marco's clients, okay Randy?"

"You bet."

"Trauma?"

"A cut and a bruise to the left side of her face, ligature marks from the ropes binding her ankles and wrists and a single gunshot, non-contact entry wound between the eyes. Lights out."

"Anything else on her?"

"No, except that we believe she's a customer of one of the other victims, Sylvia Cicerone. That's the wild-haired woman who owns a beauty shop on Miami Beach."

"Go on."

McAdams continued on with the bio on Sylvia, most of which was garnered from her thirty-two year old daughter. "She was not connected as far as we know. Her old man was a car thief but that was fifteen years ago and she never remarried. Get this, he died taking a crap in the men's room of the courthouse waiting for arraignment." It brought laughter from the otherwise somber group.

Gus Grimanski interrupted, chuckling. "The jail scared the shit out of him." Mike glanced, but did not laugh.

Randy continued on. "The daughter says her mother switched to a lesbian years ago. Says she had a heart of gold."

"Trauma?"

"A cut and bruise on her face similar to Lillie's and some deep ligature indentations from the ropes, a mouthful of regurgitation and a superficial gunshot wound to the back of her head. Doc Gavilo says she drowned in her own vomit."

"Tough way to go. Randy, I assume you are keeping a chronological lead sheet, indexing assignments and so forth."

"Shit, I've got over two hundred already and it's not even twenty-four hours."

"Al, what have you got on the grey-haired woman?"

Sanchez stood up, buttoned his jacket and faced the group. "Name is Jane Vaughn Tucker, white female, fifty-two, lives in

Cocoplum. Must have walked to the party. Married to a Fred Tucker, an antique broker who's incommunicado right now somewhere in Hong Kong with her two sons thirty and twenty-six. We figure she's either a friend of Lillie's or Sylvia's customer, maybe both. We don't know yet. We doubt that she's a player in the crime picture, just a lady in the wrong place at the wrong time."

"Trauma?"

"Ligatures, a bruise on the right side of her face and a contact gunshot wound to the right temple. Her eyes were wide open."

"And the boy? What do we know about the dead boy?"

At that moment, a secretary cracked open the door and motioned for Zeke Ferguson. The tall detective excused himself and ambled out quietly.

Speaking with a slight Spanish accent, Al Sanchez gave a brief, heartfelt narration of the boy's life according to the parents, how he loved his dog, of his homosexual lifestyle, of his ambition to one day be a movie actor and of the savage, dehumanizing death he suffered. Al was Cuban-born with charm, charisma and a voice that held the audience spellbound.

Mike was about to bring up another issue when Zeke Ferguson stuck his head back through the door and motioned him out of the room. He gestured to his audience. "I'll be right back,"

Zeke took Mike's arm, towering over his partner. "It's the kid again, Mike. It's Ken Lancaster."

"Oh no."

"Yeah. He's taken off. My boy just called. Apparently, Ken said something about testifying and not letting them find him. My kid's only seventeen. He wasn't going to butt in."

Frustrated and angry, Mike paced and balled a fist into his hand. "I knew we should have locked him up. I shouldn't have made you come to the meeting."

"Stop blaming yourself, man. Don't be so hard on yourself."

Mike searched his brain and looked at his watch. "Okay, alert all units in the district but do not, I emphasize, DO NOT put anything out on the radio. I don't want the media to know that this kid even exists. Jesus!"

CHAPTER 12

SUNDAY NIGHT

ROBYN WONDERED what was taking Beth Ann so long. It was past nine p.m. Around the corner, South Beach bustled with hordes of young people as she waited what seemed like a century in the dark alley behind the shops. The vibrator on her cell phone went off twice in thirty minutes, once to the Miami P.D., Homicide Bureau and the other to some number she did not know, but she ignored them both. The strain was unbearable. If she could only stop the trembling, she thought. She wasn't sure she could go through with it.

Sandwiched between a travel agency and a Jewish deli, "Styles By Sylvia" was a non-descript storefront that faced busy Washington Avenue at the southern tip of Miami Beach.

Two blocks to the east, in another world, the Art Deco District bustled with thousands of Yuppies and pleasure seeking tourists wandering the streets, cruising, eating, drinking and partying at the scores of restaurants and night clubs facing the ocean.

Starting in the 1980s, redevelopment successfully revitalized this once deteriorated, mile-long row of 1930s style hotels into a

Mecca for models, photographers, movie makers, musicians, artists, bikers, skaters, runaways, drugs and sex. Along with the tourist explosion came the nascent traffic dilemma for which Miami Beach roads and parking facilities were ill-equipped to meet.

People parked in any cranny they could find, figuring the fine was worth it. That was good for Robyn because her car would not draw any attention parked in the alley behind Styles By Sylvia.

Sylvia's shop was situated in the center of the block where street lights illuminated both ends of the one story building, leaving her in the darkest part of the alley. If she got caught by passing tourists cruising through, she figured she would simply claim to be an employee coming in to check her bookkeeping, then pray.

She had not been home so she was still clad in her husband's size-large shirt over her baggies and her hair pulled under a baseball hat. She stopped the car, shut the lights and assumed she was at Sylvia's door because Moshe's Deli was painted on the one beside it. She checked her watch and muttered to herself, "Come on, Beth Ann. Where are you?"

She saw that the shop's door knob had a push button lock plus a hasp and padlock. No dead bolt. She wondered just how easy it would be to break if she had to. A partly eroded decal displayed a nugatory warning that an alarm system protected the store, but the company's name was illegible. *Alarm? What do I do if an alarm goes off? What if it's one of those silent ones? Oh God, Beth, where are you?*

Her heart was pounding again just like it did in Lillie's attic. Suddenly, she heard a clinking sound from behind. She breathed deep when a grey cat jumped from the trash can behind the deli. She sat back in her car and took a long deep breath. *Okay Robyn, calm down. Stay cool. You've gone this far.*

It was another typically humid August night, and the perspiration was already trickled down her neck. A pair of headlights turned into the alley and she felt relieved to see the BMW as it neared.

"Jesus Christ, Beth, what took you so long?" Robyn asked as she walked to the driver's window, looking left and right.

"Sorry, sugar, but I spent thirty minutes on the phone before I found a locksmith who would come out tonight. He's on the way. Said he'd be here in fifteen minutes."

"I don't know about this, Beth. I don't like involving you. I mean, it's so risky and all."

"Don't worry about it, Robyn. Let's face it. You're the most exciting thing in my life anyway, so I may as well enjoy it while I can. Besides, if this guy ever gets questioned, you don't want him describing you. Me? I'm like a piece of oatmeal in the bowl. No one would ever figure it was me here."

"What if the alarm goes off?"

"Then we haul ass, Sugar. That's all." Beth Ann saw that the door to Sylvia's shop had a padlock. "Have you got a lug wrench for this car, Robyn?"

"Yes, why?"

"That padlock. You're going to have to break that padlock or I won't be able to open the door from the inside."

"Oh Jesus. I'm shaking, Beth."

“Look, settle down,” Beth whispered. “It's going to be okay. He's going to be here any minute and I said I'd be waiting out front. When I leave, you take that lug wrench and slip it into the lock and twist. Do it. Come on."

As Beth Ann drove off, Robyn watched her tail lights turn out of sight. Quickly, she opened the trunk, pulled out the iron tool, checked both directions then inserted it into the arch of the lock.

Beth Ann was right. As soon as she twisted, it snapped. She had performed step one of her first felony. As she placed the lug wrench back into the trunk, a Fire Rescue van at the end of the alley suddenly blared its siren. Robyn yelped, her body leaped and she convulsed into a mass of tremors. Her knees buckled as she slipped back into her car. It seemed like hours before Beth Ann finally returned and opened up the door.

"What took you so long, dammit?"

"Some old, lonesome Jewish guy that wouldn't shut up. I'm sorry. Come on, sugar. Let's find what you're looking for."

Like the pair of burglars that they were, they slunk past the row of old hair dryer chairs heading directly to the front register where the books were kept. As Robyn passed Sylvia's chair, she thought about the fun loving eccentric, always laughing, always sucking on a cigarette, telling dirty jokes, cussing and making deals. *My God, who would have ever thought?* Then she whispered to Beth, "That's the chair where Sylvia did my hair."

"That's nice. Shhh."

"You know, Beth. You can go. There's no sense you risking any more. I can..."

"Robyn. Shut up."

The sounds of footsteps and laughter from passing pedestrians crescendoed and then faded as they stooped behind the counter. Robyn heard herself breathing, almost panting. The taste of salt reminded her that beads of sweat had rolled down her face.

She mused over being the wife of a cop, and now she was a common burglar. She had to hurry. Next to the register lay a three-ring, loose leaf notebook just like those from real estate school. Sure enough, it recorded the appointment list for each hairdresser and manicurist for the past four months.

"This is it," Robyn whispered.

Stooping, she rapidly flipped pages until she found her name listed for August thirteenth and ripped it out. Then she figured her name would be listed on past appointments but there was no time to go page by page. She shoved the sheet of torn paper into her panties figuring she would destroy it later.

It was almost over. Robyn began wiping the book and the counter with her hanky. "What the hell are you doing?" Beth asked.

"Fingerprints, Beth. We can't leave our prints."

"We can't leave our asses in here any longer either. Let's go."

Beth tugged on Robyn's arm. As she turned, her elbow made contact with a table mirror which smashed to the floor. Frantically, they leaped and hugged.

"We got to clean this up," said Robyn, panicked.

"Sugar, I'm leaving. You comin'?"

The broken glass remained on the floor as they snuck out the rear door. Robyn slunk nervously into her Supra while Beth Ann waved goodbye and headed to her own car parked a block away. "Call me tomorrow, Robyn."

"Sure. Thanks, Beth."

Robyn did not switch the car lights on until she reached the end of the alley where she turned onto Ocean Drive and assimilated into the lines of traffic, still wiping perspiration from her face with a soggy tissue. A block south on Ocean Drive, in the center of a jam, she looked in the mirror at flashing red and blue lights coming closer from behind, silently, no siren. They were less than a block away and getting closer as traffic yielded. *My God. There must have been a silent alarm.* Instinct urged her to run for it, gun the accelerator and take her chances. It was her only chance.

Do it now, or get caught. Wait, relax. Don't panic. Act like you belong here.

Following the lead of other cars, she drove upon the sidewalk to allow the Miami Beach Police unit to pass. It turned on the very street she just came from. *Whew!*

She was about to cross the bridge to McArthur Causeway when the phone vibrated against her waist. Startled, her heart skipped another beat. It was Mike's number. Unable to stall any longer, she decided to answer and pulled into a convenience store parking lot.

A parade of delivery trucks passed by and opened her window to allow the noise. She put one hand over her ear. "Where am I? Um, I'm at a pay phone up in Aventura Mall," she lied. "How are you doing, honey? Speak up. I can hardly hear you."

In the heat of the night and over the dissonance of traffic noises, Mike rambled to his wife about the spectacular Cocoplum murders while complaining of exhaustion from only four hours of sleep in two and a half days. He said he missed her and asked if she was coming home tonight. "Yeah, honey, sure. I can hardly hear you. I'll see you later." *Don't get him suspicious.* "Give me an hour or so. I'm taking this client to her hotel."

"It's okay, baby. Right now we're searching for a witness that ran off and disappeared. I'll still be a little while. I just miss you. Are you okay?" Mike sensed the stress in her voice.

"Yeah, honey, I'm okay. Um, who's your witness?"

"Some male stripper, a black guy. Would you believe, he watched the entire killing with some girl hiding in an attic and now he's really spooked, afraid the killers are going to find him."

"I can imagine how he must feel."

"MISS JACKSON, my name is Mike Estevez and this here is Zeke Ferguson. We're both detectives from the City of Miami Police Department." Like so many times before, they held their badges to a jalousie door.

"Oh lord, what's happened to Kenny? I've been so worried. Is he all right?"

"Yes ma'am. He's all right. May we come in?"

She placed an index finger to her lips as she invited them into the house. "Please, try not to wake the baby."

Christina Mae Jackson lived in one side of a small duplex in the black section of Coconut Grove less than a mile from where these same two detectives parked Carolyn Webb's car just twenty-four hours earlier. The interior was dark and sparsely furnished, illuminated only by a small television with nearly inaudible sound. On each table sat groups of framed photographs of a baby girl with herself and Ken Lancaster holding hands, smiling for the camera. A portrait of Martin Luther King Jr. hung on the wall over a porcelain crucifix.

Small and delicate and wearing a terry robe, the men were struck by her soft, dark features, large brown almond eyes and an easy going quality about her. She seemed homey and sweet, honest, trusting.

"When is the last time you heard from him, ma'am," Zeke asked.

"Why do you want to know?"

The young woman crossed her arms under a healthy bosom and insisted with serious eyes on knowing the purpose of the visit.

The young mother was informed of the hunt for her boy friend and briefly told his role in the now famous Cocoplum murders. She said Ken worked as a male stripper for a sleazy company called

Caesar's Teasers but she was unaware his services extended any further. Mike told her nothing about his bedroom interlude with Mirage, only that they escaped together and hid in the attic.

Once she took a breath and absorbed the shock of it all, she was ready for questions. "Anything I can do to help. My goodness. Thank God, he's alive. I don't want to see Ken get hurt. I love him so much. We're going to be getting married next June you know. On our baby's birthday. Can I offer coffee to anyone?"

Zeke asked the questions. "Miss Jackson, when is the last time you heard from Ken?"

"About an hour ago." The detectives looked at each other. "He said the company was sending him upstate for a special show. Supposed to be a lot of money. We really need the money, you know." She paused and pondered a moment. "Well, I guess that was a lie."

Zeke answered, "Probably didn't want to worry you, ma'am."

"Did he say where he was going, Miss Jackson?" Mike asked.

"Didn't say, I didn't ask. He has older brothers and sisters who live all over, some in Pompano Beach, South Bay, even Lighthouse Point. He's only close with one of them. Name's Fitzgerald. Everyone call him Fitz. Maybe he would know? You know, he coulda told me about those murders and all. I'd understand."

Mike checked his Rolex. It was now ten fifty-five p.m., plenty of time for Ken to have been picked up and driven the thirty miles to north Broward County.

"Would you mind calling to check, please?"

Christina phoned Fitzgerald Lancaster in Pompano Beach who said he hadn't heard from Ken in days and knew nothing of his whereabouts. When he asked why she was inquiring, she placed a hand over the receiver and looked up to Zeke. "He wants to know why I'm asking?"

He whispered back, "Don't say anything, ma'am, about the murders. Don't tell no one."

"Just a little worried. That's all, Fitz. That's all. Thanks. Bye." She hung up abruptly.

The interview went on for half an hour as Christina did her best to cooperate. "Friends, other relatives, what does he do in his spare time? How about ex-girl friends? Where is his address book? Where does he work out?" Drink? Smoke? Drugs? Does he have a car?" A thousand questions, it seemed, with few answers.

It was near midnight when the detectives ended their inquiry and walked out toward their car. Zeke turned around and saw Christina standing on the porch under a dim yellow light. With one finger, she wiped a single tear that had nearly dropped to her lips. Her voice was barely audible. "Please find my Kenny. I know he do things sometimes, but he's a good man. He love his little girl."

CHAPTER 13

IT WAS 12:30 A.M. when Mike dropped Zeke off and headed for home. With his brain on overload, he figured there was nothing left he could do until tomorrow. The investigation machine was in full gear with another dozen detectives in the field following leads around the clock. McAdams was a loyal and capable subordinate, as was Al Sanchez. He had confidence in both.

Another briefing was scheduled with the chief in the morning and probably more press conferences. He thought about Ken Lancaster and Mirage, their uncanny survival, wondering where she was and now searching for him as well.

There was Raul Gonzalez, the buffoon who politicked his way into homicide without ever working an investigation in his entire life. He had to deal with him, but he would also try to keep him as ignorant as possible to preserve the integrity of the case.

He pondered the nuisance press and how to keep them placated which caused him to reflect on Gloria Menendez, her Spanish eyes and that porcelain complexion. A cloud of guilt came over him for even imagining another woman. He had the perfect wife at home, a perfect daughter and the respect of the law enforcement arena. It was a perfect world, indeed.

He was happy to see the red Supra in the driveway when he pulled in.

"Well, hello there, stranger." Robyn sat up in bed as though reading a book, clad in one of his faded F.O.P. tee shirts. Her long hair draped casually over a firm but modest bosom. It was the first time in two days they had been in each other's company. Disheveled and tired, he leaned to one side of the doorway and gave her the once over. He smiled. She smiled back, nervously.

"Why don't you let me make you a drink while you get comfy?" she asked

"I'm beat, baby. I've really had it. It's been a rough couple a days."

"Seems like I've heard that before," she replied, walking by him. He grabbed her gently by the arm and pulled her body to his. She stiffened, then jerked away.

"Something wrong?" he asked, quizzically.

"No, honey. Uh, I'm just a little tired, too." She gave him a peck on the lips, saying, "I'll get you that drink now."

Mike wondered why she was acting like an iceberg. "How's Corrina? She okay?" He shouted down the stairs.

When she returned, Mike saw she was not making eye contact, her movements were jerky, her smile strained, her persona detached. "She's fine, Mike," she replied with his drink in her hand. "She'll be staying at Cindy's this week. With your case load and my calendar, I thought she'd be better off. Besides, she can pig out on her mother's cooking."

"How did it go with the new client?" he asked as he hung his suit in the closet.

"What new client?"

"The client you told me about on the phone. You know, Aventura, or someplace like that." He looked at her, questioning.

She hesitated, then, "Oh yeah. It's a woman from Canada. Big bucks. Wants to invest in a motel."

"Are you sure everything is all right, baby?"

"Everything is just fine, Mike. You're working another big

murder case and I'm off doing my thing. How can it be more normal than that?"

"Come on, baby. Please don't start in."

"I'm sorry, Mike. I'm sorry."

As they lay on the bed together, Mike reached over to touch her face. "You look beautiful, baby. I really miss you, you know." He leaned over to her neck. "What's that you're wearing? Really smells good."

"Shalimar. A gift from the office."

"You seem so up tight."

"Sorry if I seem distracted. I guess we both have had a full agenda, haven't we? And, you know how I am just before my *friend* arrives."

"I told you before, Robyn, I don't believe in that shit. Women use that as excuses for..."

"Come on, Mike. Let's not get into that again. Tell me, what's going on. Tell me about your big case."

He sighed, deeply. "Oh baby, this one is a whopper. National news. What a slaughter. Four dead bodies, a house full of blood, everything smashed. Those poor people. And that new Lieutenant, Raul Gonzalez. What an asshole."

It was normal for her to ask, just as it was normal for him to confide in her. "Want to tell me about it?"

Just as he admonished his fellow workers not to, Mike began telling his wife the graphic details of the crime scene. Robyn laid back listening, forearm over her eyes, seemingly aloof.

"Poor kid, stuffed in a grand piano like a side of beef all because he took a job entertaining a bunch of sick broads." She remained completely motionless, listening. "Two of the women were laying side by side in a huge pool of blood in front of all these mirrors. I mean, gruesome. The owner was some rich old lezzy named Lillian Diefenbach. She was on her back with a bullet between her eyes."

Mike saw her lips quiver, then the bottom lip disappear under her top. He thought she was disturbed by his ugly descriptions.

"Are you okay, babe?" he asked.

"Excuse me, Mike. I have to go to the bathroom." He lay his

head on the pillow for several minutes until she reemerged with a cold, damp rag in her hands. "I have a little headache. Sorry," she said returning to bed. "Go on, Mike."

"When it was all over, this woman, Mirage, whoever she is, just split leaving the black kid all by himself. They even shot a little poodle and stuffed it between Lillie's legs." Robyn laid the damp cloth over her eyes.

"What did you say?" she asked.

"I said they killed the dog, too." Then he asked, "What's the matter with you, Robyn?"

"Nothing."

"Geez. You get more emotional about a dead dog than a dead person."

She swallowed, struggling to reply, "Well, you know how I am about animals." Then she changed gears. "Tell me about your leads. What about that black fellow?"

Mike's eyelids began to droop while his head sunk further into the pillow with every breath. "He's gone. Took off. Schizoid. That woman Mirage supposedly saw everything. Supposed to be a foxy lady but cool as dry ice." Robyn listened closely as Mike drifted off. "Can you imagine that. Some good looking chick hopping in the sack with some guy she never even met before? What a fucking whore."

She wasn't surprised. It was consistent with the Mike Estevez moral value structure. Yet, a cold chill consumed her. She swallowed, paused, then replied. "Well, I guess it takes all kinds. Do you think you'll find him?"

"Find him? Find who?"

"That guy. The witness. Are you going to find him?"

"Oh yeah. Alive, I hope, unless they find him first, then he's dead meat."

"Any leads on that girl, Mirage?"

He opened his eyes, looked at his wife sitting rigid against the pillow and asked, "Wanna make love, honey?"

"Mike, come on. You're in no shape. Tell me more about Mirage."

He closed his eyes again. "What about her?" he murmured.

"Any leads on her?"

Eyeballs curled back in his head as he strained to maintain consciousness. "Uh, she's very pretty, little red car, maybe. Got a stomach scar, something like yours, I guess. Wore a wig."

"Anything else?"

It was his final murmur before drifting off. "Fantastic body."

KEN LANCASTER CHOMPED into the pork sandwich like he hadn't eaten in twenty-four hours and washed it down with a tall glass of iced tea. Still, he wouldn't talk about it. He desperately tried to redirect his thinking, to wash his mind, but memories kept reemerging.

The Spanish voices, the ear-splitting gun shots, the dead bodies, the smell of blood, the sight of blood dripping from the grand piano. Fitzgerald sat across the kitchen table perplexed. "Gee whiz, Bro, come on, tell me what kind of trouble you in? You can talk to me."

Fitzgerald looked into his eyes and witnessed a dimension to his younger brother that he'd never seen before: panic. He reeked from wearing the same clothing for over twenty four hours. This was the same little brother that was a high school track star, who dogged his way through college nearing a Bachelor's Degree and who almost died from scarlet fever when he was twelve. He was like his own son. They were the product of the poorhouse, a runaway father and a welfare mother. It was not an uncommon story.

Ken's head felt heavy as a bowling ball. "I need sleep, Fitz. Maybe I'll feel better tomorrow. Then we can talk. Don't tell no one I'm here, please. I mean no one. Make sure Dylonna knows that, too. No one."

"Damn, Ken, I told you doing that strippin' shit was bad news, bound to get you in trouble some day."

"Come on, Fitz. Not now. It paid my tuition, didn't it?"

"Please, Bro, tell me what's wrong. It's driving me nuts. Ain't I always there for you?"

"I'll tell you one thing, and that's for sure."

"What's that?"

For the first time, Ken looked back into his brother's eyes. "Ain't nothin' I done wrong. I ain't in trouble for committin' any crime or anything like that. Just so you know. Okay?" Ken took another bite of the sandwich.

"Okay, but then..."

"Fitz, my life is in danger. I mean, big time. Just believe what I tell you. There are people out there who want to kill me. And if they found me here with you, they'd kill you, too. So, don't say nothin'. It's for your protection now also." Ken Lancaster could hardly keep his head from nodding. "Look, I'm wipin' out here. Thanks for picking me up. I need a bed. Good night, okay?"

"Good night, Bro."

Fitzgerald Lancaster sauntered into the warmth of his den, turned off the console television and lifted the Ft. Lauderdale Sun-Sentinel from atop the bar just where Dylonna always left it. He plunged into his favorite cushy chair and scanned to the sports page, as usual, still confused and pondering his baby brother's dilemma.

Ken was tired, he thought, so we'll get to the bottom of it tomorrow. It had been a long day working security patrol on the commuter trains, on his feet checking fares, smiling, never sitting, even for a meal break. It was his quiet time. As he began to unfold to another section of the newspaper, he lay his head back, just for a moment to rest his eyes. When he awoke the next morning, he looked down and spotted the huge black letters:

"NO PROGRESS IN COCOPLUM MURDERS.
CITY IN SHOCK"

CHAPTER 14

BANG! "I GOT IT!" Little Orlando shouted, excitedly. A marsh hen fluttered its wings as the two boys rushed into the bushes to fire another shot and finish it off. *BANG!*

"Okay, Orlando, come on. Now it's my turn. No fair. I get the next shot." B.J. had yet to fire the nickel-plated Smith and Wesson .38 caliber four-inch special. Pudgy and undersized for thirteen, the revolver felt too large for his small hand. When he spotted an empty beer bottle, he used both his hands to shoot. *BANG!* He missed.

"What will you do if you see an alligator, Orlando?"

"Shoot it. What else?" The Spanish boy was taller and a year older. "Listen, B.J., we're not going to be out here too long. It's too hot. Look at that sun. It must be over a hundred degrees out here. Besides, I don't want to be lunch for the mosquitoes."

B.J. was disappointed. His father prohibited guns in the house and it was the first time he had ever held one in his hands. "Just a little while longer. Come on, Orlando."

Miles of sawgrass lined the dirt and gravel roadway as the boys started back toward their bicycles parked near the Tamiami Trail. A hazy pall seemed to separate the expanse of the Everglades from the blue, cloudless sky but it didn't make any difference. In the intense heat Orlando was getting edgy.

"Hey, did you hear that?" B.J. pointed to the canal where the tail of a twelve foot gator swashed the water, breaking the eerie stillness. "Want me to get it?" he asked holding the pistol up with two hands.

"Yeah, give it a try."

BANG! "Doggone it. Missed."

"B.J., you couldn't hit the side of a house, even if you were standing inside."

Fascinated, the boys watched as the gator submerged itself on the other side. That's when Orlando spotted the murky image of a Florida license tag, then a chrome automobile bumper below the ripples. "Wow, check it out. Maybe it's a stolen car," Orlando said. "Let's get back and call the cops."

"Oh no, don't do that. Gee whiz, if my Dad finds out."

"Don't worry, he won't."

Forty minutes passed before the youngsters watched the arrival of the first Miami-Dade green and white cruiser turn into the dusty gravel road. They were responding to an anonymous call. It had come from a pay phone at Frog City, population eight, barely a rest stop along the hundred mile ribbon of pavement stretching through the heart of the Everglades known as Tamiami Trail. The caller identified herself as a girl, but didn't want to leave a name.

Twenty minutes later, a dusty blue tow truck rambled down the same roadway followed by a van from the Miami-Dade Crime Scene Bureau and then another van marked, "Police Diver". Soon after, the van arrived from Channel Seven News. It was all so exciting. From a distance, hidden by the brush of a nearby hummock, the boys watched the diver slip on his underwater suit then submerge himself in the dark waters next to the car. "God, what about the alligators?" asked B.J. in a whisper. Orlando shrugged his shoulders.

A tall female officer stood near the truck driver as the cable stretched taut, and the car began its slow exit from the canal. The odor was unmistakable. The police officer recognized it seconds after the car window broke the water's surface. "Send me Homicide," she called into her hand held radio.

Just then, B.J. and Orlando wheeled up on their bikes, pretending to be casual passerby.

"Which one of you made the call?" asked the uniformed woman looking at them scornfully.

Startled, B.J. looked up and said, "It was a girl that called, wasn't it?"

The lady cop smiled, "Well, son, how would you know that?"

THE SWARTHY, BUG-EYED CAR SALESMAN watched in astonishment as the tall Latino peeled off sixty-two thousand dollars in twenty and hundred dollar bills. Then he handed over the keys to an old Buick Regal and drove off the lot in the car of his dreams, a white 2012 Mercedes SL550 convertible. He was ready, even anxious to cruise down Calle Ocho where all his Cubano amigos, who thought him a small time coke peddler, would gawk with envy. He was in no hurry. Now, he wanted to be noticed. Javier Jimenez-Izaguirre had arrived.

He tuned to his favorite Spanish music station and raised the volume. The odometer showed only twenty-one thousand miles as Javier drove by with the top down waving at admiring senoritas, his Hawaiian shirt flapping in the breeze. On a Monday afternoon, Calle Ocho throbbed with the sounds of salsa blaring from rows of jewelry, clothing and electronics shops while thousands of Latinos walked, danced and gyrated to the infectious rhythms.

Fifty years had passed in which Miami's Southwest Eighth Street experienced a cultural metamorphosis. Once a simple business road in a southern town, it was now transformed into a total Hispanic community following a five decade explosion of Cuban immigration. Calle Ocho had become Main Street in Little Havana, a country virtually displaced within a country.

Shops, restaurants, garages and old homes were converted into retail shops, funeral parlors and insurance agencies lining both sides of the one-way street from the center of the city for seven miles to the west. Small café windows evolved as the social magnets which drew aliens and citizens together so they could chatter about Castro, the lottery, crime, family, gold jewelry, cops and the price of drugs. It had been over two hours since Javier swallowed his last jolt of Café Cubano. He turned the corner and parked beside a throng of elder Cubanos playing dominos on concrete patio tables. He offered a casual salute.

As he stood by the open café window, he exchanged greetings with a heavy set woman and sent in his order by waving an index finger, "*Café, por favor.*" He sniffed and snorted. It was high noon and the Miami sun was blazing. Beads of perspiration formed on his brow.

The second he took his first sip from the tiny cup, his first customer arrived. Then the next. Two more walked away with their daily supplies of cocaine, all thanking him and admiring his new car. Javier was an important man. A successful man.

He stood near the café for nearly half the afternoon. "I will have much more tomorrow," he told Victor in Spanish. He was a small gentleman, a regular customer who constantly wore white open collared shirts, a sport jacket and a tan brim hat. "I'll give you my cell number. Today is my last day in the streets, my friend. From now on I will have people working for me."

"Ah, *muy bien.* I am happy for you. You are moving up, eh, Javier?"

"*Si,* business is good, *amigo.*"

They each sipped from their small cups of café and smiled. Victor looked around furtively and moved closer saying, "Everybody is talking about the four gringos who were killed in the Cocoplum house on Saturday night. Three ladies, *conyo*, and a young boy. Think maybe it was a ripoff?"

Javier remained calm as a swell of emotion came over him. He was so proud, so anonymously famous. His workmanship was now national headlines. If he could only tell him about the aliens in the car.

"No," he answered staring into man in the eyes, "probably some lover that went crazy. Who cares?" He took a sip and ordered another café.

"Ah, but the rumor is that three Cubanos did it and the police have witnesses."

Javier raised his brow. "Oh, yes? That's very interesting. What else did you hear?"

Victor was talking very quietly, almost in a whisper. "Well, don't repeat me because I have contacts in the police, but there is a woman they are looking for. I think her name is Mirage. That's a funny name, eh? They say she knows everything but they can't find her."

Javier became noticeably somber. "Knows everything, huh? That's strange. How do they know about her?"

"I don't know that, *amigo.* You are right. How would they know?"

Javier's interest was piqued, but he was also cautious not to appear more interested than the average Cubano along Calle Ocho. He snorted and took another sip from the small cup.

"Ah, your police contacts are full of shit. How could they know all this?"

Victor leaned to him again. "My friend is on the payroll. He's like us. I took good care of him one time when my brother went to jail. No problem, you know, so long as the price is right. Don't tell anyone. You, well you are my friend. I trust you."

A direct source inside the police? What a dream. He needed to draw Victor in. "Ah, who cares. They were just gringo pigs." He took Victor by the shoulder and walked with him to his new car. "Listen Victor, I was thinking. How would you like to make a lot of money?"

"Money? Doing what?"

"I have many business ventures opening up, and I'm much too busy to run them all myself. I need some help. Maybe even a partnership. You are the kind of man I trust. You are smart. Are you interested?"

"Well, how much money are we talking about?"

"Good money Victor. At least a thousand a week. Maybe even more."

"Well, it sounds good, but I don't want to go to jail."

"No jail, Victor. It is all legitimate. I won't let you go to jail."

"You are an important man, Javier. I would be proud to be your servant."

"If you can come to my place, say at eleven in the morning, I will get you started. Don't worry, I take good care of you. Say, would you like to ride in my Mercedes?"

Like a fish snatching the bait, the small Latino smiled from ear to ear. He was going to be a big man now.

IT WAS SIX-THIRTY that evening when Javier humped the large breasted brunette in the penthouse suite of the Radisson Hotel overlooking the Palmetto Expressway. He was in heaven, horizontally gyrating to the stirring rhythms of Spanish music playing from the headboard speakers. Now he was rich, and stoned, and fucking a beautiful woman who he would not have to feed. She gave her name as Carlita but that was probably a lie. He had offered her some of his cocaine but she turned him down. The more he went on, the more he thought she was a lousy fuck, just laying there like a limp rag with her arms at her sides. But, who cared? He would never see her again.

Suddenly, he heard a buzzing sound; his cell phone was vibrating across the dresser. It displayed the one number he could not ignore. Reluctantly, he pushed the whore aside and reached for the phone.

"Turn on the television, you fucking asshole!" Growled the angry seaweed voice on the phone. "Channel seven."

He turned his head and whispered into the receiver. "Godammit, I tell you no call me asshole."

"Turn it on, I said!"

Javier watched in disbelief as the video footage showed a wrecker hauling the old Lincoln sedan from a remote, murky canal, water gushing from the trunk and cracks in the windows. In the background, two boys on bicycles looked on while a female police officer held a rag to her nose. The reporter was a dashing young fellow wearing an open collared sport shirt.

"...AND WE ARE STANDING WHERE THE BODIES OF TWO MEN WERE
RECOVERED FROM A VEHICLE SUBMERGED IN AN EVERGLADES
CANAL FIVE MILES WEST OF KROME AVENUE."

JAVIER HELD the phone from his ear while the prostitute sat up to light a cigarette. "*Conyo,* I can't believe this," he said to Marco.

"You fuck," barked the gravel voice. "You said they would never be found? Listen, asshole, you better find out who that broad is and take care of her. You understand me?"

Cupping the receiver, Javier answered, "I can't talk right now. I'll come over to your place."

"No fucking way, asshole. I don't want you seen anywhere near me. Never come to my place again. You hear? And don't call me on anything but my air page. Just leave a number and I'll call you back. You really fucked this whole thing up."

"Listen, Marco..."

"No, you listen! Find out who that broad is and take her out. Mirage, whatever. And don't do it in the goddam Dolphin's football Stadium on Super Bowl Sunday in front of CBS cameras. Understand, asshole?"

"I told you not to..."

"And another thing, you fucking asshole, one more fuck up and my little cassette tape heads for South America."

Call disconnected. .

Naked, Javier leaped from the bed, shouted a Spanish expletive then swung his arm whacking the whore with a backhand and a forehand as hard as he could.

"What was that for?" cried the bare breasted woman holding her face.

"For being an asshole, you bitch. Get the fuck out of here."

CHAPTER 15

IT WAS STILL DARK when Mike awakened at five-thirty that Monday morning. There was much to do, much to figure out.

What would Lillie be doing with two million dollars in her house? Who was she storing it for?

How would the killers have known it was there?

Where is Ken Lancaster and how can we hold on to him?

Why did they only leave two of their Glock semi-automatics on the scene and not three?

Whose print is on the band-aid?

Who is Mirage? And why did she go into hiding? Why the disguise?

How can I unload that jerk, Gonzalez?

Robyn appeared to be sound asleep as he quietly slipped from the bed. He donned his suit of the day with only a closet light for illumination and glanced at the phone, thankful that he hadn't been called during the night. He was trying not to wake her. He wrote a brief message on a piece of pocket sized note paper, leaned over to kiss her on the forehead and placed it on the night table. It said, simply, "I love you."

He looked in on Corrina and was surprised to see that her bed was empty. Ah, yes, he forgot. Robyn had said something about her staying at Cindy's this week. He tore out another small piece of paper and left a note on her night table. "Daddy loves you."

He phoned Al Sanchez from the kitchen. "Call Zeke and have him meet me at the office first thing," he said. "We have a big day ahead and he's going with me. Any developments during the night?"

"One thing, Mike, but I didn't think it was important enough to wake you. Sylvia Cicerone's beauty shop was broken into last night. The Beach police sealed it up, waiting for your instructions."

"Well, that's a hell of a coincidence. What was taken?"

"Don't know, Mike, but it wasn't money."

Ninety minutes later, Mike and Zeke were at "Styles By Sylvia", each holding a Styrofoam cup containing warm coffee. Two hairdressers, one a gay man, the other a lesbian, and a manicurist arrived for work unaware that their employer was among the slaughtered four they heard so much about over the weekend. The pretty black girl was only five foot tall. She strained her neck to look up at Zeke Ferguson.

"Sorry, sir, but I just do nails. Miss Sylvia, she was a nice lady, but I don't know her much. Don't think I would want to, you know? Wasn't my type, if you know what I mean."

When customers began arriving for appointments, Mike advised they were closing the shop for probate and investigative processing. First, they needed to interview every employee.

Mike took Zeke to the rear of the shop out of earshot. "You talk to the gay guy and I'll take the lezzy. You know what to ask."

"Hey, why do I have to talk to the gay guy? Come on, Mike. I really think I'd do better with the woman. You'd get more out of the fella."

"What's that supposed to mean?"

"Like, you're white, he's white and you're nice looking."

"Well, my friend, thanks a lot. That's just the reason I don't want to talk to him."

"What's the matter? Afraid he'll..."

"Shit Zeke, I'm just better at women, that's all. They kinda spill things out to me. And you're so goddam big, you'll scare the shit out of him. He'll do anything for you."

"Yeah, that's what I'm afraid of. Look at him, Mike. He's, you know, so, so fairy like."

"He ain't gonna bite, for Christ's sake, Zeke. Besides, I'm in charge here." Mike grinned. Zeke flipped his eyeballs upward in exasperation.

The three employees waited patiently at the front of the store, watching in amusement as the Mutt and Jeff investigators stood in the back whispering and flailing arms in an obvious dispute. Finally, Zeke wiggled his finger toward the group. "Sir?" he said, summoning. "Uh, may I speak with you?"

The rail-thin fellow swished over to the black giant and extended a limp hand, saying, "Yes sir. My name is Jay Markowitz. And I don't bite."

In separate corners, they grilled the employees about any suspicious people, Sylvia's connection with underworld figures, what they knew about Lillie and most important, Mirage.

"Does anything in the store appear to be out of place?"

"No."

"Is there any money missing?"

"No."

"Do any of your employees or customers drive a little red sports car?"

"No."

"Have you ever heard any reference to the name Mirage?"

"No."

The questions gushed but they were of no help. Markowitz pointed out that all customer's names were listed in the appointment book. As he leafed through the pages to show the detectives, he stopped suddenly and remarked, "My goodness, look at this. The page for last Saturday is gone."

"Any reason that an employee would take that page out?" asked Mike.

"Uh uh. It's supposed to be in there. Sylvia is going to have a fit, well, I mean, she would have, you know. Oh dear. It's so hard to believe." Markowitz sensed a flood of emotions and turned away.

Mike looked over at his partner, "Zeke, I think we might have helped the Beach P.D. to solve a burglary. You know our next step?"

Zeke did not hesitate. "The way I see it, Mirage's true name is on that missing appointment calendar. It means we talk to every employee in this shop that worked here on that Saturday. One of them must have done her hair."

"That's right my friend. Every single one."

"Well, I know one you won't talk to," Zeke said.

"Who is that?"

"Sylvia."

After discovering the missing page, Mike Estevez gently handled the spiral notebook like it was a used condom and ordered technicians to dust it for prints so they could examine its contents. They made a list of all employees who worked on Saturday the thirteenth including the three already there, plus every customer booked for the Saturdays before and after.

"We've got to go, Zeke. I have an appointment with Captain Davidson at eleven."

Mike drove the Taurus while Zeke took notes on the way back to headquarters. It was another hot, bright and sunny day. As they sped along beautiful McArthur Causeway, they both glanced over at the giant, luxurious floating hotels cruising out to sea from Dodge Island Harbor. Silence prevailed for nearly a mile before Zeke, feeling a moment of insecurity, turned to his mentor and asked, "As this case goes on, I suppose you'll hook up with Randy McAdams or someone more experienced, huh? I mean,.."

Mike shifted his eyes to the right and just listened. "You mean what, Zeke?"

"I mean, like this case is much too big and too important for a rookie. God, I hate that word. I mean for a new guy in homicide. Like..."

"Zeke, what's up my friend? You feeling unsure of yourself?"

"No, not really, just..."

"It's me then, is it?"

"I don't want to be a burden and..."

"You think I feel you are a burden, is that it?"

The big man didn't answer.

Mike looked to his right again. "Did I tell you? Just yesterday, Chief Howard was so concerned about all the heat he was taking on this case that he virtually gave me Carte Blanche."

"What do you mean by that? Carte Blanche?"

"Zeke, listen, the chief said he was pulling all stops, no sweat on overtime. This case is to be solved at all costs. I can have anybody, anywhere, any experts I want, at any cost. And that includes any partner from anywhere in the department."

"And? So?" Zeke glanced at the Cuban cop, his brow raised in anticipation.

"One more thing," Mike said with a sheepish grin. "Run Ken Lancaster's elimination prints against the bandage print. We have to eliminate that. Or find out whose it is. Got that?"

"Right." A toothy smile crossed the giant face of Zeke Ferguson as he started writing across a legal pad.

"Then we have to check with Ken's brother and his employer."

"Right."

Have Randy assign someone to interview all the shop employees and customers. Better yet, I want Al Sanchez and Phyllis Moriarty to do it. It's too important to give to just anyone."

"Right."

"Get me the name and address on the gate guard that Gus Grimanski talked to. He must have more information on the little red car. Maybe you and I will talk to him ourselves."

"Got it."

"Find out when and where the funerals will be held. We need someone there with a camera, and I want a copy of all the visitor registries."

"Okay. Sir!" Emphasis on Sir!

Then Zeke asked, "What about the news media. You're going to be hounded, Mike."

"Good point. Make sure Gloria Menendez is given a full time detective as a liaison. That guy can put out a daily release even if there's no progress. You're right. We've got to keep them pacified. And don't forget the chief. We need to throw him a bone from time to time."

"Even if it's bullshit. Right?"

"Have Randy assign someone to research Lillie Diefenbach. I mean thoroughly. I want to know what she ate for breakfast, where and when she shit, her bank records, who and what she owed, her relatives, all her friends, her doctor, her lawyer and her rabbi. Got that?"

"Looks like Randy has a head start on her already."

"You're right, but we need more."

"What about her hairdresser?" Zeke asked with a sly grin.

Mike was caught off guard. "What do you mean? Lillie's?"

Zeke glanced back to his partner with jesting eyes.

"Smart ass. We go to the M.E.'s office later and get all we can from the autopsy report. We need to check the belongings of the deceased in case there's any clues that could lead to Mirage. I also want to see if any of the bodies are still there."

Zeke opened wide and turned his head toward the driver. "Is that really necessary?"

"Yep. And tonight, my friend, we hit Little Havana. Brush up on your Spanish."

"WHAT DID YOU DO WITH IT?" asked Beth Ann.

"Tore it to shreds and threw it in a dumpster."

"You've got a thing for those dumpsters, don't you, sugar?"

"What can I say? Would you believe, I actually slept with Mike last night."

"Did you..."

"Oh no, he was too tired. So what else is new?"

Bayside Marketplace was one of those glitzy, upbeat waterfront tourist Meccas, a spacious and colorful series of two-story, open-aired structures designed to lure shoppers and diners to pricey boutiques, restaurants and bars overlooking the briny marina.

Groups of brass musicians wandered about in colorful garb, stopping here and there for photos on request, playing Spanish and Italian music and an occasional strain from a John Philip Sousa march.

They were sitting outside of the food court at a wobbly aluminum table sipping coffee, munching bagels and cream cheese and feeding crumbs to waiting pigeons. Though far from the crowds, they spoke softly.

"You feeling better today, Sugar?"

"I'm scared shitless, Beth. I know he's going to catch on. It's only a matter of time."

"The worst thing would be to panic. Go on like normal but stay close enough so you can talk to Mike and know what's happening. He always trusted you with his cases before; no reason not to now."

Beth Ann brought another two cups of coffee from the refill pot. Robyn's eyes panned to a chartered windjammer drifting out of the harbor.

"He knows that Mirage has a little red car. I don't know how, but he knows it. I told you he's good. He won't let up."

"So, there's only forty thousand little red cars in Miami-Dade County."

"Yeah, but not all of them are owned by a woman with a

C-section scar on her stomach."

"Oh. He knows that, too? How'd he find that out?"

"From Ken, probably."

"Well, you can't get rid of the car now. That would be too suspicious."

As typical business attire, Robyn wore a pants suit and her satin blonde hair in a long pony tail. More matronly, Beth had stylish horn-rimmed glasses and her dark brown hair pulled into a bun. Robyn's eyes were constantly roaming, paranoid.

"Robyn you're with me. There's nothing to worry about."

"Shit, Beth, I haven't even seen a newspaper."

"It's all that's on TV around here. It's like the Casey Anthony case came to Miami. *The Herald* has a four page spread on the lives of all the victims, their families, Sylvia's customers, Lillie's connections and a picture of the white boy's German Shepherd. It's even headlines on the front page of *USA Today*. *CARNAGE IN MIAMI*. *The Herald* says that the cops are looking for a woman named Mirage, and they even know that three Spanish men are involved."

Robyn was taken aback. "What? Are you kidding? Oh that's great. How...? My God, if those maniacs see that on TV, they'll know there's a live witness." Her hands started to shake. "That had to come from Ken. Who else but he and I knew that? Well, there's also that girl, Carol. I don't know what happened with her."

Beth watched and listened as her friend began trembling once more. "What's the matter with Mike anyway? Why the hell did they let that information out? I'm telling you, Beth Ann, I gotta do something to get Mike off track. Get him off the case, or something. This is driving me crazy, goddamn it. This is just great."

"Calm down, sugar," Beth said placing her hands on hers.

"I've tried so hard, Beth. With all the loneliness, I was still there for him. You know better than anyone. Hell, I've been with one other man in seventeen years, one time only, and that was during our trial separation three years ago." She pondered that a moment, then went on. "Trial separation. Ha. It was supposed to be six months; we couldn't stay apart six weeks."

"Well, sugar, he said he'd change, but..."

"Mike did change. He got assigned to the office heading up the cold case squad, nine to five. It was wonderful, being a family again. It was normal for a year. Then came the Liberty City child serial killings. Who did they assign? Well, you know the rest. That's all it took."

"Try to calm down, okay?"

Robyn took a sip from her cup and cringed. "Look. If those bastards find out about me, I'll be as dead as Lillie and the rest." She stood up as though to walk away, then turned and wiped a tear from her cheek. "And I've got Corrina to worry about. I can't let her get caught up in this."

"Have you talked to Charlie?" Beth asked.

"No way, Beth. I told you that."

"You know how much he cared for you. Maybe there's something...."

"I said, no way."

Beth Ann Lieberman rose, walked slowly to the railing that overlooked the marina and marveled at the colossal guitar rotating over the carousel-shaped Hard Rock Café. Several minutes of silent reflection passed as a pair of sail boats glided from the marina into the placid waters of Biscayne Bay. Robyn had collected her emotions and looked up to her friend curiously. "What are you thinking, Beth."

Beth took a deep breath, turned to her tormented chum and said, "There's only one thing you can do, Robyn. I've thought about this, and really, there is only one thing you can do."

Robyn stood, approached Beth Ann at the railing and asked, with pleading eyes, "What's that, Beth? Tell me."

"Tell him, Robyn. Tell Mike everything," she said looking directly at Robyn.

Robyn stood frozen, astonished, her mouth agape, unsure whether to feel confusion or anger. Her first impulse was to storm away and say nothing.

"What?"

"You're digging a hole, Robyn, deeper and deeper and one day, you'll never be able to get out of it. The deceit is burying you. I hate to tell you that, Sugar, because I know it's not what you want to hear, but..."

"Beth, I thought you were my friend."

Beth Ann gazed back with sympathy and said, "I am your friend, Robyn."

"Jesus Christ," she whispered, straining not to raise her voice. "Do you know, do you know what would happen? I don't dare let on that it was me in bed with that man, at a damned sex party. My life would be over, Mike would see me as some common slut. And the killers... God, they would hunt me down. My God, Beth, do you know what you're saying?"

"Robyn, yes. Your marriage will probably be over, which might be a blessing because it should have been over years ago."

"It's not just that, Beth."

"What, then? Is it the humiliation, Robyn? Well, maybe you'd have to bite that bullet. I don't see any other choice. It's going to catch up to you."

"There's also Corrina? What about my baby? Look what it would put her through. What would she think of her mother? She'd think I was a..."

"Well, that's something you might have thought about before you took the risk. She wouldn't have to know the whole story anyway."

"The killers, they'll…"

"Robyn, listen to me. You are a material witness to the most sensational murder case in the history of this city. They would protect you like the Hope Diamond for Christ's sake."

Robyn shook her head. "You're unbelievable. And you sit here and tell me you're my friend?"

"Think about it, Robyn. Think about it. You'll be free again. For once."

CHAPTER 16

MONDAY AFTERNOON

BARNIE DAVIDSON WAS an affable man but he dripped with apathy. Mike sat at a long table extended perpendicular from Barnie's while the balding captain kept glancing up at the clock. Scores of plaques, degrees and pictures of himself shaking hands with important people blanketed his ego wall; country music played softly from a small sound system atop a bookcase. He made an effort at seeming concerned.

"Listen, Mike, I know how disconcerting it must be at times, but Raul, I mean Lieutenant Gonzalez, he's basically a good man. He certainly handles his administrative duties well, his reports are excellent and he keeps me informed. That's important, you know." Another glance at the clock.

"Sir, isn't the Cocoplum case an important matter to this department?"

"Why of course, Mike."

"Then if that case is important, it is dangerous to keep Gonzalez anywhere near homicide. He may not mean any harm but he gets in the way, sir. He's unreliable and you can't trust him. I'm not saying he's dishonest. He's just plain fucking stupid."

"Those are pretty strong words about a superior officer, especially coming from a sergeant."

"Do you know that he stuck a pencil down the barrel of a suspect murder weapon on the scene? I'm talking about the Bureau Lieutenant. With all due respects, Captain, he's a goddam embarrassment, not to mention a liability." Tense, angered, Mike stood up to pace.

"Sit down, Mike. Relax. Come on."

"Captain, I don't think you realize the potential consequences of his release to the media. If those Bozos hear about the three Latinos, and I'm sure they have by now, they will know there's an eyeball witness. How else would we know that? They're probably working harder than we are at finding Mirage. And they don't have to follow the law. They don't have S.O.P.'s, Administrative Orders and Supreme Court decisions to worry about, and they sure as hell don't give a shit what the watchdogs are saying. Honestly, sir, the job is tough enough without worrying about getting stabbed in the back." There was a brief pause. "Excuse me, sir. Am I holding you up from something?"

Davidson caught himself looking at the clock again. "Oh no. Listen, Mike, you're right about that media comment. I'll talk to the lieutenant about that." The captain smiled and stood as though the meeting was nearing an end.

"Why can't you get rid of him, sir?"

"You know that answer as well as I do." The captain walked and stood over Mike's chair. "And you better get a leash on your attitude, Sergeant. It's because of shit like this that you're not a lieutenant yourself."

Mike stormed out the door, ignored Lieutenant Raul Gonzalez in his glass enclosed office and motioned to Zeke it was time to go. Captain Davidson would be on time for his Monday lunch date in the dark corner of Steak and Ale with the wife of one of his detectives.

FIFTEEN MINUTES LATER, as they traveled south to interview another possible witness, Zeke broke a long silence. "What's the problem, Mike? You want to tell me about it?"

"Forget it. I'll be all right. Just give me a few minutes." Mike was letting his partner do the driving. "You got the address for that kid? The gate guard?"

There was another hush as the two men crossed over the Miami River. Zeke looked out his window to see the same backdrop of skyscrapers, elevated trains and the glistening bay laden with skiffs and cruisers that he'd seen a thousand times over. Like always, he would compare it to the images he preferred, when Miami was the home town he grew up in, when people were friendly and he felt safe and there existed a sense of sharing a piece of paradise with your neighbor. But he would also remember the prejudice, the days when his parents drank from a fountain bearing the sign, "Colored Only", when his Mama had to leave Miami Beach before dark because she didn't have an employee I.D. card and his father's nickname among the white boys; Big Nigger. Oh well, he thought, I guess it's a trade-off. Some things were better then. Some were not. He watched Mike Estevez stew, gazing ahead not uttering a word. He could almost see his brain bubbling.

Finally, Zeke broke the silence. "You know, Mike, you got a rep. People out there talk about you."

Startled out of deep thought, Mike replied, "Oh yeah, what's that?"

"I heard, long time ago, you have a problem with the black people. They say you don't like working with black officers." Zeke thought he would have rattled his partner but he just looked straight ahead. "That true?"

"Reputations often stem from what others wish to think of you. Small minds cannot grasp complex matters so they invent rationale to justify myopic perceptions of others."

Zeke shook his head. "Huh? Does that mean yes or no?"

Mike grinned, "That's no, Zeke. That's also pretty stupid." Then

Mike turned to ask a pointed question. "You've been with me a week now. What do you think?"

"Ain't seen no signs."

"Then why do you bother to ask?" Zeke said nothing. "Let me ask you something. Why did you come into homicide?"

"Honest?"

"Yeah, honest."

"To begin with, it was money, mainly. You know, I'm over forty now. Got five, maybe six years left. This overtime can jack up a pension ten grand a year. Hell, why do you think most of the other guys are in homicide? I would have done it years ago but I had to raise kids by myself." He glanced at Mike still looking straight ahead, listening. "But you know something?"

"What's that?"

"I think I'm hooked."

"Meaning what?"

"The job, man. It's consuming."

"Okay, next question."

"Shoot."

Mike glanced up at a Metrorail train pulling into a station. "How did you get in homicide?"

"Put in the papers, got interviewed. Why, what you mean?"

"Come clean, Zeke. Did you pull any strings? You're on this job eighteen years; you know lots of people and they know you. You're well liked and you're a minority, just like me."

"Yeah, maybe. So?"

"It's not you that gets me angry. It's the fucked up system. You know how many capable people chomping at the bit for this job get passed over just to satisfy some dumb percentage quota? Why do you think that asshole Gonzalez is in here? Because he's a fucking Cuban. No other reason. And I'm a Cuban telling you that. My friend Charles Bosworth was one of the best sergeants I ever worked with in homicide until he made lieutenant and got shipped out. He put in for the lieutenant's job here a dozen times but look who they gave it to."

Then Mike remembered. "Take Sam Waters. An outstanding

detective who just happened to be black. He would have been a great homicide lieutenant but he missed the chance. The day after he was promoted, they catapulted him to major and paraded him around in all his regalia before Liberty City citizen councils and news photographers. The system didn't recognize him; they prostituted him."

Zeke remained quiet as Mike took a breather. "It's not you, my friend, so don't take it personal. You're doing what you thought you had to do. You took advantage of the system; you didn't create it. I'm just too much of an idealist."

"Well, I guess I asked." Zeke said glancing back and forth to the road.

Mike raised his arm and placed his hand on the big man's shoulder. "It's not you. Remember that. We're partners now."

Five minutes later, they pulled into the driveway of a small, stucco house in South Miami. Zeke turned to Mike, "Well, I may be an old fart and you might think I'm only here 'cause I'm black, but I'll tell you this. Before it's over, you're gonna be saying that Zeke Ferguson's one damn good homicide detective. I guarantee you."

Mike tapped his partner on the shoulder with a fist. "I have no doubts, my man."

TED GUNTHER WAS a full time student and part time employee of the Cocoplum Security Company who looked barely old enough to shave. He was absolutely awestruck by the presence of two honest-to-goodness Miami P.D. homicide detectives sucking his subconscious for details about the young woman heading for the Diefenbach house in a little red car. They showed him page after page of automobile photos from a loose-leaf notebook. It seemed to be going nowhere.

"My instructions were to simply let anyone pass through who announced they were heading for Mrs. Diefenbach's party. Those were the only two I remember. You know, when I finish my degree, I'm putting in for...."

"Think real hard; take your time," Zeke asked, "Close your eyes and try to envision her again. Her voice, her mannerism, her car. Any markings?"

"Such a looker, man. I mean my knees shook when she eye-balled me. Her nose, her lips, whew, what a woman! The car, I'm sorry. All I can tell you is that it was red, like fire engine red, and small. I'm not that up on sports cars. Well, I think there was one thing."

"What's that?"

"It had some decals on the back window. A bunch of them on the left side. I didn't see them close up. You know, I'm going to be a police officer, I hope. You got any advice on what I should do, what to study?"

"Sure. Next time. Thanks, Ted."

AS PART OF TRAINING, Mike made a point to bring Zeke Ferguson into the Medical Examiner's Office every day even if it was unrelated to any case. "Murders were the springboard that spawned the development of forensic science," he told him. "Autopsies, bodies, the study of trauma is central to the investigation of a case. There is no better way to implant, to etch it into the mind than to be there and study it first hand." Zeke called it, *"the drill."*

As they entered the hall leading to the autopsy room, the all too familiar stench of decomposition filled their nostrils. "Whoooh, yeow, it's gotta be a bad one," Zeke said as he pulled a hanky from his pocket. Impervious, Mike strolled on through the double doors.

"Wow, Doc, it is ripe," Mike commented to Doctor Gavilo who scampered around the table in his white smock and rubber gloves. Two black body bags lay on separate steel trays. "What did the county bring you today?"

As he busily arranged his tools, Doctor Gavilo answered, "Two white males, DOA in the front seat of an old Lincoln. The County had it pulled out of an Everglades canal about five miles west of

Krome, just before the Miccosukee Reservation. I'd say it's an execution. Who knows, probably drugs."

Mike mused. With a population of 2.5 million people, Miami-Dade County was listed among the most murderous regions in the United States, reporting over four hundred homicides annually, more than half drug related. Forty years ago, a body recovered from a shallow Everglades grave indicated a Mafia rub-out or the demise of a third party to a love triangle. Now it invariably pointed in one direction; Drugs.

"Who's working it from the County?" Mike asked.

"Luis Vasquez. He's on the way." The doctor looked up and asked with a grin, "Want to stick around when we open the bag?"

His eyes wide, Zeke answered with a chuckle, "No, that's okay, Doc. We got lots else to do."

"Zeke, buddy, how do you think you're going to learn?" Mike said mockingly. "Come on. We have a few minutes."

Less than forty-eight hours rotting in shallow waters under an August Everglades sun could produce the most grotesque cadavers ever to burn the lungs of a Medical Examiner. Methane gases within the tissues expand, causing the corpse to balloon with skin so taut it seems about to explode. Bulging eyeballs result from the eating away of the eyelids, and the tongue protrudes from fattened, puckered lips. But there is nothing to compare to the sickening, fetid odor, even the best dry cleaning cannot remove, that penetrates into the very fibers of a detective's clothing.

Zeke remained close to Mike in a valiant display of determination. "Anybody got a line on who they are?" he asked.

The doctor unzipped the first bag. "No, no I.D., just some gold jewelry around the neck. Can't see any markings on the skin yet. The lab people will be here to take their prints."

"How the heck are they going to do that, in their condition?" asked Zeke.

"Glove 'em," Mike answered.

"What do you mean?"

"The M.E. here will cut off the fingers and send them to the

Crime Lab. There, they will chemically treat them and after they dry, the skin will peel off all in one piece."

"Sounds gross. What then?"

"Then the I.D. man will insert his fingers into the dead man's fingers just like a glove and then roll the prints. Piece of cake."

Zeke shook his head. "Glad I'm not an I.D. man. I can tell you that."

Mike and the pathologist went on to discuss the details of the Cocoplum victims. All the bodies had been released except for Janie Tucker whose husband was somewhere in the Far East unable to be reached. The three others were long since shipped off to funeral parlors.

Small in stature but confident in attitude, Luis Vasquez arrived dressed like he was attending a wedding then introduced himself to the two City of Miami detectives. He was no more than twenty-eight years old with narrow shoulders and dark wavy hair combed back without a part. Mike thought he looked more like an accountant than a cop.

They exchanged small talk, cracked jokes about the hideous appearance of the two dead men in the bags and offered each other mutual assistance if ever needed. The detectives came from two separate and often rival agencies. Miami-Dade handled everything in the unincorporated areas of the sprawling county, which entailed about two thirds of the total population. The City of Miami department was less than half the size of Miami-Dade's.

"Do me a favor, if you will, Mike," asked the Miami-Dade detective. "Run this guy in your city files. The car was registered in this name and we have nothing on him."

"Who is it?"

"Name is Felix Armando De La Rosa, D.O.B 2/12/74. The address on the registration is 2125 Southwest Tenth Street. My man checked over there. It's an abandoned house."

"You got it."

Mike and Zeke remained at the Medical Examiner's Office for two hours researching the belongings of their victims, studying the autopsy reports and making phone calls to headquarters to check in with Raul Gonzalez and coordinate lead assignments with Randy McAdams.

"They're coming out of the walls," Randy told them. "These broads saw you on TV and suddenly there are a dozen women out there named Mirage calling in. There's another two dozen who say they know who Mirage is. Some callers want to know if there is a reward and then hung up when we say no. CNN is doing a special on the families of all the victims, and the entire media frenzy is simply driving Gloria Menendez crazy, not to mention the chief. The captain is sitting here stewing because the chief won't let him out to play golf. The chief is running back and forth getting answers to questions for the mayor, commissioners and the city manager. And they all want to talk to you."

"Any word on Ken Lancaster?"

"Not yet."

"Has Robyn called?"

"Haven't heard."

"We're heading in."

Mike and Zeke were leaving the front steps of the M.E. Office building when Zeke stopped suddenly and grabbed his arm. "Hey Mike, I just thought of something." He paused for a moment, reflecting. "Felix Armando De La Rosa." Then he repeated himself. "Felix! Get it?"

Mike studied Zeke's face for a moment then his eyes lit up. "Ah, Felix! Zeke, you're right. Ken Lancaster said he heard one of the killers was called Felix." They entered the car and Mike leaned over to his prodigious partner, "Okay, smart ass, what do we do next?"

"Ah," he said with an index finger in the air, "We compare the bullets from our victims to the bullets in these guys."

"Very good. You're doing well."

CHAPTER 17

"WHY CAN'T YOU GET RID OF HIM," asked Raul Gonzalez holding an unlit cigar.

"Funny, he asked the same question about you," replied the captain from behind his desk. "Besides, you know it's not up to me."

"I can't get along with him, Cap. He's arrogant. Everyone thinks he's such hot shit, but he's no better than anyone else. Besides, I'm the lieutenant here now. I ought to have some say so." Gonzalez mused. "So he wanted you to get rid of me, huh?"

"He's pissed off about you blabbing shit to the press. He thinks you hurt the case. Really, maybe you ought to watch what you say." Davidson leaned forward in his chair, opened a bottle of cologne from his desk drawer and stood up.

"Hey, Cap, whose side you on?"

"Side?" The captain stepped from behind his desk and sat in the chair next to Gonzalez. "Raul, let me tell you something. It doesn't matter a hill of beans whose side I'm on 'cause I'm just about that close..." He held up his thumb and index finger, "...to becoming history around here. My twenty-five are up in two months and I got about as much clout as a Chihuahua against a Grizzly bear. I'll be walking softly for the next few weeks so no one fucks with my pension. Honestly? I don't give a flying fuck about anything except getting out of this madhouse in one piece."

"Hey, Cap, no problem, okay?"

"So don't fuck with me, Raul. And you might as well figure that Mike Estevez isn't going anywhere. He's too well liked, even at the mayor's office. And you can think all you want; he's a goddam good detective. No. He's not good. He's the best. As a cop, you wouldn't make a pimple on his ass. Don't you ever forget that."

Gonzalez caught himself in a stare-down not knowing how to answer or what to say. Burning inside, he was feeling the urge to protect his dignity and then remembered Davidson was just a has-been, an old cop on the way out. His opinions wouldn't matter to anyone.

"You've got the watch tonight," Davidson barked returning to his chair. "Make sure you're available in case anything breaks. I can be reached if you need me," he added, waving his cell phone.

Gonzalez figured all bases were covered. Mike and Zeke would be out there running down informants. Al Sanchez had taken over the lead sheet from Randy McAdams until tomorrow; another dozen investigators were in the streets following leads and compiling reports and the media room was down to a handful of tired reporters waiting for any tidbits thrown their way.

Gonzalez had his cell phone and a Monday night date. The Bears were playing the Chiefs in preseason NFL. Not even a quadruple homicide in Cocoplum would keep the corpulent lieutenant from meeting his best friend at Pub El Conquistador on Flagler Street where the game would be shown on a sixty-one inch television. Besides, everyone was entitled to a meal break.

"REMEMBER MIKE," Zeke said to his partner in slow, articulated syllables as they drove into the parking lot. Gold and red flashers from the neon sign illuminated the street. *"Yo no hablo muy mucho Espanol."*

"Hey, that's not too bad. First, the Versailles. You are about to enter the most popular Latin restaurant on Calle Ocho."

A tall distinguished man with white hair slicked back in one swoop stood in the center of the restaurant wearing a blue Guayabera shirt. He clapped his hands and spoke loudly in Spanish, "*Senores y Senoras*, I am sorry to interrupt for this brief moment. I have a very good friend here who has an important message. I would like for all my friends to listen. It will only take a few minutes." He gestured to Mike. "Please, Senor, go ahead." The clatter from silverware and voices echoing off glass mirrors and tile floors came to a sudden halt. Unusual for Monday nights, the dining rooms were full.

"My name is Sergeant Miguel Estevez." He announced standing very comfortable before an audience. His strong, mellifluous voice carried through all three rooms. Pretending to understand the language, Zeke Ferguson stood near his side not understanding a word being spoken.

"As you all must know by now, we are working very hard at trying to identify the persons who murdered four innocent people in a home in Cocoplum on Saturday night. We do not want to see a repeat of these butchers' work. We are asking for help. You all know as well as I that people talk and rumors spread like a disease throughout this community. If you have any information or if you know anyone who has information concerning the motives or the people involved, I would appreciate a call. Names and identities of people with such information will be held in total confidence. I will assure you."

"Are there any rewards?" a male voice asked from the rear of the main room.

"No, not as yet."

Mike Estevez left his business card on all seventy-four tables and said to his partner, "Come on, La Malaga is next."

BY HALFTIME, Raul Gonzalez had jovially finished five bottles of Mexican beer and ordered another round for him and his fellow lieutenant, Juan Masvidal. They shared a corner of the crowded bar where throngs of intoxicated Hispanics jammed every nook and cranny to get a view of the giant screen. The air-conditioning system was neutralized by the pulsating ebullience of a hundred imbibers in such a small space where warm perspiration flowed as readily as cold *cervesa.*

The two men laughed, slapped each other on the shoulders, hoisted their glasses in a hearty "Salute", and admired the progress of the game. They were getting drunk. And they were happy.

"It seems like only yesterday you were working for me as a young patrolman. Now, I see you standing behind that Miguel Estevez on the news conference today on TV, shoulder to shoulder with the chief. Raul, you have come a long way. You are an important person now."

Raul soaked it in, stroked his thick black mustache and wiggled his oversized head in absolute arrogance. "Well, amigo, I will see what strings I can pull to get you out of Records Bureau. That is no place for you."

"Oh no, Raul, I appreciate your concern. But I am quite happy there. No need to go through so much trouble."

"You want to stay in the Records Bureau? You, with so much experience? It's a waste."

"Ah, my friend, but it has its rewards."

Juan Masvidal was a thin, balding, naturalized Cuban with a tiny mustache who carried a pack of Salems in the pocket of his Guayabera. "That Miguel Estevez, he is a good detective I hear."

"Ah, he is overrated. And a back stabber."

"Oh? Why do you say that?"

"Just today, he talked to the captain trying to get rid of me. I'm the one running this case. I'm in charge. Miguel Estevez works for me." With that, Raul emitted a raucous belch and guzzled another drink from his glass mug.

"Well, I know he is a little over-confident with his nose up in the air. I remember, three years ago I was on an interview panel when he was trying to make lieutenant. He buried himself. He went into this long speech about the evils of special treatment for minorities. What a jerk, eh?"

"I know. But he's got the newspapers, the State Attorney and the chief thinking he's Superman. There's nothing I can do. Son of a bitch." Another belch. "You know, he is not even a member of the B.L.O.?"

"I don't believe it?"

"Yes. I think he is a fucking traitor to his race."

"Race?" We are a race, amigo?" Juan snapped his head back grinning.

"Well, you know what I mean."

"How's it coming so far, Raul? You know, the Cocoplum thing? Got any good leads yet?" Think you're ever going to solve this one?"

"Well, you know we're sort of under a gag order. I Can't really discuss details with anybody. If anything got out, it could be..."

"Come on. Shit, man, you and I go back. You know you can trust me more than anyone you know. I would say nothing to anyone."

THEY HAD BEEN TO a dozen bistros and restaurants along Flagler Street and Calle Ocho. By midnight, Zeke began to show his wear while Mike buzzed with energy and tenacity, stopping and talking with Cuban citizens at each stop, getting nowhere. "You're a doggone machine," Zeke said jokingly to his partner.

"I've got an informant in here," Mike said as they pulled behind an alley in a sleazier side of town. Their unseemly incongruence took the patrons of El Colombian Pub by surprise. Pool sticks stood vertical as two dozen eyes followed a slick, well-tailored Spaniard strut through the back door into the drug haven with a behemoth black man beside him. "Stay close, my friend," Mike said to Zeke.

The only lights in the bar were situated over three pool tables surrounded by young, intoxicated, olive-skinned men wearing undersized tee shirts. A pall of cigarette and cigar smoke hung in the air as Mike motioned the crusty old bartender to turn the radio down. Zeke stood watching carefully as a number of sweat-glistened billiard players drifted back into the shadowy penumbra.

"Do you see your man?" Zeke whispered to Mike.

"You mean woman. Looks like she's not working tonight."

"Well then let's get the fuck out of here, huh?"

Mike held his hands up to the group in a half-hearted surrender motion and started to speak. "May as well make the best of it," Mike said.

All Zeke heard from that point was Spanish.

"Gentlemen, my name is Miguel Estevez. I am a homicide investigator with the City of Miami Police Department. As you know, we are working very hard trying to solve the murders of four people who were killed in the Cocoplum house last Saturday night. If anyone here..."

A muscular Latino wearing a soiled tee-shirt with a pack of cigarettes wrapped in the shoulder stood forward to stand inches from Mike. "Hey, man. Why the fuck do you come here? Can't you see we are busy?"

A hum emitted from the shadows, a hum of agreement. "Let's go, man," Zeke pleaded. "This ain't no place for us."

Mike thought about turning around but pride and utter stubbornness compelled him. The arrogant Latino walked directly into Mike's face but there was no backing down. "You fucking cops, why us? Huh? I got one question, pretty boy."

Tension rose in the air but Mike Estevez held his position.

"What is that, amigo?" Mike answered. Zeke steeled himself, watching the Latino's hands.

"Were any of those dead pigs Spanish?"

"No."

"And you say you don't know who did this, eh?"

"That's why we're..."

"Then why aren't you looking for the gringos in Dadeland, or over in Liberty City fucking with the niggers. Why are you fucking with us?" Another hum from the gallery.

One word Zeke understood very clearly. Mike heard his partner flare his nostrils and knew it was time to leave.

"Listen folks," Mike said, "I know we're grabbing at straws. If there is...."

"My friends and I don't appreciate..." As the Latino spoke, Mike and Zeke caught movement coming from the shadows as no less than a half dozen of his compadres started inching forward, into the light. "...you motherfuckers coming in here and..." The detectives started backing up, eyeballing all the cue sticks. "...hassling us just because we are..." Mike had a small stack of his business cards in his hand. He nodded to Zeke and threw the cards on the cigarette covered floor. "...Latinos minding our own..." By this time, the Latino was shoulder to shoulder with six of his friends as Mike and Zeke turned, shook their heads in frustration and exited the door. "...fucking business. Pigs!"

"Whew. I guess we dodged that bullet. Who's your snitch anyway?" Zeke asked getting into the car.

"The owner. A woman. A little rough around the edges, but a good woman. She'll know that we were here. I assure you."

"What now, boss?"

"One more stop."

IT WAS NOW WELL into the fourth quarter as the two inebriated lieutenants ordered another beer. After eleven years of career insignificance working in mundane assignments, Raul Gonzalez was glowing with pride. Now, he was an important person, the focus of much attention. And the man he once worked under, who once wrote his evaluations, who had been his mentor, was now looking up to him.

They gibbered on while watching a game they would be too drunk to remember the next day.

As the ABC wrap-up rolled and a hundred drunk and noisy Cubans started to leave the Pub El Conquistador, a bright light suddenly illuminated the entire room. A handsome man dressed in a dark suit stood at the front door accompanied by a large black man. The owner of the club lowered the TV volume.

"My name is Sergeant Mike Estevez from the Miami Police Department Homicide Bureau. As you know..."

THE EVENING WAS WARM AND QUIET when she pulled her red Supra to a convenience store just after nine o'clock. She was angry at herself for misplacing her smart phone. Only two other cars were parked, one of which surely belonged to the employee, a young dark skinned man from the mid-east. The other was another small sports car occupied by a pretty teenage girl who was obviously waiting for someone to get off the pay phone. She decided she would wait until he left.

Less than five minutes passed and the phone was hers. She amazed herself by remembering the number by heart. After fumbling and looking around nervously, she managed to insert the coin. It only rang once when the man's voice answered abruptly.

"Victoria, I told you it's over. Now, please, leave me alone."

For a moment, they could only hear each other breathing. "Uh..."

"Victoria?"

The memory of that night three years ago raced through her mind the moment she heard the deepness of his voice. It was a night she had always regretted, but repeated in her dreams a thousand times, imagining it was Mike adoring her the way he did. She pictured the gold coin hanging from his neck, resting on a chest full of thick hair and his gentle words of love, "*I was in love with you the moment I first saw you, Robyn, and forever after. It will never change. Never change. If ever you...*"

"Uh," She hesitated, her voice quivering.

"Victoria, are you all right?"

She wanted desperately to say, It's me, Charlie. It's Robyn, and I do need you now. I don't know what to do, and I need you so much. I need someone. Please help me.

She hung up.

CHAPTER 18

MIKE AWAKENED before the alarm went off. Again, she was sound asleep. The routine was like any other day, dirty clothes into the hamper, morning bathroom duties, shaving in the shower, the careful selection of attire. He dressed by the light of the closet lamp, made his morning calls, left another love note on her night stand, kissed her forehead and headed out the door. He stepped past the Supra onto the curb, started his Taurus, put it in drive and began moving forward. His peripheral vision caught it first. Then he glanced over his left shoulder, backed up the Aries in front of his driveway again and looked twice at Robyn's car. For a fleeting moment, it occurred to him, how coincidental. F.O.P. stickers, three of them.

Little red sports car. Decals on the left side of the rear window. A beautiful woman, scar on her stomach. No. No way.

"I KNOW THIS IS a bad time, Mike, but I need to take a few days. Maybe even transfer out."

"What's up, Randy?"

"Marion. She's on my case again. She just doesn't understand."

"It's a tough time, my friend. I really need you. Is it the same old problem?"

"What else? It's the hours. I tell her ten hours a day and it turns into fourteen. She waits for my days off but they never arrive. When I do come home, the cases are swirling in my head and she says I'm useless to her. I'm really torn." Mike listened intently. "I thought we had it all worked out. But lately, I can't even tell where she is half the time and I think she might be, you know, screwin' around."

"You love her, Randy? I mean, do you want to keep her?"

"She's my life, Mike. What else can I do to show it? But the truth is, I have two loves. I also love this job. Shit, it's my career."

They were in the same barren little room where Carolyn Webb had given her saucy statement two days earlier. Emotionally stressed and his mind in perpetual motion, Randy McAdams paced the floor as Mike Estevez sat patiently.

"Hell, Mike. Look at your situation. You're worse than I am with all your teaching schools and stuff. But Robyn sticks by you. Why can't Marion...."

"I have an unusual woman. All wives can't be expected to be like Robyn. I'm just lucky. What can I say."

"Shit, I could go to Missing Persons and have a nice office, nine to five, a secretary and all the time in the world to study for Sergeant. I'd be bored out of my skull." Randy stopped pacing and pondered. "What the hell is it about working homicide, Mike?"

Mike drew a wry grin. "You're a part of the police elite, and you like that. It's where you can put your intellect to work more than any other place in this job. And you're good, Randy. You're very good."

Once a computer programmer for a plastics company, it had been four years since the crew-cut detective left private industry for the lesser paying but more exciting life of a street cop. The department quickly seized his genius and placed him in Homicide where his talents were put to use indexing evidence, creating intelligence files, statistical charts, tracking reports, correlating modus operandi and preparing prosecutorial reports. Trained by Mike Estevez, he became an outstanding interrogator as well, often instructing in special schools and seminars.

A brief moment of silence before Mike answered. He raised an index finger. "Listen to what I am telling you. There is only one *numero uno.*"

"What's that?"

"Your job will only be here for a while. Your family is forever."

Mike put his arm around the distraught young man. "Look, you can do me a favor. Tell Marion you are going to stay with me for another two or three weeks then you'll take a transfer to Organized Crime Bureau. I'll help you. For now, I really need you to help me keep this case organized. Meanwhile, work closely with Phyllis and give her all your notes. Okay?"

"Sure, Mike. Thanks."

SHE LOOKED STUNNINGLY chic in a red pants suit and her black satin hair swirled into a twist. To Mike, there was something about Gloria Menendez which set her apart from other striking women. Perhaps it was her poise, her natural aura of sophistication, those dark, sensuous eyes. She mirrored his pace step for step down the hallway peppering as many questions as she could in the three minutes before he would disappear again.

"Have you located Ken Lancaster yet?

"No."

"Can I tell *The Herald* that an arrest is imminent?"

"No."

"Were there any signs of sexual assault on the women?"

"No comment."

From down the hall, he heard the captain's voice bark, "Hey, Mike, one minute please."

"Be right there."

"Can we say anything about the three Latin males?"

"Absolutely not." He strode quickly; she chased after him.

"Any news on Mirage?" She was starting to puff and her hair was falling.

"No. Gloria, I gotta go. Later, okay?"

The captain barked again, "Mike, are you coming?"

Four doors from the captain, they stopped next to an empty room.

"One more thing, Sergeant Estevez," she asked.

"Quickly, please."

She took a deep breath, looked through the detective's eyeballs then caught him off guard. "Have you ever messed around?"

His impulse was to tell her it was none of her business. He paused, drew a faint smile and answered in a low voice, "No, never." Then, he peered deep into those pristine, alluring eyeballs, slowly scanning downward to her full, red lips. She had an intoxicating aroma. Impulsively, he grabbed her arm and pulled her into the tiny, vacant interview room, startling her. She was backed against the wall now as he locked his arm around her neck and planted a fast and torrid, gaping kiss. Her knees buckled. Using a handkerchief on his mouth, he quickly reopened the door and looked back at her standing there speechless and said, "But if I did, Gloria, it would be with you."

"Thanks." *Whew*

Louder this time, the captain bellowed down the hall. "MIKE?"

"I'm coming. I'm coming."

Moments later, Mike was at the office of the Chief of Police sitting in a chair beside Captain Barnie Davidson.

"He is a security risk, Chief, period. Not because he is corrupt, I'm telling you. It's because he's stupid." Mike was being forceful, adamant.

Articulate, tall, lanky, brown-skinned and good looking, George Amos Howard the Third was the youngest chief in the history of the city. A cop with only ten years on the job, he took a meteoric rise to sergeant and then lieutenant three years later. Immediately, he rocketed to Major of Operations, placing him in charge of a division of seven hundred cops virtually a day after he was a mere shift supervisor in the streets. City hall was impressed with his master's degree in public administration along with a thick file stuffed with special credentials, none of which had anything to do with his performance in the field. Standing out, above all, was his charming, unruffled personality which drew people to him from all ethnic backgrounds.

"I'm getting calls from city hall, Mike. The B.L.O. is bugging the Mayor, the City Council and the Manager. Next I expect to see it in the papers. I don't know who he's talking to, but they're not happy with your insubordinate behavior toward a department lieutenant."

Mike twisted the rings on his fingers. "And you? What about you, Chief? Do you know what he has done already on this case?"

The chief sat behind his desk, his legs crossed and hands folded on his knees. His desk and credenza were laden with trinkets, mementos and photos presented at various award luncheons and banquets. A broad toothy smile seemed to wrap around his face.

"Captain Davidson here has kept me abreast. He made a little mistake, Mike, but you can't treat him this way. He's talking about bringing you up for disciplinary action when this case is over."

"That's fine, Chief. The State Attorney's Office may have to deal with Raul Gonzalez. My concern right now is this case. And for the life of me, it seems no one around here above the rank of sergeant really gives a shit about the murders except when it's time for press briefings. No offense, Chief."

Barnie Davidson sat quietly on a leather sofa at the side of the palatial office thinking about the passage of time.

"Mike, no one around here doubts your abilities. That's why you are given such a major responsibility like this. But, I'm afraid I'm going to have to order you to include Gonzalez in on your briefings."

"And what if he blows this case?"

"We'll deal with that."

"After the fact? I understand. Thanks for your time, Chief."

RED-EYED, RAUL GONZALEZ sat to the side of the squad room leaning his chair backward against the wall, his arms folded across his rotund belly. He never uttered a word.

"Gail Dow?" Mike barked as he held that same piece of chalk.

"The prints from the two Everglades corpses match several latents lifted from the murder scene. It was them all right. The bullet from the driver's head and the spent projectile bullet taken from the floor of the Lincoln match the projectile from Lillie's head. They're from a gun we don't have. All the other victims were shot with the guns left on the mantel."

"Sounds simple enough," muttered Estevez standing in front of the small group. "The third subject saved us from prosecuting the other two."

"A conscientious citizen, saving the taxpayer, right?" Al Sanchez's little joke drew a faint chuckle.

"Randy, what do we know about these guys?"

McAdams stood and checked his note pad. "The driver had prints on file with Immigration, came into the U.S. on a raft over six months ago. Name is Felix Armando De La Rosa, D.O.B. 2 February 1974. The address he gave in the city is a vacant house. We have no other past information on him."

"Randy, I want you to run everyone we have in file by the name De La Rosa. He had to have relatives here. Be sure you exchange any information with Luis Vasquez at Miami-Dade." Mike checked his watch. "What about the other guy?"

"Five foot ten, thin, about twenty-five years, gold chain around his neck with a religious medal, black tee shirt, no markings, no prints on file. We figure he came in illegal."

"Zeke, anything yet on Ken Lancaster?"

"Nope. But we're tryin'. Miss Jackson agreed to let us put a tape machine on her phone. She says she would call immediately. We're just standing by."

"She's in a dangerous position there. We need to put a man on her house. No, better yet, inside her house until we can get Ken back into custody."

"I'll set it up right after the meeting."

"Good. It would be a good idea to run by Ken's employer and his brother's house, just in case." Mike turned back to Randy McAdams. "What about Marco, the lawyer?"

"You already know him, Mike. Remember the Samoyez case? He was the defense attorney."

"I remember it well. A fat slob who tried to imply to the judge that I was on the take. Hey, they try anything."

"Intelligence has files on him. Ten years ago he was almost disbarred, then reprimanded for incompetence. He was charging huge fees from clients then doing nothing but showing up in court unprepared. His clientele are mostly drug defendants and most of his cases are settled. You don't see him in court very much. Judge Berretoni used to be a partner in his law firm."

"I want a list of all his clients for the last five years, okay? Any O.C. connections, Randy?"

"Only through defendants. Can't say he's a big time link."

"Personal?"

"Never married. God, who would marry that? The only thing we came up with was a news article some time back when he was caught by a reverse sting people trying to get a blow job from a street hooker for twenty bucks. The judge threw it out."

"What judge?"

"Berretoni."

"Phyllis Moriarty, you've been awfully quiet." Estevez gave his top female detective an encouraging smile. "Any word yet on the family of Janic Tucker?"

FIVE MILES TO THE SOUTHEAST, the soft motion of undulating waves crested in tranquil rhythm upon the sandy shores of Crandon Park Beach. It was nearing noon as the sun blazed through a blue sky spattered with the slow drifting movement of white, cumulus clouds. Carrying shoes, their toes sunk into the wet sand with each step.

"You know something, Mom, I think I've decided what I want to be."

"What's that, honey?"

"Psychologist. I'm going to major in psychology." They each took several steps without uttering a word. Corrina had caramel brown hair which she had grown long like her mother's. It blew gently around her face as she walked.

"Why is that?"

"There's just so much I don't understand and I want to understand.

"Like what?"

"Like, people. What is it about people? Why do people make themselves so unhappy. Like, here we are the richest society on earth in the history of the world. I mean, we have so much at our disposal. Yet, there are more bums than ever, people live in poverty, people are killing each other every day, and the ones who have everything complain about what they don't have."

"I never thought about it that way."

"Just like us, Mom. You and Dad have everything in the world to be happy about, but you're miserable. I can see it."

Corrina reached into the plastic bag and threw a handful of crushed potato chips in the air. Dozens of seagulls fluttered, swarming and squawking. Wearing dark Ray-bans, Robyn looked away toward the horizon composing herself so her daughter could not see her expression. Finally, she answered her.

"What do you mean, honey?"

"I mean, gosh, there's just nothing, Mom. I never see you guys together any more. What's happened to our family?"

Her mother found it difficult to talk. "What's going on between your father and I has nothing to do with how much we love you, you know that?"

"Sorry. But it's not a consolation. I love you, too, but I just feel so detached. I mean, both you guys always running in a thousand directions and there's nothing left for us. As a family. You know what I mean? Take Cindy's Mom and Dad. Gosh, he's a traveling salesman and she's a school teacher, but it seems they're always doing stuff together."

"Well, let's just say your father is married to his job as much as he is to me. Maybe even more. That's been going on a long time now. You might say it has come between us."

"You, too, Mom. Gee, don't blame it all on Dad. When's the last time you and I went for one of these beach walks together. A couple years? When I was smaller, we used to do it all the time. Every day, it seemed. It was so great. You and I, talking and dreaming, laughing and feeding the birds, falling into the surf with all our clothes on. Ha ha. Remember that?" There was a moment between the words. "So, why now? All of a sudden, Mom? What's with today?"

Robyn watched as a blond surfer fell from his board. He reminded her of Chad, the dancer.

"There 's been a problem. It's something I can't talk about. I just thought it would be nice. Like you said, old times."

"What's up, Mom? God, it sounds so serious. Please. Tell me."

"I want you to stay at Cindy's, for at least a little while. Until some of these problems are worked out. Okay? It's important. I'll help out Cindy's mother with expenses, you tell her that. If she doesn't mind."

"I can't. Cindy and her parents are leaving Thursday night for the Keys. She's taking off from school on Friday. Sorry. Gee, are you sure I'm not in the way?"

Robyn was struck with a pang of guilt. "It's not that, Sweetheart. It's a long story; don't worry."

They walked a while longer without saying a word. Corrina continued luring the seagulls while wondering what was on her mother's mind. They stepped around a small child sitting on the edge of the surf building a sand castle.

"Corrina, there is something I have to do. And it's going to mean I'll be very busy and I'll probably seem a little nervous and upset."

"Like you are now?"

"Maybe more. But, don't ever lose faith in me. Okay, honey? Just promise me that? Remember, I love you very much." Then she looked out over the horizon once more.

PHYLLIS MORIARITY STOOD before the group with pad in hand. "Frank Tucker and his two sons were located in a Bangkok bath house being tended by a half dozen Thai girls under the age of sixteen. I talked to the proprietor who spoke perfect English. Mister Tucker spoke with me just this morning and he's on the way. He'll be here late tonight."

"Great, Phyllis. You interview him but be delicate about Janie's, you know, little party. Find out anything that Janie might have known about Lillie's dealings with organized crime."

"Al, have you got anything new on Carolyn Webb?"

The tall Latin detective stood holding his notes. "From what we can gather, Mike, she was born and raised by her mother in Anderson, South Carolina along with a string of four stepfathers. Ran off from home and came to Florida with a group of redneck bikers in '99 and been here ever since working odd jobs until she met David Webb, the pilot she married a couple years ago. Through him, Lillie helped her get a job working in a law office. Nine months later, after a flight was canceled, he walked into his bedroom and caught her balling a pair of animal trainers from the Ringling Brother's Circus. That was that. We figure David is running shit from the Bahamas, but that's only speculation."

Mike looked to his right again at Detective Moriarty. "What about the hot line and all the mail, Phyllis? Anything promising there?"

She had a trace of a New York dialect. "You would have to ask. So far, three-hundred and fourteen crack pots, uh, I mean tipsters on the hot line recorder and a batch of mail that came in this morning. The entire population of the city thinks they can solve the case so I guess we can all go home. Right? Well, all right." No one laughed. "A half dozen envelopes were left at the front desk for you marked 'personal'. You can have those directly."

"Where are they now?"

"On your desk."

THEY SPOKE NOT A WORD as Robyn drove Corrina through the busy corridors of Miami into the suburban development called Kendall. Robyn turned up the radio to break the unnerving silence while her eyes started to well up again behind the Raybans. Corrina stared out her window, oblivious to the Spanish street vendors and the endless gauntlet of shopping plazas bordering South Dixie Highway. She wondered what was happening to her family that had long since been a dream. It was what she wanted more than anything in the world.

I have to talk to Daddy. She thought. *My Daddy. He loves me; he'll listen. He'll understand. He just doesn't realize. If he did, he would change. I know he would.* She thought about Cindy's ideal family, how envious she was, how lucky Cindy was. She looked over and saw her mother gnawing her knuckle, her mind a thousand fathoms deep. Robyn caught herself being watched.

"Do me a favor, honey."

She was startled out of her daydream. "What's that?"

"Don't say anything to Dad about our little talk today. Okay? That's, if you see him."

"Why? What's the big deal, Mom?"

"Just trust me."

HE HAD ALREADY OPENED four of the envelopes. Two contained snapshots of women posing naked cut off at the chin line. Two others were letters claiming to be Mirage. The fifth envelope was pink and square, like it once contained a Christmas card. His name was typed in bold letters on the face; *SGT. MIKE ESTEVEZ.* The meeting was over and he had returned alone to his desk. He smelled the envelope first. That was an old habit. Nothing there.

A small piece of pink stationary no larger than an index card was folded inside. On it, a puzzling message was typewritten in bold upper case letters;

FATA MORGANA LIVES WITH YOU

THAT MOMENT, Lieutenant Raul Gonzalez abruptly walked into his small office like he had something important to say, He sat down, holding an unlit cigar in between his fingers. He looked down at the envelopes as Mike was putting the pink note back inside.

"Anything worthwhile?" he asked.

"No. Just a bunch of crack pots."

CHAPTER 19

BLENDING ODORS from hot musk oil, perfumes, sweat and marijuana permeated the dark, cavernous bedroom overlooking the bay. Wide open draperies offered a panoramic night view of distant lights from Key Biscayne through double-wide glass sliding doors twenty-four stories above Brickell Avenue. The hue of tiny blue light bulbs cast an eerie glow in the mirrors. A glistening nude black girl turned up the stereo volume and returned to bed. A blonde girl, also nude, also glistening, knelt on the bed at his right side massaging more oil on his obese torso while he moaned and groaned and whimpered in euphoric ecstasy. Like a scene from legendary times when a decadent Roman aristocracy wallowed in erotic eccentricity, here was Nero, ugly but rich, virtually bathing in pleasures of the flesh bought and paid for with the proceeds of corruption.

The beat of The Rolling Stones bellowed from speakers on both sides of the king bed as Chocolate and Vanilla, as he preferred to call them, roamed vigorously with palms of warm, musk oil into every cavern of his naked body.

Oooooh!

His little pony tail untied now, leaving straggles of graying hair sopping in oil and clinging to his huge, round shoulders.

"Gimme a hit," he whispered in a soft gravel voice to the white girl, his lips pursed and wet from licking. Marco Scandiffio held a filled glass of brandy in one hand while he took turns fondling the bodies of either girl with the other. The blonde placed the glass pipe to his lips. He closed his eyes and inhaled, then held the dope in his lungs as long as he could before exhaling. While his head reeled, eyeballs floated left and right scanning the nubile torsos of Chocolate and Vanilla.

He loved every second of it, reclining there in depraved, superficial adoration. Every so often he muttered with a grin, "I want some chocolate," and the black girl would obediently straddle his belly and immerse his grotesque head between her giant, brown slippery breasts.

"Do it, come on, you know," he whispered to Vanilla. No older than eighteen, the blonde had shared his dope and his liquor and was nearly as stoned as he. Her oily hands reached into his crotch massaging the diminutive penis until it hardened into a plump, three-inch mushroom. "Ahhh," he moaned, taking a sip of Courvoisier, his head leaning back, sweating.

No sooner than the music stopped, his treasure, his personal Salome arrived through the electronically controlled door. Elated, Marco greeted her with a gaping smile and an extended hand from his king bed.

"Sorry I'm late," she said. "May I?"

"Please, my dear, my wonderful sweetheart." While Chocolate and Vanilla undressed her, slowly and sensuously caressing her milk-white body, she poured herself a glass of brandy and sucked from the glass pipe while Marco gazed at her, playing with himself. It wasn't long before she was as high as the others.

"*Bolero*, my sweet, do the *Bolero*," he said smiling with his eyebrows raised.

"First, the ties Marco."

"Oh, yeah."

Wearing sheer, pink veils, she used silk neckties to spread his arms and loosely bind each of his wrists to bronze overhead wall rings. He panted, watched in anticipation while Chocolate and Vanilla massaged on, his eyes floating back and forth, left and right to each girl. Nearly helpless now, he liked that.

"Now, the noose, Marco," she said softly with a lecherous expression. She wrapped a satin pillow case around a bungee cord to ease the discomfort. The end attached to the wall ring centered above the bed and lowered to where the noose barely reached under his flabby neck. The bondage design offered a gentle rise to his head while squeezing the blood flow from the carotid artery, enhancing his euphoria.

The girls likened him to a huge gorilla hanging from a crucifix. Ravel's *Bolero* started its opening strains and Marco looked on, sweating, panting. *Buhm...buh buh buh buhm.* Her breasts were oversized for such a thin figure as her long carrot-red hair swayed to the rhythms of her undulating body. Sheer fabric clung to her nipples as she rotated, gyrated and kicked her sinewy legs to the cadenced music at the foot of the bed. Chocolate and Vanilla sucked lips with each other across his stomach while they played with his little mushroom. The music roared on.

Buhm...buh buh buh buhm.

"Outa the way," he said to the girls blocking his view. "Gimme a hit. Aaahhhh."

The music crescendoed. Veils dropped to the floor and she danced for him naked. Marco tensed, the noose tightened and his body strained at the ropes binding his hands. "Okay, do it now," he muttered to Chocolate and Vanilla.

Buhm...buh buh buh buhm.

The black girl poured warm oil onto his genitals. His living fantasy, Salome, rolled and writhed every angle of her nakedness before his eyes while Vanilla manipulated her oil-soaked hands to massage every inch of his crotch. His little mushroom tried to grow bigger but remained flaccid. Marco Scandiffio lavished in a fifth dimension, detached from humanity, consumed by debauchery and hopelessly in love with the licentious dancing girl.

Buhm...buh buh buh buhm.

His breathing accelerated as Chocolate straddled his face and presented herself like a sponge, up and down, scrubbing and rubbing, his tongue dancing. The music crescendoed, nearly reaching peak volume. Marco groaned, mumbled with his gravel tones, "Oh yes, do it, do it."

His eyes rolled back in his head. He could feel himself losing control. He wanted to lose control. No stopping, no turning back, the incredible euphoria. The dancing girl wobbled her gorgeous breasts at him while Vanilla sucked him, one after the other as cymbals clashed and the music climaxed. He screamed, "NOW!"

The phone rang.

The girls all stopped, bewildered. The phone rang again.

"Let it ring, godammit. Come on, do it!" The music was blaring now.

BUHM...BUM BUM BUM BUHM!

Fat Marco shifted, gyrating, humping, his pathetic whining and ululations overriding the music's noise. He tugged at his overhead fetters while his elevated, rotund face grimaced from the silken garrote.

The phone continued ringing.

"Now, do it!"

BUHM...BUM BUM BUM BUHM!

As *Bolero* reached its final stanza, horns blaring, cymbals clashing and drums beating at peak crescendo, Salome finally mounted his mushroom and it was over.

"Aaaarrrgghhh."

The music stopped. Suddenly, stark silence. Then, the phone rang again.

"Answer that, godammit," he ordered his bare breasted dancer, panting. "And you there, untie me!"

"It's for you, Marco," she said in southern drawl.

Angrily, he snatched the cordless phone from her hand and screamed into the receiver, "Who in the fuck is this?"

The voice on the other end was a near whisper, barely audible. "*Oye*, Marco. I have good news. I know who ees Mirage."

"You, you fucking asshole. I told you not to call me..."

"I tell you, Marco, I go take care of Mirage. And like I tell you before, you dun call me asshole." Javier hung up before Marco could respond.

"Get me my robe." Marco had now regressed into the more familiar gluttonous slob.

With great difficulty, he exited his bed and waddled to the walk-in closet, turned on the light and closed the door. When he came out, he held two packages of wrapped twenty dollar bills totaling a thousand dollars each. Chocolate and Vanilla feverishly dressed, hoping their commitment had been fulfilled for the night. When he handed them the money he said, "Remember, girls, you've never been here in your life." In a flash, they were gone.

Then he turned to his love. "Carolyn, I want you to sleep with me tonight."

"Must I?"

"Hey, baby, ain't it worth twenty grand?"

SIX HOURS PASSED as the orange glow rose across the eastern horizon, the freckle-faced vixen tried to slip out of the bed unnoticed. He reached his mutton-like hand across and held her shoulder. "Where you going?" he asked in his seaweed voice, surprising her. His eyes remained closed.

"Got to get ready for work. You know that."

"What's the matter? Trying to impress your boss?" With his eyes still closed, he managed a salacious smile. Then he looked at her, "Twenty Gees. That ain't bad for one night's work, eh kid?"

She started dressing, ignoring the question.

"There's plenty more where that came from, toots. Look, I want for you to just come and live with me?"

She sat, her back to him, looking up toward the ceiling.

"You know I'm crazy about you. With me, the world will be yours. Whaddaya say, kid?"

From the edge of the bed, she turned her head to the fat man and asked in a serious tone, "Why, Marco? Why the killing?"

He was taken aback by her inquisitiveness. "I told you not to ask questions. It's not healthy."

"But you've got me involved. I mean, I thought I was only helping to set up a robbery, not a damn killin'. I mean, when I called your number that night, I thought it was just going to be a robbery. Nothing else."

Marco waited, carefully editing his reply. "Shit, that's what I thought, too. Those crazy fuckin' Cubans get stoned on that shit and go gun happy. Baby, honest, I didn't know they were going to do that."

"Honest, Marco?"

"Honest, baby. Hey, what did those cops ask you? I don't like that Estevez guy. He scares me. Don't you tell him nothin', okay?"

"They gave me my rights."

"No shit. They tell you why?"

"No. They said it's routine. Like they'd give the rights to their own mother."

"They didn't ask you any questions about your boss, did they? I don't need no problems."

"No, except I had to tell them where I work. I also over heard that they're looking for the black dancer, the stripper."

"Yeah, what does he know? Do you know?"

"Just that he survived somehow."

"Yeah, well, don't you worry about that. Are you sure you never saw that Mirage broad before? I mean, I don't like..."

"But, Marco, you didn't do this. You have nothing to worry about."

"If they trace to my man, they'll trace him to me. It's that simple. And then, they trace to you. You understand that? That's why you gotta keep your mouth shut. It's murder one for anyone involved, and that means you, too."

"Oh that's just great," she answered as she stood up abruptly. She waited a minute and thought to ask the one question that had been bothering her. "How come it had to be that night anyway, when everyone was there?"

Marco turned his head away annoyed. "Because they were

coming to pick up the money on Sunday morning. There was no time. Lillie only held the dough for two days. Understand, kid? Don't let it bother you so much."

Fully awakened, Marco Scandiffio listened to Carolyn as she told him about the interrogation. When it was time to leave, he bade her goodbye with another pack of fifty one-hundred dollar bills in appreciation for her performing arts.

As she drove her Mustang Cobra across Rickenbacker Causeway facing a rising sun, she had no intentions on being at her job anytime before noon. Exhausted from the emotional stress, the dancing, the dope and the miserable night with the corrupt lawyer to whom she actually owed a debt of gratitude, Carolyn hated herself. But it seemed her only avenue toward independence. Ever since that night, she had to deal with pangs of guilt, knowing she had taken part in the brutal killings of these people.

"Twenty-thousand dollars, Carolyn. All you gotta do is call my cell number before you leave the house. That way I'll know it's all set and you're outa there. Then I'll signal the guys. No problem."

She pulled quietly into the parking lot of her apartment building and slipped the sports car between a pair of Cadillacs, one gray and the other white. As she inserted the key into her first floor unit, she thought it strange that she didn't hear the usual cry of her calico greeting her.

"Tabby? Where are you Tabby Wabby?" She walked into the living room and the kitchen without turning on the lights. "Tabby? You in here, honey?" The central air conditioner suddenly clicked on. She looked behind the couch, then her screened patio. She checked her food dish, but no Tabby. Then, the bedroom.

Behind the door she spotted a pair of eel skin boots. Suddenly a powerful hand wrapped around her mouth, jolting her violently to the bed. "No screamin' Mirage, or I keel you."

She squirmed and grunted in panic, eyes darting left and right as he twisted one arm behind her almost breaking it at the socket. "If I let go, you weel no scream, right?" She shook her head vigorously. "I mean it, lady. No even talk loud. Nothin' foony." She nodded again then felt the temperature of cold steel against her temple.

When he removed his hand, she gasped, caught her breath and pleaded in a raised whisper, "Please, I'm not Mirage. I'm not who you think I am."

"Turn around," he said forcefully with his pistol pointed to her forehead. "I have to tie you. Dun worry, I won't hurt you."

"What are you going to do?" she asked pleading. "And where's my cat?"

"Be quiet."

As he bound her wrists behind her with nautical rope, she said to him again, "Look, please believe me. I am not Mirage. You have nothing to worry about with me. Look, take what you want; just don't hurt me, please. What are you going to do?"

He took a roll of three inch surgical tape and wrapped it completely around her head and mouth two times before she could make another plea. "You see, Lady, I know you are Mirage. The police know who you are. Stay still."

To no avail, she shook her head violently over and over which only pleased him and made him feel more powerful. As he bound her feet to the corners of the bed frame, she realized his intentions and began grunting desperately, squirming, writhing, eyes bugged from their sockets.

"You are very pretty, lady," he said ogling the helpless woman. "I like all your leetle freckle."

She watched in horror as he removed a steel silencer from his pocket, screwed it on to the muzzle of the Glock and laid it upon a night stand. She plunged into the pit of a deep, dark chasm looking up at the evil maniac, helplessly, pitifully doomed. Arms twisted and tied under her back, she watched his eyes scan her body from toes to breasts.

He opened his blade and cut the dress, first the spaghetti straps, then the neckline, then the skirt and then the panties. She shook her head furiously, left and right, pleading, grunting.

"I have thees big present for you," he said unzipping his fly. He grinned and he snorted, sniffed and snorted again as poor Carolyn looked up from her abyss. Hopelessly trapped, her fleeting mind raced, pleading. It was always this way, she thought. Men and her body.

Give in. Help him enjoy. Maybe you will survive this. My God, what has Marco done to me!

She felt the weight of his entire body crushing, humping, penetrating. The Glock lay on the night stand as he raped her without so much as unbuckling his belt. But he wasn't finished. There was no climax. He was still erect when he pulled out.

The madman then untied her legs, spun her onto her stomach like a rag doll and then retied her ankles to the posts. Frenzied, writhing, she remained helpless as the thumping of her heart pounded through her chest. Then he mounted her once more from behind as the cold, steel muzzle pressed against the back of her neck.

"Watch the birdie, Leetle Mees Mirage," he said. "See, I shoot two guns at the same time. Ha ha ha."

As he started to pant, she squeezed her eyes, praying, shaking her head violently.

No no, I'm not Mirage. Don't come, no...

CHAPTER 20

WEDNESDAY

AT 8:30 IN THE MORNING, Marco lumbered out of the shower with a huge terry towel wrapped around him like a Roman toga. His head reeled with thoughts of spending a holiday in Monaco with Carolyn, even if it meant blowing the entire million from the Cocoplum haul. It would be worth it. Maybe, she would come to live with him after all. He had just planted himself on the commode when the phone rang. For these anticipated moments the cordless was installed on the wall just above the roll of paper.

Before he had a chance to say hello, an accented voice said, softly, "She ees out of the peecher. No more worry. One more to go."

Blood rushed to his head. His first reaction was to call him an asshole for phoning him at home, but his usual paranoia set in. What if, by some fluke, his phones were bugged? "Uh, who is this? I don't know what you're talking ..."

He hung up.

EVEN THOUGH SHE was only twenty-nine, Dylonna Sue Lancaster was one of those traditional women who took care of her man, adored her family, raised children, taught the Bible, sewed cooked and cleaned every day of her life. She remained not only dedicated to Fitzgerald, but to anyone whom he loved, including Ken, her husband's dear and troubled brother. Indeed a dutiful woman, rich in character and obedient, she was taught to be by the minister's family that raised her in a foster home.

Rarely did she ever interrupt or take part in a serious conversation, unless approved of by Fitz. But this situation was different. She couldn't resist. She felt Ken's pain and had to say something.

"Excuse me, please. Fitz, I know sometimes I shouldn't be talkin', but this one time I just gotta say somethin'."

Ken Lancaster paced the floor of her tiny living room while her husband sat in his easy chair, following his kid brother's movements like watching a tennis volley. "Say anything you want, my honey."

She wiped her hands on a dish towel, stepped over to Ken and stopped him from pacing. "Listen to me. There is only one place to turn, Bro. The Lord is in charge here. Listen to me. Jesus is with you; he is protectin' you. The Bible says to trust in the Lord with all your heart, in all your ways acknowledge him and he will make your path straight. You must be true to yourself, Ken. Repent your sins and put yourself in the hands of Jesus."

"You don't understand, sister Dy."

She placed loving hands around his broad shoulders and looked up at Ken. "You can't run. Don't you understand? You can't run. If you run, you will run for all your life...and you have a long life yet to live."

"That's right, Bro," interjected Fitz puffing his pipe. "Listen to what Dylonna is sayin'."

Ken stopped pacing and plopped in a large chair. He was feeling the pressure. Nearly four days had passed since the murders, days he needed to collect his sanity. He knew he had to act rationally, to get his life back in focus. After all, it was not his fault. He didn't place himself in harm's way. It sought him out and now he had to deal with it.

"As soon as they, you know, them, find out I was there, they'll kill me. They'll hunt me and kill me. And what about Chrissy Mae? They may go after her."

"It's a very important case to the police, Ken," answered his brother, his pipe in teeth. "They will take care of you."

Dylonna Sue interrupted, "Jesus will protect you. You know I'll be praying for you."

Ken sat and stared into space, his mind in high gear.

Dylonna picked up a cordless phone from its carriage and brought it to Ken. "Come, Bro. First call Chrissy Mae. The poor woman must be worried to death."

MIAMI-DADE DETECTIVE, LUIS VASQUEZ arrived early at the City of Miami's Homicide Bureau to meet with Mike and go over all the intelligence information regarding the dead men found in the Everglades. Such finds were not uncommon but because they were linked to the Cocoplum murders, they would get more attention than an ordinary drug execution. Waiting with him were Randy, Zeke and Raul Gonzalez.

"*Que tal, amigo*," said Vasquez.

"Doing fine," Mike answered in English.

The five men exchanged introductions, sat at a long table and got down to business. "What have you got on these Bozos, Luis?" asked Mike.

"On one, a full life story. The other, nada." Vasquez opened his portfolio and started passing out photos.

"This is Felix Armando De La Rosa. He's thirty-eight, registered with INS as a refugee alien this past January. Came over with four other Cubanos floating on a rubber raft and picked up in Marathon Key by the Coast Guard. Since his release at Krome Avenue detention in March, there were no arrests, lived quiet as a church mouse in an apartment above a jewelry store on Flagler Street."

"Did he work?" asked Estevez.

"Odd jobs, probably under the table. The only real job we could find on him was a few weeks at the Four Ambassadors Hotel washing dishes and bussing tables. That was in June and July of this year."

Randy interrupted. "If he went through processing that fast, he must have relatives."

"I was just getting to that. We put a call in to a brother; his name is Carlos De La Rosa, lives off West Flagler in a trailer park and works as an auto paint and body man. No record on him either, except for traffic. From what we can tell from records, Felix was a quiet, law abiding alien trying to get a better life like so many other Cubans."

"What did the autopsy give us, Luis? Drugs?" It was primarily a dialogue between Mike Estevez and Luis Vasquez as the others listened on.

"That's what was surprising, Mike. The other guy, the unknown one, had high levels of cocaine in his blood. No surprise there. Felix? Nada. Clean. Not even alcohol."

Several minutes of discussion passed when a petite young woman with long brown hair cracked open the door and asked in an apologetic tone, "Excuse me. May I come in?"

"Yes, Holly," answered Mike. "What's up?"

"I've got two messages, saying they're very important. Sorry, or I wouldn't have interrupted."

"That's okay, Holly. Let's have 'em."

"A Christina Jackson called saying she heard from a Ken Lancaster? Wants you to call her back as soon as possible." She shrugged ignorantly.

Mike turned to Zeke, "That's good, eh partner? Okay Holly, what's the other?"

"Your wife, sir."

"Tell her I'll call her later. We're too busy." Mike snatched the slip of paper with Christina's phone number from Holly's hand and turned to walk out of the room when Holly called him back.

"Sir, uh, Mrs. Estevez was real upset. She says it is urgent that you call her back, like right now."

Perturbed, Mike replied, "She say why? What's wrong?"

"I wouldn't know, sir, but I think you better call her. She sounded like, real serious."

"What the hell is wrong with her? Jesus like I need this right now." Mike turned to Zeke and instructed him to call Christina while he phoned his wife. Raul Gonzalez gloated with pleasure seeing Mike in an uncharacteristic moment of consternation.

Her voice was stressed over the phone, almost choking. "Meet me for lunch, Mike. We got things to talk about."

"Baby, what the hell is with you. You know I'm in the middle of..."

"There's something I must talk to you about. It's very serious."

"Is Corrina all right?"

"Yes, she's fine. It's us, Mike. You and I."

"Robyn, can't it wait at least..."

"It cannot wait. I have to talk to you now. I mean, now!" Muffled cries were heard from a cupped receiver, clearly, dire circumstances. With the phone to his ear, he whirled in place and caught himself being ogled by two secretaries who spun away as he made eye contact. He would never show emotion in the presence of others.

"Okay, meet me at the Rusty Pelican. Noon." He hung up without saying goodbye. *"Fuck!"* he muttered under his breath as he stormed off to find Zeke.

FOR SPECTACULAR WATERFRON VIEWS, the famous Rusty Pelican ranked in the top one-hundred restaurants in the United States. Wearing her black Raybans, Robyn sat by herself at a window table near the eastern shore of Biscayne Bay and checked her watch; 1:35. All that separated The Rusty Pelican from the mainland a mile away was the expanse of lambent, choppy waters that sparkled under a dark grey cloudy sky.

She watched bikers and motorists speed across the lofty causeway bridge and then mused at the architectural wonders rising from the city so far off, penetrating the skies in an array of rainbow colors mixed with silver, white and grey like a mural painting. A sixty-foot yacht cruised by carrying sun-soaked passengers waving happily from the bow. It was overcast and humid, a certain sign it was going to rain.

Figuring she would not be going home after lunch, or perhaps ever, her clothing and other essentials were packed in the trunk of her car. She planned on spending the next few days and nights at Beth Ann's. Corrina was safe at her friend's house, at least for now.

When Beth first suggested a full confession, Robyn felt deceived and confused. As the day passed, she weighed it all and realized she had painted herself into a corner, and all was bound to come out eventually. It finally made sense. Her marriage wrecked, it was time he knew it, too.

No doubt, he would express a myriad of emotions, but she feared his anger. She would blame the champagne for her indiscretion with Ken Lancaster and see how he reacted. Above all, she needed to protect Corrina and needed the help of police in protecting her from the killers once she was identified. Worse than walking on a bed of hot coals, she thought, but it had to be done. She needed to get it over with.

Meeting him in a public place seemed best because she knew there would be no outbursts, no displays of temperament where he was so conscious of his image. Mike's perfect little world would be wrecked, so she had to keep it under control as much as possible. He hadn't the faintest idea. Today, the wife whom he cherished and believed to be so devoted would be unveiled as a common slut in his eyes. A day of personal infamy, a day that would forever seal a seventeen-year chapter in their lives.

Although the restaurant was half full of business people and tourists, the tables remained empty on either side of her table. Her watch showed one-forty. She was apprehensive he might stand her up. As she lit a cigarette, her heart skipped a beat watching the handsome, well-dressed detective weave swiftly through the maze of tables until he arrived at hers. He stood a moment with intense sapphire eyes boring into hers. Inside, she quivered with guilt.

"Sit, Mike." Her anxiety was transparent.

"You're smoking? What is this?"

"Yeah. I do a lot of things you don't know about."

"Well, my wife doesn't smoke. What the hell's gotten into you anyway, Robyn?" Mike snapped a napkin in his lap trying not to appear agitated. A smiling, East Indian waiter neared the table as he ordered a Johnny Walker Black on the rocks. "Robyn? A drink?"

"I'll just have a Diet Coke, thanks."

Throughout a long, painful pause Mike gazed contemptuously at his wife. Robyn nervously stroked her glass of water contemplating where to begin.

"Well?" Mike asked, gritting. "I'm here. It must be important so tell me what's on your mind."

"How's the case going, Mike?"

"Fine. Busy!"

She felt her eyes turn into pools of tears. Mike didn't notice until the first one rolled down below her Raybans. With a pang of sympathy, he reached over and put his hand on her arm. "Hey, baby, what's the matter? Tell me, come on. You're driving me crazy here."

She swallowed, then nearly choked on her words. "There's a problem. A really big problem. And it's going to upset you very much, but there's nothing I can do about it now except tell you."

"What is it?"

"You and I, well, you know that it's been a while since it's been right with us."

"No, I don't know. I don't know what you're talking about. Tell me."

A small commotion interrupted her words as a trio of diners were seated at the next table. Over her left shoulder she could see two of them were women. Another, a man she thought, sat almost directly behind her. She lowered her voice.

"Well, Mike," she said with a defensive chuckle while sipping on her water, "you want the good news, or the bad news?" She rattled the ice cubes.

"Come on with this already. Out with it."

The women to her left were laughing, distracting. Robyn wished they had sat elsewhere.

"Well, the good news, my dear husband, is that I will help you to solve your big case." She wiped a tear, looked at Mike and puffed her cigarette with an unsteady hand. The women laughed again. Louder this time.

"Oh, yes?" Mike's brow came together in the center. "And, the bad news is?" His hands were folded tightly on the table as his phone started to ring. Irritated, he checked the digital displaying the number of Randy McAdam's office followed by a

9-1-1, meaning the call was urgent. "Keep talking," he said.

As Robyn started to speak, the waiter approached to take their order. Mike waved him off with his free hand. "Later, please."

He flipped open a cell phone from his coat pocket and started punching numbers. "Continue, Robyn. I can listen."

Robyn had garnered a morsel of attention for a few seconds before her husband responded to more urgent matters. That was nothing new. As she raised the cigarette to her lips, trembling, it dropped to the carpet just slightly behind her chair. "Oops." "What is it, Randy?" Mike said cupping the phone, watching his wife. Then he snapped. "What? Carolyn Webb, dead?"

The cigarette rolled behind her chair. Mike continued his conversation as Robyn turned to her left and bent down to rescue the burning butt. First, her eyes blazed, then she gasped. Pale green eel skin boots, directly in front of her nose. For a moment she hoped and doubted. Too coincidental, she thought. Bent over still, she heard the familiar sound of a Latin male emit a raucous snort. Images of terror appeared in a flash.

The beetch with the grey hair. Over there, Chico. Matenla! BANG!

She rose up, begging God that it would not be him but there was no mistaking; she stared face to face with the killer named Javier.

She screamed directly into his face, startling him. He jerked backwards. Then she burst into a hysterical sequence of uncontrollable, shrilling screams, flailing her arms maniacally, knocking over a vase and water glass. Nearby diners dropped their glasses and leaped from their seats as the frantic outburst echoed through the entire room. Over the phone, Randy McAdams asked about the commotion as an astonished Mike Estevez dropped the cell phone, stood and reached over to grab his wife.

"No! No! Get away, get away!" she cried in a deafening squeal, shaking her head.

Unable to grasp her wrists, Mike glanced right and made eye contact with the man at the next table, then turned to Robyn. Simultaneously, Javier realized he was facing the detective he had seen on television and averted his face toward the window. Robyn ran hysterically through the dining room, crashing into tables as Mike chased after, drawing the attention of everyone.

Thunderclaps blared from a roiling sky as a deluge of rain suddenly burst upon the city. Robyn crashed through the front door and out to the parking lot, screaming inside herself but unable to make any sounds other than panting and hyperventilating.

In pursuit, Mike asked over and over, "What's the matter with you, Robyn? Robyn, I'm right here. Take it easy."

She collapsed to the pavement at the rear of a parked car, sobbing, her brown skirt and silk blouse soaked to the skin. Thunder boomed and rain beat down as her husband crouched over to hold her shoulders, totally confused. She wept hysterically, "Oh no, please God. Oh no."

Robyn Estevez and her husband of seventeen years on the macadam alone together, drenched, while he held her head to his chest sitting in a fresh puddle, oscillating to and fro, trying desperately to comfort her.

"It's okay, baby. I'll be with you. I love you, baby. It's going to be all right."

She sobbed and sobbed. Of all the thoughts pouring through

Mike's brain, of everything she had said, one item repeated over and over.

Well the good news, my dear husband, is that I will help you to solve your big case.

INSIDE THE RESTAURANT, the tall Latino approached the maitre d' with a lady's purse in hand saying, "I think that woman left thees behind."

"Oh, thank you, sir."

CHAPTER 21

THE FORTY-INCH, flat screen Magnavox was tuned to channel six.

"...WAS BELIEVED BY POLICE TO BE A CRUCIAL WITNESS IN THE

MASS MURDERS OF COCOPLUM UNTIL DISCOVERED THIS MORNING

BY HER EX-HUSBAND AND FORMER EASTERN AIR LINES PILOT,

DAVID WEBB. WE ARE OUTSIDE OF THE BREEZEWAY CONDOMINIUM

APARTMENTS WHERE THE BODY OF MRS. WEBB IS BEING PLACED

INTO A MEDICAL EXAMINER'S VAN. WITH US NOW FOR AN UPDATE IS

OFFICER GLORIA MENENDEZ OF THE MIAMI POLICE DEPARTMENT."

. . .

ALONE, the big man sat on a leather couch in his plush office on the forty-first floor of the Southeast Bank Building. His face flushed bright pink while his eyes remained glued to the television set. He couldn't believe what he was watching.

"Oh no," he muttered to himself. "Not my Carolyn, my Salome. That fucking asshole!"

"...THAT SHE WAS SHOT. NO MORE INFORMATION AT THIS TIME."

"DO DETECTIVES BELIEVE IT IS CONNECTED TO THE COCOPLUM
MURDERS, OFFICER MENENDEZ?"

"WELL THAT'S CERTAINLY A POSSIBILITY THEY ARE LOOKING
INTO."

"AND WILL SGT. ESTEVEZ BE IN CHARGE OF THIS CASE ALSO?"

"YES. OF COURSE, ASSISTED BY ..."

MARCO ROSE, wheezed and ambled to his desk, lifted the phone and punched seven numbers followed by seven more.

"...MORE QUESTION, OFFICER MENENDEZ. WAS MRS. WEBB, IN
FACT, THE WOMAN CALLED MIRAGE?"

. . .

"OH NO. HOMICIDE HAD BEEN IN TOUCH WITH MRS. WEBB FROM THE BEGINNING."

HIS PRIVATE LINE rang twice before he picked up the receiver to speak to Javier. "Meet me," Marco said in a low, gravel voice. "Matheson Hammock Park, same place as before. Five o'clock. Sharp."

When he hung up, a female voice over the intercom broke his train of thought. "Mr. Scandiffio. There are two detectives here to see you."

THE DISTRAUGHT, confused homicide detective had been on his cell phone in the hospital hallway talking for thirty minutes to Gloria, Zeke and Randy while nurses, doctors and aides scrambled about ignoring the handsome Cuban pacing to and fro. Then it was Lieutenant Raul Gonzalez who needed to talk to him. With his rain-soaked jacket strewn across a chair and his shirt still wet, he placed a finger in his opposite ear to deafen the noise from people chattering around him.

He was informed that Al Sanchez and Phyllis Moriarty were at the Breezeway Condominium working the death scene of Carolyn Webb along with the lab and the M.E. She had been tied spread-eagle and shot one time directly in the back of her head with a nine millimeter. No doubt about it. The same guy. But, no witnesses. They figured the killer mistook her for Mirage.

"But how would he have known about Carolyn Webb? Jesus, we're trying to keep these things under wrap."

"Don't know, Mike," answered the lieutenant.

Mike also learned that Ken Lancaster had called Christina Mae Jackson and confessed his entire role, well almost, in the

Cocoplum case which she already knew anyway. Before turning himself in, Ken told her he needed preparation, some spiritual guidance and prayer. She had promised not to tell where he was. Not yet, anyway. A twenty-four hour police guard was stationed at her house.

"One more thing," said the lieutenant, smugly. "The chief put Barnie Davidson on paid leave of absence pending his retirement. He's out of here."

"Yeah? Why? What's the story?"

"Apparently, he came on to a detective's wife and she made a complaint. I.A. went straight to the chief. So, it looks like he's worked his last day, on this job anyway."

"Who'd he....?"

"Marion."

"Randy's wife? You're kidding?"

"Randy's okay with it. He's still with us. She went to lunch with the captain a couple times trying to talk him into transferring Randy out. I guess Barnie thought she should return the favor first."

Mike Estevez was afraid to ask. "Who's taking Barnie's place?"

There was a short pause. "Guess."

Mike could sense Gonzalez's ear-to-ear grin over the phone. He hung the receiver and shuffled back into the private room where Robyn lay sedated and sleeping, then sank into a vinyl chair next to her bed. At a loss, his sense of order had shut down.

Once before, three years back, he had been burdened with the combined pressures of job and family, but they had worked it out, so he thought. Perhaps he had been blessed. Perhaps he was just ignorant. He thought about resigning from the case, from Homicide, but it was too important. He had to stay with it. He needed to regroup. He was charged with the responsibility and he had to meet it. Failure, withdrawing, did not reside in his vocabulary.

There she lay, the love of his life, the purest woman on the face of the earth, troubled so and he did not know why. He lowered his head into his hands trying to shake out answers.

"The good news is that I will help you to solve your big case."

What in the hell was she talking about? What's got into her?

Ever since Sunday she's been acting strange. He stood again to pace the floor, thinking.

He stopped at the window, his hands in his pockets and sighed, his brain consumed with all that had to be done on the case. Down and to the far right, he spotted her car in the parking lot, facing away from the building.

Little red sports car, decals on the rear window. Left side.

No way. He turned back to gaze at her in the bed.

"She had this soft voice, like she always talked in a whisper."

She had been to the Scandinavian gym on Saturday night. Of course. How stupid to even think of doubting her.

"No marks, except for that scar on her stomach."

Mike returned to the present when Doctor Paul Wembsley entered the room, chart in hand, to tell him that Mrs. Estevez was under heavy sedation and probably would not awaken until the next morning.

"I'm recommending that Dr. Gruenberg see her tomorrow, Mike. He's one of the top psychiatrists in South Florida. I think it would be wise. She's definitely suffering from a deep emotional trauma. Those are the worst kinds. I would hate to see her do anything to herself."

"Of course. Call him."

"Meanwhile, does she have any friends that can stay with her? I know how busy you are."

Beth Ann flashed through his mind. "Yes, thank you, Doctor," Mike replied.

After the doctor left, Mike leaned over his unconscious wife to whisper "I love you" then planted a delicate kiss upon her forehead.

As he started from the room, he hesitated, then looked back.

"She had this scar on her stomach..."

He stepped back to her and removed the old glossy photo of Robyn from his wallet. Quietly, he raised the sheet from the foot of the bed and firmly pressed one end of the glossy side against the big toe of her right foot, then the toe of her left foot on the opposite end.

Large ridges, probably came from the finger of a man.

"Why not the big toe of a woman?" he whispered to himself. "I hope not. God, I hope not."

He removed a tissue from the night table, encased the photo gently and slipped it into his coat pocket.

As he drove from the hospital, instead of turning to the north toward his office, he curved south toward the Scandinavian Health Spa.

A TOUGH-AS-NAILS FEMINIST-TURNED-COP, Phyllis Moriarty earned a master's degree in psychology by the time she was twenty-two but never did anything with it until she became an officer. Now, ten years later, she worked in homicide for the fabled Mike Estevez, trying to match up to expectations as she perceived them to be.

Steel grey eyes glinted under her short dark brown hair, very short, shaved above the collar with the front parted naturally in the middle. When she raised her silver badge from a black purse to the eye level of Marco Scandiffio, it seemed like his heart dropped to his ankles.

"I'm Detective Moriarty and this is Detective Sanchez. May we speak with you a few moments?"

A bead of sweat already formed on his brow. "Why, of course. What is this all about may I ask?"

"May we sit?"

Marco gestured toward the maroon leather chairs as he took his seat behind his desk.

Al Sanchez spoke first. "Mr. Scandiffio, do you have an employee here by the name of Carolyn Webb.?"

"Why, uh, yes. She is a receptionist for the office." Marco had seen the news but decided to play it dumb. He raised a water pitcher offering the detectives a glass. "Come to think of it, she hasn't been to work today."

"She's been murdered, sir. Found dead just a few hours ago in her apartment."

Marco raised his eyebrows and shook his head in disbelief. "Oh no. That's terrible. Such a nice girl. Who did it? Do you know?"

Al Sanchez continued on. "Mr. Scandiffio, we understand that Lillian Diefenbach was a client of yours, is that correct?"

"Oh yes, poor Lillie. That thing over in Cocoplum." He shook his head again. "Yes, I did some work for her. Taxes, probate, that sort of stuff. We were old friends. She was a great lady."

"Do you know what she would be doing with a large sum of cash?"

"Well, she was quite wealthy and, uh, how much are you talking about?"

"Millions."

Marco shook his head and gestured with his waving hand, "No. No idea."

Phyllis interrupted abruptly, "Sir, we are concerned about the connection between Mrs. Webb and the Cocoplum case. We think it may have led to her death. And seeing as you knew these people – worked with them as all – we have a number of questions we would like to ask you on the record."

Marco's brain bolted into high gear, wondering what they knew, how he could be implicated, if it would be unwise to answer their questions. He could invoke his rights, not answer, even ask for another attorney.

Phyllis Moriarty spoke on. "So if you would be so kind, we'd like to take a statement from you at our headquarters."

If he refused, they would surely focus on him as a suspect. After all, why would an innocent man refuse to cooperate in an investigation about his employee and a client? He dared not stonewall. It was too dangerous.

"This afternoon," she added.

Another bead of sweat glistened from his temple. "Well, I suppose so," he said in a low tone. Then he cracked a little smile. "Anything to help the police. What time?"

"We could drive you now, sir," said Al Sanchez.

"I'll take my car if you don't mind. I have a stop or two to make first. How about in one hour? Is that all right?"

"We'll see you in one hour, Mr. Scandiffio."

As soon as the cops left, Marco headed for the elevator and down to a coffee shop in the basement arcade where a pay phones was mounted on the wall outside the glass door. He punched seven numbers, waited, then seven numbers again and hung up. In less than thirty seconds, the phone rang.

"Where are you calling from?" he asked in his seaweed voice.

"A pay phone. No trace. What ees the problem?"

He cupped the receiver and spoke softly, trying to control his anger. "Listen you fucking...that wasn't Mirage you did. That was my goddam secretary. My girl. Did you hear that? What in the fuck is wrong with you?"

There was a dead pause and then, "Oh? Sorry, I thought that..."

"And now the cops are linking me up because she works for me. I gotta go downtown, all because you're an ignorant fucking asshole. Forget the meeting at Matheson. I can't afford being seen anywhere near you. I should have never..."

"I tell you many times before Marco, you dun call me asshole. Now look, I weel fix thees problem. Thees time I think I know who ees Mirage."

"She was my fucking girl, my fucking girl, goddamit!"

"I am sorry Marco...I am sorry. My source in the police tell me she was at the party and was steel alive."

"Right, stupid. Remember the girl who left the house before you went in, the one who gave us the signal?"

"Oh, sheet. That was her?"

"Yeah, that was her. A stand up little broad and you..."

"I am sorry, Marco. Thees time I weel be sure."

"And what about the nigger kid?"

"Heem, too."

"Fucking asshole!" grumbled Marco as he hung up the phone.

CHAPTER 22

THREE YEARS PRIOR, Javier Jimenez-Izaguirre entered the United States stowed amid cargo in a freighter bound from Havana to Nassau and then Nassau to Miami. Raised by his older brothers in a town called Sagua La Grande on the northern coast of Cuba, Javier never rode in an automobile newer than a '57 Chevy until he disembarked at the Port of Miami in June of 2010.

While in Cuba, he had resorted to violence now and then. It all began one night when he watched his older brothers beating a kid to death on the wharf. He was ten. It was a memory that had always fascinated him, to see a living, breathing, thinking human transformed into a lifeless carcass. At times, he would ask his oldest brother if they would do it again, but he was told that it was done for a special reason and to stay out of trouble.

Since arriving in the states, he worked several jobs off the books in hotel kitchens and car washes but survived mostly on income from small time drug sales, a few burglaries and an occasional robbery through which he became acquainted with a camarilla of Hispanic thieves and killers.

Once he was questioned by police about a prostitute's murder. She was found tied and shot in the same flea bag hotel where he lived one floor up. That's when he met Marco Scandiffio, champion of the guilty, defender of crime, lover of debauchery, ever ready to take on the law providing profits deemed palatable.

For a five thousand dollar retainer, Marco prevailed on call for Javier at the sound of a touch tone. When Javier thought he was under suspicion, Marco notified his contact in city hall and had them call off the dogs. His man was innocent, he said, simply a law abiding resident of the same hotel. No evidence existed. The case drifted into obscurity as Miami's Homicide Bureau underwent a deluge of riots and murder cases that same year. Javier remained a non-entity within the community where he used any one of a dozen aliases.

Some thought him a madman and perhaps he was, but he endured, focused and undeviating in remaining undetected. Killing had become intoxicating. The more he killed, the higher his thrill; it was almost recreational.

At four in the afternoon, Victor appeared at his modest second story apartment on Douglas Road across from the dog track. Javier felt strong and confident after having snorted another line of cocaine. The day reigned full and eventful, killing who he thought was Mirage and then celebrating by purchasing two beautiful *senoritas* for bed. The crazy lady screaming in his face and creating such a scene in the restaurant almost ruined his high. *Who was she?*

Later, he learned it was not Mirage that he killed after all. Thus, two witnesses still remained, both capable of putting him in prison to rot for life. That would not stand. He had too much living left. After all, he was now a millionaire in America.

As Victor knocked, Javier was musing over the photo on the lady's driver's license. Lovely he thought, much lovelier than the contorted, grimacing face he viewed in the restaurant. Before inserting the license back into the fold, he committed her information to memory.

Robyn Saunders Estevez, 8250 S.W. 85th Terrace.

No need to rush into things, he thought to himself, especially if she has anything to do with that cop. He had to find out for sure.

"This weekend, Victor, I will be moving to a new address. I am leaving this shit hole."

Like an obedient acolyte, Victor stood while Javier, smoking a cigarette, sat pompous upon a recliner chair with his legs crossed to show off his precious boots. "You are a successful man, Javier," he said slightly bowing, smiling.

Javier unfolded a wad of twenty dollar bills and snapped off five thousand dollars and handed it to the little man. "What is this for?" he asked, his eyes aglow.

"I want direct contact with the police department, Victor. Put me in touch with your man."

AT TWILIGHT, Mike Estevez entered the headquarters building through the basement to avoid being seen. He stopped at the canteen where he selected a ham and cheese hoagie from the vending machine and a soda. He figured the gang must be out in the streets working leads for he was all alone in his office. He had time, precious time, to think and eat the only food since early breakfast that day.

He wondered about Marco's statement and how he figured in the whole mess. He thought about what information Felix De La Rosa's brother had to offer, where Ken Lancaster was, how he would handle Raul Gonzalez as an acting captain, why and how Carolyn Webb was killed, how the killer knew about her, how Randy McAdams was holding up, Zeke, Phyllis, the Chief, the media, Robyn, and Mirage. Yes, Mirage. No, it could not be. But what if it was?

He looked out his window at the coral pink Miami Arena and watched as a Metrorail train pulled into the adjacent station.

"I will help you to solve your big case."... "Little red car, decals on the rear window, left rear"... " Scar on her stomach"... "No Daddy, she's at Scandinavian, you know that."... "Sorry, Sergeant, no record of Mrs. Estevez here last Saturday night."

He tried to imagine his wife at a lurid sex party making love to a man she didn't even know, then hiding with him in an attic while three crazed killers went about murdering four people in cold blood. His daughter's mother. No, not Robyn. It couldn't be. But what if were true?

His marriage would be shattered. The tabloids and the media would have a field day, smearing his picture, Corrina's and Robyn's on the front page of every super market reading rag while CNN and the networks would make mince meat of his reputation; television docudramas, *60 Minutes, Inside Edition, Anderson 360,* all probing his career, his precious image falling in shambles, facing department humiliation. If there were ever a trial, it would engage the nation's attention, and they would relive it over and over again. They would hound Corrina, his wonderful Corrina, who would endure enough by dealing with the truth. Poor Corrina.

How could this happen, mi Padre? How could this happen? Could it be true?

If only he had listened to his father and become a doctor. If only his father could still be there for him. Like so many times before, he envisioned him lying in the casket as his loving son wept, promising to avenge.

In the quiet of his little office, he opened the center drawer to his desk and lifted the pink card.

FATA MORGANA LIVES WITH YOU.

What crack pot sent this? What the hell does it mean? Mike opened his dictionary and flipped to the letter "F" and there it was.

"n. A Mirage (Italian, Morgan Le Fay) the mirage was attributed to her witchcraft."

"FATA MORGANA – Mirage, lives with me?"

He replaced the dictionary and reached into his pocket where he gingerly pulled out the old glossy photo of Robyn wrapped in tissue, held it carefully by the edges. She looked radiant in her ski outfit, the sun shining on her golden hair, pure white slopes in the background.

He hesitated, thinking. His first impulse was to wipe it clean and place it back into his wallet, like nothing ever happened, to protect her, and Corrina, and his own precious reputation. Perhaps, this was one case that should not be solved.

Yet, he remained the consummate cop. He opened a manila folder, gently inserted the photograph and laid it in the midst of loose papers in the bottom left desk drawer.

After a pair of rapid knocks, Randy McAdams entered without waiting to be invited. "Jesus, Mike, you look like death warmed over. Are you okay?"

"Oh yeah, Randy. Hey, how are you doing? I heard what happened."

Randy took a chair in front of Mike's desk and slumped in exhaustion. "Can you believe that old jerk, putting the move on my old lady?"

Mike tried to shift the focus from his own problems as he answered Randy. "Yeah, but what was the deal with her going to lunch with him?"

"Mike, I think we've worked it out. Marion admits she was wrong, but she said she was desperate to save our marriage. Going to lunch with Davidson was her idea, to plead with him to give me another assignment in this place." He paused, tilted his head back and sighed. "I guess I didn't realize how serious it was."

"What are you going to do, my friend?"

"We worked it out. I'll work this case with you to the end, Mike. But it's my last. I promised Marion. Anyway, it's time for me to start studying for sergeant, right?"

Randy recognized the distraction, the distance in Mike's eyes. He asked, "How's Robyn?"

"Fine. A little under the weather, Randy, but she's fine." *Got to change the subject.* "Tomorrow, Randy, I want to go to Ken Lancaster's work place, Caesar's Teasers, is it? They may have info on where we can find him. Tell Zeke. Right now, I'm wiped out."

"Lieutenant, uh, Acting Captain Gonzalez has set up another critique and a briefing. Nine a.m. sharp. The chief is going to be there."

Mike raised his eyebrows and looked up again at Randy, "Can

you believe it; that fucking asshole Gonzalez has been put in charge?"

"What a joke. But it's temporary, Mike. You can work around him."

"Yeah, I know."

THE LITTLE RED SUPRA was conspicuously missing when he pulled into his driveway. Corrina wouldn't be there either. A small night light from the front bedroom cast a bluish hue through the vertical blinds, which was noticeable when he turned off the car's lights. A dark, overcast night and Robyn had not left the yellow porch light on. Conflicting emotions of love and confusion consumed him, as well as anger, despair and determination, wanting to rid himself of her yet protect her as well. That's if! *If*, it were her. How could she? What got into her? Why? Why?

Within fifteen minutes of Mike making a phone call, Ernesto Garcia knocked at his door. He was a broad shouldered, barrel-chested Cuban in his mid fifties who had left the department ten years past. Mike always liked Ernie since he first knew him as his instructor in the academy. He was a good soul, a little ignorant and naive perhaps, but a good soul.

Mike remembered Ernie's familiar beefy handshake. "It's been a long time, my friend."

They shared a Johnny Walker Black on the rocks sitting in the family room as Mike explained that he had reason to fear for the safety of his wife. "I don't want to say more than that. But believe me, Ernie, it's serious. Can you help me?"

"For you, Mike, I am at your disposal."

"She is in Mercy Hospital, Ernie, room 632. Be there tomorrow, before ten a.m. checkout."

CHAPTER 23

BEFORE HER EYES COULD OPEN, antiseptic hospital odors piqued her consciousness so she lay quietly and listened a while. She heard no sounds other than the shuffling of footsteps outside the room which broke the silence. The first person Robyn saw at seven thirty in the morning was Beth Ann Lieberman sitting on the vinyl chair working on a needlepoint. Deep in concentration, Beth hadn't noticed that Robyn opened her eyes. Suddenly, out of the silence, Robyn murmured, "I guess I blew it, huh?"

Beth laid the project in her lap, reached over and touched Robyn's arm, "How're you feeling, Sugar?"

"Like shit. How long have I been here? Where's Mike? Is he here?"

"Mike is working. I'm here to be with you. What happened anyway?"

Robyn asked Beth to raise the level of the bed. Then a drink of water. "What do you know, Beth? What did they tell you?"

"Only that you went berserk for no reason at The Rusty Pelican and they couldn't calm you down. Hell's bells, Sugar, I thought maybe he went to hurt you after you told him."

"Never told him. I couldn't spit it out."

"So, what triggered the..."

"I saw him. My nose was inches from his nose, and he saw me, too."

Beth sat on the edge of Robyn's bed. "Saw who?"

"Him. The guy." She spoke in a near whisper. "That goddam maniac who killed Lillie and the others."

"Oh, no wonder, oh my gosh, Robyn, I hope he didn't know who you were." She laid a comforting hand over Robyn's hand.

"How could he? He wouldn't know me from anyone; he'd never seen me before. But he sure as hell must be wondering who I am now."

"What'd he do, you know, when you lost it in there?"

"I have no idea. All I know, Mike was talking on the phone when I dropped this cigarette and that's when I saw him. I lost control. I was so scared, Beth. The next thing I remember was Mike holding me in the parking lot with the rain beating down on us."

A large, buxom grey-haired nurse rushed through the door brandishing a thermometer and blood pressure cuff. Beth Ann stood off to the side. A few minutes passed before they were alone again.

"Well, Mike may not know about it all, but he sure as hell knows something's wrong, I can tell you that. He must be baffled." Then she mused a moment. "Just think, Beth, for the first time in his life, Miguel Estevez, ace detective, is baffled. Ha."

"You still have to tell him, Robyn."

"No way. Uh uh. I can't. Not now. I tried, but right now I think I'd rather take my chances and keep my fingers crossed. Seeing that, that monster, face to face. I thought my heart was going to burst out of me. I mean all I could think of was his eyes and a gun to my head. Maybe Mike and I, well, we'll just break up, and he'll think it's just the job and all." She stopped a moment to ponder, then, "Do you have any idea what he's doing today?"

Beth Ann hesitated because she knew her answer would trigger another episode, but she couldn't hide it. "Well, my bet is that he's on that new case."

Her brows curled together. "New case? What new case?"

"Yeah, it's all over the news." Beth sighed and took her hand back. "Sugar, one of the girls from the Cocoplum party was found dead in her apartment, shot."

"What?" Robyn raised up from her supine position, stiffening, no longer relaxed. "Who? Carol?"

"Yeah. That's her. Carolyn Webb."

"Oh, my God!" Robyn raised her hand to her mouth, her eyes welled up. The images began to reappear as she visualized Carolyn dancing with the nude white boy named Chad. Then, Chad's blood-soaked body crumpled inside a piano. Then Janie. *BANG!* "Beth, oh, that's terrible," she said straining.

"Easy, Sugar. Don't get all excited again, please. There's a psychiatrist coming this morning to talk to you. Mike asked for him. He's supposed to be the best in his field. Maybe it would help if..."

Robyn interrupted her. "Give me my clothes. Now!"

WITH THE CONVERTIBLE'S TOP UP, and tinted windows tightly closed, the white Mercedes stopped at the corner of north-east Seventh Avenue and Fifty-Second Street. As usual, he wore another Hawaiian shirt, only with more gold showing on his chest hair and a pair of wrap-around Polaroids. He watched the old white frame house in the center of the block but saw no movement for thirty minutes. Only one vehicle, a black pick-up truck, remained in the driveway. He was in one of the older, deteriorated residential sections of Miami situated on the cusp of "hooker alley" only three miles from downtown, a stone's throw from busy Biscayne Boulevard. No signs indicated a business operated from the house. He had called Caesar's Teasers an hour earlier, certain he had the right address.

Finally, a young white woman, blonde and skinny, emerged and drove off in the pick-up truck. It was time to make his move.

Javier approached a white smudged door in need of paint and knocked.

A portly little man about forty with a New York accent and black permed hair sat behind a dilapidated, wooden desk in what once was a formal dining room. "Come in, dammit. What took you so long?" said the voice from inside.

Javier stepped into a small enclosed porch cluttered with wrought iron furniture stacked to the ceiling and then into the living room where he approached the desk. "Hey, you're not from Sonny's. What's up, Bub?"

Javier looked around the disheveled room, unimpressed, then back to the little man. "You have a dancer; hees name, I theenk, is Lancaster. A black man?"

"So what's it to ya? He's quit, anyway. Hey, you from the cops?"

Javier didn't like him. He was crude, insolent, disrespectful. Javier deserved respect. "I want to know where he ees."

"Yeah, so do I. Sorry, Bub, we don't give out that information, unless of course, you're with the cops. We always cooperate with the cops." The pudgy little man looked up at Javier sensing this was going to be a problem. "Hey look, I'm very busy here."

"Thees ees Caesar Teaser? No?" Javier looked around.

"Yeah, you got the right place, but unless you got business with us..."

Certain that they were alone, Javier pulled the Glock from his waist band and pointed the silencer muzzle directly at the man's forehead. His face turned tomato red as two hands shot high above his head. "No, please, don't. Whatever you want."

Javier was in charge now. No more disrespect. "Your personnel file, *amigo.* Now!"

Slowly, deliberately, Anthony Augustus "Tony" Portelli stood with hands held high over his head, eyes darting back and forth, slowly leading Javier to a rusty, grey cabinet in the second room where he pulled the second drawer. Trembling with fright, he thumbed through a number of tabs and then lifted a folder marked Lancaster. Nervously, he sputtered, "Here, here it is. Take it and..."

BANG! For a millisecond, Tony Portelli felt pins and needles at the base of his skull, then blackness. The killer jumped back to avoid blood on his boots then, wallowing in power, gloated proudly at his latest victim.

Two minutes later, as he strode across the street toward his Mercedes, a yellow Toyota pulled up to the house with a little sign on its roof, *SONNY'S. WE DELIVER.*

ZEKE AND MIKE were sitting in the corner of the headquarters' canteen exchanging ideas when they spotted Lieutenants Raul Gonzalez and Juan Masvidal standing at the counter. They each ordered a tiny cup of café Cubano then sat at an opposite corner table. Deep into a hushed conversation, they gibbered and gestured to each other in some obvious disagreement.

"That's the lieutenant from records, isn't it?" Zeke asked.

"Yeah. He and Gonzalez are old buddies. They always talk like that. It's ethnic, my man. We Cubans are like the Italians. We can talk without talking." A little smile crossed both their faces.

As a crowd grew, Gonzalez and Masvidal ceased their conversation and bumped into Chief Howard on the way out the door. Brisk and cheery, the chief took a chair and greeted Mike and Zeke with a generous smile. "How're you doing, boys?" he asked. The chief looked like he had stepped out of a *GQ* cover page, wearing a brown, pinstriped suit with a paisley tie against a pale blue shirt and a generous, reeking splash of Polo cologne.

"Just fine, boss," said Mike. Zeke nodded.

"You look a little tired, Mike. I heard your wife, well, she's not feeling well?"

"She's fine, Chief." He diverted the conversation. "And how are you holding up under all this?"

"Well, I guess it comes with the territory. Listen, before you start the critique, can we talk? Just you and I." Zeke caught the hint and politely excused himself.

Howard saw the fatigue in Mike's eyes. "Are you all right Mike? I mean, really? You look tired, man."

"I got problems, boss. I mean, big problems you don't want to know about."

"What problems?"

"Problems everywhere I look, at home, this case, my supervisor, name it. You just don't know, boss. Gonzalez does not belong in this unit. And he should never have been made an acting captain. His head is the size of a Goodyear blimp."

"Sorry 'bout that, but for now there's nothing I can..."

Mike interrupted, "Why? Because he's a Cuban? There are other Cuban lieutenants, Chief."

"Look, Mike, you know how it goes. He's strong with the B.L.O. and the Miami-Dade County Latin Coalition. Its president calls city hall, city hall calls..."

"Calls you, and you're obligated."

"Something like that. It's life in the big city."

After a brief pause of exasperation, Mike changed the subject. "Chief, just so you know, this is between us, okay?"

"Sure, what's up?"

"I want out of homicide after this case. I've had it."

"Mike, I'm only putting Gonzalez there in an acting capacity until we find another captain. It's only temporary. Don't worry. I'll make sure he leaves you alone and..."

"That's okay, boss. But I'm still out of here. I gotta grab a life before it passes me by." Mike checked his watch. "It's nine, Chief. You coming to the critique?"

"Wouldn't miss it."

THE SQUAD ROOM maintained its customary disarray, papers strewn over every surface, phones ringing and computers clicking to the nimble fingers of secretaries in the adjoining room. Mike had his entire group waiting, some standing, others leaning, sitting on chairs and edges of desks, all holding note pads, portfolios and eight by ten photos. No one was without a pen in hand.

Besides the Chief of Police, there was the grey-haired Chief of

Detectives whose primary role in all of this was to administrate resources. Raul Gonzalez sat in the front of the room, his arms folded across his girth. All the primary investigators, Randy McAdams, Zeke Ferguson, Al Sanchez, Phyllis Moriarty and Luis Vasquez from Miami-Dade were there as well. Gail Dow represented the lab. I. Richard Jacobson, the prosecutor, arrived the same time as Mike.

With his head still mired at Mercy Hospital and at The Rusty Pelican, Mike was having trouble concentrating on the bombardment of new information. Then he pointed.

"Phyllis?"

"Carolyn Webb, White Female, thirty-three years old. She was found by her ex-husband, who was still a regular visitor, so he said. He was pretty upset, Mike."

"Go ahead."

"Anyway, she was tied to the four corners of the bed on her stomach with her skirt pulled above her butt and her panties cut away. One single nine millimeter slug passed directly through the back of her head. The shell ejected to the right of the bed on the floor."

"Raped?"

"Undoubtedly. Semen was found in the vagina. We're taking it to the lab for blood grouping, DNA and all that."

"Forced entry?"

"Must have used a lock pick. Nothing. No marks."

"Al, what about witnesses, neighbors. Anyone see, hear anything?"

"Nothing. Except a Mrs. Weinberger in apartment 312 claims that she came home in the morning from an overnight stay at her daughter's and another car was parked in her assigned space. She says it happens all the time and the condo association does nothing about it. Really, Mike, a witch if I ever met one."

"What kind of car?"

"Doesn't know…says it was a white convertible."

For the moment, Mike was feeling back into the groove. "Neighbors heard nothing?"

"Her only neighbors are snowbirds. They're not here in the summer."

"What was she doing just before she was killed?"

"No way to know that, not now anyway."

Phyllis Moriarty interrupted. "I think she had just come home, Mike. She still had a dress on and fresh strap marks on her feet from her slings. Her entire ring of keys was on the floor at the entrance to the bedroom."

"How long had she been dead?"

"At one p.m., the M.E. said she was dead about three to four hours. That puts the murder around nine or ten."

"What did David Webb tell you?"

"It's a mess, Mike. He spilled everything he knew, and it's complicated. It involves Lillian Diefenbach, Carolyn, Marco Scandiffio, himself, drug running and money laundering. He's coming clean and wants Carolyn's killers to pay. I'll give you more details later."

"Interesting. What did you get from Marco?"

Phyllis answered. Everyone in the room listened intently as more intricate details of the murder investigation unfolded. "Well, Mr. Slimeball showed up an hour late for his statement and then told us nothing. He was a waste of time."

"So what did you expect?"

"He says that he only knew Carolyn as an office receptionist, that he hired her as a favor to Lillian. My guess, Mike, is that he's in the middle of this somewhere. There are just too many coincidences. He's such a disgusting slob. You know what he did? Right in the middle of the statement, he lists to one side and blows this whopping fart. I mean it was like he revved up a motorcycle." The room broke out in uproarious laughter. "He cracks this ugly grin and then, get this, lights a match to kill the smell. Prune-lips Penny, well, she didn't know what to do."

The laughter was contagious and despite her efforts, Phyllis broke into her own fit of cackling. Mike smiled, chuckled and allowed the levity to run its course.

"Wouldn't surprise me at all if he were involved." Mike turned to Randy and asked, "Have we got a printout on all his clients? The last five years, maybe?"

"No, but we will now," Randy said sitting on the edge of a desk.

"Good. I want a full read on everyone he's connected to, especially if they're Spanish. Get together with the Organized Crime Bureau and see what they have on file."

Zeke raised his hand. "Yes, Zeke?"

"Mike, wasn't there a city murder case, maybe two years ago, where some girl was tied to a bed and shot? There was a bulletin on it when I was in uniform, but I don't remember anything more."

Mike put his thumb and forefinger to his head trying to concentrate, all the time thinking to himself; *Do I really want this solved?* "Sounds familiar. Al Sanchez, do you remember?"

The Spanish detective with hair parted in the middle alerted. "Yes, I remember, a Dominican prostitute at some flea bag hotel. I think Charles Bosworth handled it before he got promoted. Then it just sat on the shelf. It's still open so there must be a file."

"Al would you follow up on that?"

"Sure thing."

"Zeke, what's the latest on Ken Lancaster?"

"I think he'll be calling us pretty soon. He talked to his fiancé, Christina. He's trying to get up the nerve to come in. Still don't know his whereabouts."

"I'm still concerned. Later, we'll go to his employer and see what help we can get there."

He switched over to the detective from Miami-Dade and his older partner. "Luis, glad you could be here. Any help from the brother of Felix De La Rosa?"

"Name is Carlos De La Rosa, age thirty-eight. A hard working paint and body man who came over in a boat in May of 1998. No police record other than traffic since he's been here but I think he was a member of Alpha 66, you know, the anti-Castro group. He was real close to his kid brother."

"Does he know anything?"

"Says that Felix wouldn't have hurt a flea. Last week Felix said that he was going to make some big money soon and then they were going to bring their mother to the United States. That's all he wanted, to bring his mother here. No wife, no kids, just a brother and a mother. Carlos had no idea who he associated with outside of his job."

Mike looked up at the only person present from forensics. "Gail, I want the projectiles compared with the ones from the heads of the two guys in the Everglades."

"Right."

"Any prints in the house?"

"From preliminaries, looks like hers and her ex-husband's. Nothing else of value."

The vibrator on his cell phone buzzed against his belt. The digital read-out was a number strange to him. He turned his head to the Assistant State Attorney. "Dick Jacobson, you got anything?"

"Sounds like it's all under control. Call if you need me."

"Lieutenant?"

Gonzalez nodded.

"Chief Howard?"

He nodded. Then Gonzalez interjected, "Hey Mike, you haven't discussed the leads on Mirage?"

"Oh yeah." Mike's heart pounded at the sound of her name. "Randy? Phyllis? Zeke?" Mike was relieved. There was nothing.

As soon as the meeting was over, Mike called the number on his phone. It was Ernie Garcia at a Mercy Hospital pay phone.

"She was gone by the time I got here, Mike. Sorry."

He turned his back to the secretaries and spoke low but firm. "Jesus, she was supposed to be there until ten. She had an appointment with a shrink. Get over to the house, Ernie. Find her. Don't let anything happen to her."

He hung up in frustration as Raul Gonzalez approached him with a slip of paper. "Here's a fresh kill. Just called in from communications. Man, shot dead on Fifty-Second and northeast Seventh. Body found by a delivery boy. You handle."

"Jesus Christ, Raul, what's the matter with you? Can't you see I'm buried here? Get off my back."

"It's the owner of Caesar's Teasers."

CHAPTER 24

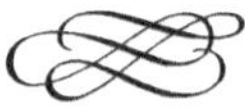

SOUTHEASTERN BREEZES from the bay swirled their hair, causing Beth Ann to hold her skirt as they stood outside Mercy Hospital's guest parking lot. "Beth, where's my wallet?" she asked frenetically as she started opening the door to the Supra. Robyn rummaged through her purse. The wallet was gone.

"I don't know. Who drove your car to the hospital?"

"It had to be Mike. But he wouldn't take my wallet. I don't even know who brought my purse from the restaurant."

Frustrated, Robyn slung the leather bag through her driver's window. "I don't know, I don't..." An ominous thought struck her.

"What are you thinking, Robyn?" Beth envisioned the wheels turning in her head.

"When I ran out of the restaurant, I don't know where my purse was. I always place it on the floor next to my..." A cold chill overcame her. Her facial muscles dropped as she turned to look into Beth Ann's eyes. "My God. He's got it. He's got it, Beth."

"Who, Sugar?"

"Him! The one."

"Come on. You don't know that for sure."

"That means he's got my address. Oh my God. Where's

Corrina? What day is this?" Her face flushed, Robyn scanned the parking lot, fearful, frightened, more paranoid than ever.

"It's Thursday."

"She's coming home tonight. Corrina's coming home."

Beth Ann watched as her friend trembled, then composed herself. Robyn straightened her hair with two fingers as a warm gust of wind ruffled her skirt. She was adamant now, and forceful, grasping for thoughts. She realized that Beth Ann was being sucked into the middle of the conundrum with her. "Beth, listen, you better stay away from me. You understand that? Thanks for your help, but you have to stay away from me. You hear me? It's for your own good."

"THE NIGGER EES HIDING. But I know where he leeve."

Marco waddled angrily about the office with the phone to his ear then issued an order, "Give me a number."

Javier spoke seven numbers. "It ees a pay phone."

Ten minutes passed until Marco Scandiffio arrived at the basement arcade to use the pay phone. It was mid afternoon outside the coffee shop with very little passing traffic. Cupping the receiver, he furtively scanned the marbled hallways and spoke softly. "Don't you ever, *ever* again call me at my office. Do you realize that the cops are already questioning me? What the fuck are you, some kind of loose cannon?"

"Now, I think I know who ees Mirage and..."

"Look, you fuck, from this moment on, I don't know you and you don't know me, got that? You've already wasted my girl and got the cops snooping around. You don't fuckin' exist. Is that clear, asshole?"

"I tell you before, you dun call me asshole. I dun like it."

Marco worked hard at restraining his temper, and managed a phony smile at a waitress passing by. He coughed, wiped his mouth and spoke again, even softer. "Now you listen, and listen good this time. I'm not going to repeat it. I know this system better than you. I know these cops and I know these judges. You are buying us first class tickets to death row. Do you understand? No more killings. *Comprende?* It's bringing too much heat. We'll take our chances with those goddam witnesses, but no more killings. And don't ever call me again. Is that clear?" He spoke in slow, distinct syllables, "You... Fucking...Ass...Hole!"

He slammed the receiver to the carriage.

THE MEDIA HADN'T TIED IT together yet, so there was little coverage outside the small dilapidated frame house on Fifty Second Street. Yellow barrier tape sealed off the street as a half dozen police cars, marked and unmarked, were parked in scattered directions, across neighbor's yards, atop sprinkler heads and foliage. Gloria Menendez wore a blue blazer with white pants and her jet black hair in her regular French twist. Mike Estevez couldn't help but notice. Everyone else did. Waiting outside in case reporters asked questions, she chatted with the uniformed men.

"Zeke, this is yours," Mike said as they stood over the supine body of Anthony Portelli lying amid a cluster of files and papers, eyes fixed to the ceiling. Zeke nodded with uncertainty, afraid to let on he was feeling overwhelmed. He was still Mike's "rookie" in training and he was being handed a whodunit linked to the biggest case in Miami history. What if he couldn't match up to it? Then, words of comfort. "You will be fine, Zeke. I'll be there for you, you know that."

"What would Lieutenant Gonzalez say?" asked the big man.

"Whatever the chief tells him to say. Now, let's get to work."

Mike went outside to use his cell phone while Zeke gave instructions to the forensic technicians, telling them to look for employment files bearing the name *Lancaster.* He then went outside to question the delivery boy from Sonny's who was stationed in one of the uniformed cars. Next, the distraught, strung-out girl who just arrived back at the house driving Portelli's pick-up truck. She leaned against the police car smoking and biting the corners of her knobby fingers, saying that she always called him her old man though they weren't married. "He was a good guy. What can I tell ya? Poor bastard. Now what am I gonna do?"

The forensic technician waved Zeke to the front door. "Nothing here on Lancaster," said the Latin fellow no older than twenty-five. "The folders on each side of the L-A-N's were wedged up as though the file next to it had been removed."

Meanwhile, back in the Ford Taurus, Mike left several messages on his home voice mail and another message at the real estate office in a futile attempt to locate Robyn. He called Ernie Garcia who said he was still sitting across from his house, waiting for a red Supra to drive up but, so far, nothing. Who would she call? Who would she trust? He tried to reach Beth Ann Lieberman at her office, on her cell and at her house where he spoke to her husband, Sam. Nothing.

It's out of hand. There's a homicidal maniac out here and Robyn's in danger. So is Corrina. Play it cool here. I've got to protect her. What if the department ever learned that I knew and I did nothing? It's obstructing justice, interfering with an investigation. Imagine that. Me? Interfering? I can't believe this is happening. Why? Why did she? How could she?

He was startled out of his thoughts by Zeke leaning over his car. "You okay, Mike?"

"Sure, how's it going?"

"Looks like another nine-millimeter, only this time to the back of the head. The girl wasn't here. She's no help. Didn't even know Ken Lancaster. No help from the neighbors either."

"Is that it?" Mike looked off into the distance.

"You didn't ask me about the kid who found him. Hey, you're slipping, Mike."

"What about him?"

"Didn't see anything. Just walked in when no one answered the knock and there he was. He did say he saw a white convertible turning the far corner when he drove up to the house. He has no idea what the make was."

Mike reflected, not saying a word. His mind and his heart were on overload.

"Hey, Mike, that fits with Mrs. Weinberger over at Carolyn Webb's. You know, the white car in her space?"

"Right, Zeke. Very good. What's next?"

"Sure you're okay, Mike? Sorry, but you just don't seem with it." Zeke set his huge hand on Mike's shoulder.

"Just a lot on my mind. So what's next?"

"I have to call Christina Jackson."

"Ken's girl. That's right." Mike raised up back into reality, back into the case. "Call her and get someone over there, like now! That crazy mother fucker..."

"Easy, man. Remember, we've got a twenty-four hour watch going on there."

"Oh, yeah."

"But if she knows, she better tell us where he's at or he'll be joining Mr. Portelli in there."

Mike paused and gazed straight ahead. "Doesn't it strike you strange, my friend?"

"What's that?"

"How did he beat us here?"

KEN LANCASTER TOLD Fitzgerald and Dylonna that he would return to Miami and face the music. But that's not what he did. Fitz dropped him off at the Tri-Rail commuter station with the intent of Ken making his way home but, again second thoughts as he pondered the court testimony, the embarrassment, the shame and the dangers.

Images flitted through his mind; the evil gun-waving Spaniards, the shots, screams, furniture smashing, the smell of the blood, the crazy one laughing, and Mirage, her intoxicating smells, her warm bloodedness and then her cold bloodedness.

He gazed out of the window at the nothingness passing by, cogitating, vacillating and mulling over Dylonna's words of love and inspiration. But Dylonna was not the one in that attic. The quivering inside of his stomach erupted again. By the time the train crossed into Miami-Dade County, wrought with fear and uncertainty, he figured it was better to be a live coward than a dead witness. He still needed more time.

Ken disembarked at the Golden Glades station and walked the half mile to check into a safe motel in North Miami. Then he called the one he loved.

"Chrissy Mae, you know if anything happens to me, you know I love you, I mean I love you with all my heart, and our little girl. I'm so sorry this all happened. I feel so guilty, so wrong, so dirty."

"Ken, please come home." She started sobbing over the phone. "I love you, too, and it's okay. I forgive you. Please come. I'm so worried. Where are you?"

"I will. I will. Maybe tomorrow, but I just got to get it together first. Please understand, Chrissy."

There was a short pause. "I'm taping this call, Ken. The police asked and I said it was okay."

"You mean I'm being traced?"

"Oh no, honey, not that. Just tape recorded." Then she heard a sound from the front door. "Just a minute, Ken. Someone's here."

Ken held on to the line for over a minute when another familiar voice came on the line and said, "Ken, this is Zeke Ferguson, listen to me, son..."

Dial tone.

ABOUT FOUR-THIRTY ON that warm and muggy Thursday afternoon, Robyn and Corrina Estevez pulled into Alligator Jake's Motel and Restaurant on Tamiami Trail deep in the heart of the sprawling Everglades thirty-three miles west of Miami. The afternoon thunder boomers had left the pavements steaming as the blazing summer sun reappeared in the western sky.

Other than an old, rusty blue and white Ford pickup parked in front of the office door, no other cars appeared in the lot. Separated by the office in the center, the motel consisted of an old one-story building shaped like a boomerang where all the rooms faced the main road. To the west, a smaller house served as an Indian gift shop and a seldom frequented eatery that specialized in fresh, deep-fried catfish caught in the motel's back yard.

As Robyn turned into the driveway, Corrina looked up at the large faded green and yellow sign that read, *AIR BOAT RIDES* and asked, "Here? We're staying here? Why here?"

"Jake's an old friend, Corrina."

"Mom, when are you going to tell me what's going on? Like, you know, I really don't want to be here."

"Trust me."

Robyn pulled her Supra to the front, ordered Corrina to wait and then walked swiftly to the office. She never removed her Raybans. The screen door slammed behind her. "Ah, Mrs. Estevez, how good to see you. A pleasure."

An aging Miccosukee, Alligator Jake once thrilled tourist audiences with his skill at wrestling twelve foot alligators in the village three miles to the west. Then his reflexes slowed with the passage of time and one afternoon, he found his forearm crushed in the jaws of a young gator they called Hercules. That became his last day in the pit. He could only extend a right elbow to Robyn as she walked through the door. For seven years now he had operated the motel and restaurant with his wife and twenty-four year old son, Robert. As tourists flocked during the winter season, they hired on more Indian employees to help with the air boat rides.

"It has been a long time, Jake. You are looking well." She forced a smile. "Jake, I need a room and the use of a telephone for my daughter and I, uh, I have no money with me right now but I'll pay."

"Misses, please don't worry. I know you are good. It is no problem." Though he was curious, Jake would ask no questions. He was lined and leathered, looking much older than his fifty-nine years though his long black hair showed only sparse streaks of grey.

In her real estate endeavors, Robyn would often entertain clients and prospective customers by offering tours of the Glades and using Jake's air boats for thrilling, fifty mile per hour excursions across the sea of grass. Jake saw her at least three or four times a month during winter. She was a good customer.

"Just fill out this registration, Misses," he said.

"Would you mind, Jake?" she asked looking through her dark glasses, "I'd rather not."

The Indian paused, peering into her eyes. The lady was in trouble. He would help and not ask.

"Cell phones cannot get a signal out here. There is a land line telephone here in the office. The door is open. You use it anytime you want. Tell me and I will leave. It is no problem for you, misses."

Robyn's bags had been packed since she had decided to confess to Mike at The Rusty Pelican. Corrina carried a small overnight bag which she kept at her friend Cindy's. They each tossed satchels on the floor as Robyn flopped upon a twin bed with her hands over her forehead. Safe at last, at least for now, she thought. No one would ever trace her here. Even if just for a day or two, until she could work it all out in her head. Who knows, maybe she would tell Mike after all, but not now. The crazy one had her wallet. He knew where she lived and she was certain he knew she was Mirage.

Corrina swelled with frustration and anger as she stood at the inside of the door asking one more time. "Mom?"

"Okay, honey. I have a lot to tell you. I just hope you'll understand."

CHAPTER 25

ONLY FIVE DAYS BEFORE, Mike had been a happy police detective with a secure, loving family and the envy of hundreds in the local law enforcement arena. The world was perfect and Miguel Estevez sat on top of it. Now, four people were dead at Cocoplum in the most bizarre and sensational crime in Miami's history and his life had turned upside down. Carolyn Webb's murder posed a grim omen that the killer still stalked the surviving witnesses. Since the homicide at Caesar's Teasers, Mike figured the killer probably knew the home address of Ken Lancaster who, like Mirage, was still missing.

Meanwhile, Mirage might very well be the pseudonym for Robyn Estevez, wife and mother of his child. A killer with an uncanny knack for obtaining inside information lurked and stalked. Mike could not turn to the department for fear of unveiling Robyn. On top of it all, Randy McAdams had his own marital problems, he had a rookie detective to train, a teaching seminar in Orlando in two weeks, the media haunting him, a department demanding results and an incompetent, egomaniacal lieutenant breathing down his neck. For Mike, the whole situation made it a really bad week.

It was dusk, nearing eight p.m. on Thursday evening. Mike took the wheel of the car and drove to his own townhouse, leaving Zeke somewhat bewildered at such a waste of time when there was so much else to do, leads to follow, evidence to sort, witnesses, autopsies, reports, background on the victim, and on and on.

"Wait in the car here, Zeke. Get your lead sheet organized; I'll be right back." Zeke was facing the garage door of a townhouse in Kendall as Mike hustled across the street toward an old gray van parked off to the side. Through his side view mirror, Zeke watched him stand at the driver's door talking to a man at the wheel.

"No red car, no any car. *Nada, Miguel,*" said Ernesto Garcia to his long time friend. "I have not taken my eyes off your house. No one has been here."

"I've got to find her, Ernie. I think she is in danger."

"In danger from who, *amigo?"*

"I can't tell you that. But trust me. Listen, you stay here a while longer until I tell you, okay? You have my cell phone. You call me if anyone comes. If you see anyone else around the house, find out who it is. But be careful. Understand?"

"*Si.* For you, anything. You know that."

Mike reached through the window and shook his left hand while drawing a faint smile. "Right, Ernie, and we'll settle the bill later." Ernie chuckled.

Appearing frazzled, Mike ran back to his car. "I've got to go inside just for a minute, Zeke. Want a cup of coffee, water? I don't have chocolate milk."

Zeke accepted, not so much for the drink of water but concern over the odd behavior of the normally unflappable sleuth. Once inside, Mike entered Corrina's room to search for an address book or any other source to locate Cindy's house. His cell phone rang. He saw Randy's number appear at the office. He called out to his partner in the living room. "Hey, Zeke, how about phoning Randy back for me. See what's up, okay?" Mike found the little red phone directory in Corrina's night stand drawer. In spite of her poor handwriting, he could make out one listing for a Cindy Harbolt. She lived on the west side of Kendall, five miles away.

"What did Randy want?" Mike asked, seeming distracted.

"Well, the chief is asking for anything to tell the press, Gloria Menendez is looking for you, Lieutenant Gonzalez wants you to call him, Luis Vasquez from Miami-Dade is asking for you and Al and Phyllis want to meet us at La Malaga. They have important information." Zeke looked at Mike and shrugged. "It's your call, boss."

Mike called and pacified Chief Howard for the next five minutes. Gloria Menendez could wait. Raul Gonzalez uttered something about demanding to be informed and issued a direct order to meet him at Pub El Conquistador later that night. The walls, it seemed, were closing in. Everything started to run together, blurred, indistinct. But Robyn remained all-consuming. He couldn't think of anything else.

Mike rushed through his house looking for any signs of where his wife may have gone. Nothing. He checked drawers, closets and clothing. When he looked in the bathroom trash can, he stopped, gazed and sucked a deep breath. There were the two Hershey Kisses, still in foil wrap. He lifted them, gazed and pondered a moment, then placed them in his coat pocket.

"I thought we were going to meet Al and Phyllis?" Zeke asked as Mike drove west on Kendall Drive.

"We are," Mike replied.

"But this is the wrong way, that is, unless the geography changed drastically around here in the last couple of hours."

"I'll just be a few minutes. Be patient with me, okay man? It won't take long."

Uncharacteristic anxiety dulled Mike's eyes. Zeke sensed something very serious, a deep obsession he couldn't share. For the first time since working beside Mike Estevez, Zeke felt alone and unprotected, unsure of himself.

"Why don't you tell me what's going on?" Zeke asked. "Honest, I can handle it." He was trying to be a friend.

"Nothing. Everything's okay. Just got a little problem here. Be over with it in no time."

Mike pulled in front of a two-story home in West Kendall. "I'll just be a minute," he said, leaving his partner sitting in the driveway.

"Sorry to trouble you, Mrs. Harbolt. I need to talk to my daughter Corrina, is she...?"

"Robyn was here about three-thirty, Mike. She picked Corrina up outside the house and never came in. Is everything all right?" asked Stella Harbolt holding her white velour robe with her hair bundled inside a turban.

"Oh yes, I just needed to see her a minute, uh, to give her an allowance. You know."

"My husband and I were supposed to take the week-end off but he suddenly took ill and..."

"Sorry, I hope he's okay. I have to run along. Thanks again."

BAREFOOT IN HER MIAMI DOLPHIN'S football jersey and white jeans, Corrina sat bewildered on the edge of her bed in the tiny motel room. She watched her mother pace incessantly, to and fro, smoking one cigarette after another, stopping every so often to answer her questions. The television hummed in the background.

Robyn tried to relay as many truths as possible without telling everything. After all, Corrina didn't need to know that her mother had an intimate moment with a stranger. And, she didn't need to know that her mother felt unwanted by her father or the gross neglect for so many years. All she had to know is that her mother attended a risqué party and inadvertently became a secret witness to the Cocoplum murders. Now, somewhere out there, people wanted to kill her, too.

Poor Corrina, she thought. So innocent, so naive, yearning for love and family stability and now caught in the web of this horrible nightmare. "We have to protect ourselves, honey. That's all. We won't be here long. I promise."

"This is unbelievable," she murmured to herself. "So this is why you've been acting like a nut this week."

"Corrina, please, I've got enough to handle. Look, I know you might not understand, but..."

"How could you? I mean, Daddy loves you; he loves us so

much." Tears welled up in Corrina's eyes as Robyn leaned against a soiled wall near the bathroom, her golden hair fallen, unmanaged. "I mean, I know he's always busy and all that, but that doesn't mean he doesn't love you, or me. I know he loves me. I know it."

"I know it, too. Believe me, I know it." She exhaled a lung full of smoke and sighed. "But your mother's only human, and I have needs. I wanted some fun, because we seem to have lost all the fun in our lives. That's all. It's been so long since your father and I shared anything that could be called fun and I've been feeling lonely. It was a mistake, that's all. There are things you just don't know."

"Did you, you know, do anything, like, with any guy or anything?"

Robyn took a nervous puff from her cigarette and looked directly at her daughter. "No."

"Why couldn't we go to Grandma's or someplace besides this, this dump?"

"Because, sweetheart, this is one place no one would figure we're here." With a heavy shroud of remorse, Robyn gazed at her teenage daughter sitting on the bed holding her arms across her chest, confused. She had plunged her child in the center of this dilemma, a dilemma she could have averted had she simply said *no thanks* to Sylvia Cicerone. "Look, sweetheart, I'm really sorry about all this. I'm really sorry." Robyn felt the controls uncorking. She wiped a single tear from her cheek but another followed.

"It's okay." She could see her mother trembling, standing alone, smoking, looking away. She was always so beautiful, so envied, so absolutely perfect. It was so hard to see her like this, surrounded by a pall of smoke, a blathering, sniveling wreck.

"Corrina, I love you. I just need you to help me through this for now. And I have to protect you. Just try to understand."

Corrina's eyes welled again and her heart pounded as she watched Robyn break into shambles. She approached, took the cigarette from her quivering fingers and placed it in the ash tray. Weeping now, Robyn buried her face in her hands. She dropped her head onto her daughter's shoulder and felt the welcome warmth of her embrace. They stood, mother and daughter, holding one another, alone and afraid in the corner of a filthy motel room in the Everglades, each wailing and sobbing. As Corrina stroked the silkiness of her mother's hair, she whispered into her ear, "I love you, Mom. I'll be here for you. It'll be okay. It'll be okay."

ZEKE COMMANDED THE WHEEL AGAIN as they headed for Calle Ocho to meet Al Sanchez and Phyllis Moriarty. Mike was punching numbers on his cell phone when Zeke asked, "Aren't we going to see Gonzalez first, you know, at Pub El Conquistador, like he said?"

"Fuck him. Al and Phyllis are more important. Later, if we have time." Mike felt focused again. At seventy miles per hour on the Don Shula Expressway, he pressed the little phone to his ear. "Luis, what's up, my friend?"

Luis Vasquez and his Miami-Dade partner had been beating the bushes around Calle Ocho for information on the activities of Felix De La Rosa but were coming up with very little. Everyone who knew Felix thought he was a gentle but diligent man, a Castro hater who loved America and was determined to bring his mother over from the island. As far as they all knew, Felix did not use drugs, drink alcohol, gamble or steal. He was strong and powerful enough to win all the arm wrestling matches every Friday night in the patio next door to the Copa Cabana. Chico, on the other hand, remained an unknown. They had talked to a hundred people along the strip, and they all knew plenty of coke-heads called Chico.

As Mike pocketed his phone, Zeke pulled up to La Malaga Restaurant on Calle Ocho. Al and Phyllis waited anxiously at a square, wood-top table in the first dining room. Flamenco guitars and stomping dancers echoed from the nightclub in the adjoining room, the music loud enough to drown their conversation from any neighboring table.

Mike motioned the waiter to send over a bottle of red wine. Zeke settled for white milk.

Running her finger across a note pad, Phyllis spoke first. "Margarita Ceballos, Dominican Female twenty-three, found tied to bedposts on her stomach, naked, shot in the back of the head in room 204 at the Santa Ana Hotel on First Street, July tenth a year ago. It's a typical flea-bag hangout for junkies and hookers."

Zeke and Mike both leaned forward. "No shit?" Shades of Carolyn Webb's murder scene entered their thoughts.

Phyllis had the undivided attention of her table. "The case is unsolved, went absolutely nowhere. Charles Bosworth and Angel Diaz handled it and then three days later were called off to work the riots."

"Any suspects at all?"

"No. According to the file, there was hardly any work done on it at all. When the riots were over, hell Mike, you remember, they had a backlog of new cases waiting for them."

"Boy, do I remember," Mike said nodding his head.

"But there is one interesting point." She sipped wine from her glass as the waiter arrived to take their orders, interrupting the continuity of conversation. The moment he left, Phyllis continued on. "The day after they canvassed the hotel, Bosworth got a call from an attorney saying if he wanted to talk to his client, to call him first. Otherwise, he was to, and get this; 'stop harassing his client'."

Mike raised his brows. "Who was Charles supposed to have been harassing?"

"Some Cuban named Javier Izaguirre, probably an illegal. Bosworth had him in his notes. But he wasn't a suspect; he just lived in the hotel one floor up. Must have been paranoid about something, wouldn't you think?" Phyllis curled her lips into a smirk, looked over at her partner asking, "You want to tell them the rest, Al?"

Zeke and Mike turned to Al Sanchez. "Well?"

"Guess who the lawyer was?"

Mike knew immediately. "You're shitting me."

"Yep. The fat man himself."

Zeke was feeling pretty good about himself. After all, he was the one who unearthed the old case at the meeting.

They all clinked glasses as Mike Estevez toasted, "Well, I guess we got us a bona fide suspect."

Mike's brain launched into high gear once more as Zeke turned to Phyllis, asking, "Where is this guy now? You know, Javier something? He got a record?"

"Can't find a thing on him, but that doesn't mean we're not going to."

"Okay, guys," Mike said, "first we need blood grouping and DNA on the semen to see if we're on the right track. Then we need to go back to that hotel and trace Javier Izaguirre. I'll get with Bosworth and see if he can give us a description. Work your informants, ask everyone in the neighborhood, the store and shops, clubs and whatever."

"There is one person who knows him for sure," Zeke said.

"Who's that?"

"Who else? Marco Scandiffio."

"That's right. Phyllis, you and Al head over to his office in the morning like you're working on Carolyn Webb's case. Try and segue into the Margarita Ceballos murder and see if he remembers who he was representing then." Mike changed gears and turned to Zeke. "Who've we got watching Ken Lancaster's house?"

"Different guys. I think Gus is going to be there tomorrow."

"Any progress yet on Mirage?" Al Sanchez asked, turning toward Mike.

The question hit Mike like a sledge hammer. He stared at Al for a moment to see if it were rhetorical, if he were being baited and then glanced at Phyllis and Zeke. For a moment, it seemed they were peering into the privacy of his brain. He had to harness his paranoia. "No, nothing." His was the pain of truth, as well as the pain of lying.

"Al, you and Phyllis can do me one favor."

"Sure, Mike, name it."

"Go meet Lieutenant Gonzalez. See what he wants. He said he'd be at the Pub El Conquistador."

The conversation abruptly halted as four very hungry detectives began devouring platters of shredded pork with onions and chicken and yellow rice with black bean soup and side orders of plantains. "I feel like I haven't eaten in days," Zeke grumbled as he ordered another glass of milk.

"Enjoy, my friend," Mike replied. "It may be days again."

The silence opened the window to his inner thoughts once more. He ate heartily but constantly envisioned Robyn and sensed deep feelings of guilt by carrying on a charade. He hid intimate knowledge that everyone else should know, and he was being selfish, obsessed more over the embarrassment, his precious image, than facing truth — a gut-wrenching quandary with irresolvable conflict in values. Where is the final priority, he wondered? And he knew, the longer the charade, the deeper the pit.

HE STRUTTED BACK AND FORTH in his dingy apartment, spotting himself in the mirror every so often to point the Glock semi-automatic and then admire his good looks, snorting, sniffing and talking to himself. "That's the last thing they saw," he said pointing the gun once more in the mirror. "Ha!"

He felt strong, powerful and indestructible but the high was beginning to wane. He needed more cocaine, but his supply was depleted so he headed out into the dark, humid streets. Minutes later he felt secure again, carrying five grams back to his apartment where he promptly snorted two little spoons.

His demented mind fleeted with instant replays of the exciting murders at Cocoplum.

How could those filthy aliens overlook the people in the bedroom? Then it would have been six killed. It would have been perfect. But no, we were in a hurry. We should have searched the house as soon as we got in. Stupid! Now the black boy is hiding. The pig knows he is a dead man.

He stopped again to study his face in the mirror; Hawaiian shirt unbuttoned, eyes glazed from drugs, unshaven and stinking from not bathing for four days. He combed his hair and thought about the woman in the attic, the woman named Mirage. He had killed the wrong woman.

But who cares. She was just another whore. But that woman in the restaurant, the pretty one, she screamed when she saw my face. This must be the woman. But she is with that detective so I must be certain this time. Do not hurry.

Javier opened his dresser drawer where he pulled a red suede ladies' wallet from below his underwear. Snorting, coughing, sniffing, he plopped in the recliner chair and studied her credit cards under the light of a floor lamp.

Ah, better leave this alone. Besides, now I am a millionaire. Who needs to steal credit cards any more?

He flipped through her photos all neatly inserted inside clear plastic sleeves. Young Mike Estevez in a blue uniform, then another photo more recent, wearing his customary double-breasted suit. Two pictures of a baby girl and another of a teenage girl with long brown hair and braces on her teeth. Behind that, the woman and the detective standing next to a red Toyota Supra with a group of little round stickers on the back window.

This must be her car, he thought to himself. *His would be a detective's car.*

He studied her driver's license and admired the woman's beauty from the photograph. Her long blonde hair framed her face differently than the pony tail she wore at The Rusty Pelican. She was not as he remembered, her contorted face, screaming, racing and plunging hysterically through the restaurant. He found a car registration, insurance cards, several scraps of paper with hand-scrawled notes folded with the money which only amounted to two hundred and twenty dollars. In another compartment, her business cards, ah, a real estate lady, as well as a dozen cards from other businesses, restaurants, lawyers, insurance men, auto repair, a beauty salon on Miami Beach and a motel near the Miccosukee reservation.

His energy surged once more. He stood to resume pacing, snorting and admiring himself in the mirror. He lit a cigarette and turned his thoughts to Marco Scandiffio, the man who made him a millionaire. He thought deeply about him, visualizing the fat, slobbering pig who waddled like a duck. But, still, Marco set it all up.

Marco was his friend and his protector, who he should appreciate, who calls him *asshole.*

Always Asshole! I am not an ASSHOLE!

Anger swelled as he paced again, back and forth and then he started talking out loud. "Fuck him. Who cares? Fucking pig. Who is he to call me an asshole?" He threw her wallet into the wall, knocking over a table lamp, papers and cards scattering around the floor.

Javier stopped once more to spoon another small snort of cocaine, then examined himself once more in the mirror and aimed his Glock.

ASSHOLE!

CHAPTER 26

ATOP THE SATIN BEDSPREAD, Mike awakened fully dressed with the exception of his jacket and holster, both of which were strewn across the living room couch. He looked at the digital clock, amazed that it read 7:47 a.m. After rubbing his eyes, he bounded from the bed into the bathroom and washed his face with cold water to stimulate his head into consciousness. He had never slept with his clothes on and he felt disgusted with himself, falling apart, losing control. He recognized flaws now in his own self image. This had to stop.

Finally, he regrouped and reflected on the night before, the door to door, bar to bar questioning, the prostitutes, the druggies, cab drivers and poor Zeke backing him up like a loyal soldier, at such a disadvantage not understanding the language. He wondered what Gonzalez wanted at the Pub El Conquistador but figured that Phyllis and Al would let him know. Ken Lancaster was still missing. Robyn and Corrina were missing. He had a staff of detectives to guide, a press corps and a chief to placate, a mad killer to locate and people to protect from further killings.

In the final stage of getting dressed, he was lacing his wing-tipped shoes when the phone rang. It was Robyn.

"Mike?" Her voice quivered. "I just wanted to..."

He alerted immediately, jumping to his feet. "Where are you?" he asked authoritatively. He hadn't given her a chance to say anything.

"Mike, just listen."

The pulse in his temple beat a fierce tempo. He stood and paced and altered the phone from ear to ear, emotions filled with anger, disgust and relief all at once.

"I just wanted to tell you that Corrina is with me and she is all right. Don't..."

"Robyn, I have to know where you are. Why are you doing this? What is going on, tell me?" Did he really want to know? What if she blurted it out? Should he let on that he knew?

"There are problems, Mike, you know that as well as I..."

"What problems, Robyn? Tell me. I want you to tell me."

After a long, breathy pause, she replied. “I'm sorry. I'm so very sorry. Please...”

“Robyn...I...”

“I know I was weak, but I'm also human. You've been living in your own world, Mike, a world that got out of hand, a world that no longer included us. And I faltered.”

“Please, Robyn, tell me where you are.”

“Listen to me, my darling. No matter what happens, you must know...I love you, more than I love life itself...”

Pacing, Mike swung around in frustration as his eyes started to well up.

“Let's not give it all up. Not seventeen years. Mike, please; I'll change if you will. I'll walk a mile if you'll just step one inch.”

He plunged into a chair, his face covered by one hand, while the other hand gripped the phone. Thoughts of Ken Lancaster swirled through his head.

“I know you can't think straight with everything going on. But you will. And you'll realize how much I love you. I'll always love you. Please don't hate me."

"Why?" he asked in a whisper.

"I can't...I can't talk long. Just try to understand. Corrina is fine and..."

"Tell me where you are."

"No, not now." She had only called to alleviate any worries about Corrina, but she found herself gushing at the sound of his voice.

"Robyn, I have to know, where you are. I must know."

"Not now. I can't"

"When are you going to call me again? Please Robyn, we need to protect you."

"Protect? Protect me from what?" Her voice choked.

"From danger, what else?"

The call disconnected.

He beat the phone receiver angrily on its carriage as he shouted her name over and over again, Robyn! Robyn! Godammit! He lost her. She was in control. His caller I.D. registered "unknown." When the phone rang once more, he jerked the receiver, thinking it was her, but it was only a friend calling for Corrina a call that ruined any chance of tracing Robyn's number. Frustrated, he flipped though pages of their Rolodex stopping at the name, *Lieberman.*

"Sam, sorry to bother you. Is Beth Ann there?"

"Went off to the office early today, Mike. Say, how are..."

He hung up.

A press conference with the chief was scheduled at nine but he would have to be late. In less than five minutes, Mike drove the four miles to the B & S Realty office in West Kendall not far from Cindy Harbolt's house. The glass door flew open, startling Beth Ann alone at her computer.

"Mike. What's going...?"

"Beth Ann, where's Robyn?"

She felt awkward being face to face with Mike for the first time since learning of Robyn's distress.

"Honestly, I don't know. She's not home? What's wrong?"

"Beth, don't lie to me." She recognized panic in his eyes. He did not seem like the same Mike Estevez she'd known before. "She's my wife, and I want to know where the hell she is. Now!"

"Hey, easy. Back off. Don't raise your voice to me."

He caught himself and eased back. "Sorry."

"I know she's away, Mike, but she honestly did not tell me where she was going. I can't tell you something that I don't know."

"Why, Beth Ann? Did she tell you what is going on?"

She turned to conceal her reddened face. "No."

At that point, Mike glanced around the room and stormed toward the glass door. But an object captured his attention. On Beth Ann's desk, sandwiched between a dictionary and a novel by James Patterson, he spotted the spine of another book with a familiar title: *The Fata Morgana,* by Leo Frankowski. Not a word transpired as he looked deep into the eyes of Robyn's best friend who met his stare with a sly grin. So many answers, so little words. The glass door flew open again and Mike Estevez slid back into the Taurus.

IT WAS NINE A.M. sharp when Maggie Lou Johnson slipped her pass key into the twenty-fourth story condo apartment. It would be the same as every Monday, Wednesday and Friday, cleaning luxurious domiciles for single men, executives and businessmen entrusting her to tidy up, make their homes presentable for whoever may visit in the evening. A professional maid for thirty years, Maggie never once missed a day of work. She swabbed toilets in her sleep, polished furniture, cleaned glass and vacuumed carpets until it was no more than auto-pilot. She would enter a door with her rolling equipment cart then glide through the day dreaming of how life should have been, how it never would be and thank her God for her health, her children and her grandchildren.

This day started no different than any other. She laid her keys on the marble book shelf near the door and went on to dusting, singing every step of the way. An alto in the First Baptist Church in Naranja, a suburb nearer to Homestead, she loved singing hymns and revival tunes best, especially the revival tunes. They made the days pass swiftly. They made her smile. "Praise the Lord, yeah!"

The living room appeared in its usual condition, unkempt, disheveled, pillows awry, ash trays full, the smell of liquor and marijuana pervading the air. She paid no particular mind to the lady's purses on the floor next to the sofa. What he does is his business, she thought.

Dirty dishes, pizza boxes, stem glasses and garbage overflowing from the trash can cluttered the kitchen. Nothing new. It's like this every time, she thought to herself. That's why he hires a maid.

Usually she started in the kitchen and left the bedroom for last. But this time, she thought some dishware or glasses might be near the bed, so she opened the door to the master bedroom. At first she paid no mind to the rhythmic flickering of a strobe light. But as she walked further through the passage past the bathroom and closet, a mirrored disco ball reflected hundreds of tiny rotating lights across walls, ceilings and furniture. She sensed something unusual, something different, strange, eerie. A pungent odor pervaded the air, a familiar odor she couldn't identify immediately. She looked toward the bed, gasped as nausea churned in her stomach. The room turned around and around, her head spinning. Then her knees buckled and she collapsed to the floor into darkness.

AL, RANDY, PHYLLIS AND ZEKE all stood off in the rear to watch Mike Estevez and Chief Howard handle the press conference. The meeting room, nothing more than a mini auditorium for holding training seminars and briefings, bulged at the seams with the press corps. Besides the police and city executives, reporters from no less than five television stations and numerous newspapers jammed the small space. Cameras and tripods lined the rear pass-through, essentially blocking any foot traffic.

Though exhausted, Mike regrouped and looked immaculate once more. He stepped up between Chief Howard and Raul

Gonzalez and waited behind Gloria. His image, as always, took precedence.

"You're late," growled Chief Howard forcing a smile to the audience.

"Sorry."

For the first few moments Gloria presided at the podium to make introductions, then turned the meeting over to the chief.

"Ladies and Gentlemen, I just want to make a brief statement before turning this over to Sergeant Estevez, who as you know is in charge of this investigation."

From the corner of his eye, Mike saw Randy McAdams suddenly turn and leave the room. The chief continued to talk. A few more moments passed and he saw that Al Sanchez and Phyllis Moriarty had also disappeared.

Randy McAdams reentered the rear of the room and gave Mike a nod, summoning him. He looked for a passageway and spied an opportunity between a cluster of female reporters.

Mike leaned over to a startled Raul Gonzalez and whispered, "You handle it." He tapped the chief's arm, uttering an inaudible then surprised everyone by bolting from the podium through the gaggle of reporters and quickly into the adjoining offices where he could talk with Randy McAdams.

The confused police chief announced, "Sorry, ladies and gentlemen, perhaps the sergeant has a personal emergency. Lieutenant Gonzalez here will brief you."

"What's up, Randy?" Mike asked.

"There'll be no interview with Marco Scandiffio today."

THE PRESS CORPS gravitated to Mike Estevez like rats to the Pied Piper of Hamelin. As soon as the first reporter saw him scurry from the building with his squad of detectives, they knew more news existed. To his chagrin, Raul Gonzalez found his media briefing drastically shortened as all the reporters and photographers bailed out after two short questions to which they knew the answers anyway.

When Mike and Zeke pulled up to the towering Seascape Condominium, a rescue unit in the driveway was loading a gurney holding a weighty, gray-haired woman, oxygen mask to her face. "Who is she?" Mike asked of the female officer standing post.

"The maid, sir. She fainted when she discovered the scene. When she woke up, she ran screaming through the lobby and then fainted again. I was unable to talk to her, not now anyway."

As they stood in the elevator ascending to the twenty-fourth story, Mike noticed Zeke looking at him, realizing he was on edge, not acting his normally composed and organized self. "It's been a helluva a week, eh boss?" Zeke said.

"You don't know, Zeke. You don't know."

The macabre crime scene almost rivaled Cocoplum. Odors of musk oil blended with alcohol, marijuana and human blood reeked throughout the apartment. Splattered with the rotating, sparkling lights like a million comets in the darkness, Marco Scandiffio sprawled naked in the center of the bed; a reclining Buddha with his hands tied and arms spread overhead, bulbous head hoisted by a homemade noose, grotesque face frozen in a hideous grimace. Blood from a single gunshot wound spilled down his forehead and over open eyes, rendering luster to his gaze into nothingness. His fleshy stomach seemed covered in a marbleized pattern of blood until Mike looked closer. There, scrawled in blood upon dead Marco's giant gut, a single word:

A S S H O L E.

Chocolate and Vanilla, each naked, each beautiful, rested in crimson pools on the carpeted floor, one on each side of the bed, their faces buried and draped in hair and gore. Vanilla had been shot one time directly in the face. Chocolate got it twice, once directly between the breasts and the second in the forehead. Their skins emanated the wax-like sheen of bodies fully stiffened in rigor mortis, dead at least eight hours.

At the opposite wall a blue light flickered from the large television with no sound. Later, the lab technician would find a porn video still in the VCR of a dancing nude named Carolyn Webb. The only traces left by the killer, it seemed, consisted of four ejected nine-millimeter casings, all on the floor soaking in Vanilla's blood.

Mike, Zeke and the young, Spanish lab technician, the one who had responded to Anthony Portelli's murder, stopped what they were doing to absorb the grisly ambience, gazing for several minutes at a scene they would never forget. Mike turned away somberly, "Let's get to work."

Al and Phyllis arrived to canvass all the apartments for anyone who may have seen or heard anything the previous night. Randy McAdams headed for the law offices of Marco Scandiffio with the prosecutor, I. Richard Jacobson, to secure files, records, clients and any information that Marco's secretaries would have. Raul Gonzalez had arrived at the crime scene but was chased out by Mike Estevez who told him he was needed at the office to handle the press. When Gonzalez gave a direct order to allow him in, Mike escorted him by the arm to the foot of the bed for a thirty-second review and then said, as diplomatically as possible, "Raul, don't let this bother you, but we have a lot of work to do and, frankly, you're in the way."

Lieutenant Charles Bosworth, once a crack homicide investigator until he was promoted and sent back to patrol, came to the scene at Mike's request. Lean and trim with a boyish quality looking far younger than his forty years, Bosworth's hair draped to one side like Will Rogers and his leather shone like a polished mirror. Good friends and colleagues in the old days, Charles and Mike often shared responsibility for training new men and teaching seminars.

"I'm going to ask to have you detached to work with us, Charles. This Cocoplum thing is getting out of hand."

Out of earshot, the two stood outside on the wrap-around terrace overlooking the bay. "So you think this is connected to that?"

"They are all connected, Charles. Cocoplum, Carolyn Webb, Anthony Portelli and now Marco and his two whores. Shit, that's nine dead, plus the two guys in the car and the killings are not over. There will be more, unless we get lucky soon."

"Well, if you ever find Mirage, or whoever she is, you'll have your eye witness, won't you?"

Mike was stunned by his reply. "Eye witness? How do you know that, Charlie?"

"Sorry, Mike, but it's around. Everyone knows."

"Don't get me wrong, my friend; you I trust. It's just the rest of the world. We were trying to keep her a secret. So much for that."

"What makes you think that Marco is connected to Cocoplum?"

"Well, to start with, he was Lillie Diefenbach's lawyer." By the time Mike finished explaining the criminal network of activities and the details of the week of horrors, Bosworth felt like he was back home again. "How can I help, Mike?"

"Do you remember the Margarita Ceballos murder?"

He searched his mind a moment. "The prostitute at the hotel. Sure. Wild scene, tied up on her stomach, shot in the head, semen in her vagina. We figured the guy shot her the moment he got his rocks off."

"The Carolyn Webb murder scene was a carbon copy."

"No shit?"

"Yeah, no shit. And the blood grouping from the semen on both scenes is the same. Did you ever work up any decent suspects or informants on that case?"

"Mike, I'll be honest." Charlie posed an embarrassed grin. "It was one of those cases when the sky fell in on us. You remember. Murders were raining out of the sky and then the riots."

"How well I know. But maybe you remember the fellow who lived upstairs from her?"

Bosworth laid his knuckle to his chin, pondering, then, "Oh yeah, I remember that guy. I was trying to work him up as an informant until I got a call one day." Instantly, a light bulb went off in Bosworth's brain. "Wait...damn, it was Marco Scandiffio. Yeah, he called to tell me to stop harassing his client." Bosworth chuckled. "Can you believe that? What an asshole."

"Yeah, a fitting epitaph as well. What did you do after that? Do you remember?"

"Nothing. The case went to the winds. Later that same day, I was wearing a helmet and toting a shotgun and riot shield in Liberty City."

"Charles, tell me about that guy."

"Nice fella, I thought. Seemed personable and all. Cuban, spoke some English, tall, maybe six two, thin, had a long skinny nose, black hair worn down to the collar."

"Name?"

"It's in the file, in my notes, I'm sure. Ah. Javier, I think."

"How about Javier Izaguirre?"

"That's it. Why?"

"Is there any record on him, any photos?"

"Honest, I don't remember."

"We need a picture, Charlie. I'll call the artist. Are you up for it?"

"No problem."

Two hours passed as Bosworth and a police artist sat outside the elevators on a vinyl cushioned bench working up a charcoal sketch of the man named Javier. Gloria Menendez, stunning as always, took charge of the press and remained unnoticed and unspoken to by Mike. Detectives and lab personnel packed the crime scene pursuing evidence under Mike's direction. This time the diligent, meticulous, incise investigator who dazzled his colleagues with an incredible nose for sorting out puzzles roamed from room to room, fidgeting as if in a fog. He phoned several times to call anyone and everyone who might know where Robyn would be. For Mike, it was instinct, like an actor who had repeated his lines for a thousand shows. He caught himself going through the motions of searching and probing the entire apartment before realizing that his actions were simply automation.

Each passing minute and hour, his gut twisted with conflicting emotions of hate, love and guilt for holding back. Forget the marriage; she was a material witness who saw four innocent people murdered in cold blood and then walked away in the pursuit of anonymity. Now that killer had killed again and again, a killer whom she could identify, who would continue to kill until he finished them all. Who is it, then, that should be standing trial? Does guilt not attach as well to the protectors of the guilty? She, at least, had an excuse for she fled for self preservation.

But what of me? What is my excuse?

As the technicians buzzed about dusting for prints, collecting blood samples and drawing sketches in the gruesome death chamber, Mike Estevez stepped inside one more time and stood at the foot of Marco's waterbed. He looked down at Marcia Brundage, alias Vanilla, and saw her as a once living human being. At this time yesterday, perhaps, she was driving her sports car over the Rickenbacker Causeway on the way to Crandon Park Beach, happy with herself, looking for that silver lining like so many others. She may have been a hooker and many had passed harsh judgment on her character, but she still remained a feeling, hoping woman with a full life ahead. Then he looked at the floor and pitied Lorraine Cherry, alias Chocolate, a beautiful, sinewy girl with long straight ink-black hair who, like Marcia Brundage, her hopes and dreams snuffed away by a mad man's bullets. How many more? Who would be next?

"Everything all right, Sergeant?" asked the technician.

Mike jerked his head. "Yeah. Yeah, everything's fine."

DETECTIVE GUS GRIMANSKI sat in Christina Mae Jackson's little house on Grand Avenue feeling like an Indian in a synagogue waiting, endlessly it seemed, for the phone to ring. It was three in the afternoon and she had just put her baby down for a nap. He had been guarding the house since seven a.m. and wouldn't be relieved until seven that night. Such tedium made for a very long day, particularly when no meaningful conversation transpired between he and the young black lady.

Gracious and hospitable, she bored Gus with her loving references to Ken, her baby and the dear Lord. Gus would rather have been discussing the line on the upcoming football games or in front of his Magnavox washing down a bowl of boiled shrimp with a cool beer. Worse yet, she would not permit smoking in her house, so Gus had to trot out on the front porch every thirty minutes for his regular dose of nicotine.

That's when he really felt out of place. In this section of the Grove, whites only passed through on their way to or from the business area. Naturally, he felt conspicuous, standing in front of Christina's duplex, a corpulent white man wearing a tie and polyester jacket. What else would he be, but a cop?

Gus may have been one of the friendliest, happy-go-lucky guys in the department but never a candidate for upward mobility. He functioned as the consummate journeyman, someone to go out and dig the trenches, do the dirty work and follow orders from those either smarter or more motivated. He rarely had to think; it was always done for him. A more astute officer might have initially noticed the white Mercedes convertible driving by. The third time, when Gus was outside smoking just before going off duty, he thought it odd seeing this strangely familiar car with its tinted windows and a white man at the wheel, maybe a pimp or drug dealer.

Like a good officer, he eyeballed the tag number and wrote it down in his tiny notebook after he went back in the house. *LWY 10W.* Ten minutes later, with the notes safe in his breast pocket, he exchanged "howdys" with his relief officer, got into his car and drove home for a cool beer and a bowl of shrimp.

CHAPTER 27

AT NOON the uniform squad room had mostly vacated at the Miami Police Headquarters building. Lieutenant Charles Bosworth sat alone at his steel desk inside a small cubicle laboring over a difficult performance evaluation, debating whether to recommend the demotion of a newly promoted Sergeant. He tried to ignore the phone, but by the fourth ring, his concentration jarred.

"Lieutenant Bosworth. May I help you?"

A long silence. Bosworth stared at the receiver, about to replace it on the carriage when he heard a woman's voice. "Charlie?"

"Victoria?"

She spoke softly, almost a whisper, "It's not Victoria."

He looked at the receiver again and asked, "Who is this?"

"I'm in trouble, Charlie. I don't know what to do."

Then he knew. "Robyn!" He stood up. "Robyn, you said you'd never see me again."

"I know, Charlie. And I meant it. But, right now I got a big problem, and I need a lot of help."

"Is it Mike?" Bosworth closed his door and sat on the edge of his desk.

"Well, kinda. But, I mean it's real complicated."

"Where are you?"

"I can't tell you."

"Does Mike know where you are?"

"No. Listen to me, Charlie. You can't tell him that you've talked to me. I'm going to tell you something and you have to promise me that you'll not say a word to anyone."

"What is it?"

"Promise?"

"Okay. Promise. What's wrong?"

"I know you're a cop and all that, but really."

"I won't say anything. What's wrong?"

He could hear the tremor in her voice as she hesitated. "I'm Mirage. Charlie, I'm the one they're looking for."

Bosworth felt the blood drain from his head. "What?"

"That's right. It's me. And I'm stuck. I don't know what to do."

"You? You were in that house?"

"I know what you're thinking, Charlie. Please, please don't judge me. Not now. Please. I'm trying to survive this nightmare. And I've got Corrina with me."

"I don't believe what I'm hearing. Do you know what that means, Robyn?" He waited for a response but there was none. "You're a material witness. You have to come forward."

"I can't. There's Corrina. Mike will hate me. The killers will come after me. My life is over." She began to cry again. "My life is over."

Bosworth sensed the gravity then realized she had just locked him into an untenable position, compromising his career over the love of a woman he could never have. He sat speechless when, suddenly, a knock resounded at the door. It swung open before Bosworth could respond. A tall, thin officer with stripes on his sleeve smiled and waved.

"Anytime you're ready, Lieutenant."

Bosworth waved him off. "I'll be with you in a minute."

"Look, Robyn. You've got to tell me where you are."

"No. I'm safe, for now. I just want to know I can call on you? I may really need help."

"Always, Robyn. I told you that three years ago. Look, I have to go right now. I'm on days, early shift. Call me at home tonight."

"Remember, Charlie, you promised."

"Don't worry." He couldn't break his promise. Neither could he trash a career. He hung the receiver and gazed at it for several seconds until the knock at the door again.

FROM INSIDE THE dusty office window, she could see Alligator Jake and his son loading boxes onto his pickup truck. Every time she used the phone, Jake would oblige and find work to do elsewhere. She thought about the call she had just made and prayed that Charlie Bosworth would not succumb to conscience and unveil her to the world. She knew him well. He was honest and straight forward as any cop, and she was sorry now that she had weakened. She shouldn't have involved him. If Charlie ever exposed her, he would also be disclosing his past with her, though only a one-time tryst, a brief interlude of lust and desire brought about by circumstance. She and Mike were separated then; yet, Charlie's greatest fear, Mike would find out.

She lit another cigarette and watched the Indians working on the air boat outside, then thought about Corrina alone in her room.

ALL THE FRAMES and plaques had been removed from the captain's office, leaving a spray of gaping nail holes in three of the walls. The background of country music had surrendered to the beat of salsa and Lieutenant Raul Gonzalez relished in his glory, leaning as far back in the huge, swivel recliner as it would allow, his feet crossed at the ankles atop the corner of the massive desk.

"Maybe you forget, Mike," he said chewing on an unlit cigar, "I'm in charge here. I'm the acting Captain, and I want you to know that I'll be filing disciplinary papers for your insubordinate behavior."

Mike remained mute at the end of the long table set perpendicular from the center of the desk. Gonzalez leaned the back of his head into folded hands, his elbows at full mast. "I'm considering demotion."

"So, demote me." Mike offered a small gesture with the palm of his hand and looked away from the lieutenant. It was not the reaction Gonzalez expected or desired.

"Godammit, Mike, you have ignored me, disobeyed me and kept me out of the loop this entire investigation and I don't appreciate it. You wouldn't be this way if John Sox were still here."

"That's right," Mike answered, softly. Deep circles under his eyes revealed weariness.

"Then why me?"

"Because you're an incompetent." Gonzalez looked at Mike in disbelief. "Well, you asked."

"Hey listen, I don't care if you don't like me, but I still hold a position..."

"I don't dislike you, Raul. I just feel this urge to vomit every time I'm in your presence. Does that clear it up?"

"Godammit, I told you to meet me at the El Conquistador last night and you sent over Al Sanchez. If I wanted to see Al Sanchez, I'd call for Al Sanchez."

Mike checked his Rolex. It was after seven, time to hit the streets. His team of detectives waited for him outside the office.

"And then you treat me like trash on the Scandiffio crime scene."

"That's right."

"Well, it's goddam embarrassing."

"Is there anything else, Lieutenant? I have things to do."

"You'll sit there until I say..."

Mike rose from his chair, buttoned his jacket to walk out of the door. Gonzalez stood abruptly, and with his cigar still wedged in his fingers shouted, "Get back here, you mother fucker! Get back here! Now!"

Al, Randy, Phyllis and Zeke all turned away feigning work as Mike stepped from the door, ignoring the lieutenant's shouts. Gonzalez followed him. Mike winked at Al Sanchez and moved his lips, "Come on, let's go."

"Don't you do this, Mike. Don't you dare ignore me, you mother fucker!"

Mike paced down the hallway following his squad of people as Gonzalez charged after, spewing mucous from his nostrils, screaming, "You mother fucker, I said stop!"

When Gonzalez grabbed his arm from behind, Mike stopped suddenly, spun around and peered deep into the angry lieutenant's eyes. He glanced to his team, looking at Al Sanchez and said, "See this? Lieutenant assaulting a subordinate." He peered back at Gonzalez who was flushed, trembling, eyes no more than four inches from Mike's. In slow, gradual syllables, through gritted teeth, Mike warned, "Get your hands off me, or I will drop you here and now."

Gonzalez ran back to his office like a mad hen. Mike turned to Al Sanchez and asked, "What did he want last night anyway?"

"Nothing, just information."

"What was he doing?"

"Sitting, getting bombed with that Lieutenant Masvidal...you know, from Records."

Randy McAdams remained at the command center controlling leads while Mike and his primary investigators immersed themselves back into the night life of Little Havana, tracking down informants, dopers, hookers, thieves, merchants and any other would-be citizen who might seem talkative. They each carried a copy of the composite drawing of a swarthy Latino with a thin face, skinny nose, deep set eyes and dark hair worn down to his shoulders. Chief Howard thought Charles Bosworth's value in uniform patrol took precedence over the Homicide Task Force so the request to have him detached was denied. "We cannot deplete our uniform forces any further," emphasized the chief.

Despite the activity, not a moment passed when Mike Estevez could erase the haunting images from his brain: Robyn with Ken

Lancaster; Corrina's peril; the mad killer. In slips of the tongue, he called Phyllis "Robyn" no less than three times. Zeke pleaded with him repeatedly to come clean, "Come on, Mike. You can't go on like this. You're just not yourself and it shows, man."

"I'll be all right, partner. Come on. Let's hit another bar."

"It's your old lady, isn't it, Mike?"

"Yeah, something like that. Not to worry; all's under control."

It was after midnight. The four of them had struck out and Mike told Al and Phyllis to call it a night and get ready for a big day tomorrow. Then he turned to Zeke and said, "One more to go, my friend."

Mike raised his cell phone and started talking. "Consuella, my love, it's Mike...Yeah, you heard, eh?...Sure you can see me sometime. How about in five minutes?...Behind in the alleyway...*Luego*."

Zeke looked at Mike warily as he drove the Taurus. "Not that place again?"

"*Si, Senor*, The El Columbian. Last stop, Zeke."

About fifty, plump, half Haitian and half Puerto Rican and fluent in four languages, a tough but personable woman who had a weakness in her heart for the handsome Miguel Estevez, she leaned over into the driver's window and smacked Mike a big smooch on the lips. "Now, we can talk," she said wearing a big, red painted smile. "Who is your friend?"

"Zeke, meet Consuella. Consuella, this is Zeke." Then he said to Zeke, "She owns this place."

"Big son a bitch, ain't he?" she said with laughing eyes. "What can I do for you?"

Even though she had closed the door, Latino music blared from the club. No lights glowed anywhere near the alley, which would have left them in total darkness if not for a full moon. He reached to his seat and lifted the composite. "Ever see this guy?"

She squinted, trying to make the best of the light from inside the car. "Shit, looks like another Cuban to me."

"About six two, thin, lanky, skinny nose."

She continued squinting. "Shit, Mike. That narrows it down to about a half million. I bet you're going to tell me he speaks Spanish, too."

"We think his name is Javier. Think hard, Connie."

"Javier." She examined the drawing again. "Javier. I know a Javier who is tall. Yeah, he's got a real fucking pencil for a nose. A coke head."

"Where?"

"Where do you think? The streets, what else?"

Sensing his first good lead, he peppered Consuella with a barrage of questions about where, when and with whom this fellow was ever seen but she could only recall him as a loner, a stand-out in a crowd. "Kind of weird, you know?"

"We need him, Consuella."

"Is this about Cocoplum and the others?"

"Yeah. Real important. Dinner at Versailles is on me."

"Give me a little time. I'll call."

It was one thirty a.m. when Mike dropped off his weary partner in the employee's parking lot, telling him to call Christina Jackson first thing in the morning. Alone again with his tormented mind on overload, Mike entered the quiet headquarters' building, offered a cordial greeting to the young officer on the desk and headed for the solitude of his third story office.

In the darkness, he wracked his brain for over an hour, spinning his chair, standing, pacing, sitting, talking to himself, weighing consequences, thinking of his image, cursing and asking, *why? Why?*

As though moved by an outside force, he pulled open the lower left drawer. He did not want to look; he did not want to know absolutely. But his hand raised the manila file folder and placed it on the desk. He stared at it contemplating.

It's still possible the print is not hers. Maybe this is all in my head!

But then, why is she in hiding? Why did she say, "I know I was weak...I faltered." Then, before that at The Rusty Pelican, "I will help you to solve your big case." Why did she go hysterical?

The moving picture of that scene flashed through his brain, a maniacal Robyn raising up after dropping a cigarette and then screaming into the face of a strange man. That man. Wait a minute. Mike stood up from his chair, put his hand to his head and took a mental snapshot of the startled man, the Spanish man sitting with the two women.

The man with the thin nose.

Then he reached into the desk drawer to look at the composite drawing.

His hair is a little shorter. But the picture, the features. It's him! That's why Robyn went ballistic. It was Mirage face to face with the killer. My wife!

He ruminated for several minutes before opening the file folder, gently lifting the tissue and gazing at the fine, soft features of a beautiful smiling blonde woman who had been his wife for seventeen years. No wiping it clean. It was time.

He spun the Rolodex file, lifted the receiver and with great reluctance and called the Identification Unit. "Mark, I know it's late, but would you mind? I think it's important."

A cop buff all his life, Mark Sanders lacked the height and the color for eligibility in the sixties when blacks were only hired sparingly and short people were considered handicapped. So, he went on to study fingerprint identification and pulled twenty years with the FBI reading loops, whirls and deltas before taking a pension and hiring on with the city of Miami.

He loved his job, loved being a part of law enforcement and sustained a special admiration for Mike Estevez who always treated him like he was special. When he strolled into Mike's office at two thirty in the morning wearing blue jeans and a tight fitting tee shirt, he was not greeted by the customary bear hug. He saw stress in the flashy Cuban's eyes. "What have you got, Mike?"

"For now, Mark, don't ask any questions. Just trust me, okay?"

Sanders looked at Mike quizzically. Such a portentous remark, so unlike Mike Estevez.

Resolved to the inevitable, Mike gingerly handed the tissue-encased photo over to the fingerprint expert. Sanders then pulled another photo from his brief case. It was a black and white of the patent print on the evidence bandage taken with oblique light under laboratory conditions. He placed it next to the photo of Robyn. She was a beautiful lady, he thought. But, as Mike requested, there would be no questions. He dipped his fingerprint brush into a jar of black powder and then stroked lightly across, barely touching the glossy print of Robyn Estevez. Two bold prints developed instantly.

"These are good, Mike," Mark said as he peered though his little glass. "Now let's compare."

Mike felt his heart skip a beat, his head pulsating. He placed a hand across his eyes, not to watch Sanders at his craft. Mark leaned his head down and then uttered, "Uh huh."

"Well?"

"This one here; it's a perfect match. Looks like you got your man."

It may be that Mike already knew, but in truth, it had not been a certainty. Now, all doubts were erased. In that moment, it felt like every ounce of energy sapped from his body while a sledge hammer pounded inside his chest. He gazed down at the black and white photo of the bandage and remembered picking it from the closet floor. Then it struck him. Robyn always had problems with ingrown toenails. He reflected even deeper, realizing now that it was his Robyn who had been there giving herself to another man. How was he to know? Why didn't he see the signals? How stupid, how blind could he have been? He recalled her words.

"I'll always love you. Please don't hate me...I'll walk a mile if you'll just step one inch."

Mark Sanders watched quietly as the deflated man gazed into space. Despite the curiosity, he dared not ask. Obviously, this situation impacted personally. Finally, he broke the silence. "What do you want me to do, Mike?"

With a hand cupped over his mouth, Mike knew he had now crossed the line of no return. He choked the words, "I'll let you know."

JAVIER COULD NOT SLEEP and he needed more dope. Visions of Mirage and Ken Lancaster stirred his anger. The all-consuming frustration made him sick. He abhorred the feeling of being powerless. They were out of reach, inaccessible.

Like a hungry tiger, he now savored the sweet blood of the human animal. He had more than tasted the kill, he had become intoxicated with his ultimate supremacy, the power to control the destiny of another human, the power to award life or death. Everyone out there in the world, he thought, was alive at his behest for at any given moment, he and he alone could decide who would be snuffed away next. And he remained safe in anonymity for those who knew him that way were all dead.

Neon signs from the nearby dog track illuminated his room through a curtained window as he lay in bed mulling over his next move. He had to know for sure before going after the cop's wife. But his skin crawled, his nose dripped and pain gnawed in his stomach, terrible pain. He rose, stumbled into his bathroom and spooned two snorts of cocaine, then checked himself out in the mirror.

Supreme, he thought, but not supreme enough. It was uncommon for Javier to handle desperation.

CHAPTER 28

SATURDAY

KEN LANCASTER HAD SPENT a sleepless night in the motel writing long rueful letters to Christina, Fitzgerald and Dylonna and his dead mother, confessing all his sins and cleansing his spirit. He promised he would never again dance naked for women nor take any other woman to bed but his loving wife to be.

In the letter to Christina, he proposed that they get married right away without any further delay and have more babies. He would get a good job, a legitimate job, even if it did not pay as well. He would finish school and go on to be a physical therapist. That paid good money. Then they could move to the suburbs and buy a four bedroom house with a swimming pool. He repeated his love for her over and over, tears dripping upon the blue ball-point ink, begging for forgiveness, for another chance.

It was eight o'clock on Saturday morning, nearly a week since that fateful night in Cocoplum. He called Fitzgerald to ask that he be at his side when he turned himself in to the police, for he knew it was what he had to do. He needed a strong shoulder to lean on, someone to pick him up in case he fell down, someone he could trust.

The journey started with an argument before they ever left the motel room, an argument in which Ken prevailed. Fitzgerald insisted that his brother first call Zeke Ferguson and head for the police station. But Ken was determined to face Christina before anything else, to give her his letter and beg forgiveness.

"Hey, Fitz, it's me goin' through all this. You have to let it be my call. Okay, man?"

Finally, Fitzgerald relented. "All right Ken," he said, "I'll take you straight to your house but you gotta call her first. You know? It's only fair."

"Okay, Bro."

GUS GRIMANSKI STOOD on the front porch of Christina Mae Jackson's house shuffling his feet and holding a coffee mug in one hand and a cigarette in the other, dreading ten more hours of utter boredom. He looked up to the east and saw that the sun was already ablaze, portending the day to be another scorcher. The cup was to his mouth when he heard the phone ring from inside. He figured another one of Miss Jackson's church friends, but he had to check it out. It came with the job.

By the time he entered the door, she held the telephone to her ear with one hand with the baby cradled in her left arm. "Ken, oh honey, are you all right?"

Gus fiddled with the voice recorder, frustrated that he had already missed the early part of the conversation. He stood by and listened.

"It's okay, baby…We'll talk when you get here...I'm so glad you've come to your senses...It wasn't your fault, I know that…Yes, there is a policeman here, but it's just for protection...The baby's fine...When? ...You're on your way? ...How long will it take you? ...I love you, too."

A broad smile wrapped across her face as, elated, she turned to Gus. "He said half an hour. I have to clean up."

"Yeah, good, well I better call Mike and Zeke and let them know."

As Gus lifted the phone and Christina turned toward the bedroom, a voice bellowed from behind.

"You dun call nobody! Poot the phone down!"

Gus froze. Christina held her mouth, gagging, eyes large as ping pong balls. He hadn't turned around yet but Gus knew. He pondered going for his gun, then thought twice. What if he got the woman killed? No heroics, not now. Not Gus Grimanski, anyway.

"Poot the phone down, I said."

Christina's voice quivered. "He's got a gun."

For a second he pondered a fast 9-1-1 call but thought twice and lowered the receiver to its carriage, slowly.

"Turn 'round, real slow like. Poot your gun on the table, pig. No scream or I keel you both."

"Oh my baby," cried Christina as Gus raised his hands, slowly rotating and then facing the Latino standing tall at the kitchen entrance. Silhouetted by light from the rear jalousie door which was still ajar, his left arm extended, he aimed the Glock directly at Gus's head.

"Please, don't hurt my baby," Christina said again, whimpering, cradling the child.

Gus carefully lifted the two-inch revolver from his waist band, holding it with two fingers by the butt, all the while watching the eyes of the madman. Christina gasped when he dropped it on the coffee table.

"Both you, in the other room. Now!"

"Do as he says, ma'am."

Gus Grimanski wasn't so stupid not to realize he faced a lunatic who was already responsible for the killings of eleven people in a week. So what's one or two more? The little house was a certain death trap, and he would never be leaving alive.

Absolute fear overwhelmed him. As he herded with the frenetic black woman into the tiny bedroom, his heart pounded through his chest, his head spun. But he alerted and caught himself before losing control. If any chance at all, he had to stay conscious. He looked down at the old alarm clock on the night stand which read nine-seventeen and remembered that Ken Lancaster would be arriving in less than thirty minutes.

"Where ees the nigger boy? Your life for hees life. I dun kid around." Snort! Desperation spewed from Javier's quivering voice as he hacked and snorted. He reached with his free hand to close the window's vertical blinds.

Christina would never tell even if she knew. She, too, glanced at the clock and saw that it was nine-twenty. In less than half an hour, Ken would walk into a trap. Then she thought about her baby and started crying, "Oh, not my baby, please. We don't know where he is. I wish I did know."

They stood trembling with their backs to Javier, Gus' hands atop his head and hers holding the baby. They faced a bright yellow wall smothered with pictures of Jesus Christ, Martin Luther King and an array of black people known only to Christina. Javier barked, "You, pig, on your knees. Now! No fooking 'round or I keel you. You know I keel you." Snort!

His voice snarled strong and harsh. When Gus dropped to his knees between the bed and the front wall, the baby started crying in Christina's arms. She panicked again, wailing, "My baby! My baby!"

Kneeling with hands raised, his back to Javier, Gus broke into a deluge of perspiration, shaking, pleading, "No, no, hey, listen buddy, uh, we got the house surrounded. You'll never get..."

"Shut up! No boolshit with me. Where is the fooking kid?"

The strident shrill of the crying baby penetrated his ear drums. With the gun pointed at the back of Gus' neck, Javier poised a piercing look into Christina's eyes and ordered her to put the child into the bassinet on the opposite side of the bed.

"Honest," she said as she laid the baby down, whimpering, "We really don't know. Don't hurt my baby."

"Okay, then we wait for heem." Javier paused, appeared disoriented, waved his gun from Christina to Gus and ran his other hand through his hair. "You, pig, on your feet. Take off your tie and your shirt." Gus staggered upward, sweating, shaking. Then he turned to the woman, "You, beetch, lay on the bed. The pig is goin' to tie you. No foony business."

Gus glanced with one eye at the clock. It was nine twenty-six. Another twenty minutes before Ken would arrive. Another twenty minutes until they would all be dead.

Javier closed the door behind him, still brandishing his pistol toward Gus Grimanski. The small room seemed even smaller with barely enough room to navigate three desperate people. "On the bed, beetch!" he said. "And no scream or I shoot. You, pig, all your clothes, off!"

The crazy man's eye glinted as Christina caught herself losing her breath, gagging on her tears. She curled up, trying to face the direction of her crying baby. Gus shed all but his underwear as fast as his trembling hands could move. Javier motioned to remove his Jockey shorts as well. In seconds, he was standing in the raw before Christina and Javier, two-hundred and fifty-five pounds of sweating flesh, his hands pointed to his ears.

"First, her hands," he ordered Gus. "Use your tie." As Gus leaned over the terrified woman, his mind passed through a lifetime. Then he thought about his teenage kids, his wife, Sarah. And he thought about death and prayed for no pain, no suffering. He heard the gunman bark another order. "No, not like that. Poot her on her stomach, tie one hand there and the other hand over there." The man's lips curled into a vile grin.

"How?" he whimpered.

"How you say? Spread eagle? Do eet. Now! Use your shirt."

Constant wailing from the baby intensified the unnerving climate of terror. Javier was piqued now, lost in his own world, stepping side to side, agitated, trying to keep himself under control. He dismissed the piercing shrill of the child while carefully watching Gus' every move. Then he ogled the pretty black woman lying there sniveling, writhing in terror. She wore a simple one piece linen dress. A feeling of power surged within him. How easy she will be, he thought.

Gus pulled her left hand and knotted the necktie to the corner of the frame. Mucous dripped down her face as she asked the man with the gun, "What are you going to do? Please don't."

"Shut up!" At that moment the phone rang, and they all looked at one another. It rang again and they could see the crazy man's confusion. Then it rang again and Gus said, "Look, buddy, if it's my office, they'll know something's wrong."

Javier stood bewildered, holding the gun, unable to make a decision. He had not counted on interruption. He had plans. And no one, nothing ever stood in his way. Finally, after the fourth ring, he ordered Gus, "Peek it up. Give it to her. No foony business or I shoot right in the phone."

On its fifth ring, Gus handed the phone to Christina's free hand as she lay on the bed half restrained. She hesitated, then, "Hello?"

The baby cried in the background as she tried to compose herself. She never took her eyes off the gun. "Yes, Jane, uh, I'm not feeling..."

It was a friendly neighbor who was telling her about a white convertible around the corner at the side of her house, curious as to its owner. Gus looked at the clock. It was nine thirty-seven. Seven or eight minutes to go. His heart pounded even harder.

Javier motioned with his gun to get off the phone. Christina shook her head but inwardly she was stalling for time and glad that Jane prated on. Gus stood beside her, petrified, his hands up to his ears again. Finally, the neighbor said she could hear the baby crying in the background, apologized and hung up. Christina continued to hold the phone to her ear uttering little responses like "Yes, Jane" and "I see" until Javier caught on and ripped the phone from her hand.

"I told you. No fooking around. Now, tie her other hand over there. Use the belt."

The clock's hands now pointed to nine-forty. Gus started to walk around the foot of the bed to reach the other side but that would put him too close to the gunman. Javier told him to cross directly over Christina with his blubbery, hairy, sweat-soaked body. Minutes, perhaps even seconds and it would all be over; the two of them sobbed. "Oh no, please."

"Do it! Now! Pig!"

Gus held his black leather belt on one hand as he crawled on hands and knees across Christina's legs to reach the other side. It was seconds until death and he knew it. That stark realization triggered his impulse as he suddenly whirled and crack-whipped the forty-six inch strip of leather, rapping the knuckles of Javier's gun hand with the pewter buckle.

Caught completely off guard, Javier wrenched in sudden excruciating pain. The gun flew airborne, caroming off a small dresser to the terrazzo floor, sliding under the bed. Gus leapt upon the Latino like a grizzly bear, bringing him to the floor. The baby wailed on as Christina screamed, her one hand still tied to the corner of the bed, her other reaching toward the bassinet. It was now or never.

"You mother fooker!" grumbled Javier as he struggled.

Then he felt the power of a huge fist plow onto his cheek bone. Slippery from perspiration, Gus crawled, his genitals dangling over Javier. Javier attempted to punch Gus, but the large man was too heavy. He felt another crushing blow to his cheek. Now powerless without his gun, Javier was no match for the likes of a Gus Grimanski so he took the single opportunity to escape.

Cupping both his fists together, he came down upon Gus' testicles with all his strength. A grunt, then a howl as Gus grabbed his groin, losing his breath and all his power long enough to permit Javier to rise and kick him once with the sharp point of his boots.

With Gus on the floor wracked in pain, Javier erupted into a frenzy trying to locate his pistol. Gus rose to his knees and wrapped his arms around Javier's legs in an attempt to tackle him down. Now impotent and vulnerable, suddenly afraid that someone, anyone would come in and he would be without his gun, his power, Javier reverted into total confusion, pulled open the bedroom door and broke loose from the slippery man, smacking him with a backhand across the eye. He ran through the house shouting Spanish expletives which no one understood.

Still wincing from smashed gonads, Gus tried to chase but crumbled under the pain and the realization that he could not engage a foot chase totally in the nude. Christina stopped crying and watched in silence as the crazy one scrambled out of the bedroom. Then they heard the jalousie door kicked open, ricocheting off the house.

It was over. They were alive. The baby still howled and they could hear a car door slam and a motor start outside the window. Gus remained on his knees moaning, while Christina lay motionless, holding her breath. Another few seconds passed when she whispered, weeping, choking, "Thank you, Lord. Oh thank you."

Gus grunted back, "Hey, how 'bout me?"

"Oh, thank you, too, sir."

A minute later, still catching his breath, his body cloaked in utter exhaustion, Gus staggered over the side of the bed, naked, ugly, sweating and his eye bleeding. As he leaned over to untie Christina's one hand, he looked up toward the doorway and saw Ken Lancaster and another black man standing agape, staring at him. For seconds that seemed like hours, no one spoke a word.

still panting, Gus said, "Really. It's not like what it looks."

CORRINA THREW A PEBBLE into the marsh to see the ripples radiate. Then another. No movement, no birds, no gators, not even an insect in the damp heat, like a sauna as the sun blazed from high up in a cloudless sky.

"Do you love Daddy?"

As they sat upon an old cypress bench under the shade of a thatched chickee, Robyn gazed out into the wilderness through her dark glasses and gave no answer. Corrina studied her mother for a moment then looked away in the same direction.

"You're not going to answer me?"

A long silence before Robyn answered, "It's not an easy question."

She tossed another pebble into the water, this time nearer the air boat moored to the crooked dock. A small fish broke the surface to investigate and then disappeared. "How can you not know? I mean, you either love someone or you don't."

"I always loved your father, Corrina. Ever since the day I first saw him. When he first looked into my eyes, something burst inside of me. A magic. I can't explain it."

"But do you still love him now?"

There was another short hesitation. "Yes. But that doesn't mean we can be together." Robyn felt a breaking surge within, but recaptured her composure. "Corrina, after you want something so bad for so long and it never comes to you, you begin to realize that it will never be. When that happens, there is a choice. Either live with it or change it. You can't do both. I tried. That was my mistake."

"I don't understand. Is it his job?"

Robyn reached over to touch the soft skin of her daughter's face. "Listen, honey, your father is the most wonderful man in the world and you should be proud of him. You should treasure him. He loves you dearly; don't ever forget that."

"But he loves you, too."

"Yes, I know."

"But not how you want to be loved, huh?"

"Well, I guess I want to feel like I'm the highest priority in his entire life and it's just not true. That's the way it is. So, that's why I went back to work and started making my own friends and went on with a life outside of your Dad. I had to. I always hoped it would change one day, but it won't. I am his love, perhaps, but the job is his passion."

"What's going to happen?"

"I don't know. Right now, I just don't know."

Corrina ambled over to the edge of the dock to peer into the murky water. A pair of small bass swam underneath the dock, then out of sight. She threw another pebble, further this time and a blue heron flapped its way up to a low altitude and settled off into the distance.

CHAPTER 29

WEARING AN UNCHARACTERISTIC open collared shirt, no tie, no jacket, Mike arrived at Chief Howard's private home shortly before eight, despondent, pondering how he would explain this horrible embarrassment. Baring a toothy smile, Nancy Howard, the chief's wife, opened the door before he knocked, ushered Mike inside and led him into a Florida room surrounded by jalousie windows. The house smelled of strong coffee and fresh paint.

"Please excuse this mess. We're doing some remodeling, as you can see. I've made coffee," she said with another pleasant smile. "Can I get you donuts? Something to eat?"

Mike sat on a patio chair and raised the palm of his hand, shaking his head, "No. Thanks."

"George, uh, the chief will be with you in a few minutes."

George Amos Howard the Third lived in a1950s model, stucco, three-story house in the south end of town not far from the causeway entrance to Key Biscayne. A traditional Florida neighborhood, streets lined with coconut palms and middle class blacks, whites and Hispanics coexisted in relative harmony not far but sufficiently away from the more crime ridden areas of Miami. Obviously, a number of renovations were under way as ladders, paint cans, drop cloths and other tools cluttered the hallway.

Nancy was an amiable, heavy-set, caramel-skinned woman who seemed a bit older than the chief. They had only been married for seven months.

Mike had called Chief Howard earlier that morning, stating his urgency to speak to him without delay and in person. He would not be attending the scheduled nine o'clock meeting at headquarters with Howard, Gloria Menendez, Raul Gonzalez, and the Chief of Detectives, Herb Stanley.

In a few minutes, the spry young chief stepped into the room knotting his tie, extended a hand and then noticed the look on Mike's face. "You look tired, Mike. No, not tired, bummed out, like you just lost your best friend."

"Yeah, well something like that."

"What's up?"

Mike sensed the chief's pressure and knew he was short on time. He waited as Nancy Howard entered carrying a tray of coffee and donuts. She could tell the famous Cuban detective seemed uncomfortable initiating the conversation in her presence. She quickly excused herself.

"You're going to have to take me off the case, boss."

"Not on your life, Mike. Come on, it's..."

"There's a major problem." He hesitated, swallowed, then looked directly into the chief's dark brown eyes.

"Look, if it's Raul..."

"It's not Raul. It's my wife. She's involved in the case."

Howard stopped and looked at Mike with curiosity. "Robyn, involved? How?"

Mike hesitated, "Robyn, my Robyn, she's Mirage."

Howard set the cup back into its saucer, his face registering disbelief. "What's that?"

"Yeah. It's true. No matter how hard I try, I can't change it. I thought you ought to know."

"How do you know? Did she tell you?"

"No. We haven't talked. As a matter of fact, she's in hiding. I don't know where she is. She's afraid the killer will find her."

Astonished, the chief stood up, paced the floor and sat again while Mike just gazed into his coffee cup. He thought about the impact. "How do you know?"

"Her toe print matches the bandage found at the murder scene. There are other reasons. There's more proof, but that's the kicker. Sorry."

"Shit. I'm the one who's sorry. I don't know what to say. I don't even know what to do."

"First thing, boss, you have to take me off the case as lead investigator."

Howard obviously stopped to ponder the new and devastating information. "That means that she..."

"Believe me, I know what it means."

"I didn't know you two were having any problems."

"That makes two of us."

The chief paused once more, digesting the shocking revelation. "Who knows about this? Have you told anyone?"

"Just Mark Sanders from I.D. He made the match but he's on hold until he gets the word." Mike tried to stay composed, in control, infinitely professional. "I would appreciate that only a few people know, just those who must. I don't want this to leak out."

Since Mike arrived, the phone had rung a dozen times. Nancy took messages while the two men talked.

"Mike, do you realize that this makes her a material witness who is evading the law, a material witness to a major crime. She has to come forward."

"Do you also realize, Chief, it makes her a hunted witness, hunted by a man who has already killed eleven people this week alone, that we know about?"

"She must be quite frightened I'm sure but..."

"She's hiding with Corrina which means that my daughter is also in jeopardy. Chief, I don't know where to find them, but I will. Not because I'm Mike Estevez the detective, but because it is my daughter and..." He paused, swallowed and took a deep breath as the chief listened on. "And my wife."

"Well, the way I see it, we have two very important tasks at hand: first, the safety of the witnesses who are in jeopardy; second, to preserve the integrity of the investigation. What about the other witness? The black kid? Any leads?"

Mike hesitated. His mind flew into images of Ken Lancaster trying to make love with Robyn. "We're working on it."

"Well, I guess you're too personally involved now..."

"I've asked you to remove me, at least as the lead investigator. If it ever goes to court, I'd be a prejudiced witness. It's just as well. After this, I won't be working homicide any more. This is it for me. I just have to see this out."

"Mike, I need you to stay close, to still work with the squad. I couldn't think of anyone I'd rather have on a case like this. So don't feel like I'm forcing you."

"Thanks, I'll keep that in mind."

"Who do you think should take over as lead from here on?"

"Zeke has worked the closest with me, but he's still breaking in, you know what I mean? Perhaps Randy or Al. Either one would be great. But they should keep Zeke involved. He's got a lot of potential."

"Well, I'll have to discuss this with the lieutenant."

Mike felt a stroke of heat rise to his neck. "That's another thing, Chief. Get rid of him, please. I'm telling you, he's poison. Find another minority if you have to, but get rid of Raul Gonzalez."

"Well, I know you two don't get along."

"Chief, there's a lot of inside information that's spilling out, information ending up in the wrong hands. Jesus, how do you think the killer found Caesar's Teasers? No one had that but us. I don't know if Gonzalez is responsible, but I can't think of anyone on this case whom I wouldn't trust, except him. Believe me."

"Well, there are things that, perhaps, you don't understand."

"You mean like 'politics?' Like he's connected'?"

"Easy, Mike."

Mike rose to his feet, sensing his temper boiling inside. Tempted to ask the chief who was really running the department, he thought twice, realizing Howard was doing the best he could with the cards he was dealt.

"I think I better go. If anyone needs my help, have them call me."

"What are you going to do, Mike?"

"Find my kid and your material witness before the killer does."

The telephone rang again as Mike strode off into the living room heading for the door. Then he heard Nancy shout from across the house, "George, they say it's an emergency."

"Emergency, emergency. It's always a damn emergency."

NO LESS THAN nine marked and unmarked police cars jammed the alleys and sidewalks surrounding Christina Jackson's house when Mike pulled up in his Ford Taurus. Passing motorists slowed to gander at all the activity; crowds of pedestrians gathered behind yellow barrier tape. Zeke already awaited his partner. He sensed a strange aloofness as Mike acted somber and unusually quiet, barely greeting him when he passed through the door. Chief Howard, looking dapper in a blue pinstriped suit, arrived in his own car.

The inside of the tiny duplex seethed in a state of pandemonium. Gus Grimanski, now dressed and licking his wounds, sat upon the sofa surrounded by a uniformed patrolman, a medic, a photographer and Al Sanchez. Fitzgerald Lancaster ranted from room to room, cursing police for locking Ken in the back of a patrol car like a common criminal. Nearly catatonic, lying on her bed, Christina awaited an ambulance to take her to Jackson Memorial Hospital for evaluation, her baby currently in the capable hands of Jane Sorrels, a friend and neighbor.

Mike's interest in the case had shifted now. No longer the slick homicide detective dogging a mass murderer, he was present as a damaged husband and a desperate father focused on finding his wife and daughter and saving their lives. But that's not how others perceived him. Not yet. Except for the chief, no one knew. The resources of the department continued at his disposal and he intended to use them. As he listened to Gus whine, the chief whispered to him, "I thought you were taking yourself off the case."

"I'm going to find my wife and my kid."

"Raul is en route. I'm going to tell him to put Al in charge. What do you think, Mike?"

"Fine. Do it. Can you still let Zeke stay with me?"

"Do whatever you have to do. I'll work with you."

"You're still keeping Raul around, huh?"

"That's life."

Mike knew it was only a matter of time before it would be common knowledge among insiders, particularly the team. No sense holding back, not if he wanted to use the department resources to find his family. Time to suck in the pride. No more waiting. Mike pulled Al and Zeke to the second bedroom where they could be alone and then abruptly shocked them with his candid revelations. As expected, they appeared dumbfounded and embarrassed for him. Once over the initial jolt, they offered their friendship and to help him at all costs.

"The chief wants you to handle the case, Al. And I agreed."

"Well, thanks, but what are you...?"

"I'll work with you because I still have to find them. But all the coordinating of leads, assembling of evidence, interviewing witnesses is under you now. Just bear with me if I need your help. Okay?"

"Okay."

Zeke felt suddenly detached, like a soaring kite that had just lost its string. "What about me, Mike?"

"I need you with me, my friend. If you don't mind."

Revealing a full set of pearly whites, Zeke replied, "Mind? Me, mind?"

An impatient Fitzgerald broke up their huddle as he barged through the door asking what was going to happen to his brother.

Al spoke up, officiously, "Well, sir, he is a material witness to a homicide. We have to take him downtown for statements and photo line-ups, whatever, then we'll release him to your custody. The most important thing is that he isn't in jeopardy. Can you provide him a safe haven until we catch this animal?"

"Yeah, sure. Of course, man. We'll have Christina and the baby stay with us a while. Not a problem."

"Very good."

Fitzgerald then disappeared to talk to Ken who was still waiting in the back seat of a uniformed police car.

Mike turned back to Al and Zeke, wiping his brow with the back of his hand as he babbled on. "We got to find this fucking madman. He's going to get to Robyn and Corrina unless we nail him. Look, talk to Gus again. He's so fucking stupid, he wouldn't remember the guy's name if he told him."

"Be nice," Al countered.

"Pick his brain again. He was there with the guy. There must be something."

In the next room, Gus glowed from all the praise extended him by the young chief who said he would be nominated for a service award. A hero now, Gus valiantly saved three lives, including his own and did not embarrass the department in the meanwhile. Al grilled him once more, reviewing the nightmarish episode in detail minute by minute. This time, he remembered a piece of information left out the first time around.

"There was a phone call. Yeah. It rang, and she talked on the phone to someone. I picked it up and he told me to give it to her. Christ, I was hoping it was you guys."

"Who was it? Do you know?"

"I don't know. That asshole kept waving that fucking gun at me and that's all I could think about. She pretended to talk even when the other party had hung up and he was pissed about that."

"What was Christina saying? Do you remember anything?"

"Naw. Well, wait a minute. There was something. Yeah. Jane. She called her Jane, I think it was Jane, or something like that."

Five minutes later, Mike Estevez and Al Sanchez were at Jane Sorrel's house which sat catty-cornered across the street from Christina's. She was a thin, pleasant woman who wore her hair in corn rows covered by a red and white bandanna. When Al asked her about the phone call, she said she'd already told the uniformed officer about it when she went to get the baby. "Please tell me again, ma'am?"

"All I saw was this fancy white car, a convertible parked around the corner next to Chrissy Mae's house and I was wonderin' if it was, you know, if it was all right."

"Tag?"

"Didn't look at no tag."

"What kind of car?"

"Big one. Looked foreign, maybe. That's all I know."

"Then what?"

"Well, I talk to Chrissy Mae but she sounded like she had a headache and all, and she was all messed up with the baby cryin' and all. So I let her go. That's all there was."

"Did you see anyone in the car?"

"No. Can't say as I did."

The humid morning in Coconut Grove continued warm enough for all the well-dressed detectives to shed their jackets, loosen ties and complain about sweat-soaked shirts clinging to their bodies. Television cameras traced their every step as the two men left Jane Sorrel's house to amble back across the street again. Christina had already been taken away. Fitzgerald stood outside as Ken lingered in the patrol car listening to the police radio. Gus Grimanski was being driven to Jackson Memorial for treatment of minor cuts and bruises while the chief offered a few comments to the media.

As they stood outside the front door, Al said, "The gun was under the bed, Mike. We'll have ballistics compare it to all the murder projectiles this week." Al saw that Mike's concentration was drifting. "And you, Mike. What can we do, anything? What are you going to do now?"

"I have to stay loose in case Robyn calls. I can't miss her call. I'll be in touch."

Zeke Ferguson helped to secure the duplex and arrange the delivery of Gus Grimanski's car to the hospital. While rummaging through a large, brown polyester sport jacket for Gus' car keys, Zeke found a small pad. "Look at this," he said to Al. "He actually carries a notebook."

"Anything in it?" Mike asked

"Grimanski? Are you kidding? Wait, here's something." Zeke opened the first page and saw a tag number scrawled in wriggled numbers: *LWY 10W.*

"What do you think?" said Al chuckling. "Blonde or redhead?"

Mike spoke. "Al, you take the jacket to Grimanski at Jackson Memorial and I'll take Zeke with me. I'll be at home. Okay? And whatever happens, my friend, please, stay close. Call me. Don't leave me hanging."

"You got it."

They were pulling away from the house when Raul Gonzalez blazed into the driveway hailing for Mike to wait. With Zeke in the passenger seat, Mike sat with the motor running while Gonzalez scrambled across the yard. Gonzalez injected his round, mustachioed face through the window, "Mike, I decided you're off this case. I know all about your old lady and you're out, do you understand?"

Mike stared contemptuously at the lieutenant for several seconds, put the car in reverse and jammed the accelerator, causing Gonzalez to snap his head back.

"Think about it, Zeke," Mike said as they sped off.

"What's that?"

"You're still going to be stuck with that fucking jerk."

CHAPTER 30

THE RAT WAS BACK in his hole pacing again, stopping now and then at the dirty mirror hung over the dresser. This time it was not to admire his good looks, but to pule over his unwelcome disfigurement. The left side of his face had turned blue and swollen to the size of an orange. *"Conyo. Maricon!* That moother fooker!" He snorted and slobbered and beat his fist against the wall until someone on the other side echoed with a wall beating of their own. "*Callarte come mierda*" he shouted back.

How could he have let that pig take his gun? How could he have been so stupid? Now, two more people are left alive, people that have seen him, people who must die along with the rest.

Angry and confused, agitated from lack of drugs, Javier savored the blood and visualization of his victims' death moments. The pleasure of killing was insatiable, addictive, almost as good as dope. But he needed more dope and he needed another gun, neither a problem on the streets so long as he had money. And Javier had money.

At high noon Javier left his apartment, heading for the home of a man known to him only as Salvo. On the way, he would buy five grams of high grade cocaine from his number one supplier behind the dog track and toot a full load which made all the pain, shakes and worries disappear. By the time he arrived at Salvo's, he floated on top of the world again.

"Where did you get the black eyes?" he asked Javier with a grin on his face.

"Car accident. Never mind. What do you have for me?"

"It will cost you two thousand dollars, Javier," said the slovenly Colombian who stank of body odor. Bare-chested, wearing Bermuda shorts, he sat on the edge of the sofa and opened the small box on the coffee table. "I want cash. That includes the clips. Bullets are extra."

"What happened to all the Glocks," he asked.

"They were a hot item. Long gone. This is all I have for now."

The weapon was a steel blue, Smith and Wesson, nine millimeter semi-automatic, not much different than the Glocks except heavier, threaded for a silencer and the serial number eradicated.

"Ah, this is good," said Javier. "Do you have the silencer, too?"

"That's another thousand, senor."

"No problem. I'll take a box of bullets with it. May I see?"

"Of course."

Standing, Javier took the weapon and looked it over, rubbing and caressing it as though it were fine silk. With his left hand, he raised and aimed at a cookie jar in the nearby kitchen, then pulled on the trigger to simulate firing, feeling the weight and the fit in his hand, imagining the kick when the bullet fired. As Salvo watched, he screwed the silencer on and aimed again at the cookie jar, remarking to Salvo that it was much heavier that way.

"Where is *Senora* today?" he asked.

"Shopping, what else. Do you have the money, Javier?"

"*Si, amigo.*" At that moment, Javier slammed a clip into the grip, pulled the slide, whirled and pointed the elongated barrel directly at Salvo's head. He never winced.

"You are not the first to come here and play games, you asshole. Give me the money and get the fuck out of here."

Asshole? Javier waited for the man to shake, to fear, to plead for his life. He wanted Salvo to see his power, but Salvo was a hardened old man whom he could not ruffle. Finally, Salvo looked up into Javier's eyes and asked, "Well, are you going to give me the money or what?"

"Si, Senor."

PHFFT! The crazy Cuban watched in fascination as Salvo grabbed his chest and looked up at Javier, utterly amazed that he would pull the trigger after all. Salvo gurgled, gagged and could no longer breathe. As he faded back into the sofa, it seemed he never took his eyes off Javier. So easy. He raised his Smith and Wesson one more time and passed a silent bullet through the dead man's forehead, then walked out the front door, savoring a fresh kill. A contented man, he had his dope, his gun, his power and his mission.

"PULL IN HERE," he said to Zeke motioning with his hand. They were the first words Mike had spoken since they left Christina's house.

Zeke cut a sharp left turn across the eastbound traffic lanes of Calle Ocho, suddenly finding himself transmuted within the beautifully manicured and spacious grounds of St. Francis Cemetery. Following Mike's hand directions, he zigzagged through and around the manicured memorial park until he heard him in a low voice say, "Stop here. Wait for me. I'll be right back."

Zeke looked over his shoulder through the car window watching Mike, without jacket and tie, step over to a grave marker inscribed simply:

JORGE ALFONSO PEREZ-ESTEVEZ
3 Dec 1935 - 21 May 1996

OUT OF EARSHOT, Mike knelt and made the sign of the cross.

My father, oh father, why must you lie here? Why did He take you. You had so much to live for? I cannot express in words the emptiness left inside of me,how my heart yearns for your wisdom, your guidance and your comfort. Help me, Father, to overcome and see me through this nightmare. I have never felt so lost. What should I do?

He paused for several minutes without saying a word, without thinking, just absorbing. In the midday Miami heat, he gazed for minutes at the headstone imagining his father's words, reaching, hoping for his message. Finally, in Spanish…

"Dear God, I pray to you, it has been long since I have asked for your help. Perhaps I am not worthy for I have sinned and I have not turned to you in many years but that does not mean that I have stopped loving. You have taken my father from me. Please, I beg you, protect my little girl and my Robyn. Give me the strength to lead and to be worthy again of your love. Don't let them be harmed. Please, don't take them now."

Another long silence blanketed the car as they drove off toward Mike's townhouse. His pain was obvious. Nothing Zeke could say would lighten the heartbreak or alleviate the humiliation. After a time of personal reflection, Mike finally spoke.

"He was shot, Zeke. Two little punks, black kids, for a lousy twenty bucks and a wrist watch."

Zeke waited for Mike to continue but he just stared out the window.

"They ever catch 'em?" he asked.

"Nope. Dead. Just like that," he said snapping his finger, "Sixty years old and thirty years of healing and saving lives eliminated at the whim of a couple of scumbags. Poof. You're gone."

"Was it a city case?"

"Yeah. Another one of those cases in May of '96 when drug wars, riots and Miami's crime rate exploded all at once. One of the kids was overheard calling the other "Shamu", you know, like the whale. It's probably a street name. They weren't more than fourteen or fifteen then. Hell, nobody would ever recognize them now."

"Shamu? Never knew any kids by that name and I was on the streets a long time."

Mike deliberately changed the subject. "What have you done with Ken Lancaster, Zeke?"

"He's at the State Attorney's Office giving statements. He's under tight wraps, not to worry."

"And what about Grimanski? Who's watching him?"

"Don't know. Why?"

"Gus eyeballed the killer. It makes him another witness. That crazy fucker will try to take him out, too."

They finally pulled into Mike's driveway, her driveway, and he thought about her red Supra, the decals and the guard at Cocoplum. And he thought about her and the way it used to be.

"What do you want from me, Mike?"

"Be there when I need you and I have a hunch I'm going to need you."

"IT'S DRIVING ME CRAZY, MOM." I'm bored out of my mind in this place. Please, I can't stand it. Isn't there somewhere else we could go?"

"Better to be bored than to be dead, honey. Just another day or two...and if they haven't caught that guy yet, we'll head for Uncle Dennis' in New York. We'll have to find a way to get money first."

Corrina, feeling claustrophobic, walked nervously in and out of the little room, threatening to jog the thirty miles back to Miami if she had to. Tensions were rising while a gamut of emotions—love, hate, fear, loneliness and guilt—clouded Robyn's abilities to think rationally. She looked up at her beloved, innocent little girl and hated herself for what she had done and for sucking her into the abyss with her. But it was too late.

"Just let me call Daddy, Mom. I'll talk to him. He'll understand. Gosh, he must be worried sick where we are."

Robyn peeled her eyes to the television hoping and praying to see a news bulletin announcing the case had been solved and to see that monster manacled and dragged into the jail. Nothing, yet. Her idea of hiding out on the fringes of the Everglades might have been impulsive, but they were safe and they could trust Jake; no one would ever suspect their location. The isolation tested both their nerves, and she sympathized with Corrina's feelings.

"I'll make a call, Corrina. Maybe we can leave here tonight. It's not a promise, but I'll try. Okay, honey?"

Corrina simply shook her head as she watched her mother crack open the door and peer out before donning her sunglasses and scurrying the hundred feet or so to the office.

"May I use the phone, Jake?"

"No problem, misses." Jake turned off the small television before getting up to leave. Everything in the office, including a folding chair, comprised old cypress or pine wood. She could write her name in the dust atop the counter.

Frustrated, she could only reach Charlie's voice mail. She listened nervously to his terse, authoritative message, waited for the beep, started to speak, choked on her words and hung up.

Oh shit. What if he's got caller I.D? Oh my gosh, that's right. All he's got to do is hit star 69 and he'll access this number. Damn!

CHAPTER 31

MIKE HAD BEEN ON THE PHONE all day at the townhouse going through Robyn's telephone directory, hoping to find anyone who would have a clue to her whereabouts, but to no avail. He called her office, asking employees to search her desk for client's names, friends and business references. He also contacted her brother in Syracuse, as well as Corrina's friends listed in her phone book. He thought about searching county wide for her car, but he knew that would be tougher than finding a minnow in the Atlantic.

While monitoring the police radio, Zeke stayed wired to headquarters, usually speaking to Randy McAdams because the rest of the gang stayed out on the road. The investigation seemed at a standstill. Robyn had not called. Frustration swelled. At four-thirty the phone rang once more and, as usual, Zeke picked it up. It was Randy.

"What?" Zeke could not believe what he was hearing. "Randy, you're kidding?"

Mike emerged from the bathroom and saw Zeke's expression.

"You know how Mike is. He's going to have a conniption."

Zeke looked to Mike and shrugged. "Has he thought that out,

Randy? I mean, you know, the consequences and all?" ..."Yeah. I'll tell him. See ya." Zeke sighed and put his hand to his head in utter grief.

"What's up?" Mike asked.

"You better sit down, Mike."

"What's the matter? What's going on, tell me."

"It's Gonzalez."

"What now?"

"He's going on the air with it."

"With what, for Christ's sake?"

Zeke shook his head in exasperation. "About your wife."

"What?"

"They're going public, TV, radio, newspapers, everything looking for Robyn Estevez, alias Mirage. Her picture and all, at six o'clock."

Mike's eyes bulged as far as his lids could permit. He strode angrily to the phone and started punching numbers, muttering to Zeke, "Oh no, they're not."

He nearly blew Randy's ear off. "Who in the *fuck* decided that?"

"Mike, take it easy."

"Who?"

"Lieutenant Gon..."

"Where's Chief Howard? Does he know about this?"

"Yeah. He's going along with Gonzalez. He'll be there for the press conference."

In exasperation Mike growled, "That's my wife you're talking about. My wife and kid."

"I know, Mike. We talked to him, Al and I both. We tried to talk him out of it. We told him all the negatives, how it would put her and your kid in jeopardy and all."

"And what did he say?"

"Just that he's the boss now. You're out of the picture, too close, too personally involved and all that."

"Where is he?"

"In his office."

"Transfer me in to him."

A knock at the door and Zeke went to take in the two pizzas ordered thirty minutes before. The aroma of tomato sauce, oregano and cheese filled the house. Mike waited, regrouping his emotions in the hope of talking with Gonzalez on an intelligent plane. He spoke with restraint.

"Hey, Raul, yeah, *que tal* to you, too." His face burned. He could envision Raul's smugness, the absolute epitome of arrogance. "What's this about putting out a press appeal on my wife?"

Raul answered, blustering, "It's absolutely necessary, not only for the case, but for her own good. And the chief agrees."

"May I say something?"

"Sure Mike, go ahead. But it's not going to change anything." Gonzalez gloated, having finally reached a higher pinnacle than the esteemed Mike Estevez.

"Raul, listen, she has not been identified yet as Mirage to anyone outside of our own investigators and Dick Jacobson, so why expose her to the entire county, especially the killer? What if he's watching?" It took all the restraint he could muster not to scream aloud.

"We figure that anyone who has seen her will call in and maybe tell us where she is, then we save her ass, okay? Who knows, Mike, maybe she'll see it and come in on her own."

"You don't have any pictures of her so how can...?"

"Oh, yes we do. A very nice one. It just has a little bit of fingerprint dust on it."

"Raul," Mike shouted, with emphasis. "Don't do it!"

"It's a done deal, Mike. She is a material witness fleeing from the law. I'm in charge now and..."

"You're signing her fucking death warrant, you stupid son of a bitch."

"Now, now. Let's not be insubordinate. Like I said, you're too emotionally..."

Mike couldn't hold it any longer. "She's with my kid, fuckhead! My only daughter! You'll get her killed as well!"

Mike could imagine Gonzalez grinning. "I can't talk to you this way, Mike."

He hung up.

Zeke, nor anyone else, had ever seen rock solid Mike Estevez in a rage, throwing books and magazines and cursing in mixtures of English and Spanish. When he finally calmed himself, he felt embarrassed. "I'm sorry," he said. "I guess my image is getting a little stained."

"Never," answered Zeke. "Don't worry about it, man. I understand what you're going through."

"Find me the chief, Zeke. Call him, dispatch him, do anything, but find him. If I have to, I'll call the mayor myself. I've got to stop this."

It would be no use. Chief Howard listened patiently for ten minutes before telling Mike that he was still going to give Gonzalez his backing. "Mike, listen, maybe you're a bit blinded by being so close to the situation," he said.

"I want you to know, boss, that I'm going over your head. I'm going to call the Mayor."

"Be my guest, Mike. He already knows about it."

After thirty minutes of the bureaucratic telephone shuffle, he finally reached the mayor who interrupted a staff briefing once he knew it was Mike waiting on the line.

"I know, Mike. I know. Your father and I were the best of friends. He saved my life. But this is something I can't interfere with. It's police business. You have to understand that."

"Mayor, it is a matter of life and death. Chief Howard is taking advice from a B.L.O. implant who doesn't know what he is doing."

"Well, maybe it's not such a bad idea, Mike. She might come forward."

"Thank you, Mr. Mayor." It was no use.

Mike had exhausted all means at canceling the press release, even to the point of trying to coerce the production managers of television stations who knew him so well.

Robyn had yet to call. Beth Ann claimed she had no idea of her whereabouts. Exasperated, defeated and strangely powerless, Mike sank into his large cushy chair with his first glass of Johnny Walker Black on the rocks and pressed the "on" button of the remote. Zeke settled on the sofa. It was five o'clock.

"Look, Mom. That's you!"

Robyn could hardly believe her eyes. Her photograph from five years ago at Aspen, her golden hair shining bright against the backdrop of glistening white slopes, covered the entire television screen. "How did they? I don't believe this. Why that son of a..."

"Mom!"

"...ARE SEARCHING FOR THIS WOMAN WHO IS BELIEVED TO BE THE

THE MYSTERY WITNESS IN THE COCOPLUM MURDERS KNOWN AS

MIRAGE. THIS WOMAN IS NOT A SUSPECT, REPEAT, NOT A SUSPECT

IN THE MURDERS BUT IS A MATERIAL WITNESS TO THE CRIME."

"You know what this means, honey?"

"What's that?"

"*He* might be watching this."

"Who?"

"Who do you think? That killer."

"...HAS LEARNED THAT HER TRUE IDENTITY IS MRS. ROBYN

ESTEVEZ, WIFE OF THE FAMED MIAMI HOMICIDE DETECTIVE MIGUEL

ESTEVEZ. SHE IS PRESENTLY BELIEVED TO BE WITH HER DAUGHTER

CORRINA ESTEVEZ, AGE THIRTEEN..."

. . .

"Oh my gosh, I hope they don't have a picture of me, too."

"...AND IN HIDING SOMEWHERE IN MIAMI-DADE COUNTY. SHE
DRIVES A 2012 RED TOYOTA SUPRA WITH THE LICENSE NUMBER CPO
47X. ANYONE HAVING INFORMATION OF HER WHEREABOUTS
SHOULD CALL THE MIAMI POLICE DEPARTMENT HOMICIDE BUREAU
IMMEDIATELY. POLICE ARE CONCERNED FOR THE SAFETY OF THESE
WOMEN."

"Mom, are we getting out, or what?"

"I hope so, honey. I'm trying to phone a friend for some money. Right now, all we can do is wait." Riveted to the television, they watched as a male reporter stood on the steps of Miami's police headquarters next to a plain clothes Spanish cop she had never met before.

"WITH US NOW IS LIEUTENANT RAUL GONZALEZ OF THE MIAMI
HOMICIDE BUREAU WHO IS HEADING UP THIS INVESTIGATION."

"Heading up? Where's Mike?"

"LIEUTENANT, CAN YOU TELL US HOW MRS. ESTEVEZ CAME TO
BE INVOLVED IN THIS CASE?"

. . .

He cocked his head and looked at the camera as he answered the question.

"NO I'M SORRY. THAT IS STILL CLASSIFIED INFORMATION."

"WMIA NEWS HAS LEARNED THAT SERGEANT MIGUEL ESTEVEZ IS NO
LONGER ASSIGNED TO THIS CASE. IS THIS TRUE?"

Robyn gasped and put her hand to her open mouth.

"YES."

"DO POLICE SUSPECT THAT THE SERGEANT WAS IN ANY WAY
INVOLVED IN THE MURDERS?"

"Are you shitting me? This is too much. I can't believe I'm hearing this."

"You are, Mom. Believe me, you are."

"OH NO. BUT IT IS URGENT THAT WE LOCATE MRS. ESTEVEZ
AS SOON AS POSSIBLE FOR HER OWN SAFETY."

. . .

"IS THERE ANY CHANCE THAT SERGEANT ESTEVEZ CAN BE
REACHED FOR COMMENT?"

"THAT IS UP TO HIM. HE PRESENTLY IS AT HOME."

"WHAT A JERK. What did he tell them that for?"

An official police photo of Mike Estevez blanketed the screen while the reporter narrated a short dissertation on his illustrious career, highlighting the serial killings of five children in 2008 which he was credited for solving. It culminated in a death sentence for an itinerant dishwasher.

"He's the most handsome man in the world, isn't he, Mom?"

She nodded her head, silent.

The reporter went on to quote department officers who said they considered Mike Estevez their role model of an investigator; totally honest, unflappable, tenacious and intelligent. Film footage flashed, Mike giving a lecture to a community college graduating class where he hammered away at the principals of integrity and image. Then the reporter switched back to a live shot of Lieutenant Gonzalez who reluctantly parroted all the accolades.

"That's the guy Mike was having so much trouble with," Robyn said.

They changed channels to another local broadcasting station and saw her picture again, then again, and again. For certain, it would be on the front page of tomorrow's *Miami Herald.*

Robyn wanted to make another call to Charlie but was afraid of being traced back to Alligator Jake's. Going on the road was risky, but not as risky as everyone finding out her hiding place.

"Get in the car, honey," she ordered her daughter. "We're going to another phone somewhere. Hold on. I'll be back in a sec; I have to see Jake and get a piece of cardboard."

"Can I get a Big Mac, Mom?"

"You know I have no money."

At dusk she pulled into a small rural convenience store twenty minutes east along Bird Road. Winding through heavy traffic, she somehow felt refreshed back within population. Wearing a scarf and sunglasses and with a Lost Tag sign covering her license plate, she fumbled for quarters while keeping her eye on Corrina.

"Duck when I say duck," she had told her.

She punched seven numbers.

"Miami Police, Lieutenant Bosworth speaking."

"Charlie, it's me!"

"Robyn? Thank God, you called. Are you okay? Where are you?"

"Did you see the television report?"

"Yeah. Pretty stupid, eh? All the more reason, Robyn, you must turn yourself in. It's your only safe way. Call Mike, talk to him. He'll understand. Nothing will happen to you."

"No, no. Charlie, listen to me. I need money. I have to get out of this state as soon as possible. I'll cooperate after I can get out of here. Right now, I need five hundred dollars."

"Tell me where you are."

She paused and breathed deeply. "Can I trust you?"

After a hesitation, he replied, "Sure. I'll help you. Because it's you. But it's against my better judgment."

At that moment, she saw a police cruiser pull into a restaurant parking lot across the street, followed by another. She could be spotted easily. She knew there were bulletins out on her car. Her heart raced. Blood rushed to her head.

"Robyn? I'll help. Where are you?"

She started to weep once more, her voice trembling. "Charlie. You know those things you keep in that glass mug behind your desk?"

"Yeah?"

"If anything happens to me, you know, please, give Mike two of them. Tell him they're from me."

"What?"

"Just do it, please."

"Where are you, Robyn."

Two more cops exited the restaurant across the street and looked her way. Her heart pounded against her ribs.

"Robyn?"

She hung up.

IT WAS JUST AFTER SIX when Al and Phyllis arrived at the hospital emergency ward to see Gus and turn over his car and clothing. His injuries were nothing but superficial scratches and bruises, no reason for the doctors to hold him overnight.

Gus still whimpered about the humiliation, standing naked before Christina Jackson, berated by that mad Cuban waving a gun. He asked to be relieved of the miserable detail so he could return to the Burglary Squad where his menial job involved the inventory of stolen merchandise by telephone and day dreaming about next weekend's football games.

The emergency room brimmed with the hustle-bustle of doctors and nurses scampering about and the general chaos of patients shifting around in poorly defined queues, all bearing facial expressions of frustration. Many had been there for an entire day untreated, regardless of their malady.

"Your keys are in your jacket, Gus." Al handed the blue sport coat to the corpulent cop as he arose from the waiting room chair. Phyllis stood to the side.

"Yeah, thanks guys."

"I want to make sure the only item in your jacket was your little note book, nothing else. That right?"

"Yeah. That's right."

"We noticed a tag number jotted in your book. Anything important?" Al Sanchez and Phyllis Moriarty smirked, thinking it belonged to a blonde or a redhead and waited to hear how Gus would weasel out of the question.

Gus stopped to think a minute, then looked inside to refresh his memory. "Oh yeah, I took down this number from some car that passed the house every time I went outside for a smoke."

"What car was that?"

"It was a Mercedes convertible. I figure it's a pimpmobile. Vice might want to check it out."

Al looked at Phyllis, then Gus. "What color was it, Gus?"

"White." Gus saw a sudden interest in Al Sanchez's eyes.

"You're kidding? When did you take the number down?"

"Yesterday, in the afternoon sometime. Why? You figure it might be the guy?"

"You know, Gus," Al said with a wry grin, "there's something about the way you fuck up and come out smelling like a rose. You may have solved us a major homicide."

"No shit? Really?"

Al instructed Phyllis to run the tag by phone, but not over the radio for the world to hear. Minutes later she came back with her yellow pad in hand. "It's registered to a Javier Izaguirre, D.O.B. 17 November 1984, at 651 Southwest 37th Avenue, apartment 210."

"Let's go."

CHAPTER 32

SATURDAY, 5:30 p.m.

"MIKE, THIS IS Charlie Bosworth. Can you come over to my office?"

"My friend, look, I'm in the middle of a major case here, and I've a lot going on. Can it wait until…"

"No, Mike. It can't wait."

Stunned, Mike replied, "Why can't you talk to me now?"

"I must talk to you in person. It's about Robyn."

"Robyn?" Mike hesitated, confused. "I'll be right there."

Frazzled, bewildered, obsessed, the last person on Mike Estevez's mind in the middle of all this chaos was Lieutenant Charles Bosworth. Yet, the mere utterance of Robyn's name, saying "It can't wait" propelled his Ford Taurus through the city streets with his blue flasher atop the roof at twenty and thirty miles over the speed limit.

He parked in the chief's space and hurdled three steps at a time, racing up the stairs, barging through Bosworth's tiny office.

Charlie remained seated, unruffled by the sudden intrusion. It was expected.

"What's up Charlie? What about Robyn?"

"Sit down, Mike." Charlie said grimly, hands folded.

"Don't tell me you found her...Jesus Christ, is she all right?" He began shouting. "Charlie, my God, is she...?"

"Mike, please. She's all right. Sit down."

"How do you know? What do you mean she's all right...?"

"Damn it, Mike. Sit! I've got something to tell you."

Mike paced the floor for another few seconds, took hold of his emotions, finger-combed his hair into place and plopped in a straight back chair. "Shoot. What is it?"

Charlie gazed into the eyes of his good friend, wishing this had never been necessary.

"Mike. Oh, Geez. This is going to be a little rough. Remember when you and Robyn went on a trial separation three years ago? You guys were split a couple of months or so."

"Yeah. So?"

"There was a boat cruise. Robyn was on it. I was on it too. It was a pure coincidence."

Chill bumps raced up Mike's neck. Incredulously, he looked at Charlie

"Mike, we talked and had a few drinks, and, honestly, all she could talk about was you and your career, and before we knew it..."

"You? You did my wife?"

"Mike..."

"My wife went to bed with my best friend? I don't believe this."

"Godammit, Mike, there's a lot more to this story if you'll just calm down. This is not easy for me either."

"Yeah. I bet it's not."

"It was a one time thing, brought on by moonlight, loneliness and booze. Later, she told me how guilty she felt and would have nothing to do with me. Not that I didn't try. I really do care for her."

Reticent now, Mike stared at the floor, gazing up at his friend now and then. "I don't believe this," he muttered.

"We talked. We talked a lot. She loves you, Mike, and no one else. But she's all bottled up, being left alone all the time, competing with your job and the desire for a normal family life. It's true, Mike.

You've always been married to homicide first. You've neglected that woman."

"I give her everything she wants."

"Everything, but yourself, Mike."

"I'm getting out of here."

"Mike, she called an hour ago asking me for help."

"Called you, huh? Not me, her husband."

"Yes. She's frightened and she's ashamed. I'm breaking a promise by telling you. She wants money to get out of the state."

"She told you where she is?"

"No. But I traced her call from a pay phone at Teague's Convenience Store on Bird Road. She's out in west Dade somewhere."

Mike buried his face into his hands as stark silence suddenly paralyzed the atmosphere. Both men grappled with their emotions. Mike pondered all the information, the news of her tryst with Charlie, that she would call him first for help, all the time hoping to find them before the killer did. He looked up at Charlie just as his friend began to speak.

"Please, Mike. Don't hate me."

"That's the same thing she asked me."

Mike looked at Charlie with disgust in his eyes, turned and headed for the door. "Well, you let me know if she calls again, okay? There's someone I have to see."

Just as he slammed the door shut and headed down the hall, Mike heard Charlie holler, "Mike, wait! Come back!"

"What is it?" Mike asked, poking his head back in the door.

Charlie walked from around his desk and extended a closed hand to his friend. "Here. Robyn asked me to give you these; they're from her."

Two Hershey Kisses.

"WE'VE GOT AN ADDRESS, Mike, but I think we better go for a search warrant first. Like, what if..."

"Fuck the search warrant, Al," Mike retorted in a brusque tone.

"There's no time to waste so get over there now. Just consider it a hot pursuit thing, whatever. Time is too important to be squandering when lives are at risk. You've got to get that son of a bitch."

The cell phone cut in and out as Mike sped north along I-95 heading for the east-west expressway in Fort Lauderdale. He was on a new mission, something he had to do. Something long overdue.

Al continued. "I'm having Randy send me a couple extra detectives, plus uniform and S.W.A.T., in case it gets nasty."

"Do it."

"The office is going haywire, Mike. Gonzalez has no idea what he's doing, running around barking stupid orders, driving Randy and everyone else crazy. I've got the entire squad tied up on two other cases besides this one, and there's absolutely no one left to check out some hot lead on an old whodunnit from years back."

"What lead?"

"Some stoolie in the Broward County Jail says he knows who killed a guy in a robbery a few years ago and he's ready to finger him. Wants a break on his sentence."

"Black or white?"

"Black"

"Break Zeke loose. He can handle that by himself. He needs to go to Fort Lauderdale anyway to talk to Ken Lancaster's brother.

Al interrupted. "Wait. Now they just got a new homicide and there's absolutely no one to handle it."

"Where? Who?"

"Some gun mule over on North River Drive. Shot twice in his house. The wife found him."

"*Conyo*. The shit is hitting the fan. Listen Al. Robyn called someone from a pay phone at the Teague Convenience Store on Bird Road near the turnpike. Any chance you put someone over there for a surveillance?"

"Jesus, Mike. Who?"

"Okay. Okay. I understand. Look, I'm going out of town a few hours. I'll be on my cell phone. Just go get that mother fucker!"

"We're heading over to that apartment now. We'll let you know what happens."

“If anything pops about Robyn, call me right away.”

“You got it.”

As soon as he hung up, Mike started punching new numbers. It was Ernie Garcia. "*Que tal, amigo.* Are you available?"

"For you, anytime. Are you still looking for your wife?"

"Yes. I think her best friend may know where she is. Her name is Beth Ann Lieberman. Robyn made a call from a pay phone not far from her house.”

Mike gave the particulars to the private investigator who immediately set up a stake-out of the real estate woman who, as it would turn out, still had no knowledge of Robyn’s whereabouts. Mike checked his watch. It was six forty-five.

BY SEVEN-THIRTY, Al Sanchez and Phyllis Moriarty had mustered three uniform units, a lab unit, a S.W.A.T. team of four sharpshooters and a host of detectives, all of whom were stationed into place around the modest two story apartment building facing Thirty-Seventh Avenue. En route, Gonzalez radioed a message to withhold all activity and to stand by until he arrived. They looked for the white Mercedes SL550 around the parking lot, but it was nowhere to be found.

They had no photograph of Javier Izaguirre other than the composite drawing as described by Charles Bosworth. Tallahassee computers showed he had a driver's license, but no one was available on a Saturday to FAX a photo. Several of the apartment dwellers stepped out onto the catwalks to see the hullabaloo as the flurry of cop activity drew hundreds of Hispanic denizens out from their cozy abodes. The sounds of Spanish music blared between the buildings in the gathering dusk.

Al wanted to get going for fear the media would soon arrive, further complicating the situation. He and Phyllis spoke to several gawkers out on the catwalks but only one, the manager, would admit knowing Javier Izaguirre. Some residents had seen the white Mercedes parked at the building as recently as that very day. For that short week, it stood out like an elephant in a pony stable from all the smaller and older cars.

Lights blazed behind drawn shades in apartment 210, a second story corner unit facing the parking lot, and television sounds carried to the outside. The S.W.A.T. team positioned a man on either side of the jalousie door which was the only entrance. Two other S.W.A.T. members positioned themselves with rifles, one behind a van and the other from the opposite corner of the parking lot behind a tree. At the rear of the apartment under two windows and a twelve foot drop to the asphalt, another uniformed man, armed with a shotgun, hid in the shadows.

Al Sanchez secured a pass key from the manager so it would not be necessary to break doors or cause unnecessary damage. As he and Phyllis crouched on the catwalk outside the apartment, pistols drawn, Lieutenant Gonzalez pulled into the parking lot from the street. "Well, we waited until he arrived, "Al said, "Let's go."

Phyllis inserted the key, turned the lock and heard the button unsnap. One S.W.A.T. officer quickly opened the door while the other darted inside, followed immediately by another. Al and Phyllis went in last. The searched all rooms and closets; Javier was not there.

Within seconds, Raul Gonzalez barreled through the door in a huff, weapon in hand and announced he was taking over. Laughingly ignored by Al and Phyllis, they searched drawers, closets, trash cans and clothing for any clues to the whereabouts of Javier Izaguirre. The S.W.A.T. group repositioned themselves outside the door to await further instructions.

A pervading stench of body odor dominated throughout the entire apartment. Phyllis said it smelled like someone hadn't taken a shower in a week. Both rooms were in disarray, papers, cigarettes, ashes, dirty clothing strewn everywhere on floors, chairs, beds, and tables. Walls hadn't been cleaned or painted in years. "Mike should be here," Phyllis said. "This is his case."

"Yeah, too bad," answered Gonzalez with a grin as he checked the refrigerator.

"Hey look at this, guys." Al was at the night stand near the left side of the queen-sized bed where he lifted a maroon purse containing nothing but a handkerchief, lipstick, a few coins and a stray business card embossed with the name: Robyn Estevez, Real Estate Agent. "If you had any doubts, forget 'em. He's our man."

"Call Mike, "Gonzalez ordered. "See if he's heard from his old lady yet."

With the landline phone in his hand, Al winked at his boss and said, "First, Lieutenant, there's a little something Mike taught us."

He pushed the button marked redial and waited, listening. After four rings, an officious female voice answered, "Miami Police Department, Records Bureau, may I help you?"

Al looked back at his boss again and tried to hand him the receiver. "Whadaya know, Lieutenant. He's been calling our Records Bureau."

An ashen expression blanched Gonzalez's face. He swallowed, blinked and dismissed the phone, stuttering. "Can't be."

The officious female voice could be heard through the receiver, "Hello! Hello! May I help you?"

Al spoke and asked, "Whose number is this, please?"

"Sir, the phones have all been switched over to the main floor. Lieutenant Masvidal is not in today."

"Well, well. Looks like we may have our police department leak right here. Lieutenant Masvidal." Al raised one eyebrow at Gonzalez. "Your good friend, right?"

JAVIER APPROACHED the expressway overpass crossing Thirty-Seventh Avenue near his apartment; a police cruiser raced past, exiting the ramp. Thinking quickly, he figured he better not exit but, instead, check out the happenings from a lofty vantage point. He parked off the road shoulder, walked back to the bridge where he could see his building a block away under the sodium vapor lights. Several cars parked in the building's lot looked like unmarked police cruisers, most backed in. A block away, in a service station, he spied two marked police cars.

Shit!

If it wasn't for that Mirage woman, he'd have nothing to worry about. Too many cops. Now he couldn't go home. He had to find a place to bed for the night.

He walked back to his car and fumbled through his pockets for Victor's address. Ah, there it is. Then he rummaged through the ladies' wallet which he had taken with him. Earlier, he had checked out a real estate office and a south Dade County townhouse address, but he knew she wouldn't be there. As the highway traffic whizzed by, he dumped all the wallet contents onto the seat, throwing the leather billfold out the car window. He headed for Victor's house.

CHAPTER 33

MORE THAN TWENTY YEARS had passed since the two-lane ribbon of pavement traversing the Everglades from Ft. Lauderdale to Florida's west coast was known as Alligator Alley. Others dubbed it the Highway of Death in honor of dispatching at least one commuter a week into an early grave. In 1992, t had been widened into a seventy-eight mile segment of the I-75 highway connecting Miami to Naples which was Mike Estevez's destination on that Saturday evening as he faced a magnificent orange fireball descend over the horizon.

For seventy-eight miles, except for one gas station, he'd see not a single shopping center, farm, motel, flea market, house or factory building as the vast sanctuary for birds, deer and reptiles spread in every direction as far as the eye could see. He was apprehensive, uncertain, even fearful of seeing *her.* It had been over fourteen years. Perhaps she was not even there any more.

His world was in chaos, Robyn and Corrina missing, a killer on the loose, his marriage in shambles, and now learning that his best friend had been intimate with his wife. Yet this journey was something he had to do, to resolve internal turmoil once and for all.

Over and over, he found himself beating on the steering wheel, talking aloud to himself, yearning to understand.

How could she do this? Of all people, Robyn! I would never have known if it weren't for a fluke. Cocoplum. How stupid. *How could I be so ignorant? So blind? There must have been signs; why didn't I see them? Jesus Christo, Robyn, I've loved you more than life. There could never have been another woman for me; you were my all, my everything. I gave to you my very soul. Why? What did I do other than set you upon a tower of pedestals? Oh God.*

As the sawgrass whizzed by at seventy-five miles per hour, he reminisced, thinking of the good times, hearing her soft, delicate, playful voice. *"You have fat ear lobes, but I love them anyway. They're a part of you."... "You've made me the luckiest woman in the world. I would not exist without you, Mike. I am so lucky."*

Sure. That's why you've been screwing around, jumping in bed fucking absolute strangers.

He caught himself veering off the roadway then checked his rear view mirror. He caught his breath and thought about seeing *her.*

Two hours passed before arriving at the east end of Naples where he would search in the darkness for a double-wide mobile home at the Manatee Mobile Home Park off Seminole Avenue. It was a well kept neighborhood, quiet, each unit clean and manicured. He slowly passed by the yellow trailer marked *314* wedged amid an identical row. A dark, battered '02 Mercury Marquis was in the carport. He could hear music of the '70's from the trailer across the street. Impaled into her front lawn, a green and white sign which read *For Sale,* and he wondered if *she* even lived there any more. Only one way to find out.

He stepped upon the front porch, faintly heard the stereo sounds of a Spanish guitar. It was her music. She was there. He took a deep breath. When he rapped on the jalousie door, the music stopped. His heart rose to his throat as footsteps approached. A yellow porch light blinked on, then the cranking of glass slats, a long pause.

"*Dios mia, Miguel.* Is that you?"

"*Si, Mama.*"

"Miguel, uh..."

"May I come in, Mama?"

The door opened but the woman had already turned her back and walked away, her hands to her face. He stepped inside and waited for an invitation to come further. She wept into the palms of her hands, mumbling in Spanish as she moved into the tiny living room, then she turned and faced him, wiping tears with a tissue. "Well, Miguel, after fourteen years, can't you at least give your mama a hug?"

His face was solemn and she could see he was shrouded in guilt. He stepped toward her, looked into her aging eyes and asked, "How are you, Mama?" Her once long and beautiful shining black hair had turned completely gray. She was hardly recognizable, he thought, but would never say that. With reserved enthusiasm, he extended his arms and took his mama to his bosom and then waited as she cried.

"So, have you come to condemn me to my face, Miguel, or to forgive me?"

He understood but ignored the question. He sat uncomfortably at the edge of an easy chair and she in her swivel rocker next to him.

"No, Mama. How have you been, really?"

"You want to know how I have been? Why now? Why all of a sudden now you want to know how I have been? Tell me, what brings you here Miguel?"

He rolled his eyes upward and turned the rings on his fingers. "I see the trailer is up for sale?"

"Sam died six months ago, Miguel."

"Oh, I'm sorry to...."

"No you're not." Her lips pursed as she snapped back at him. "Cancer. It was long and hard. He was a good man." She turned, gazed intently at Mike with piercing eyes. "I have a granddaughter whom I have never met. Tell me, is she well?"

"Corrina, Mama. She's thirteen and she's wonderful." Mike could see she started to choke up again. He took a deep breath in exasperation. "Look, Mama, I don't want to upset you. Maybe it's better that I did not come."

"You treat me as though I do not exist on this earth for fourteen years, my own son, my only son and then show up from somewhere in the world and you don't think I should not wonder, perhaps be a little bitter?"

"Yes. You're right."

"So tell me, which is it?"

"Which is what?"

"Are you here to condemn me or forgive me?"

"Neither, Mama. But I am seeking the truth."

"The truth about what, my son?"

"About you, and Papa. You know."

She sighed and looked into the deep dark eyes of her son and saw that he was troubled. Then, she rose and turned toward the kitchen asking, her back to Mike, *"Cafe con leche?"*

"Si, gracias."

Moments later she returned with a tray, raised her brow and asked, "Robyn. How is Robyn?"

He saw his mother looking at him, through him, as though she already knew. Mama always had a sixth sense, some uncanny ability to read a person, to know what was churning inside behind the mask of iron. He couldn't bring himself to answer.

"Ah, I see," she said. "So, it has happened to you?"

He was taken aback by her insight. "Robyn, well Robyn is in a problem. Have you heard the news reports from Miami?"

"I watch Oprah, I watch Geraldo, I watch old movies and I do not watch news. News is never good, so why watch it?" She paused and then asked, "What has happened, Miguel?"

"Mama, I need to know some things, some things I never asked about before. I just reacted and, maybe, I never gave you a chance."

"So you want to know. Now you want to know."

"Papa was a great man. I could never understand why you..."

"Betrayed him? Is that the word you're looking for?"

"I suppose."

"What makes you think I betrayed your father, Miguel?"

"Papa was still warm in his grave and you were at the altar with Sam. What was it? A couple of months?"

"I see." She lowered her head, sipped from her tiny cup, then set in back on the table. Unashamed, she looked directly into her son's eyes and said, "What you are thinking, Miguel, is true. Sam was my lover for five years before your father died. Is that what you want to know?"

It was her bold candor, not the revelation itself that stunned him. They stared at each other a moment and then he asked, "It's not the *what* mama, it's the why. Didn't you love Papa? Wasn't he good to you?"

"Yes. Just like you are no doubt good to Robyn. You are responsible, capable, supporting and faithful, right? You do all the right things, don't you, Miguel?"

"Yes, Mama. I try."

"Let me ask you a question, son. If God came to you and said, 'Miguel, we here in heaven must cut back on the love budget. No longer can you have it all. You must make a choice. Your career or your woman.' Now, if God really said that, you would be faced with a tough decision. Right? You would never be a homicide detective again or never again be with Robyn. One or the other. You might think, 'well, I could always find another woman, eh?' But at the same time, you would still have a job, but not the position that competes with your woman. What would you keep?"

Mike hesitated for a brief second. "There would have been no question. Robyn, of course."

"Did she ever know that? Did she ever feel that?"

He pondered a moment and looked into his cup of cold café. "So, that's why you...."

"Your father was a great man, Miguel. And I did love him, no matter what you think. But I was not his first love. And I needed to feel that I was his first love. There were times we would be making love and he would say things like 'pass the scalpel' or 'give me fifty cc's of adrenaline'. I was his object of responsibility, social correctness and tradition. I represented the way life was supposed to be. I satisfied his pursuit of image."

"Papa didn't love you?"

"Oh yes. In his own selfish way, he loved me. He loved me for himself. Not for me."

"So that's why you went out and started..."

"Sam was the only one, Miguel. Sam was there, and he thought I was pretty damned special, and I liked that. I liked that a lot. I worked for Sam for two years before we ever even thought about being intimate, but when the barrier was broken, my heart absorbed all his love like a dry sponge."

"Then why did you stay with Papa?"

"Well, I suppose you could say it goes back to how we were all raised. You know. The family and all that. Besides, I would not have done that to your father. It would have devastated him and then he would have lost us both. Me and his career."

She watched her son turn his head away and she could see his neck turning pink.

"Think about her, Miguel, as a human being, a deep feeling woman who craves your love, your treasured, so elusive love."

"How did you know?"

"I am your mother."

WHEN MIKE ARRIVED home from Naples just before midnight, he found a note left by Zeke; he was exhausted, no new developments had emerged and he had gone home for the night. Mike already knew about the raid on Javier's apartment from cell phone contact with Al Sanchez.

There were three messages on his voice mail, two from Randy McAdams and one from Chief Howard asking that he return the call as soon as possible. He poured himself a double-sized scotch on the rocks and collapsed in a reclining chair. The house seemed more empty than ever before. It would never be the same.

During the long two-hour journey back home, his mind raced in a thousand directions with images of his Robyn and then his mother flashing through his thoughts. He felt relieved that she had shared her feelings and the darkness within her past in the hopes that he would finally accept and forgive her; yet, he rued over fourteen years wasted, having turned his back on a mother who loved him so much. His passionate loyalty to a revered father blinded him all these years, and now he knew the truth. His father wasn't perfect after all, a profound revelation.

Not perfect.

The image of her saying goodbye at the door step, asking if it would be another fourteen years, was etched deep within his heart. He'd been close to saying he was sorry, but not close enough. Mike Estevez never said he was sorry.

He took a sip from his tall glass, checked his watch and lifted the phone. He knew she'd still be up.

"Just wanted to let you know I'm home safe, Mama."

"Thank you my son."

"One more thing, Mama. I forgot to tell you."

"And, what is that?"

Mike held the receiver close to his heart, swallowed hard and waited until he could regroup his emotions.

"Miguel? Miguel? Are you all right?"

"*Lo siento, Mama. Lo siento mucho.*" (I'm sorry, Mama)

"*Yo siempre te querre, mi hijo.*" (I will always love you, my son)

He phoned Randy McAdams and caught up with the details about the search of Javier's apartment. When he called the chief, his wife answered and said he was asleep. He poured one more drink and looked over at his suit jacket draped over the arm of a chair, picked it up and reached into the side pocket. He gazed at the two Hershey Kisses for an eternity, it seemed, until he collapsed into a deep slumber, never leaving the large recliner chair the entire night.

CHAPTER 34

SUNDAY MORNING

ROBERT HAD BEEN WORKING MOST of the day on the three airboats, making certain they were in top running condition for the tourist season. Meanwhile, his father tended to the motel affairs. During off season, tending to the motel generally entailed watching movies, soap operas and talk shows. On one airboat, Robert dismantled the entire aircraft engine, cleaned its inner workings, replaced a number of bolts, spring and gaskets and put it all back together again. The other two were newer and needed only routine maintenance, like waxing propellers and changing oil.

His mother was spending the day at the tribal counsel three miles to the west, sewing garments with other women and serving food and drinks to the men while they discussed various important topics; operation of the casino, the small police department, preservation of the Miccosukee culture and the selling of cigarettes.

When Robert called out for some tools, Jake left the office and brought a ratchet wrench set to his bare-chested son who was clad in nothing but Levi jeans and new sneakers bought at Walmart. He was a well built, handsome Native with black shoulder-length hair tied back by a colorful headband. It was ten-fifteen in the morning as he breathed a daily dose of swamp aroma while the vast sea of grass glimmered under a rising sun that would blister the long August day.

Rather than hand Robert a wrench, Jake seized the opportunity to immerse his own hands into work. "This one is low on gas," he remarked in Native tongue. "Tomorrow morning, bring it to the pumps."

Moments after Jake stretched out upon the aluminum deck and began unscrewing one of the plugs, the exterior bell sounded from the building. It was the office phone.

"Would you get it for me?" asked Jake.

Robert jogged to the office, picked up the receiver and answered perfunctorily, "Alligator Jake's, may I help you?"

"Mrs. Robyn Estevez, please?" It was a male voice.

"One moment."

ROBYN TRIED CALLING Charlie twice in thirty minutes, both at his office and his residence, only to reach his answering machine each time. She left a message saying she would call back, left the motel's phone number and her room. At this point, she had to trust him. He had promised he wouldn't betray her.

Bored and restless, Corrina sat up in her bed flipping channels between religious services and a rerun of *Wheel of Fortune*, but her mind fixed on convincing her mother to leave this godforsaken place and return to civilization.

"Who is it you're trying to call, Mom?"

"A friend. Honey, it won't be long now. I'll have some money. We hardly have enough gas to get back to Miami, much less out of state. And my purse, well, it's gone. We're flat broke."

"Yeah and I'm hungry. What are we going to do?"

"As long as we're here, we can eat at Jake's. We'll eat, don't worry."

"The food's icky. I hate it." Corrina remained quiet a few moments pondering her mother and father, thinking about her future. "You know, Mom, I was thinking..."

Robyn lit another cigarette, stretched her legs out and leaned back against her pillow. "What's that?"

"I don't think I'll ever get married."

"What makes you say that?"

"'Cause I never want to go through the pain I see you going through. You and Dad, the perfect couple and now, crash! What good times you guys ever had could not have been good enough to be worth this. I mean, like, I'd rather live without romance than have a lifetime of hopes and dreams vanish like they were never worthwhile."

"Corrina, when love strikes, it isn't something you buy or leave on the shelf. It consumes you and then you're driven by the passion of the moment, like a bee to honey, like the sea responds to the pull of the moon. No, I don't regret the good years. I wouldn't trade them for anything, just like I wouldn't trade you....."

Corrina started to interrupt when a knock sounded at the door. Robyn rose from her bed, pulled the curtain slightly and saw that it was Robert. He said that a man was on the phone for her. She donned her sunglasses, ran to the office and picked up the receiver, softly, cautiously, "Hello, Charlie?"

Dial tone.

"Oh shit!" she exclaimed under her breath. "We were cut off." She walked out the rear door to the waterway where Robert was back at his airboat and asked if the party left his name.

"No ma'am." He paused to look up and admire her long golden hair wistfully move in the soft breeze, her tiny waist and her perfect heart-shaped buttocks formed into tight blue jeans.

"Was it a man?" she asked.

"Yes ma'am. He asked for Mrs. Robyn Estevez. Why? What's the matter?"

"Got cut off."

"That happens a lot here, ma'am. He'll call back; just stay by the phone. You can answer it. If it's for me or my father, just let me know."

Robyn immediately tried calling Charlie at both his numbers, but to no avail. He undoubtedly had a cell phone but she didn't know that number.

After another ten minutes of pacing, she called Charlie one more time from the office. This time, he answered.

"Oh Charlie, thank God. Do you have the money?"

"Five hundred, like you asked. What now?"

"Can you bring it to me?"

"Well, I guess. Where are you, anyway?"

"It's way out on Tamiami Trail, seven miles past Krome Avenue on the left before you get to Shark Valley and the Miccosukee Village. Alligator Jake's. You can't miss it. We're in 107."

"Got it."

"I was beginning to wonder if you were going to call back at all. Maybe, you decided to break your promise."

"Don't worry. I'm going to help you, Robyn."

It was a moment of relief. Then she remembered to ask, "Hey, why didn't you call back?"

"Call back? Call back when?"

"After we got cut off?"

"Cut off? What are you talking about?"

"Didn't you call me here about twenty minutes ago?"

"Hell, no."

"You're kidding? Then who was..."

"Does anyone else know you're there?"

"No one. Absolutely no one, Charlie." Robyn searched her brain for an answer but it was impossible. Only Charlie had her number.

"What's going to happen after I give you the money?" he asked, stalling.

"We're outa here. We'll be going up to my brother's in Syracuse for a couple weeks until they catch him. We just can't stay here."

"Honestly, Robyn, you really should come forward. It's your only way of being protected. Mike will understand."

"I can't."

"What about us, Robyn? If you and Mike are..."

"Please, Charlie. I was afraid of misleading you. I shouldn't have. I just didn't know who else to call. Don't let this hurt your feelings, but there is no us. Please understand."

She shifted restlessly, wondering if the other caller was Mike, if he had found her somehow. Irritated and confused, she wished for the conversation to end. Then she glanced out the dark, dusty office window and noticed a white convertible turn slowly from the roadway and lumber into the parking area. Her eyes followed the car as she tried to get Charlie to hang up.

"You can't go on like this, Robyn. You must..."

The car was obviously expensive and out of place in such a dusty, old, dilapidated motel. Tinted windows prevented her from seeing if it were a man or a woman driving.

"...think of Mike and what he's going through, and Corrina.."

"Charlie, there's a car here. I think I gotta go..."

"What car?"

Stepping to her right out of view, she recognized him the moment she saw the top of his head rise over the driver's door. Then, the Hawaiian shirt, the tall, lanky gait, the deep-set evil in his eyes.

"Oh my God, it's him!" she exclaimed into the phone just before it dropped onto the carriage. "How did he find me? Oh no, we're going to die."

A renewed surge of panic shot through her body as she watched him stroll slowly toward the office. She ducked below the counter and spotted the rear door leading out to the waterway. Crawling on hands and knees, shaking and praying, she managed to creep outside. She thought about Corrina alone back in the room. She had to get her out.

Jake and Robert were finishing their work on the airboats and never noticed Robyn as she slunk along the back wall of the motel to the end unit. A loud bell rang outside and she knew it was him at the office. Peering around the corner to the front catwalk, she saw the coast was clear to scamper the twenty feet to room 107 and Corrina.

"What's up, Mom?" she asked as Robyn ducked inside.

In a frightful panic, she ordered, "Come with me, now. Now! Don't ask questions. Hurry." She grabbed her daughter's hand, snatched her from the bed and out the door, checked to her left then ran to the right and around the end of the building. Corrina was dumbfounded but asked no questions.

By now, she figured, he must be confronting Jake at the office. Robert stood tall on the deck of the airboat. Holding hands, hunched and running, they leaped onto the boat, jolting the young Indian. "Robert, get us out of here. Now!"

His brows curled, confused, Robert stammered, "Ma'am?"

"There's no time to explain. There's a man coming to kill me. Please." He saw they were petrified, trembling hysterically, and he knew it was urgent. He looked back to the motel and thought about his father. Then she said with gritted teeth, "Robert, please hurry. He's got a gun!"

Corrina crouched and huddled in her mother's arms as the thunderous, ear-splitting engine roared behind them. They took off and sped west then southwest as birds of all colors and sizes darted from hummocks, branches, knolls and swamp marsh into the air toward safer, quieter feeding areas. Robert, his black hair flapping violently in the wind, stood at the helm in front of the propeller, confused, wondering about his father.

The airboat raced to speeds of seventy miles per hour. Above the roar, he shouted to them, "I'm going to drop you off on an island about a quarter mile up, then go back and check on my father. You'll be safe."

Minutes later, Robyn looked back and gasped at the sight of another airboat in pursuit. Crouched at the foot of the aluminum bench, she held Corrina tightly, as tight as her arms could, sensing her life in complete jeopardy. She screamed to Robert, "How fast can you go?"

"No faster," yelled Robert looking down at them. "This is the old motor."

They zoomed at breakneck speed, smashing head-on through a forest of tall sawgrass, only to see it fold under the speed of the flat bottomed craft. The deafening, ear-splitting motor roared on, wind raging. Robyn looked back again; the other airboat had gained distance. "Please, please!" she screamed.

"Mommy! Mommy! I'm scared," Corrina cried.

"Hold on," Robert shouted as he made a sudden turn to the left and back to the right again. He gunned the motors once more, racing toward a large hummock thick with foliage, a popular haven for gators and crane birds. He ducked the raucous machine through dense trees and bushes into a canal-like opening, out of view. Quickly, he shut off the engine, the silence sudden and eerie as they crouched, listening to the stillness.

Seconds passed before the faint sound of the second airboat engine approaching from the east, louder and louder. Soon, the roaring engine seemed to be on top of them. Robyn and Corrina shivered and held each other. The engine reached full crescendo, continued on beyond the hummock, fading off and soaring upon shallow waters to the west. The killer had passed by.

"What now?" asked Robyn, crouching with Corrina.

"I think I can get you back to the motel. I have to save my father."

With the other boat out of earshot, Robert restarted his airboat, raced from the hummock and throttled easterly into the wide open spaces in the direction of the motel. Once again, the raucous engine was deafening as the wind blew violently. They soared at full speed, sixty, then seventy miles per hour, airborne at one point and nearly flipping over when Robert failed to see the thick branch of a fallen cypress. They accelerated across the vast wilderness until they neared the motel, to safety at last.

They looked up at Robert, who was pointing to his right. The madman, holding a pistol to Jake's head, sped at them from an angle. Robert paralleled Tamiami Trail two hundred yards to his left, searching for spaces between the Australian pines lining the highway, an avenue of escape, perhaps.

Finally, there was no time for hesitation, only a gamble. Cautious of the two-way traffic buzzing along Tamiami Trail, he aimed for an opening between the trees, checked oncoming vehicles and banked the airboat to the left, sliding across the paved roadway and into the north side of the wilderness. Following, Javier and Jake traversed the same highway, barely missing a tractor-trailer which jack-knifed into an oncoming Corvette. The explosion sent a pillar of smoke rising two hundred feet into the air.

Still in pursuit, the madman's airboat gradually gained as they raced toward the setting sun, closer and closer until they could see the silver glimmer from Javier's gun reaching out to shoot. Robert tried to zigzag but to no avail. He looked across the sea prairie for another hummock, but they were all too far off.

Jake's boat pulled nearly even but remained a hundred yards to their right as Javier screamed at the old man to steer closer, pressing the gun to his head. Holding on with his right hand, Javier reached with his left and fired one shot toward Robert's air boat. The bullet ricocheted, twanging off the aluminum deck next to Corrina. Mother and daughter screamed again.

Suddenly, a roar sounded from above as the thump, thump, thump of a Jet Ranger helicopter descended over both speeding airboats. Then another. And a third. With their hair blowing violently, Robyn and Corrina looked up to see the markings of Miami and Miami-Dade Police Departments flying at one hundred feet, speeding along side and over the airboats. They looked to the left and on Tamiami Trail saw no less than a dozen police units with flashing lights driving parallel to their path. A public address system blared above the roaring boat engines.

"DROP THE GUN OR YOU WILL BE SHOT! DROP THE GUN AND RAISE

YOUR HANDS!"

"That's Daddy!" Corrina shouted excitedly to her mother.

The detective on the public address system spoke again.

"STOP THE AIRBOAT. PUT DOWN YOUR GUN. NOW!"

Confused, Javier glared upward again and again at the hovering whirlybirds, staring wildly at the flack-jacketed officers poised with long barreled weapons aimed at him. He grabbed Jake as a human shield, the muzzle again to his head. Then he fired a wild volley of shots at the flying machines. As the airboat swerved, Jake seized a moment of distraction, broke away from his captor and dived into the marsh.

Alone now, Javier took the helm and accelerated north and away from the roads, roaring as fast as the boat would go, sixty-five miles per hour into the sprawling glades, firing more shots at the cops overhead.

The whirlybirds kept pace. Suddenly, the boat sputtered and slowed. Javier frantically searched for the controls, glancing repeatedly at the persistent flying machines, pointing and pulling the trigger of a now-empty gun. The boat had simply run out of gas. Javier was a sitting duck, trapped by ten thousand square miles of barren wilderness.

"DROP THE GUN AND PUT YOUR HANDS IN THE AIR! NOW!" blared the voice from above.

In an audacious act of defiance, Javier flung his weapon toward the helicopter; it fell with a splash into the marsh thirty feet away. Shouting expletives in Spanish, he twisted and turned, looking for a way out, but there was none. Sharpshooters aboard the choppers held their fire as the man was now unarmed.

Suddenly, one helicopter lowered to within twenty feet of the airboat as Mike Estevez ascended the pulley, holding with both hands, his hair whipping violently in the wind. As Mike jumped onto the platform, he reached for his gun, but Javier retrieved a hunter's knife from inside his eel skin boot and lunged at the detective. Eyes bulging, brandishing the blade, left, right, up and down, he screamed over and over, "I'll keel you."

When Mike finally had his gun in hand, the crazy one whipped the blade across his wrist rendering the semi-automatic a watery grave within the marsh. Blood gushed from Mike's hand.

Javier lunged wildly, nicking Mike in the thigh, but the movement gave him a chance to grab Javier's arm and wrestle him to the deck. Grappling, punching, the knife inches from Mike's face, the craft tipped. They both rolled into the marsh and under the airboat where they disappeared into the murky water.

Robyn and Corrina, along with Jake and Robert, looked on

helplessly from the other airboat, now fifty yards away. Both men were suddenly out of sight for what seemed like an eternity.

"Daddy! Daddy!" cried Corrina at the top of her voice. Robyn hunched on her knees, petrified, her eyes glued to the calming waters around the empty airboat. A S.W.A.T. member started rappelling from the helicopter toward the craft. Just as the cop set foot on the deck, the water broke ten feet away.

Exhausted, bleeding, swamp-soaked, Mike Estevez emerged in the four foot depth of water and grass, hair draped over his eyes, gasping for breath. Corrina and Robyn screamed. Jake and Robert hooted and hollered.

Mike raised one arm then hoisted the lifeless body of Javier Izaguirre to the surface with the other, his own knife impaled into his chest.

CHAPTER 35

With the spectacular demise of Javier Izaguirre, Corrina and her mother breathed a huge sigh of relief. But the ordeal had not ended for Robyn Estevez. The airboat ride back to the road remained a long, arduous half mile for the wife of the famous homicide detective.

She had not yet faced him since he discovered her involvement in the case and now it was inevitable. She wondered how he was going to respond, if he could ever forgive her or love her again, or if he would hate her forever.

She dreaded what surely lay ahead, the certain accusations that if she had come forward, perhaps other lives would have been saved, like Carolyn Webb, Anthony Portelli and the girls with Marco Scandiffio. If she had her own gun, she thought, she could end all the torment on her own and save everyone more grief and humiliation.

Corrina stood anxiously the entire ride back to the docking area as Robyn sat quietly behind dark glasses, clasping her arms across her abdomen. The moment Robert moored the craft, Corrina leaped onto the old, cypress deck and searched the span of grass for her dad.

Marked and unmarked police cars, as well as news media vans setting up their antennae, blanketed the roadway. Three helicopters still hovered over the site of the abandoned airboat a half mile to the north. Robyn remained seated until a uniformed officer presented a hand to help her off the craft.

The staging area teemed with uniformed cops and plain clothed officers perspiring profusely under a scorching midday sun. As she was escorted toward a waiting police car, she waved off several officers who asked if she needed medical attention. Then, the youthful chief of police pulled up in a black Ford Crown Victoria amid the huge assembly, greeted by an entourage as he stepped out. Her heart raced faster as she spotted Charlie Bosworth standing across the street talking to two men.

When the sounds of helicopter rotors grew louder, she turned and saw an aircraft approaching with a body basket hanging low from its belly. As it approached the road, she looked on with quiet resignation, knowing this was the lunatic whom she watched in terror murder four people in cold blood only a week earlier. Seeing the knife handle protruding from the dead man's chest, she averted her face. A unformed officer offered her a seat in his car, but she refused.

Moments later, the familiar roar of an airboat engine filled the air. She looked over her shoulder and saw Robert at the helm, nearing rapidly, his black hair whipping in the wind. Behind him, Mike slouched, drenched, hair lank, holding his right hand, craning his neck, his eyes searching the crowd.

The time had come.

AS SOON AS MIKE arrived at the dock, two officers greeted him with first aid kits and began treating the wound on his hand. He panned for any sight of Robyn, but he couldn't see her amid the pandemonium. Corrina suddenly burst through the crowd and grabbed her father around the neck.

"Daddy! Oh, Daddy! I'm so happy you're okay."

Still sopping wet and not yet recovered from the underwater engagement, Mike held his little girl close, relieved she was unhurt, safe. At least a dozen officers surrounded him, including Chief Howard.

"It's over now. Are you okay, honey?"

"I'm fine, Daddy. Are you okay?"

"Ah, my hand's cut. No big deal. Where's your mother?"

Corrina pointed across the roadway toward a parked marked police cruiser with its flashers swirling. Wearing her sunglasses and standing alone with her arms folded, Robyn looking anxiously in his direction. The moment he saw her, she turned away. The chief started to speak but Mike ignored him.

Once the bandage was secure, Mike started walking toward his wife, riveted. Nothing else in the world existed for him at this moment. "Sorry, boss. No offense, but I've got something more important right now."

SHE HAD NO IDEA what was to come, but it was sure to be a moment she'd never forget for a lifetime. Wrought with a mélange of emotions—fear, anxiety, love, desperation—she felt her body tremble out of control the moment he started her way. She wished she could just run, but there was nowhere to go. She thought of standing up to him, being headstrong and placing the guilt on his shoulders, but this was not the time or place, not after he barely survived a near death encounter with the crazed killer.

Halfway toward her now, walking faster. Instead of looking away, she removed her sunglasses and peered directly into his eyes, ready for whatever the consequences. He'd never hit her before. He rarely ever raised his voice, but she knew he had a temper. Her heart nearly exploded, her eyes swelled with tears, her hands trembled while trying to control her tears. Mike never took his eyes away from hers as his walk accelerated into a limping run the last few steps.

What's he going to say? What am I going to say? Oh no, please God.

Exhausted and drenched, he stopped directly before her and

said not a word. Still catching his breath, he stared deeply into her pleading eyes for what seemed like an eternity. To her utter amazement, his lips began to quiver and tears formed in his bloodshot eyes. He raised his arms and embraced her with all the power left in him.

"I'm sorry, Robyn," he whispered into her ear, holding her face, kissing her lips, patting her golden hair.

She couldn't believe it.

"I'm so sorry, Robyn, my love," he repeated, over and over, holding her like he'd never let her go.

"Oh Mike, Mike...I love you so. I'm sorry, too."

"I love you. I never want to lose you."

"My darling. Hold me. Never let me go."

Corrina rushed to the blissful reunion, jumping up and down like a pogo stick, clapping her hands. She embraced her parents together as they all wept with joy.

CHAPTER 36

"ARE YOU SURE I can't talk you out of it, Mike?" asked the chief as he leaned back on his swivel chair, feet atop the desk.

Mike stood before him, hand bandaged, left eye swollen, wearing only a rust-colored polo shirt and jeans, and smiled. "Thanks boss, my mind is made up. I really don't care where you put me for now. I've got some mending to do at home."

"I'm taking Gonzalez out. Seems he's been a bit loose-tongued with a certain lieutenant in the Records Department who is no longer with us. I'm putting in Charlie Bosworth as the new lieutenant." The chief raised his brow anticipating a different reply.

Mike drew a wry grin. Had he been told this information two days ago, before all the revelations, he would have jumped for joy, knowing Gonzalez was finally out, knowing his capable friend Charlie was to head homicide. "Charlie's the best, Chief. But, I'm outa here. I just have to get some of my things out of the office and take a few days off before you reassign me."

"How's Public Information sound to you? You have a good presence and the media likes you."

"That's great."

The two men remained quiet for several seconds before the chief stood and shook hands with his esteemed detective. "Good luck, Mike. And, thank you."

It was time to pack up and leave his homicide career behind him. Perhaps now, he would make that long delayed effort to promote his way up, become an executive and make the same money without working eighty hours a week. Yet, the thought of being a desk jockey the rest of his career was not appealing. He relished being centered amid the action, with the people of the city, solving problems and dealing with major crimes. Alas, he figured, he would simply have to adjust.

Gloria Menendez, ravishing as always, escorted him part of the way down the hall, posing inane questions and probing the rumor that he was about to become her new boss in charge of the Public Information Office. Suddenly, out of nowhere, Zeke Ferguson grabbed one arm and jerked him into the men's room.

"Hey, Zeke, what's up? You gettin' funny or what?"

"Jesus, I've been trying to get you all day. Don't you ever answer your cell phone any more? I even left messages on your home number."

"My days in homicide are over, my friend. No more of this shit for me. I've talked to the chief and I'll be going to P.I.O. in a few days."

"That's what you think."

Mike's brow curled as his eyes came together. "Why?"

They stood at the urinals, not to piss, but to act like there was a reason to be there in case someone walked in.

"Remember that snitch you sent me to see in the Broward Jail?"

"Yeah? What about him?"

"You know, the one who's fingering the trigger man on some old murder case?"

"Yeah, so?"

"His name's Shamu!"

His head spun toward Zeke. Then he looked away and rolled his eyeballs. "Don't tell me. Is it...?"

"May of 1996. Victim's name was Estevez."

Mike rolled his eyes in amazement. "You know something, Zeke. You are one damned good homicide detective.

"Thanks. You still leaving homicide?"

For no reason, Mike flushed the urinal. "Well, I guess I better call the chief."

THE END

www.ingramcontent.com/pod-product-compliance
Lightning Source LLC
LaVergne TN
LVHW091110080826
845145LV00008B/1866

9780994980991